Voices from Twentieth-Century Africa

Voices
from Twentieth-Century
Africa

Griots and Towncriers

SELECTED
WITH AN INTRODUCTION BY
Chinweizu

faber and faber
LONDON · BOSTON

First published in 1988
by Faber and Faber Limited
3 Queen Square London WC1N 3AU

Typeset by Input Typesetting Ltd, Wimbledon, London
Printed in Great Britain by Richard Clay Ltd, Bungay, Suffolk

This collection © Chinweizu, 1988

British Library Cataloguing in Publication Data
Voices from 20th century Africa: griots and
towncriers.
1. Literatures.
Anthologies
I. Chinweizu
808.8'9896

ISBN 0-571-14929-4
ISBN 0-571-14930-8 Pbk

Dedication

In honour of

Okot p'Bitek (1931–82)

Master poet, and crusader for an African Cultural
Revolution that would Africanize all centres of
culture in Africa by opening them to the vitality of
Africa's traditional artists.

*And in honour of two founders of
influential institutions which have nurtured
African literature in this century:*

Alioune Diop (1910–80)

Founder of *Présence Africaine* (1947); Chairman of
the first World Festival of Negro Arts, Dakar (1966);
and organizer of other literary congresses and
cultural societies;

and

Chinua Achebe (1930–   )

Master novelist, and founding editor of the
Heinemann African Writers Series (1962); founder
of *Okike: An African Journal of New Writing* (1971);
founder of the Association of Nigerian Authors (1981).

Epigraph

It is important that in Africa we should have our own culture as the dominant factor in our national cultural centres; and not the reverse . . . Take the situation at the university, for example. There you have professors and lecturers who are virtually ignorant of African music and poetry, and who purport to teach these subjects, while in the countryside you have the real masters of these subjects. The great African dancers and singers, the carvers, the pot-makers and the story-tellers are in the countryside. And they are kept out of our schools and colleges and universities . . . In the educational section, break down the walls that surround our schools and universities, and let the people who know our culture teach our people. Let us Africanize our curriculum in a meaningful manner. Let African culture form the core of our curriculum and foreign culture be at the periphery.

Okot p'Bitek, *Africa's Cultural Revolution*

Editor's Note

Each entry in the anthology is identified by a title (asterisked if this has been supplied by the editor); author's name, if known - if unknown then the ethnic group (in italics) from which it was collected has been given instead; and (in brackets) the country of origin of the author or the country or region in which the ethnic group is to be found.

Wherever possible the name used for an ethnic group or country is one that is accepted by its members. Thus, for instance, South Africa is listed as Azania, South West Africa as Namibia; Bushmen is replaced by San, and Hottentots by Khoikhoi.

Contents

PART TWO: The Local and Intimate Turf

PART THREE: Fields of Wonder

INTRODUCTION

Redrawing the Map of African Literature

In the conventional, official perception, which is shared by Africans and non-Africans alike, African literature is a new and fledgling product of the twentieth century; it is written in European languages, by and for a Western-educated African elite; its pioneers are the Senghors, Achebes, Soyinkas, Ngugis, Netos and p'Biteks; its use is mainly academic, to add a dash of local flavour to a standard classroom diet of Western literature; and its coming of age was marked by the award of the 1986 Nobel Prize for Literature to one of its pioneers. In specialist, academic circles, that picture is supplemented by knowledge of works in African languages, which were written, starting in the nineteenth century, in the shadow of Christian missionary publishing; and by knowledge of a handful of writings published in Europe and the Americas by slaves and ex-slaves of African origin from the sixteenth century onwards.

However true it may be of African literature created under European dispensation, that conventional picture gives an incorrect portrait of African literature as a whole. It confounds a part with the whole, passing off a small grove of young trees grown from transplanted, hybrid saplings as the entirety of a vast and ancient forest. It leaves out literature written in African languages before the coming of Arab and European invaders; it leaves out the oral literary tradition; it ignores the non-academic, social and cultural uses to which the bulk of African literature has been put in African societies since the beginning of African civilization some 5,000 years ago. The result of such major omissions is a gross distortion. To accept that conventional picture of what African literature is, and is used for, would be like accepting that its new sprouting horn is the entire ram.

An example of those distortions is the notion that African literature is a fledgling, twentieth-century phenomenon. This false notion is predicated on the false idea that African literature in modern European languages exhausts the canon of African literature. But, as a matter of fact, African literature (i.e. literature written by Africans, for African readers, in African languages) is at least as old as the Pyramid Texts of Pharaonic Egypt; it is, thus, older than European literature by some 2,000 years. Some of its early output, like Aesop's (i.e. the Ethiop's) Fables, were exported to Europe where they fertilized the literary imagination of Ancient Greece. Others helped to shape the style and content of the earliest Hebrew literature. The Senegalese Egyptologist, Cheikh Anta Diop, observed that 'certain Biblical passages are practically copies of Egyptian moral texts'.[1] The American Egyptologist, James Henry Breasted, supplied a famous example. Concerning Pharaoh Akhenaton's great hymn 'the Splendour of Aton', he observed:

The one hundred and fourth Psalm of the Hebrews shows a notable similarity to our hymn both in the thought and the sequence, so that it seemed desirable to place the most noticeably parallel passages side by side.[2]

For an accurate conspectus of African literature, one must, therefore, look beyond the confines of academic literature, and take into account those works which find, and have found, audiences outside the ivory tower. When we include the output of the oral literary tradition, the output of 5,000 years of writing in African languages, as well as the non-academic works of entertainment being produced in European languages by African writers, we find (1) that the extant corpus of African literature is much greater, and more varied, than what the official view would lead one to believe; (2) that, given its various strands and antecedents,[3] twentieth-century African literature is not a fledgling offspring of European literature; rather, it is a continuation (partly but only partly) in European languages, of a 5,000-year-old indigenous African tradition; and (3) that, from the gamut of its actual functions in African societies, African literature is used, not principally as flavouring in an academic diet, but for the larger cultural purpose of

---

[1] Cheikh Anta Diop, *The African Origin of Civilization*, Westport, Connecticut, Lawrence Hill & Company, 1974, p. xv.
[2] J. H. Breasted, *A History of Egypt*, London, Hodder and Stoughton, 1920, p. 371.
[3] See Chinweizu et al., *Toward the Decolonization of African Literature*, Enugu, Fourth Dimension, 1980 (London, KPI, 1985), pp. 25–32.

instructing Africans in African humanities. There is thus more, far more, to African literature than what the Nobel Prize recognized.

The job of correcting the distortions perpetrated by the conventional academic view dictates the two main concerns of this anthology, namely (a) to encourage a more accurate and comprehensive view of African literature, by drawing unapologetic attention to the non-academic bulk of twentieth-century African literature; and (b) to begin a process of supplying to the general public a body of African literature which reflects African history, which is rooted in the structures of African life, which makes manifest the values of African civilization, and which can, therefore, be used for instruction in African humanities. Let us consider these aims and why they are vital.

African literature: Popular vs. Academic

The conventional view of African literature needs to be corrected, not only for the sake of accuracy, but also because, as we shall see, it has permitted Euro-assimilationist junk, in the guise of 'serious literature', to be upheld as the flower of African literature. Those obliged, in schools and universities, to gnaw through such unreadable but prestigious stuff, regard it as an implement of torture, and many develop an allergy to anything called African literature. 'If this is the best of African literature, why bother with any of it?' is their quite understandable reaction. As a result, most Africans stay ignorant of that non-academic bulk of African literature which could enrich their lives.

The wide spectrum of non-academic or popular literature (popular in the sense of being adapted to the taste and understanding of the general public) is made up of what academics variously tag 'folktale', 'cheap, escapist trash', 'entertainment' and 'vernacular literature'. It is contrasted with the 'serious literature' to which academics devote their lofty attention.

'Folktale' refers to all of oral literature (orature) from proverbs to epic cycles, even when these have been written down. Academic disdain for it even extends to such contemporary writings as those of Amos Tutuola which continue, in written English, the ancient oral and moral tradition of African heroic epic. 'Entertainment' and 'cheap, escapist trash' refer to romances, war adventures, crime and sex thrillers (such as Cyprian Ekwensi's *Jagua Nana*, Eddie Iroh's *Forty-eight Guns for the General*, Naiwu Osahon's *Sex is a Nigger*). 'Vernacular literature' refers to works written in African languages (e.g. Swahili, Somali, Hausa, Sotho, Xhosa, Zulu); they are regarded by literary academics as some sort of half-way house between 'folktale' and 'literature', even though they have thriving audiences among those literate in their respective African languages.

'Folktale' constitutes the bulk of African non-academic literature of the twentieth century, and possibly of all of twentieth-century African literature. An estimate of its abundance may be made from the quantity of material collected in those few African languages in which some systematic effort has been made to write them down; by noting that each such collection is but a small part of the orature in its language; and by considering that each African society has its own corpus of 'folktale'. If all the 'folktale' of Africa were written down, the total would, I believe, easily dwarf the rest of twentieth-century African literature.

This 'folktale' is oral; it is composed in African languages by artists who work within ancient African traditions of eloquence and rhetoric; it is consumed by local African audiences during story-telling sessions, in work-places and on playgrounds, during courtship and wedding ceremonies, during ceremonies for births and deaths, and as parts of religious rites. Such uses make it an integral part of the fabric of personal and social life, quite unlike academic literature which is a sideshow that is brought into the African's life mainly for classroom purposes.

African popular literature, being mostly 'folktale', is thus an unabashedly functional literature through which the outlook and values of its makers are manifest, and through which those of its hearers and readers are shaped. To understand how this major component of twentieth-century African literature has been kept out of official view, we must examine current academic prejudices and how they determine what literary academics have projected to the world as African literature.

Eurocentric literary academics, in and outside Africa, have long been prejudiced against oral works; against works in African languages; against works by anonymous authors; against works by and for the non-elite 'folk'; against works of 'impure' or 'applied' literature which address themselves to social issues of the moment. On the other hand, they have a strong prejudice in favour of written works; in favour of works in European languages; in favour of works by named individuals; in favour of works by and for members of an elite; in favour of works of 'pure' literature which are said to divorce themselves from 'local' and 'social' issues and to aspire to 'universality'; in favour of works which supply material for detached aesthetic contemplation by the isolated scholar; and particularly in favour of works which conform to the aesthetic and thematic criteria of Euromodernism – criteria that embody the anti-popular, anti-scientific, and anti-industrial animus of the European Romantic movement of the last two centuries.[4]

When applied to African literature, these prejudices yield curious results. For example, a play is not considered drama, and so is not part of 'literature', until its words are written down and published. But even when an African oral performance is transcribed and published, it is dumped into the wastebin of 'folktale' since what the folk produce for their own consumption cannot be 'literature'. It is in this kind of way that the prejudices against the oral and the folk combine to throw out from the academic corpus the products of the fictional imagination of some 95 per cent of the African population. Conversely, only literary artefacts from the minority culture of the Westernized African elite, who make up about 5 per cent of the African population, are admitted into the academic corpus of African literature.

From among the works of this minority culture, the prejudices in favour of Euromodernist aesthetics help academics to uphold as exemplars of African literature what are indeed Euro-assimilationist[5] works by Africans. They take particular satisfaction in works of

[4] For an extended exploration of these prejudices in operation, see Chinweizu et al., ibid., especially pp. 32–98 and 147–61.

[5] Euro-assimilationism in African academic literature is the equivalent of the phenomenon in Afro-American music where black artists 'cross over' to white audiences by adjusting their musical style, themes and stage manners to suit the prejudices of white audiences, usually to the disapproval of their Afro-American audiences. In its more general manifestation, Euro-assimilationism was the cultural policy of colonial education, especially in the colonies of Portugal and France where the products were called *assimilados* or *evolués*. In the British colonies, the most Euro-assimilated earned the nickname 'Black European'. The phenomenon, alas, endures in post-colonial Africa in both its blatant and subtle versions, in academic as in general culture.

'pure' literature, i.e. those which have attained 'universality' by strictly adhering to Euromodernist aesthetics, and which embody the anti-African, and even the racist, prejudices of the West. It is thus that the most blatantly anti-black and anti-African of this 'pure' literature is paraded as the flower of African literature, while the authentic core of African literature is shunted out from the academic purview under the guise of 'folktale'.

To appreciate how topsy-turvy all this is, it is vital to look at a few examples. The reader is invited to judge for himself which, in each of the following pairs of passages, is African literature and which is Euromodernist jargon.

A1:   Hirsute hell chimney-spouts, black thunderthroes
      confluence of coarse cloudfleeces – my head sir! – scourbrush
      in bitumen, past fossil beyond fingers of light – until . . . !

      Sudden sprung as corn stalk after rain, watered milk weak;
      as lightning shrunk to ant's antenna, shrivelled
      off the febrile sight of crickets in the sun–

      THREE WHITE HAIRS! frail invaders of the undergrowth
      interpret time. I view them, wired wisps, vibrant coiled
      beneath a magnifying glass, milk-thread presages

      Of the hoary phase. Weave then, weave o quickly weave
      your sham veneration. Knit me webs of winter sagehood,
      nightcap, and the fungoid sequins of a crown.[6]

A2:   A baby is a European
      he does not eat our food:
      he drinks from his own water-pot.

      A baby is a European
      he does not speak our tongue:
      he is cross when the mother understands him not.

[6] Wole Soyinka, 'To my first white hairs', *Idanre and Other Poems*, London, Methuen, 1967, p. 30.

A baby is a European
he cares very little for others:
he forces his will upon his parents.

A baby is a European
he is always very sensitive:
the slightest scratch on his skin results in an ulcer.[7]

B1:   Gone, and except for horsemen briefly
       Thawed, lit in deep cloud mirrors, lost
       The skymen of Void's regenerate Wastes
       Striding vast across
       My still inchoate earth

       The flaming corkscrew etches sharp affinities
       (No dream, no vison, no delirium of the dissolute)
       When roaring vats of an unstoppered heaven deluge
       Earth in fevered distillations, potent with
       The fire of the axe-handed one

       And greys are violent now, laced with
       Whiteburns, tremulous in fire tracings
       On detonating peaks. Ogun is still on such
       Combatant angles, poised to a fresh descent
       Fiery axe-heads fly about his feet

       In these white moments of my god, plucking
       Light from the day's effacement, the last ember
       Glows in his large creative hand, savage round
       The rebel mane, ribbed on ridges, crowded in corridors
       Low on his spiked symbols

       He catches Sango in his three-fingered hand
       And runs him down to earth. Safe shields my eaves
       This night, I have set the Iron One against
       All wayward bolts. Rumours rise on grey corrugations,
       The hearth is damped

---

[7] Ewe orature (Togo), 'A Baby is a European', in Ulli Beier, *African Poetry*, Cambridge University Press, 1966, pp. 64–5.

In gale breaths of the silent blacksmith
Cowls of ashes sweep about his face. Earth
Clutches at the last rallying tendrils
A tongue-tip trembles briefly and withdraws
The last lip of sky is sealed

And no one speaks of secrets in this land
Only, that the skin be bared to welcome rain
And earth prepare, that seeds may swell
And roots take flesh within her, and men
Wake naked into harvest-tide.[8]

B2:   Kounadi, the eldest of the servants,
said to the queen, going against the rule
forbidding anyone to pronounce her name: 'Saran,
good, kind Saran, with whom are you in love?
with a spirit of the palace of King Solomon
or an heir to the throne of the Pharaohs of Misra?'

'No,' replied Saran. 'The one I love
is not a spirit of the elements, nor a prince of Misra.
He is born of a Bambara woman.
He grew up on the banks of the Dioliba
and played under the *balanzas* of Segou.
I am in love with the prince Da.'

'Da Monzon! He who has come to besiege Kore Douga?'

'Yes, him. I cannot prevent myself loving him.
It is something too powerful for me.
I am ashamed of myself, but I can neither resist it nor remain
    silent.
That is why I am telling you this mortal secret.
The choice is yours: either you help me to reach Da
or you go and denounce me to Kore Douga.
If you choose the second solution

---

[8] From Wole Soyinka, 'Idanre', in *Idanre and Other Poems*, London, Methuen, 1967, pp. 61–2.

know then that Douga will have my head shaved;
he will dress me in rough bark and
will weigh me down with ignoble chains
as before he weighed me down with gold and silver and pearls.
You will see me collapse under the whip
and then my head will be cut off and thrown to the crows.
But before the end, when my mouth is bleeding, my teeth
broken, when I am dying of thirst,
I shall refuse the water offered me by a kind soul.
Give me Da, I shall say, I am thirsting for him;
water cannot quench my soul!'

Kounadi looked at her companions:
they were all weeping sincere tears.
Kounadi began to cry as well.[9]

A1 and B1 are excellent pieces of 'African literature' as academics
understand the term; they have been praised by academic critics and
blurb writers, and they belong to the output to which the 1986 Nobel
Prize for Literature was awarded by the Royal Swedish Academy. A2
and B2 are pieces of African orature, and belong among what academics
disdain as 'folktale'. To see why works like A1 and B1 should win the
highest acclaim from the Royal Swedish Academy, and why A2 and B2
are banished from academic view, let us note a few things.

Note that A1 was composed in a European language (English); it is
a rather obscurantist and indecipherable specimen of 'Hopkins' Disease'
poetry,[10] which puts it in the best tradition of Euromodernist poetry; it
provides ample opportunity for academic explication and exegesis; its
style appeals to the taste of Western academic literati; and, above
all, in its orgy of self-contempt, it panders to the blancophilia and
negrophobia of Western racism. To decipher the poem is to realize that
Soyinka compares his own black head to a chimney in hell belching
smoke, and likens it to a scourbrush dipped in hot, sticky and messy
coal tar. And lest you should miss the object of such contemptuous

[9] From 'Monzon and the King of Kore', a Bambara epic of Old Mali, *Présence Africaine*,
No. 58 (1966), pp. 105–6.
[10] See Chinweizu et al., op. cit. pp. 172–83.

images, he reminds you, rather excitedly, 'my head sir!'. Having further likened his own black head to a fossil, he begins to field images of such life-giving things as milk and rain; and he deploys lively images of corn stalk and crickets in the sun, to describe the objects of his capitalized thrill – 'THREE WHITE HAIRS!' The subliminal and symbolic implications of these contrasting images are that whiteness is alive, rejuvenating, resuscitating and good; and that blackness is dead, hellish, fossilized, coarse and messy. A question must be raised here. Does a welcoming of one's white hairs call for a derogation of one's black hairs? If not, why this voluntary exhibition of contempt for things black? This all suggests that the author of this confessional poem, though a Black, is so thoroughly Euro-assimilated that he responds to black and white with the impulses of a white racist! Vorster, Botha, Hitler and other white racists would be flattered to read the poem, and would gladly hail the poet as an auxiliary Bantu spokesman for white supremacy.

The Ewe oral poem 'A Baby is a European', in contrast, quietly mocks the haughty, aloof behaviour of the European colonizers in Africa. Though quite comprehensible, though informed by accurate observation of the parties being compared, and though it subtly and cleverly makes its point, it cannot hope for an unbiased, artistic appraisal from Eurocentric and blancophile academics.

'Idanre', a twenty-five page work of verse, is one of the few works of contemporary African poetry to have been declared an epic by academic critics.[11] Such lofty regard for it may not be shared by the non-academic reader who finds its graceless grammar and its confused jumble of images difficult to understand. When compared with 'Monzon and the King of Kore', those unaddicted to Euromodernist taste are likely to dismiss it altogether as literary junk.

For those who wonder why, despite its vitality, its moving style, and its important theme, 'Monzon' goes unappreciated by academic literati, one should point out how it violates several academic prejudices. It originated in the oral tradition; it was composed in an African language, and by an unnamed author; and it is a piece of 'applied' or 'impure' art since it is a didactic story about an act of treason, inspired by uncon-

[11] See Chinweizu et al., ibid., p. 147.

trolled love, which is punished by its beneficiaries. For such 'failings', it cannot be admitted into the academic canon of African literature.

By the way, were the prejudices against oral, folk and 'impure' compositions applied to European literature, these are some of the works which would be banished from the European canon: the Homeric epics, Greek and Roman myths, Celtic legends and Teutonic sagas, the Hebrew creation myths, the Psalms, Ecclesiastes, etc. After all, they either began as oral compositions, or as products of folk imagination, or they are instructional and didactic. Which just goes to show how fatuous these academic prejudices are, and how inconsistently they are applied.

Some of these prejudices have come under vigorous attack in the last few years. One important result is that the academic prejudice against the oral is breaking down, albeit slowly, with the notion of orature (oral literature) gaining acceptance. As a result, some items have been grudgingly rescued from the 'dustbin' of 'folktale', and now wait in the antechamber of Oral Literature for possible admission into the Great Hall of African Literature, whenever the Eurocentric keepers of the gates see fit to admit them.

The differences highlighted by the above pairs of passages indicate the nature of the gulf between Africa's academic and popular literatures. The irony of the situation is that it is academic literature, with all its Euro-assimilationist characteristics, which has been given official status, and which dominates the curricula of African schools and universities, whereas Afrocentric, popular literature languishes in the shadows, a barely noticed outcast from where it ought to reign.

Ending this anomalous situation demands changes in the official view of what African literature is. The prospect of stimulating such changes is based on a belief that if readers had a more comprehensive and representative introduction to African literature, they would not be put off, and might even get to like it. Pressure from such readers, it is hoped, would eventually bring about changes even in the ivory tower. Towards that end, this anthology dispenses with current academic prejudices, and adopts a democratic view of what literature is. It accepts contributions from the oral and written parts of the tradition; from the elite and the folk traditions; from works composed in both African and non-African languages, provided there is no reason to believe that their

African authors pander to the anti-African, and even racist, prejudices of non-African audiences.

One result of this approach is that about one half of the items in this anthology comes from the oral and folk literatures of Africa. Another is that blatantly Euro-assimilationist works have been excluded. Those with a genuine interest in African literature would agree that, instead of listening to 'black Europeans' talking to Europe, in apprentice diction, and about an Africa which European racism is flattered to imagine, we should listen to Africans talking to Africans about the world. After all, those interested in British literature do not waste their time on what some Sinophile Britons have written for Chinese readers about the type of Britain that Chinese chauvinism has been pleased to imagine; they read what Britons have written to other Britons about the world. Now to a consideration of the second aim of this anthology.

Literature and the Humanities: the Scandal in Africa

'People create stories create people; or rather stories create people create stories.'[12]

– Chinua Achebe

'Why should there not be "African humanities"? Every language, which means every civilization, can provide material for the humanities, because every civilization is the expression, with its own peculiar emphasis, of certain characteristics of humanity.'[13]

– Léopold Sédar Senghor

What kind of people we become depends crucially on the stories we are nurtured on; which is why every sensible society takes pains to prepare its members for participation in its affairs by, among other things, teaching them the best and the most instructive from its inheritance of stories. These are usually drawn from both the factual and the imaginative literature bequeathed by its ancestors, namely, its songs, poems, plays, myths, epics, fables, histories, cosmographic speculations and philosophical conjectures. At the core of such stories are creation myths

---

[12] Chinua Achebe, 'What has literature got to do with it?', Nigerian National Merit Award Winner's Lecture, 1986.
[13] Léopold Sédar Senghor, Prose and Poetry, selected and translated by John Reed and Clive Wake, London, OUP, 1965, pp. 53–4.

which give the members of a society their identity and their historical anchor in the universe. Speaking of creation myths, Chinua Achebe said:

So important have such stories been to mankind that they are not restricted to accounts of initial creation but will be found following human societies as they recreate themselves through vicissitudes of their history, validating their social organizations, their political systems, their moral attitudes and religious beliefs, even their prejudices. Such stories serve the purpose of consolidating whatever gains people or their leaders have made or imagine they have made in their existential journey through the world.[14]

A society's collection of stories, especially those it considers classic (i.e. of first class), plays a fundamental part in imparting its values and cultural personality to its members. In ancient Greece, the Homeric epics provided the basis of education in what the Greeks considered civilized, as opposed to barbarian, conduct. In old China, the Confucian classics were the foundation of cultural education. In the Arab world, the Koran, which is the central text of Arab religion, together with the Hadith, provides the basis of cultural education. The Old Testament Bible, especially its first five books, the Pentateuch, has shaped the identity and outlook of Jews down the millennia. In modern Europe and the Americas, the classics of Greek, Roman and Hebrew literature, together with the classics of modern Western literature, are at the core of the humanistic instruction which moulds the identity and values of the educated Westerner.

Faithful to this sensible practice, pre-colonial African societies brought up their members on their own inheritance of classic stories. But in neo-colonial Africa today, the classics bequeathed by pre-colonial African societies have been denied a comparable role in official culture. They are generally excluded from the curricula of schools and universities, leaving the Western inheritance of classic stories as the basis of humanistic instruction for the African elite-in-training. If African stories are used at all, they are mostly works produced under European dispensation. Thus, drama syllabuses cover a 'tradition' that is alleged to run from Aeschylus, Euripides and Aristophanes, through Shakespeare, Molière and Lope de Vega to Shaw, Brecht and Soyinka. Poetry

[14] Chinua Achebe, op. cit.

syllabuses proceed from Homer, Virgil and Horace, through Chaucer, Villon and Dante, to Yeats, Rimbaud, Eliot, Senghor and Okigbo. Those who organize such syllabuses do not appear to notice any anomaly in a 'tradition' which simply tags a few twentieth-century Africans on to the tail of the European tradition.

Such practices indicate that, in the official view of Africa's literary and educational bureaucracies, the study of the humanities is the study of Western humanities, and of whatever has been spawned by them in Africa since the European invasion. That is the scandal of the humanities in Africa – that the literary tradition of Europe, rather than the even much older African literary tradition, is the basis of humanities instruction in post-colonial Africa today.

To appreciate fully just how absurd this is, one need only observe that Africa is probably the only continent where, in the official elite culture of its indigenous peoples, the humanities are taught through materials imported from alien conquerors, without coherent reference to the classics of its own pre-colonial civilization. If matters are to be put right, the classics of 5,000 years of African literature, as selected down the millennia by African assessors, should form the tradition to which the best of twentieth-century African works are appended. The drama tradition would run from the Ancient Egyptian sacred drama *The Triumph of Horus*, to J. P. Clark's *The Wives' Revolt*; the poetry tradition from the Pyramid Texts of Ancient Egypt to Senghor and p'Bitek; and the narrative tradition from such Ancient Egyptian stories as 'The Eloquent Peasant' and 'The Lion in Search of Man', down to those being invented by the Achebes and Tutuolas.

One of the sources of that absurd 'tradition' is the entrenchment in Africa, since colonial times, of the Eurocentric definition of the humanities as the branches of learning concerned with ancient Greek and Latin cultures. Despite the fact that humanity includes all of humankind, the study of non-European cultures does not qualify for a place in Eurocentric humanities! The implicit notion that non-Europeans are somehow less than human is partly responsible for relegating the study of non-European cultures to other disciplines: Oriental Studies for Arab, Indian, Chinese, Japanese and other Asian cultures; Anthropology for the allegedly primitive cultures of Africa, pre-Columbian America, Oceania, etc. The most serious consequence for African education of this European cultural chauvinism is the teaching of Western humanities as if they were the only and universal humanities. To root such consequences out, the Eurocentric notion of humanities must be repudiated, and the notion of African humanities must be entrenched in Africa.

To accept Senghor's point about African humanities, and Achebe's point about stories creating people creating stories, is to realize that African stories, wherein the characteristics of humanity are given an African emphasis, should be used to create African people to create African stories. The core of the collection of such stories would be classic or first-rate works which express what Africans have felt and thought about their lives and societies and the world, particularly in the classical periods of African civilization, such as Pharaonic Egypt, pre-Islamic Nubia, the West African empires of Ghana, Mali and Songhay, etc. Only when such materials are assembled, can African humanities (instead of European, Arab or any other non-African humanities) have pride of place in the education of Africans. As I have argued elsewhere, 'If charity is to begin at home, then the sensible procedure is for Africans to master African literature, philosophy, history and cultural traditions before venturing to study those of other lands.'[15] In other words, African education ought, properly, to be based on a tradition of African humanities.

The imperative to assemble the classics from 5,000 years of African literature may be best understood by reference to the sculptural, architectural and ornamental arts. Anyone who has felt the arresting presence of the classics exhibited in 'Treasures of Ancient Nigeria – Legacy of 2,000 Years', or in 'Treasures of Tutankhamun', or who has seen the pyramids and other monumental architecture of the Nile Valley, thereupon acquires a sense of an African tradition that is second to none in the world. He is thereafter unlikely to be impressed by African imitations of Picasso, Rodin and Le Corbusier, not even if the cultural czars of Europe should mischievously heap their praises and prizes on such imitations. By standing on the shoulders of an excellent African tradition, the African sculptor can confidently face the world, and create without an inferiority complex.

[15] Chinweizu, *Decolonizing the African Mind*, Lagos, Pero Press, 1987, p. 271.

In contrast with that situation in the sculptural arts, some of the pathetic features of twentieth-century African literature, such as the Hopkins' Disease brand of poetry, are traceable to the lamentable fact that the masterpieces of 5,000 years of African literature have not been made the starting point of literary education in Africa. One of the aims of this anthology is, therefore, to make a small contribution toward harvesting Africa's literary classics. It is not claimed that the works here are Africa's classics of the twentieth century; far from it! The aim in selecting them is simply to open our eyes to the diverse fields where we must go and search for the classics of African literature.

In the passage which serves as the epigraph to this anthology, Okot p'Bitek advocated, as a way of instigating an African cultural revolution, that we 'break down the walls that surround our schools and universities, and let the people who know our culture teach our people'. What might result were that indeed to happen in literature?

Imagine that the gates of Africa's universities are thrown open, and that master singers, story-tellers, poets, orators and theatre groups from Africa's villages and towns take over the lecture halls, auditoriums and open fields of African campuses and begin to recite, read and perform in the languages spoken by Africans. Imagine that they are joined by the handful of African story-tellers, poets and drama troupes from within the universities, who carry on in the languages imposed on Africans by foreign conquerors. Imagine that, in a drawn-out literary festival, they present works commemorating national and continental events; works for social ceremonies like births, weddings, deaths, planting and harvesting; and that, every evening, they entertain and instruct their audiences with plays, fables, epics, adventure stories and tales of all sorts. Imagine that their audiences are drawn from the entire society, including villagers, townsfolk, and campus intellectuals. Imagine also that the best of the works presented are chosen by the votes of the assembled populace, and are then put together into a book.

Before such audiences, the authority of foreign critics and prize-givers would evaporate; their lordly pronouncements would carry no cultural authority whatever, but would be recognized as utterances by insolent outsiders meddling in a family gathering. Consequently, the works selected by the festival would reflect what African societies, rather than foreign mentors, consider the best to be.

A book made up of winning works from such a festival would be an alternative to existing anthologies which rarely look beyond the academy for entries or critical judgement when they assemble works of African literature. The book would be, quite naturally, dominated by the output of the traditional masters of the word; after all, they vastly outnumber the academic writers in Africa today, and they are more in tune with the taste of the majority of Africans. It would be dominated by works in which a majority of Africans would take pleasure; those works which give the impression of being addressed to non-African audiences and prize-givers would find no place in the book if, in calculating to please alien masters, they become stylistically strange or unintelligible to the African audience, or are loaded with anti-African prejudices which violate African self-respect. Such a book would give a foretaste of what African literature would look like when it is eventually Africanized by the type of cultural revolution which Okot p'Bitek demanded.

This book has been conceived in the spirit of what Okot p'Bitek advocated, namely, a surge of popular, traditional culture into the centres of the official, alienated, and neo-colonial culture of Africa's state elites. Like that imagined festival, it attempts to present African literature from the viewpoint of the general, unalienated African audience, and not from the viewpoint of the Western mentors to whom Africa's official literature has hitherto been attuned. In particular, it does not accept the authority of alien pundits and prize-givers, from the Nobel Foundation down, and has not been swayed in its selections by reputations based on their mischievous, neo-colonial accolades. As a result, an unusually large proportion of its contents (roughly one half of its 186 items) comes from traditional literature that was composed in African languages. All of which help to make it an anthology unlike any other now available.

Features of the anthology

The title, selection principles, and organization of this anthology call for some explanation.

In traditional Africa, griots and towncriers have long been archetypal masters of verbal communication. The towncrier carries salutations and, with quickening oratory, declares to the community the hot issues of the moment; the griot hands down the communal memory from generation to generation, thus instructing his hearers in the African humanities.

While the role of the towncrier probably needs no explanation, that of the griot may not be familiar to the reader. The word griot (probably of Franco-Portuguese derivation) has come to be used to denote a specialist musician-cum-narrator of the type found in the Malinke culture zone of West Africa. The Malinke (alternatively known as Mandingo) are to be found in Senegal, Mali, Guinea and Burkina Faso – countries which today occupy territories that belonged to the ancient African empires of Ghana, Mali and Songhay. The Malinke griots were advisers to kings and praise-singers to princely families; they were preservers of the traditions, and from them were selected private tutors for young princes and nobles. For millennia, and in all parts of Africa, counterparts of the Malinke griots have enlightened and entertained their audiences with songs, stories, epics, admonitions, histories and moral instructions. They have transmitted the classics of African societies and, taken as a functional group, they have served as traditional Africa's informal academy of the humanities.

Between them, griots and towncriers have preserved and transmitted much of the flower of what Africans have said to Africans about the world. It is proper, I believe, for them to be honoured in the title of an anthology which stresses the social context and humanistic functions of African literature.

The selection has been guided by the following principles:

1) That each work of literature is a historical artefact. Its production and consumption are acts within the social history of its originating community.

2) That while the making of a literary work may be purely an act of self-expression, its presentation to an audience is an act of public communication; and in so far as publication is expected to elicit varied responses from the public, and usually does, literary works are an integral part of public conversation.

3) That the hallmark of a good piece of literature is neither its form (e.g. whether it is versified or uses rhymes), nor whether it conforms to any given models or definitions, but whether it is a

moving or memorable utterance which touches the reader or hearer emotionally, intellectually, morally or aesthetically. The more moving or memorable it is, the better it is, the classics being those which exhibit this power in the highest degree, and which, by their enduring relevance, invite repeated reading or hearing.

4) That works composed for African audiences, by Africans, and in African languages, whether originally oral or written, constitute the historically indisputable core of African literature. To that core must be added works composed for African audiences, by Africans, in those non-African languages which African communities have been obliged, by foreign conquerors, to employ.

5) That communities of alien conquerors, or of their alien camp-followers, do not qualify as African, regardless of how long they have expropriated parts of the continent and settled there. Hence, the literatures of Arab and European settlers are excluded. (It should be noted that the literature of the Berbers is represented. Though submerged and dispersed by 2,500 years of successive European and Arab conquests, they are indigenous to North Africa. They are a North African counterpart of the blacks of Azania/South Africa.)

6) That the emphasis, in an anthology of this sort, is on letting the reader into the twentieth-century African conversation about the African experience of life. The anthology therefore includes not only works composed in the twentieth century, but also African works, from any other period, which have enjoyed a twentieth-century African audience. Examples of these are the epics, fables and religious materials handed down from previous centuries.

7) That the interest of this English-language anthology is to harvest only such pieces as have been effectively rendered in English.

The resulting selections contain African responses to diverse facets of life. These include war, power, religion, affairs of state; African landscape, flora and fauna; work, adventure, leisure; birth, death, courtship, marriage, child-rearing and the other enterprises of the hearth; flood, famine, drought, and other disasters; as well as travel to foreign lands. The literary genres represented include short stories, epics and novels (in extracts), parables, fables, myths, songs, boasts, satires, dirges, and epigrams.

Out of concern for the humanities, the entries have been organized to facilitate insight into values which Africa's masters of the word have manifested in their communications. I have chosen to divide human concerns into these broad areas: the arena of public affairs, the domain of intimate matters, and the field of more distanced phenomena — human, environmental and cosmic. The eleven thematic sections of the anthology have, accordingly, been grouped into three parts named 'The Arena of Public Affairs', 'The Local and Intimate Turf', and 'Fields of Wonder'.

African life in the twentieth century has been dominated by foreign conquest and foreign rule, mainly by Europeans, and secondarily by Arabs. These have provoked political and cultural nationalisms which have brought political independence to most of the nations created by foreign rulers. The African experience of relations between rulers and ruled has undergone changes as the pre-conquest rulers were superseded by the foreign rulers who, in their turn, were replaced, at independence, by the new African elites. War has been a recurring feature of African life in this century. The initial wars of resistance to foreign conquest, the wars of liberation which helped bring independence, as well as the post-independence wars between African armies, have provided themes for Africa's masters of the word. Examples of their output on such aspects of the African experience are grouped under 'The Arena of Public Affairs'.

As everyone knows, life in the personal sphere is dominated by births and deaths, by the events of growing up, by instruction in the ways appropriate for membership in one's community, by work and play, and by the complexities of relations between the sexes. Works on such matters are grouped under 'The Local and Intimate Turf'. Works on matters which lie outside the arena and the hearth are gathered under 'Fields of Wonder'.

It would be useful to note the impact of social organization on the production of various kinds of literature, by comparing the contributions to some parts of this anthology by traditional and state-elite cultures. The latter dominate in 'The Arena of Public Affairs', reflecting the sociological fact that affairs of state have been removed from previously autonomous local communities where traditional culture held sway, and are now firmly in the hands of state-elites. In writing about what their social position thrusts centrally into their lives, members of state-elites have produced most of the literature dealing with colonial conquest and colonial rule, the alienation it caused in their lives, and the political and cultural nationalism which it provoked.

In contrast, works from state-elite culture do not dominate in 'The Local and Intimate Turf'. After all, everybody, elite or not, urbanite or villager, has a social life, a work life, a personal life. If anything, state-elite writers are underproductive in this area because their lives have lost those special structures which demand that the main events of personal and community life be celebrated with new works. For instance, since planting, harvesting and hunting have become marginal to their urban and bureaucratic lives, one would be surprised if they produced a lot on such themes. Besides that, they have been underproductive on themes associated with those events which they still celebrate (like weddings and birthdays). Most appear content to utilize European wedding marches and hymns ('Here Comes the Bride', 'O Perfect Love'); European birthday songs ('Happy Birthday to You'); European lullabies and children's songs ('Baa Baa Black Sheep', 'Frère Jacques'); and Euro-Christian funeral hymns ('Nearer My God to Thee', 'Sleep On, Beloved'). Many do so in the belief that using these European works of literature makes them 'civilized'; and that using traditional African lullabies, wedding songs and dirges would be 'uncivilized'.

A similar observation may be made about the relative contributions of traditional culture and state-elite culture to the section on Cosmic Mysteries. Here the traditional producers dominate, since the elites, having adopted as 'gospel truth' the Hebrew and Arab myths embedded in the Christianity and Islam to which they have been converted, have abandoned interest in speculation on gods, cosmic mysteries and other extraordinary occurrences.

Needless to say, this is an anthology, not just of African academic literature, nor just of African popular literature, but of both, for only in that way can it contribute to dismantling the wall which literary academics have erected between the two. The only kind of works which have, on principle, been excluded from consideration are those which are blatantly Euro-assimilationist. I believe that works by Africans which pander to white racism, or which emulate the obscurantist and uncommunicative styles of Euromodernism, belong, not to African literature, but in some appendix to an anthology of European literature.

This anthology ought to interest those who are free from Euro-modernist aesthetics and its affectations; and those who are free to look at literature with fresh eyes, and who let each work speak for itself, without being bamboozled by the reputation of its author, or lack thereof. But those brought up on the Euromodernist notion that a passage must be the indecipherable outpouring of genius, divine spirit, or semi-divine shaman for it to be 'literature', are unlikely to be impressed by what they find here – intelligible works produced by ordinary, mortal craftsmen for mortal readers. Similarly, those who are indoctrinated into the delusion that a work is not 'literature' if the average newspaper-reader can understand and enjoy it, without help from academic interpreters, will not find here the jargon to which they are addicted. Likewise, the post-modernists will not find here poems or novels whose 'meanings' are other poems or novels; nor will they find works generated by the 'anxiety of influence', but only works shaped by life. As for those who believe that, as the cliché has it, 'literature is language', they will be disappointed since this anthology operates on the ancient principle that literary quality is not a question of using 'sophisticated' language to say next to nothing, but of how well matter and manner combine to produce memorable utterance.

Finally, this anthology is not likely to appeal to those African Ph.Ds who have been, through no fault of theirs, aesthetically miseducated on a narrow diet of Euromodernist works. Their sensibility may be likened to that of a child who grew up confined to a dank, unlit cellar; when he is brought into the open air and bright daylight, he would have to be cured of his sensory deprivations before he can appreciate the diverse sights, sounds and aromas of the world. For such African Ph.Ds, I would recommend, as therapy, that they read a work like *Limits of Art*, edited by Huntington Cairns.[16] It is an anthology of what Western critics of the non-modernist tradition, from Aristotle down, have declared the best of their literature, and why. They will learn why certain passages by Homer, Catullus, Sappho, Anacreon, Martial, Juvenal, Chaucer, Dante, Villon, Heine and others down to James Joyce are considered classic. Exposure to a non-modernist tradition whose authority their Eurocentrism is likely to accept, should get them to appreciate that there

[16] Princeton University Press, 1948.

is far more to literature than is contained in the Euromodernist dungeon. Thereafter, our Euromodernist Ph.Ds might be better able to appreciate the kinds of works in this anthology.

A word on translations

It is inevitable that translations should play a decisive role in any presentation in one language of works which were originally composed in the hundreds of languages which Africans have used to communicate with one another. This fact may cause disquiet to those who thoughtlessly bemoan what is inevitably lost in translation, and who do not give appropriate recognition to what comes through. It ought, therefore, to be noted that what gets lost in translation tends to be such language-specific features as rhyme, rhythm, assonance and metric patterns which may not be reproducible in a language with different resources. On the other hand, much gets conveyed by competent translators, particularly the sense and force of a passage. A good example of this is the spectacular case of the Bible, which has been translated into virtually every language in the world. If what comes across is memorable, felicitous and moving, and if it retains the sense and something of the style of the original, then the result, I believe, is as good as can be had.

Conclusion

In the last analysis, an anthology represents the personal taste and the public aims of its compiler. This anthology consists of works in which I take pleasure, in which I find instruction, and which, I believe, others will enjoy if they are interested in the texture and flavour of African life, and in the artistic spirit of twentieth-century Africa.

Concerning its public aims, this anthology aims to stimulate a displacement of Euro-assimilationist, academic literature from its dominant place in Africa, and to help replace it with the Afrocentric, non-academic literature which, by rights, should form the mainstream of African literary culture. As Okot p'Bitek rightly insisted, Africa's literary academy needs to open its gates to all types of African popular literature if it is to be vitalized, if it is to become relevant to African life, and if it is to be cured of the Eurocentric sterility which its narrow diet encourages.

If this anthology can help to end the official disregard for Africa's non-academic literature; if it helps to end the impression that African literature is merely a third-rate appendage to European literature; if it can help persuade the African reader that African literature can be fun, can be instructive, can play a vital role in his life and his consciousness, and is not simply an instrument of torture that is gleefully used on him by sadistic professors; if it contributes to winning for African literature a wider and more appreciative readership, I shall be quite satisfied.

I should add that this anthology embodies the Pan-Africanist cultural standpoint which is articulated in *Toward the Decolonization of African Literature* (1980); however, I must also stress that it is *not* the long-awaited Volume II of that work. That anthology of 5,000 years of Pan-African literature is, alas, yet to be completed.

Chinweizu, Lagos, November 1987

PART ONE

The Arena of Public Affairs

I — THE AFRO-EURASIAN ENCOUNTER

The Rout of the Arabi*

A moon went by, and another, and all in all four moons went by. Then, one bright sunny morning four sea canoes were seen far out at sea. They were coming nearer and nearer, but as yet we could not recognize whose they were. The sign of Dom Manuel was a black piece of fabric flying on a pole, and all his canoes carried this black flag. Mandlenyati shaded his eyes and told us softly that they were indeed the war canoes of the Man of Steel.

Zulu shouted an order to his warriors and a great smoky fire was lit, so as to give off a pillar which could rise like a cloud into the sky. It was our agreed signal that we were still in the same place and that we welcomed them, having much to trade.

Suddenly a strange thing happened – a most unexpected thing. From the tops of the canoes, and from the masts, there came flashes as of brightly polished bronze winking in the sun. We watched, puzzled, and then a small boat left the largest and newest-looking canoe. As it made towards the land, we descended the hill and ran to the shore, Maneruana with us. The boat came fast, its oars like the legs of a strange sea insect as they lashed the placid sea to foam. There was Dom Manuel with his red sash and the red plume on his helmet waving in the breeze.

I noted with surprise that nearly all of his men now wore corselets of iron. He himself was a pillar of steel in the stern of his boat. It ground into the sand and the Potugiza climbed out, those wearing steel making deep imprints with their boots in the sand.

There was a grin on the face of Dom Manuel as Maneruana interpreted his words: 'Dom Manuel says he greets you all and he has come in peace. This day he has the honour of proving his friendship to the Zulus. He says you must put that smoky fire out, as a mighty band of Arabi slavers is nearby. This band of Arabi has heard of your gold-mine and the other treasures you have here. It is said that one of your own Zulus has given this information to the Arabi. For several moons the Arabi have been banding together and marching through the forests. They could by now be even half a day's journey from here. They want to slaughter the Zulus, take as many slaves as possible, and capture your wealth. Dom Manuel has come to lend a hand of strength to the Zulus and will fight by their side.'

We were thunderstruck at the news.

This was incredible – a Zulu conniving with the Arabi for the destruction of the Zulus. But how did Dom Manuel come to know all this. I asked Dom Manuel to enlighten us, through Maneruana.

'Dom Manuel says the Potugiza settlement of Beyira is very big and there are many people there, both Potugiza and Arabi. His men, whose duty it is to spy for him so that he will best know which ships are laden with riches for him to rob, found a rumour flying around among the Arabi merchants. The rumour spoke of a fabulous gold-mine in the south, worked by a migrant tribe called the Zulus. The great leader of the slave raiders, Ben Sayyid the Terrible, sent messages to all his Arabi friends to rally to his assistance. Every Arabi criminal has taken up arms and has joined Ben Sayyid. Dom Manuel has had his men out spying on these Arabi, and he has followed them for some time along the coast. He says all preparations for war must be made immediately.'

Zulu lifted his great horn and blew a long blast. The Zulus had been keenly awaiting this sound for a long time, and their keen ears picked it up across the length and breadth of the area they occupied. The blast conveyed only one message: 'To me – to me – all Regiments.'

We then watched as the men of Dom Manuel disembarked and there were close on five hundred of them. They wore steel cuirasses and helmets and they carried tremendous weapons which looked like a combination of spear and battle axe. Some carried the dreaded weapon called the *isibamu* which makes a terrible noise and belches fire and smoke. It is said that this weapon can hurl a heavy bead across a great distance, much further than a sling can hurl a slingstone. The men carrying these weapons did not wear body armour, only helmets, and they also carried horns by their sides containing the magic powder which causes the mighty belch of fire.

But there was a yet more incredible sight. A great ugly boat approached the shore carrying but a few men. Most of the space on the boat was taken up by one of the ugliest things we had ever seen. The thing was like a huge long clay pot, but made of thick bronze and mounted on a large flat piece of wood with two strange round things on either side. The thing sat there in the boat like a nightmare from a dark land. Maneruana explained that it was a very big version of the *isibamu*, but we called it the Beast.

The Beast was trundled off the boat across a flat piece of wood and we could tell by the ruts it made in the sand just how heavy it was. It took twenty-five sweating Potugiza and forty sweating Zulus to manhandle the thing through the loose sand on to firmer ground. They pulled and they pushed and cursed in their respective languages, and by midday the Beast squatted obscenely right in the centre of the Zulu village.

We watched as the Beast was prepared for battle. A Potugiza with an unpronounceable name made it eat a quantity of black soot-like powder – the magic fire powder – and its wide mouth yawned hungrily. The Potugiza and an assistant pushed a wadded piece of skin down its throat —. with a long stick. It was then fed a heavy ball of metal, also pushed in with the same long stick.

'They are feeding the Beast . . . it must be very hungry,' remarked the dwarf Malevu, who had watched everything carefully and who was growing rather fond of the Beast. Dom Manuel suggested that we lay a trap for the Arabi and ordered that the tracks of the Beast be erased; that a hut be built over it with a door at its mouth, and that a *kaross* be placed over the door.

Zulus and Potugiza took to the forests, leaving only two Zulu regiments and the servants of the Beast to defend the kraal. Zulu went with the units into the forests and I took command of the regiments in the kraal. The Potugiza had moved their war canoes to the south so that the Arabi would suspect nothing.

We waited for three days and the enemy did not appear. Zulu sent scouts all over the land and these brought no news of the enemy's whereabouts. This was greatly puzzling, and it was not till the fourth day that we received the explanation. A warrior came with the astonishing news that the Arabi were pouring out of the mouth of our mine, right behind our lines.

I searched with my mind far back into the past and something flared like a mighty sun in my memory – the Tagati mine had another entrance. Whoever it was playing traitor among the Zulus must have discovered the second entrance and also disclosed this information to the Arabi. The story behind all this, as we learnt it afterwards, was incredible.

The Arabi were massing at the mouth of the mine and Zulu ordered us to attack them immediately before more of them could come through. The Zulus rushed through the forest in a savage tide, accompanied by a group of Potugiza armed with 'bursters'. A hail of throwing spears tore into the Arabi, who were now trapped in the depression near the mine. Some of the Arabi had 'bursters' too, and there was a series of savage explosions as these were discharged at the Zulus and the first Bantu ever to die before this terrible weapon fell in this battle. A great clamour rose in the forest. Surprised by this strange way of making war, the Zulus turned and fled.

The Potugiza were on their own now, brave men with their 'bursters' keeping up a savage reply to the Arabi from behind rocks and trees. Zulu tried to rally his regiments and a terrible disaster loomed darkly over all the tribe and its allies.

Dom Manuel came up with the rest of his men. But their long, unwieldy weapons slowed their march through the bush. It was a time of peril and uncertainty. Taking advantage of the scattering of the Zulu regiments, the Arabi tried to break out of the depression and it was then that a miracle happened – a double miracle. A withering hail of Bushmen arrows tore into the enemy.

The Arabi fell and died in agony on the ground. Again and again the hidden Bushmen fired a rain of arrows into the confused Arabi, and it was then that Vura-Sereto and the Nana-Cwedi came into the attack – a shocking thing which the Zulus never expected. I had not known this, but each of the Nana-Cwedi was a peerless woman archer.

With those bursts of hellish missiles the Arabi fell back into the depression and into the mine in a howling rush. The Potugiza came up and their weapons roared.

The Zulu regiments rallied, shamed by the fact that the situation had been saved by unknown Bushmen and the Moon Women. They roared into the depression to close in on the Arabi. A terrible battle raged in the confined space, but the Arabi had the courage of cornered rats; they fought with a ferocity typical of the murderers they were. They cleaved the skulls and lopped off the limbs of their attackers with long curved swords, even while they were being overwhelmed and killed like dogs. The Zulus were like demons running amok; they were cold in their determination to wash their shame off in Arabi blood, and in their own. They cheered those of their own comrades who fell and the wild, terrible warcry of charging Zulu suicide squadrons rang loud in the air.

More Zulus raged into the depression, and still more. The Arabi were sent reeling back into the mine. It was then that Vura-Sereto came with her second surprise. She had positioned her archers so that each had a command of the entrance to the tunnel and now they were raining arrows into it, denying the Arabi the opportunity to enter. She was also denying an outlet to the bulk of the Arabi force still underground. Then she brought forth burning trees and bundles of grass, launching them down the slope above the mine into the entrance. Tree after tree was rolled over and a breeze fanned the flames, sending a blast of heat and smoke into the mine. The Arabi in the depression were slaughtered mercilessly to the last man.

'My lord, Dom Manuel says that we have only destroyed a fraction of the Arabi. He says that we must keep the fire at the entrance burning and fed with green branches to fill the tunnels with smoke. He says that Ben Sayyid is not among the slain and he must still be with the main body of his men.'

'Tell Dom Manuel that we honour him and thank him for his wise advice. Tell him that his wisdom is as great as his courage is formidable. Tell him that it is our resolution to hunt the Arabi down to the last man so as to redeem our shame at wavering in the face of the Arabi bursters.'

'My lord, I know where the Arabi are. Skiwa the Bushman and his friends here will guide us thither.' That was the soft voice of Vura-Sereto. 'I suggest an attack with all the forces available.'

'It shall be done, Goddess, it shall be done,' replied Zulu.

'My lord, Dom Manuel suggests that we bring the great Beast with us. He asks that cattle be used to haul it,' said Maneruana. 'He says also that this is going to be the great battle and with this battle we must feed Ben Sayyid, Stealer of Men, to the vultures.'

In the bustle of preparations that followed I sought out Skiwa and asked him to explain the sudden presence of a hundred Bushmen, led by him, in the battle at the mine. The little yellow man cocked his head to one side and said he had known of the presence of these Bushmen for a long time. They were living in the other entrance to the mine and were very cross when the Arabi came to disturb them. He also told me that for many nights a band of Zulus, led by an old woman, had been visiting the mine. They had visited the mine the day the Potugiza came with the storm, and they were then accompanied by Luamerava.

A sickness overwhelmed my heart and I walked over to where the Potugiza were inspanning the great Beast. Dom Manuel was with me, also Maneruana. I saw Maneruana stoop and pick up something from the ground and stare at it for a long time.

'What is that, Maneruana?' I asked curiously.

'It is a fragment of the thing I once saw carried out of this kraal, on the night I arrived here.'

I recognized it immediately as a fragment of one of the Ma-Iti clay coffins from the mine. 'Who were carrying out a clay coffin from the kraal?'

'Do you know nothing about it, my lord?' she asked in great surprise. 'Luamerava said it was yours. It was in the hut that was given to me the first night. I was wondering what the Zulus were doing with such a thing in their midst when Luamerava came in. She said I was trespassing in one of your forbidden huts and that I was to leave the hut immediately. Five other Zulu men then came in, removed the coffin and took it right out of the kraal. I was curious and asked her about this strange behaviour. She flared into murderous anger, saying you had instructed her not to answer any questions about the coffin and that anybody interfering must be killed. She stabbed me with a sharp meat knife, but Luanaledi turned up just in time to save me.'

'Maneruana,' I said, 'I swear by all that is holy that I know nothing about this affair. I can see that there is a great treachery afoot. The leader of this dark affair is the one who directed the Arabi to the mine and this village.'

Then the quiet, half-caste woman gave me yet another surprise. 'I know who the leader is, my lord. I thought you knew too. He led the group who removed the Ma-Iti clay coffin. It is Gawula, the Rainbow Induna.'

'What!'

'My lord, when Luamerava came with the five men, when they were still outside the hut, I heard Gawula say something about a messenger having already been sent and that things would soon start happening. And as they carried the clay coffin out he was speaking to somebody inside it . . .'

She suddenly fell on her knees, her eyes wide with fear. I could see from her eyes that she was looking at somebody behind me and I knew what was coming even before I saw the spear hissing past Maneruana's neck. I spun round and sent my own spear straight at the attacker, who was almost outside the gate. There was a thud and a loud, gurgling howl as my spear found its mark.

I lifted Maneruana and we ran to the gate. There lay Gawula; he was already dead for my spear had penetrated his heart.

I was beside myself with anger and frustration – at myself and at all the miserable creatures who laid foul plots and wove intrigues in the dark to smash my plans for building up a strong Zulu nation. I strode across to the huts that formed my home and I found Luanaledi standing there with all her dogs round her.

'Child, I want you to guard Maneruana with your life and you must confine Luamerava to her hut. I shall deal with her after I return from the battle. But to make sure, I am going to tie her up. Is she in her hut?'

'I think so, father.'

I bade Luamerava come out of her hut, and she came forth, great with child. Even in her pregnancy her beauty was astounding, second only to the fairest of the Nana-Cwedi, Letakisa the Sparrow. 'What is this evil you are now mixed in woman? How many times must I go on forgiving you?'

'I cannot help myself, lord; I really cannot help myself . . .'

Before I knew what was happening she was away, running as fast as a pregnant woman can run. I was so surprised that I did not move for some time. I stood paralysed as I watched her run, eight moons pregnant, straight for the pen which housed my vicious bull, Ntontozayo. The bull was in a very wicked mood that day and had to be kept penned up. He spied Luamerava and a film of savage anger clouded his eyes. There was a sound like thunder as he smashed out of his pen and dry dung, dust and splitered poles exploded into the air. Luamerava was tossed into the air like a beautiful, helpless doll . . .

I managed to control the bull and I recovered Luamerava. She was badly injured across her stomach. I wrapped her in my battle *kaross* and gently carried her back to her hut.

Luanaledi's voice was cold as she said: 'Why did you not leave the bull alone, father . . . she deserved what she was getting.'

'Get away, child, and leave me alone!'

'You love this slatternly thing, don't you, father?'

Another voice intruded softly: 'My lord, I am yours to command. Say what you need . . .'

'Bring much water, Maneruana, much hot water, quickly.'

We saved Luamerava, but she has lost her baby.

The battle has been raging for a full half-day now, and many men are dead – mostly Arabi. As I come through the bush I am in time to see the Arabi ranks break for the last time and shatter before the combined Zulus, Potugiza and Bushmen. Here and there I see a Potugiza lying in all his steel amongst dead Zulus and Arabi. Bursters roar and their voices are the voices of triumph, for they are now mainly Potugiza weapons.

The Potugiza are fantastic fighters and terrible in battle. This open country is ideal for them, for they are advancing in solid ranks with their long *halabadas*, as they call their fantastic war weapons, part-spear and part-axe.

Then it happens, right in front of my eyes, at the foot of the hill on which I am standing. There is a bright flash of flame, followed by a loud thunder, and a cloud of smoke rises in the valley. A group of Arabi which have just formed up is clawed to pieces as something unseen tears into it. Bodies are hurled in all directions, legs and arms flying through the air. The same thing that has struck them causes a mighty fountain of dust and rock where it strikes the slope of the hill further back. The Beast has spoken.

I run down to it, and watch the crew feeding it again. It squats there in its artificial nest and glares malevolently. There is one Potugiza who is in charge of the whole thing and next to him stands Malevu, his one eye bright with excitement. Two of the Potugiza are behind the Beast, and one holds a small burning torch. The leading man raises his fist and shouts: '*Fuwego!*'

The one with the torch touches the brazen Beast behind and once more the flame licks out of the mouth. The noise is very sharp and terrible to hear, and the smoke is thick. Again the Arabi are scattered in all directions and the Zulus take advantage of the confusion.

I notice something which makes me feel sick; there are a number of our Bantu fighting side by side with the Arabi — black men wearing Arabi clothes and Arabi weapons against their own people. Tears of sorrow mist my eyes and a strange feeling falls over me — something tells me I am seeing the death of my race. The Bantu race is dying a slow spiritual and physical death; it may yet take hundreds of years. The Potugiza, fighting at our side this day, is but the first raindrop of a mighty deluge that will burst upon my fatherland and ruin it utterly within the next few hundred years. It will become a flood of foreign peoples. There is nothing I can do to stop the flow of the River of Fate.

I look up at the heavens and in the brilliant colours of the westering sun I see the road I must take. I see the future laid bare and the noise of the battle dies away in my ears. A vision opens itself to my eyes: I see my race sink in spirit to the lowest depths. I see evil, war and bloodshed; I see fantastic things that I cannot as yet understand, and I see things that are still a thousand years in the future. A voice reaches me from the depths — the Voice of the Ultimate reaches my soul:

Oh Eternal Wanderer, oh greatest Vagabond of Time
You whose weary, deathless feet must tread the path you see,
Be strong and be of courage, weep not like a widowed wife,
Nor be like fairest Amarava lost in the Forests of Time;
I have designed for Man a pattern and have set for him a path.
In my hands the life of worlds and all the tribes of Man
Are traces in eternal lines which none but I can e'er erase;
What I say shall happen, truly it will come to pass!
For I am the Chief Eternal — Monarch of the Realms of Time.
The Black Race of Tanga-Watu has been willed by me to fall
And sink for fifty centuries in slimy pits of Death—
To sink for years five thousand into degradation's Lake—
To wallow like a warthog in the pool of Evil's Mud!

All the other human races shall deride the Bantu Tree;
They will spit in sullen contempt at the feet of all your kind,
And their voice of loud derision unto all the stars shall rise.
The world, in scornful laughter, shall deride the Bantu face
And spit upon it and strike it many blows.
Then I, the Lord Eternal, shall lift high the Bantu hand;
And build for her a village out of rainbows and of stars—
Crown her with a silv'ry glory high above the nodding stars—
There to reign, a Mighty Empress, until Time shall flow no more!

There was a deep silence in my heart as the voice ended and the vision faded. The noise of battle filled my ears once more and my eyes were opened to see the final rout of the Arabi and the Bantu traitors with them. They dropped their swords and spears and shields as they ran, seeking safety in the hostile bush. They found nothing there but arrows waiting for them and they died in droves like helpless, yelling goats.

I saw the huge Dom Manuel strutting like a wild bull in front of his bristling ranks, thumping Zulu lustily on the back. I heard their loud laughter dimly across the distance.

Back in my hut, as night fell, Ben Sayyid was brought in and thrown contemptuously at my feet in a big red bundle. I looked for a long time into his cruel face with its hooked nose, black brows and glossy beard. And he glared savagely back at me from narrowed eyes. He did not realize that I could speak his language and he was visibly surprised when I greeted him:

It took him some time to recover from this. When he did so, he spoke thus: 'Dog of an unbeliever . . . soulless heathen *Kafur*!'

'A truce to your insolence, Sheik; I can easily order you killed.'

'Kill and have done,' snarled Ben Sayyid. 'Allah has willed it.'

'Allah has willed nothing of the sort, you putrid Arabi rat! You are defeated and your verminous followers are all dead. What now, Ben Sayyid?'

'Allah willed it thus . . . that is all.'

'Did your Allah will that the great Ben Sayyid should run like a skulking coward and not die with his men as all true leaders should? You are a coward, Ben Sayyid; your evil heart is quaking with fear even now. Tell me, why does your race abduct thousands of my people and sell them into slavery?'

'You *Kafurs* are not people,' snarled the Arabi. 'It is the will of Allah and the Prophet that we catch you and sell you, for you are not people . . . you have no souls. Allah gave you to us for servants.'

The Spirit of Anger filled my soul and I rose to my feet. I bent over him and struck him on the side of his face with such force that he rolled over completely. I felt a burst of heat above my head and I knew that the Light of the Immortals was flaring out from my hair. There was a deeper fear in his eyes.

'You are . . . you are a *jinni*!'

'Yes, I am Lumukanda, the Lost Immortal!' From a Ma-Iti jar, one which Zulu had given me, I took a handful of old gold coins and another of diamonds. I told the Arabi to take these and begone. He lay there incredulous, his mouth open as if he could not believe his ears.

'I spoke to you, spawn of a whore of Zanzibar! I told you to take this rubbish and be gone from here.'

'You are giving all this to me?'

'Arabi,' I said to him, 'your race sets much store by these things which you think are precious and which you call wealth. This is nothing but metal and useless stones from the earth. On the day you die you would not be able to purchase a single extra breath of air with this rubbish. If I were to cut off your hand now, this rubbish would not help you to buy another hand.

'Arabi, your race has killed, cheated and lied for this rubbish, which we give to our children to play with. You have depopulated vast areas of my fatherland because of this filth from the rocks and river beds of the earth. I am giving you this and letting you go to show you that I can afford to be merciful even to a rat like you. I am giving you the very rubbish you came all the way to get, and for which you sacrificed the lives of a few thousand human beings. It is written on the Web of Time that your cursed race, together with other races equally evil, will overrun this land and enslave my people. But it is also written that one day your cursed race shall grovel at the feet of my race and on that day, Arabi, your descendants shall pay in blood and tears for the crimes *you* are now committing in this land. You say only you have a God, Arabi, but your god is a murderer and a low assassin, like yourself! You say you have a God, Arabi, but your god is a demon, for no true God would ever condone what you are doing in my fatherland. Your religion is a lie! Your god is false! Take your weapons and begone!'

'I go now, wizard, *jinni* . . . whatever you are. But we shall meet again one day. By the Prophet, we shall . . . meet again.'

'Lord, where have you been?' Her voice is soft in the night.

'I have been out in the forest, Vura-Sereto, and in my Cave of Prayers.'

'I have something to tell you. Two things happened after our return from the battlefield and they need both your and my attention immediately. There is evil afoot, Lumukanda, and terror walks the night. Disaster has struck the Zulu people.'

'What happened, wife? What has happened?'

'Luanaledi was attending to Luamerava in the hut, and she sent Lulama-Maneruana to the river for water. She did not return and with a wide search one of the Nana-Cwedi found her . . .'

'Is Maneruana dead?'

'No, my lord, but she is mutilated. This is a serious loss to the Zulu tribe. Her wonderful tongue, which could speak the language of the Potugiza so well, has been cut out . . .'

'What!'

'That is not all, my lord. One of the Nana-Cwedi, Letaka, saw a strange figure leap over the palisade not so long ago and news has now reached us that two women have been found strangled in their huts and ten children are missing from different homes. Panic is beginning to mount among the Zulus.'

I feel weak, utterly helpless, and unable to think. My mind reels and my thoughts are scattered.

'What can be happening, wife? What does all this mean?'

'I have called a gathering of the Wives. Come, husband.'

Two days later Zulu held a great feast in celebration of his victory and in honour of Dom Manuel, our noble Potugiza ally. Twelve oxen were slaughtered and beer was plentiful. There was feasting and there was noise and laughter. But there was also a note of sadness – Lulama-Maneruana was not there to interpret for us. Dom Manuel told us in sign language that he would be sailing away that evening, but would return again in a year's time with even more trade than he had brought with this visit.

That year was a year of peace among the Zulus, and a year of hard work. We cultivated vast areas and planted the tobacco weed. The year also saw the rapid recovery of Lulama-Maneruana and the slow recovery of Luamerava.

We managed to destroy all the Zulus who had taken part in treachery. They were all together, on their knees before the strange alien goddess *Tagati* in the mine. There was a fire by which we could see some of the remains of the ten missing children. In one corner stood a broken Ma-Iti coffin.

On a roughly built altar something lay covered with a *kaross*. I tore the *kaross* off, and there was a corpse, a mummified corpse from the clay coffin, of a Ma-Iti woman who had died 2,000 years ago. Even as I stared at it, Vura-Sereto struck it and a great part disintegrated into dust.

'You fools,' cried Vura-Sereto. 'You forsake your own ancestors to worship a foreign deity! You turn your backs on your own religion to worship something you have stumbled across in this mine by accident. Now behold, you are left with no goddess, but a crumbling corpse.'

'We . . . we cannot understand,' cried one of the women. 'The Snake Mother was alive, and was speaking to us only a few moments ago!'

We left them in the cave like a row of stiff statues. Outside Vura-Sereto said to me: 'This mine has served its purpose; we have enough gold to trade with the Potugiza for years. I am going to close both entrances. Men of future generations will perhaps rediscover this mine and marvel at the twenty dried bodies they will find in here.'

With these words she raised her arms, and a mighty landslide covered both entrances.

Vusamazulu Credo Mutwa (Azania)
Extract from 'Luanaledi's Discovery'

The Death of Richard Corfield

You have died, Corfield, and are no longer in this world,
A merciless journey was your portion.
When, Hell-destined, you set out for the Other World
Those who have gone to Heaven will question you, if God is
    willing;
When you see the companions of the faithful and the jewels
    of Heaven,
Answer them how God tried you.
Say to them: 'From that day to this the Dervishes never
    ceased their assaults upon us.
The British were broken, the noise of battle engulfed us;
With fervour and faith the Dervishes attacked us.'
Say: 'They attacked us at mid-morning.'
Say: 'Yesterday in the holy war a bullet from one of their
    old rifles struck me.
And the bullet struck me in the arm.'
Say: 'In fury they fell upon us.'
Report how savagely their swords tore you,
Show these past generations in how many places the daggers
    were plunged.
Say: ' "Friend," I called, "have compassion and spare me!" '
Say: 'As I looked fearfully from side to side my heart was
    plucked from its sheath.'
Say: 'My eyes stiffened as I watched with horror;
The mercy I implored was not granted.'
Say: 'Striking with spear-butts at my mouth they silenced
    my soft words;
My ears, straining for deliverance, found nothing;
The risk I took, the mistake I made, cost my life.'
Say: 'Like the war leaders of old, I cherished great plans
    for victory.'
Say: 'The schemes and djinns planted in me brought my
    ruin.'
Say: 'When pain racked me everywhere
Men lay sleepless at my shrieks.'

Say: 'Great shouts acclaimed the departing of my soul.'
Say: 'Beasts of prey have eaten my flesh and torn it apart
    for meat.'
Say: 'The sound of swallowing the flesh and the fat comes
    from the hyena.'
Say: 'The crows plucked out my veins and tendons.'
Say: 'If stubborn denials are to be abandoned, then my
    clansmen were defeated.'
In the last stand of resistance there is always great slaughter.
Say: 'The Dervishes are like the advancing thunderbolts of a
    storm, rumbling and roaring.'

Mahammed Abdille Hasan (Somalia)

An End to Sovereignty*

Ezeulu often said that the dead fathers of Umuaro looking at the world from Ani-Mmo must be utterly bewildered by the ways of the new age. At no other time but now could Umuaro have taken war to Okperi in the circumstances in which they did. Who would have imagined that Umuaro would go to war so sorely divided? Who would have thought that they would disregard the warning of the priest of Ulu who originally brought the six villages together and made them what they were? But Umuaro had grown wise and strong in its own conceit and had become like the little bird, nza, who ate and drank and challenged his personal god to single combat. Umuaro challenged the deity which laid the foundation of their villages. And – what did they expect? – he thrashed them, thrashed them enough for today and for tomorrow!

In the very distant past, when lizards were still few and far between, the six villages – Umuachala, Umunneora, Umuagu, Umuezeani, Umuogwugwu and Umuisiuzo – lived as different peoples, and each worshipped its own deity. Then the hired soldiers of Abam used to strike in the dead of night, set fire to the houses and carry men, women and children into slavery. Things were so bad for the six villages that their leaders came together to save themselves. They hired a strong team of medicine-men to install a common deity for them. This deity which the fathers of the six villages made was called Ulu. Half of the medicine was buried at a place which became Nkwo market and the other half thrown into the stream which became Mili Ulu. The six villages then took the name of Umuaro, and the priest of Ulu became their Chief Priest. From that day they were never again beaten by an enemy. How could such a people disregard the god who founded their town and protected it? Ezeulu saw it as the ruin of the world.

On the day, five years ago, when the leaders of Umuaro decided to send an emissary to Okperi with white clay for peace or new palm frond for war, Ezeulu spoke in vain. He told the men of Umuaro that Ulu would not fight an unjust war.

'I know,' he told them, 'my father said this to me that when our village first came here to live the land belonged to Okperi. It was Okperi who gave us a piece of land to live in. They also gave us their deities – their Udo and their Ogwugwu. But they said to our ancestors – mark my words – the people of Okperi said to our fathers: We give you our Udo and our Ogwugwu; but you must call the deity we give you not Udo but the son of Udo, and not Ogwugwu but the son of Ogwugwu. This is the story as I heard it from my father. If you choose to fight a man for a piece of farmland that belongs to him I shall have no hand in it.'

But Nwaka had carried the day. He was one of the three people in all the six villages who had taken the highest title in the land, Eru, which was called after the lord of wealth himself. Nwaka came from a long line of prosperous men and from a village which called itself first in Umuaro. They said that when the six villages first came together they offered the priesthood of Ulu to the weakest among them to ensure that none in the alliance became too powerful.

'Umuaro kwenu!' Nwaka roared.

'Hem!' replied the men of Umuaro.

'Kwenu!'

'Hem!'

'Kwezuenu!'

'Hem!'

He began to speak almost softly in the silence he had created with his salutation.

'Wisdom is like a goatskin bag; every man carries his own. Knowledge of the land is also like that. Ezeulu has told us what his father told him about the olden days. We know that a father does not speak falsely to his son. But we also know that the lore of the land is beyond the knowledge of many fathers. If Ezeulu had spoken about the great deity of Umuaro which he carries and which his fathers carried before him I would have paid attention to his voice. But he speaks about events which are older than Umuaro itself. I shall not be afraid to say that neither Ezeulu nor any other in this village can tell us about these events.' There were murmurs of approval and of disapproval but more of approval from the assembly of elders and men of title. Nwaka walked forward and back as he spoke; the eagle feather in his red cap and bronze band on his ankle marked him out as one of the lords of the land – a man favoured by Eru, the god of riches.

'My father told me a different story. He told me that Okperi people were wanderers. He told me three or four different places where they sojourned for a while and moved on again. They were driven away by Umuofia, then by Abame and Aninta. Would they go today and claim all those sites? Would they have laid claim to our farmland in the days before the white man turned us upside down? Elders and Ndichie of Umuaro, let everyone return to his house if we have no heart in the fight. We shall not be the first people who abandoned their farmland or even their homestead to avoid war. But let us not tell ourselves or our children that we did it because the land belonged to other people. Let us rather tell them that their fathers did not choose to fight. Let us tell them also that we marry the daughters of Okperi and their men marry our daughters, and that where there is this mingling men often lose the heart to fight. Umuaro Kwenu!'

'Hem!'

'Kwezuenu!'

'Hem!'

'I salute you all.'

The long uproar that followed was largely of approbation. Nwaka had totally destroyed Ezeulu's speech. The last glancing blow which killed it was the hint that the Chief Priest's mother had been a daughter of Okperi. The assembly broke up into numerous little groups of people talking to those who sat nearest to them. One man said that Ezeulu had forgotten whether it was his father or his mother who told him about the farmland. Speaker after speaker rose and spoke to the assembly until it was clear that all the six villages stood behind Nwaka. Ezeulu was not the only man of Umuaro whose mother had come from Okperi. But none of the others dared go to his support. In fact one of them, Akukalia, whose language never wandered far from 'kill and despoil', was so fiery that he was chosen to carry the white clay and the new palm frond to his motherland, Okperi.

The last man to speak that day was the oldest man from Akukalia's village. His voice was now shaky but his salute to the assembly was heard clearly in all corners of the Nkwo market place. The men of Umuaro responded to his great effort with the loudest Hem! of the day. He said quietly that he must rest to recover his breath, and those who heard laughed.

'I want to speak to the man we are sending to Okperi. It is now a long time since we fought a war and many of you may not remember the custom. I am not saying that Akukalia needs to be reminded. But I am an old man, and an old man is there to talk. If the lizard of the homestead should neglect to do the things for which its kind is known, it will be mistaken for the lizard of the farmland.

'From the way Akukalia spoke I saw that he was in great anger. It is right that he should feel like that. But we are not sending him to his motherland to fight. We are sending you, Akukalia, to place the choice of war or peace before them. Do I speak for Umuaro?' They gave him power to carry on.

'We do not want Okperi to choose war; nobody eats war. If they choose peace we shall rejoice. But whatever they say you are not to dispute with them. Your duty is to bring word back to us. We all know you are a fearless man but while you are there put your fearlessness in your bag. If the young men who will go with you talk with too loud a voice it shall be your duty to cover their fault. I have in my younger days gone on such errands and know the temptations too well. I salute you.'

Ezeulu who had taken in everything with a sad smile now sprang to his feet like one stung in the buttocks by a black ant.

'Umuaro Kwenu!' he cried.

'Hem!'

'I salute you all.' It was like the salute of an enraged Mask. 'When an adult is in the house the she-goat is not left to suffer the pains of parturition on its tether. That is what our ancestors have said. But what have we seen here today? We have seen people speak because they are afraid to be called cowards. Others have spoken the way they spoke because they are hungry for war. Let us leave all that aside. If in truth the farmland is ours, Ulu will fight on our side. But if it is not we shall know soon enough. I would not have spoken again today if I had not seen adults in the house neglecting their duty. Ogbuefi Egonwanne, as one of the three eldest men in Umuaro should have reminded us that our fathers did not fight a war of blame. But instead of that he wants to teach our emissary how to carry fire and water in the same mouth. Have we not heard that a boy sent by his father to steal does not go stealthily but breaks the door with his feet? Why does Egonwanne trouble himself about small things when big ones are overlooked? We want war. How Akukalia speaks to his mother's people is a small thing. He can spit into their face if he likes. When we hear a house had fallen do we ask if the ceiling fell with it? I salute you all.'

Akukalia and his two companions set out for Okperi at cock-crow on the following day. In his goatskin bag he carried a lump of white chalk and a few yellow palm fronds cut from the summit of the tree before they had unfurled to the sun. Each man also carried a sheathed matchet.

The day was Eke, and before long Akukalia and his companions began to pass women from all the neighbouring villages on their way to the famous Eke Okperi market. They were mostly women from Elumelu and Abame who made the best pots in all the surrounding country. Everyone carried a towering load of five or six or even more big water pots held together with a net of ropes on a long basket, and seemed in the half light like a spirit with a fantastic head.

As the men of Umuaro passed company after company of these market women they talked about the great Eke market in Okperi to which folk from every part of Igbo and Olu went.

'It is the result of an ancient medicine,' Akukalia explained. 'My mother's people are great medicine-men.' There was pride in his voice. 'At first Eke was a very small market. Other markets in the neighbourhood were drawing it dry. Then one day the men of Okperi made a powerful deity and placed their market in its care. From that day Eke grew and grew until it became the biggest market in these parts. This deity which is called Nwanyieke is an old woman. Every Eke day before cock-crow she appears in the market-place with a broom in her right hand and dances round the vast open space beckoning with her broom in all directions of the earth and drawing folk from every land. That is why people will not come near the market before cock-crow; if they did they would see the ancient lady in her task.'

'They tell the same story of the Nkwo market beside the great river at Umuru,' said one of Akukalia's companions. 'There the medicine has worked so well that the market no longer assembles only on Nkwo days.'

'Umuru is no match for my mother's people in medicine,' said Akukalia. 'Their market has grown because the white man took his merchandise there.'

'Why did he take his merchandise there,' asked the other man, 'if not because of their medicine? The old woman of the market has swept the world with her broom, even the land of the white men where they say the sun never shines.'

'Is it true that one of their women in Umuru went outside without the white hat and melted like sleeping palm oil in the sun?' asked the other companion.

'I have also heard it,' said Akukalia. 'But many lies are told about the white man. It was once said that he had no toes.'

As the sun rose the men came to the disputed farmland. It had not been cultivated for many years and was thick with browned spear grass.

'I remember coming with my father to this very place to cut grass for our thatches,' said Akukalia. 'It is a thing of surprise to me that my mother's people are claiming it today.'

'It is all due to the white man who says, like an elder to two fighting children: You will not fight while I am around. And so the younger and weaker of the two begins to swell himself up and to boast.'

'You have spoken the truth,' said Akukalia. 'Things like this would never have happened when I was a young man, to say nothing of the days of my father. I remember all this very well,' he waved over the land. 'That ebenebe tree over there was once hit by thunder, and people cutting thatch under it were hurled away in every direction.'

'What you should ask them,' said the other companion who had spoken very little since they set out, 'what they should tell us is why, if the land was indeed theirs, why they let us farm it and cut thatch from it for generation after generation, until the white man came and reminded them.'

'It is not our mission to ask them any question, except the one question which Umuaro wants them to answer,' said Akukalia. 'And I think I should remind you again to hold your tongues in your hand when we get there and leave the talking to me. They are very difficult people; my mother was no exception. But I know what they know. If a man of Okperi says to you come, he means run away with all your strength. If you are not used to their ways you may sit with them from cock-crow until roosting-time and join in their talk and their food, but all the while you will be floating on the surface of the water. So leave them to me because when a man of cunning dies a man of cunning buries him.'

The three emissaries entered Okperi about the time when most people finished their morning meal. They made straight for the compound of Uduezue, the nearest living relation to Akukalia's mother. Perhaps it was the men's unsmiling faces that told Uduezue, or maybe Okperi was not altogether unprepared for the mission from Umuaro. Nevertheless Uduezue asked them about their people at home.

'They are well,' replied Akukalia impatiently. 'We have an urgent mission which we must give to the rulers of Okperi at once.'

'True?' asked Uduezue. 'I was saying to myself: What could bring my son and his people all this way so early? If my sister, your mother, were still alive, I would have thought that something had happened to her.' He paused for a very little while. 'An important mission; yes. We have a saying that a toad does not run in the day unless something is after it. I do not want to delay your mission, but I must offer you a piece of kolanut.' He made to rise.

'Do not worry yourself. Perhaps we shall return after our mission. It is a big load on our head, and until we put it down we cannot understand anything we are told.'

'I know what it is like. Here is a piece of white clay then. Let me agree with you and leave the kolanut until you return.'

But the men declined even to draw lines on the floor with the clay. After that there was nothing else to say. They had rebuffed the token of goodwill between host and guest, their mission must indeed be grave.

Udueuze went into his inner compound and soon returned with his

goatskin bag and sheathed matchet. 'I shall take you to the man who
will receive your message,' he said.

He led the way and the others followed silently. They passed an ever-
thickening crowd of market people. As the planting season was near
many of them carried long baskets of seed-yams. Some of the men
carried goats also in long baskets. But now and again there was a man
clutching a fowl; such a man never trod the earth firmly, especially when
he was a man who had known better times. Many of the women talked
boisterously as they went; the silent ones were those who had come
from far away and had exhausted themselves. Akukalia thought he
recognized some of the towering headloads of water pots they had left
behind on their way.

Akukalia had not visited his mother's land for about three years and
he now felt strangely tender towards it. When as a little boy he had first
come here with his mother he had wondered why the earth and sand
looked white instead of red-brown as in Umuaro. His mother had told
him the reason was that in Okperi people washed every day and were
clean while in Umuaro they never touched water for the whole four days
of the week. His mother was very harsh to him and very quarrelsome, but
now Akukalia felt tender even towards her.

Uduezue took his three visitors to the house of Otikpo, the town-crier
of Okperi. He was in his *obi* preparing seed-yams for the market. He
rose to greet his visitors. He called Uduezue by his name and title and
called Akukalia Son of our Daughter. He merely shook hands with the
other two whom he did not know. Otikpo was very tall and of spare
frame. He still looked like the great runner he had been in his youth.

He went into an inner room and returned with a rolled mat which he
spread on the mud-bed for his visitors. A little girl came in from the
inner compound calling 'Father, father.'

'Go away, Ogbanje,' he said. 'Don't you see I have strangers?'

'Nweke slapped me.'

'I shall whip him later. Go and tell him I shall whip him.'

'Otikpo, let us go outside and whisper together,' said Uduezue.

They did not stay very long. When they came back Otikpo brought
a kolanut in a wooden bowl. Akukalia thanked him but said that he
and his companions carried such heavy loads on their heads that they
could neither eat nor drink until the burden was set down.

'True?' asked Otikpo. 'Can this burden you speak of come down before me and Uduezue, or does it require the elders of Okperi?'

'It requires the elders.'

'Then you have come at a bad time. Everybody in Igboland knows that Okperi people do not have other business on their Eke day. You should have come yesterday or the day before, or tomorrow or the day after. Son of our Daughter, you should know our habits.'

'Your habits are not different from the habits of other people,' said Akukalia. 'But our mission could not wait.'

'True?' Otikpo went outside and raising his voice called his neighbour, Ebo, and came in again.

'The mission could not wait. What shall we do now? I think you should sleep in Okperi today and see the elders tomorrow.'

Ebo came in and saluted generally. He was surprised to see so many people, and was temporarily at a loss. Then he began to shake hands all round, but when Akukalia's turn came he refused to take Ebo's hand.

'Sit down, Ebo,' said Otikpo. 'Akukalia has a message for Okperi which forbids him to eat kolanut or shake hands. He wants to see the elders and I have told him it is not possible today.'

'Why did they choose today to bring their message? Have they no market where they come from? If that is all you are calling me for I must go back and prepare for market.'

'Our message cannot wait, I have said that before.'

'I have not yet heard of a message that could not wait. Or have you brought us news that Chukwu, the high god, is about to remove the foot that holds the world? If not then you must know that Eke Okperi does not break up because three men have come to town. If you listen carefully even now you can hear its voice; and it is not even half full yet. When it is full you can hear it from Umuda. Do you think a market like that will stop to hear your message?' He sat down for a while; nobody else spoke.

'You can now see, Son of our Daughter, that we cannot get our elders together before tomorrow,' said Otikpo.

'If war came suddenly to your town how do you call your men together, Father of my Mother? Do you wait till tomorrow? Do you not beat your *ikolo*?'

Ebo and Otikpo burst into laughter. The three men from Umuaro exchanged glances. Akukalia's face began to look dangerous. Uduezue sat as he had done since they first came in, his chin in his left hand.

'Different people have different customs,' said Otikpo after his laugh, 'In Okperi it is not our custom to welcome strangers to our market with the *ikolo*.'

'Are you telling us, Father of my Mother, that you regard us as market women? I have borne your insults patiently. Let me remind you that my name is Okeke Akukalia of Umuaro.'

'Ooh, of Umuaro,' said Ebo, still smarting from the rebuffed hand-shake. 'I am happy you have said of Umuaro. The name of this town is Okperi.'

'Go back to your house,' shouted Akukalia, 'or I will make you eat shit.'

'If you want to shout like a castrated bull you must wait until you return to Umuaro. I have told you this place is called Okperi.'

Perhaps it was deliberate, perhaps accidental. But Ebo had just said the one thing that nobody should ever have told Akukalia who was impotent and whose two wives were secretly given to other men to bear his children.

The ensuing fight was grim. Ebo was no match for Akukalia and soon had a broken head, streaming with blood. Maddened by pain and shame he made for his house to get a matchet. Women and children from all the nearby compounds were now out, some of them screaming with fright. Passers-by also rushed in, making futile motions of intervention.

What happened next was the work of Ekwensu, the bringer of evil. Akukalia rushed after Ebo, went into the *obi*, took the *ikenga* from his shrine, rushed outside again and, while everyone stood aghast, split it in two.

Ebo was last to see the abomination. He had been struggling with Otikpo who wanted to take the matchet from him and so prevent bloodshed. But when the crowd saw what Akukalia had done they called on Otikpo to leave the man alone. The two men came out of the hut together. Ebo rushed towards Akukalia and then seeing what he had done stopped dead. He did not know, for one brief moment, whether he was awake or dreaming. He rubbed his eyes with the back of his left hand. Akukalia stood in front of him. The two pieces of his *ikenga* lay where their violator had kicked them in the dust.

'Move another step if you call yourself a man. Yes I did it. What can you do?'

So it was true. Still Ebo turned round and went into his *obi*. At his shrine he knelt down to have a close look. Yes, the gap where his *ikenga*, the strength of his right arm, had stood stared back at him — an empty patch, without dust, on the wooden board. 'Nna doh! Nna doh!' he wept, calling on his dead father to come to his aid. Then he got up and went into his sleeping-room. He was there a little while before Otikpo, thinking he might be doing violence to himself, rushed into the room to see. But it was too late. Ebo pushed him aside and came into the *obi* with his loaded gun. At the threshold he knelt down and aimed. Akukalia, seeing the danger, dashed forward. Although the bullet had caught him in the chest he continued running with his matchet held high until he fell at the threshold, his face hitting the low thatch before he went down.

When the body was brought home to Umuaro everyone was stunned. It had never happened before that an emissary of Umuaro was killed abroad. But after the first shock people began to say that their clansman had done an unforgivable thing.

'Let us put ourselves in the place of the man he made a corpse before his own eyes,' they said. 'Who would bear such a thing? What propitiation or sacrifice would atone for such sacrilege? How would the victim set about putting himself right again with his fathers unless he could say to them: Rest, for the man that did it has paid with his head? Nothing short of that would have been adequate.'

Umuaro might have left the matter there, and perhaps the whole land dispute with it as Ekwensu seemed to have taken a hand in it. But one small thing worried them. It was small but at the same time it was very great. Why had Okperi not deigned to send a message to Umuaro to say this was what happened and that was what happened? Everyone agreed that the man who killed Akukalia had been sorely provoked. It was also true that Akukalia was not only a son of Umuaro; he was also the son of a daughter of Okperi, and what had happened might be likened to he-goat's head dropping into he-goat's bag. Yet when a man was killed something had to be said, some explanation given. That Okperi had not cared to say anything beyond returning the corpse was a mark of the contempt in which they now held Umuaro. And that could not be overlooked. Four days after Akukalia's death criers went through the six villages at nightfall.

The assembly in the morning was very solemn. Almost everyone who spoke said that although it was not right to blame a corpse it must be admitted that their kinsman did a great wrong. Many of them, especially the older men, asked Umuaro to let the matter drop. But there were others who, as the saying was, pulled out their hair and chewed it. They swore that they would not live and see Umuaro spat upon. They were, as before, led by Nwaka. He spoke with his usual eloquence and stirred many hearts.

Ezeulu did not speak until the last. He saluted Umuaro quietly and with great sadness.

'Umuaro kwenu!'

'Hem!'

'Umuaro obodonesi kwenu!'

'Hem!'

'Kwezuenu!'

'Hem!'

'The reed we were blowing is now crushed. When I spoke two markets ago in this very place I used the proverb of the she-goat. I was then talking to Ogbuefi Egonwanne who was the adult in the house. I told him that he should have spoken up against what we were planning, instead of which he put a piece of live coal into the child's palm and asked him to carry it with care. We all have seen with what care he carried it. I was not then talking to Egonwanne alone but to all the elders here who left what they should have done and did another, who were in the house and yet the she-goat suffered in her parturition.

'Once there was a great wrestler whose back had never known the ground. He wrestled from village to village until he had thrown every man in the world. Then he decided that he must go and wrestle in the land of the spirits, and become champion there as well. He went, and beat every spirit that came forward. Some had seven heads, some ten; but he beat them all. His companion who sang his praise on the flute begged him to come away, but he would not, his blood was roused, his ear nailed up. Rather than heed the call to go home he gave a challenge to the spirits to bring out their best and strongest wrestler. So they sent him his personal god, a little wiry spirit who seized him with one hand and smashed him on the stony earth.

'Men of Umuaro, why do you think our fathers told us this story? They told it because they wanted to teach us that no matter how strong or great a man was he should never challenge his *chi*. This is what our kinsman did – he challenged his *chi*. We were his flute-player, but we did not plead with him to come away from death. Where is he today? The fly that has no one to advise it follows the corpse into the grave. But let us leave Akukalia aside; he has gone the way his *chi* ordained.

'But let the slave who sees another cast into a shallow grave know that he will be buried in the same way when his day comes. Umuaro is today challenging its *chi*. Is there any man or woman in Umuaro who does not know Ulu, the deity that destroys a man when his life is sweetest to him? Some people are still talking of carrying war to Okperi. Do they think that Ulu will fight in blame? Today the world is spoilt and there is no longer head or tail in anything that is done. But Ulu is not spoilt with it. If you go to war to avenge a man who passed shit on the head of his mother's father, Ulu will not follow you to be soiled in the corruption. Umuaro, I salute you.'

The meeting ended in confusion. Umuaro was divided in two. Many people gathered round Ezeulu and said they stood with him. But there were others who went with Nwaka. That night he held another meeting with them in his compound and they agreed that three or four Okperi heads must fall to settle the matter.

Nwaka ensured that no one came to that night meeting from Ezeulu's village, Umuachala. He held up his palm-oil lamp against the face of any who came to see him clearly. Altogether he sent fifteen people away.

Nwaka began by telling the assembly that Umuaro must not allow itself to be led by the Chief Priest of Ulu. 'My father did not tell me that before Umuaro went to war it took leave from the priest of Ulu,' he said. 'The man who carries a deity is not a king. He is there to perform his god's ritual and to carry sacrifice to him. But I have been watching this Ezeulu for many years. He is a man of ambition; he wants to be king, priest, diviner, all. His father, they said, was like that too. But Umuaro showed him that Igbo people knew no kings. The time has come to tell his son also.

'We have no quarrel with Ulu. He is still our protector, even though we no longer fear Abam warriors at night. But I will not see with these eyes of mine his priest making himself lord over us. My father told me many things, but he did not tell me that Ezeulu was king in Umuaro. Who is he, anyway? Does anybody here enter his compound through the man's gate? If Umuaro decided to have a king we know where he would come from. Since when did Umuachala become head of the six villages? We all know that it was jealousy among the big villages that made them give the priesthood to the weakest. We shall fight for our farmland and for the contempt Okperi has poured on us. Let us not listen to anyone trying to frighten us with the name of Ulu. If man says yes his *chi* also says yes. And we have all heard how the people of Aninta dealt with their deity when he failed them. Did they not carry him to the boundary between them and their neighbours and set fire to him? I salute you.'

The war was waged from one Afo to the next. On the day it began Umuaro killed two men of Okperi. The next day was Nkwo, and so there was no fighting. On the two following days, Eke and Oye, the fighting grew fierce. Umuaro killed four men and Okperi replied with three, one of the three being Akukalia's brother, Okoye. The next day, Afo, saw the war brought to a sudden close. The white man, Wintabota, brought soldiers to Umuaro and stopped it. The story of what these soldiers did in Abame was still told with fear, and so Umuaro made no effort to resist but laid down their arms. Although they were not yet satisfied they could say without shame that Akukalia's death had been avenged, that they had provided him with three men on whom to rest his head. It was also a good thing perhaps that the war was stopped. The death of Akukalia and his brother in one and the same dispute showed that Ekwensu's hand was in it.

The white man, not satisfied that he had stopped the war, had gathered all the guns in Umuaro and asked the soldiers to break them in the face of all, except three or four which he carried away. Afterwards he sat in judgement over Umuaro and Okperi and gave the disputed land to Okperi.

Chinua Achebe (Nigeria)
Arrow of God, Chapter Two

Song after Defeat†

Old woman:
Diossé has lost men for nothing.
Where did you leave your men?
Where did you leave your fighting men?

Spirit of Diossé:
Let me alone. I am trying to find my way.
Go ask the Whites,
Go ask the soldiers,
And look at the bank of the dry watercourse.

Old woman:
Diossé did not run away, but lost his fame.
Samba ran away. Whites are brave men.
Samba was afraid,
Samba of Massantola is not a man.

Girls:
Samba and Diossé unleashed war for no reason,
They took our elder brothers to be killed for nothing.

Old woman:
Now I have no son; now I shall have nothing to eat,
I shall have no clothes . . . and I am old.

Girls:
Old woman, don't cry.
We will marry, we will feed you.
Don't cry, we will take good care of you.
Forget Samba and Diossé, they are criminals.

Bambara (Mali)

---

†Composed in 1915. The chiefs Samba and Diossé had revolted against the French and were defeated on the bank of a dry watercourse. Diossé escaped to a stronghold with some followers, then blew it up, killing himself and them. The song was composed by an old woman whose only son was killed in the revolt.

Memorial†

O you who ride to Segotta, the fighting men who set out for there full of life have not come back.

Berber (Morocco)

Colonizer's Logic

These natives are unintelligent –
We can't understand their language.

Chinweizu (Nigeria)

My Name
Nomgqibelo Ncamisile Mnqhibisa

Look what they have done to my name . . .
the wonderful name of my great-great-grandmothers
Nomgqibelo Ncamisile Mnqhibisa

The burly bureaucrat was surprised.
What he heard was music to his ears
'Wat is daai, sê nou weer?'
'I am from Chief Daluxolo Velayigodle of emaMpodweni
And my name is Nomgqibelo Ncamisile Mnqhibisa.'

Messia, help me!
My name is so simple
and yet so meaningful,
but to this man it is trash . . .

He gives me a name
Convenient enough to answer his whim:
I end up being

---

†On a battle between Berbers and French, fought in 1911.

Maria . . .
I . . .
Nomgqibelo Ncamisile Mnqhibisa.

Magoleng wa Selepe (Azania)

My Cousin Mohamed
(Excerpt)

Listen!
You Mohamed and I
Are not brothers,
You're the son of my aunt —
You're my cousin!

Long ago your Arab father came,
Also he came with the Holy Koran
And his traditional ways,
But without a mistress or a wife!

Your father came to live among friends,
Not his slaves,
For the Africans are always generous
And useful friends
Until they are offended by despising
Their traditional ways . . .

So despite his colour, or creed,
Your father was free
To surround himself with lovely maids!

And then he began to study
The existing tribes and clans,
And concluded that the Arab
Was culturally and racially superior
To the African Man!

So, he proceeded to propagate Islam
Along with his traditional ways.

Islam and Arabism
The jihad men† thought invincible!

But all the Africans,
Those men who were charcoal black
From every tribe and clan
Came and assembled,
They fixed their vision on a gigantic idea
To survive collectively . . .

They said to themselves:
'If the Arabs have come to claim
This African Land,
No doubt they will have it pretty rough!'

But then,
Continuing their assault
The Arabs wiped out thousands of the African males,
And took the women as their slaves
With whom they freely mated!

This is the version of the story
Of conflict between the Africans and the Arabs
The Arab historians do not tell.

And so,
You cousin Mohamed in the Northern Sudan
Are an offspring of my slave-aunt,
Who in her wretchedness stooped to conquer
By blood strength . . .
A reality as large as the Imatong mountain!

You are no longer
A pure Arab, like your father . . .
You are the hybrid of Africa,
The generous product
Of many years of bloody war

†Jihad – a holy war; and jihad men are men believing in holy war.

On the African Land,
Your African Motherland!

My cousin Mohamed
Thinks he's very clever . . .
With pride,
He says he's an African who speaks
Arabic language,
Because he's no mother tongue!

Again, he says,
It is civilized to speak Arabic!

Among the Arabs,
My cousin becomes a militant Arab –
A black Arab,
Who rejects the definition of race
By pigment of one's skin.

He says,
If an African speaks Arabic language
He's an Arab!
If an African is culturally Arabized
He's an Arab!

My cousin claims
That Islamic Religion is a property
Of the Arabs!

He says,
God revealed the Holy Koran in Arabic . . .
And it cannot be translated
To other languages,
Because God has forbidden to do so!

He says,
Muslims must know Arabic
Because it is the language of the Holy Koran,
And the Holy Koran is the vehicle

For the Arab culture,
Because the Arabs are God-chosen people!

My cousin says,
The Africans have no culture!
The Africans have no history!
The Africans have no religion!
The Africans have no one language!
The Africans are uncivilized!

He says,
It is his duty to extend
The Arab sphere of influence
Into Africa!

He claims that,
Egypt is already Arab!
Libya is already Arab!
Tunisia is already Arab!
Algeria is already Arab!
Morocco is already Arab!
Mauritania is already Arab!
Somalia is already Arab!
Djebuti is already Arab!
Sudan is already Arab!
And soon,
Western Sahara shall be Arab!
Eritrea shall be Arab!
Chad shall be Arab!
And if God's willing,
Ethiopia shall be Arab!
Let the whole African continent
Become an Arab continent,
So that its people can be civilized!

My cousin is deafened
By Orouba:†

†Orouba – cultural Arabization of non-Arab people.

To be an Arab is right!
To be a Muslim is right!
If an Arab/Muslim kills you during jihad,
He has secured his place in paradise!
If you kill him,
All the same, he goes to Heaven
For furthering Islamic cause!
In other words,
My cousin wins both ways!

His opponent has no alternative,
But to submit!

And so,
Like Zionism, or Apartheid,
Orouba has become a racist ideology!

S. Anai Kelueljang (Sudan)

Veteran's Day

And because somebody
fired a gun
at somebody else
at Sarajevo
but more because
of a man named Darwin
who said his daddy
was an ape
and proved it in a book;

therefore did the nations
fight amongst themselves
to see who was fittest to survive
and killed a few million people
among whom were Africans
conscripted to serve;

bloodied, that is, to prove a point

concerning civilization's
monkey-mongering ways.

Ifeanyi Menkiti (Nigeria)

Meka's Medal*

The bugle sounded and there was a roll of drums. One of the enormous white men came toward M. Pipiniakis.

'It is him, the great white Chief!' thought Meka. He had never seen anything or anybody like him. All that he noticed were the voluminous folds of skin under his chin that almost concealed the knot of his tie.

The great Chief was speaking to M. Pipiniakis, as if he were speaking to someone who was deaf. M. Pipiniakis stood as still as a statue. When he had finished the Chief took a medal from a small case which M. Fouconi's assistant held out for him and pinned it on to M. Pipiniakis's breast. Then Meka saw the great Chief grasp his shoulders and put his cheeks one after the other against the cheeks of the Greek. At each movement the folds of skin under his chin trembled like a withered dun-coloured breast.

Then it was Meka's turn. The white Chief stood in front of him and began to shout. As he opened and shut his mouth his lower jaw went down and came up, puffing up and then deflating the skin under his chin. He took another medal from the case and came towards Meka, still talking. Meka had time to notice that it was not the same as the Greek's medal.

The white Chief was now at his shoulder. Meka looked down at him just at the moment when he was pinning the medal on to his breast. He could feel the hot breath through his khaki jacket. The Chief was sweating like a wrestler. It looked as if it had been raining over his back. A large damp patch stretched from his shoulders down to his buttocks.

Meka wondered anxiously if he was going to push his damp turkey-crop against each shoulder as he had done with M. Pipiniakis. He breathed again when the white Chief, after he had pinned on the medal, took a few steps backward and shook his hand. Meka's hand swallowed up the hand of the Chief like a scrap of damp cotton rag.

Meka squinted down at his chest. The medal was certainly there, pinned on to his khaki jacket. He smiled and lifted up his head. Then he noticed that he was singing under his breath and that the whole of his face was beating time. His body was swaying in spite of himself and his knees bending and stretching like a spring. He no longer felt any pain. He could not even hear his bones cracking. The heat, his need, the pain in his feet, as if by magic they had all disappeared. He looked down again at the medal. He could feel his neck growing. Yes, his head was climbing up and up, up to heaven like the Tower of Babel. His forehead reached the clouds. His long arms gradually rose like the wings of a bird poised for flight.

'It is a long time before the pot where the goat is cooked loses the smell,' he said to himself. Who said that the Mekas were finished? Was there not one of them, himself, Meka, the one African of Doum decorated by the Chief of the white men? Yes, he was known in Timba, his name had crossed the seas and flown over the mountains and come to the ear of the great Chief of the whites, who had sent another great Chief to decorate him at Doum. The whole world knew this, the whole world had seen how the very hand of the High Commissioner had pinned the medal on to his chest.

The great Chief of the whites, together with his second in command and M. Fouconi and his assistant, stood in the middle of the courtyard, facing Meka. M. Fouconi beckoned the interpreter that Meka had met a few days before in his office. The African interpreter, his pith helmet in his hand, ran over to Meka and told him that the Chief of the whites invited him to drink and eat for the whole day and the drinking was to begin at the African Community Centre. Meka tossed back his head to indicate assent. The interpreter told him to go over and stand with the officials and M. Pipiniakis. Meka with his head held high went across the courtyard and, not deigning to stand beside the Greek, took up position by the side of M. Fouconi's assistant.

The bugle sounded. The soldiers began to march off to the sound of the Marche Lorraine. They turned their head sharply toward the Chief of the whites who had brought his hand up to the peak of his kepi.

Deeply impressed, Meka watched with bulging eyes the fine rifles that passed to and fro in front of him. Who could resist the sons of Japhet? He thought of his old kaffir musket. To think his father had wanted to fight it out to the end against the whites with that! He looked for the smoke bomb which Ignatius Obebé had talked about, but not one of the soldiers was carrying the great black ball which his imagination pictured. Meka began to count the rifles in his mind. He lost count, tried to begin again, lost count again. Then he thought about the gorillas, the unclean creatures that devastated the banana groves. If he was given one of these rifles being wasted here – just one – the gorillas would know who they had to deal with. He made up his mind that he would ask the great Chief of the whites for a rifle. What would it cost him to make a present of just one of them? The idea grew so in his mind that he began to look from the great Chief of the whites to M. Fouconi and then back. He caught a withering look from the assistant. Meka moved his lips and took a step forward. The assistant signalled to him with a sharp gesture to step back. Meka felt a great throbbing in his feet. He passed his hand over his face. The assistant shrugged his shoulders and took no more notice. Meka's throat was constricted. He brought his heels together and leaned forward a little to watch the last of the rifles disappearing. When he stood up again he caught another withering glance from the assistant. Meka felt this urgent need return.

Kelara had watched her husband presented with his medal through eyes damp with joy. When the white man shook Meka's hand she thought her heart would stop beating.

'There's somebody,' they were saying. 'You can't say we haven't got a great man at Doum.' Then some troublemaker said, 'I think they ought to have covered him with medals. That would have been a bit more like it! To think he has lost his land and his sons just for that . . .'

That was the false note that quenched all Kelara's enthusiasm. It was then that she knew that her sorrow was still sharp and that nothing could ever make up for the loss of her two sons. She unknotted her neckerchief and pushed it into her mouth so that she could not cry.

'What's wrong with the old woman?' someone asked. 'Is she ill?'

A woman held her by the shoulders. Kelara started to weep with all her heart on the woman's shoulder, and the woman started to weep with her. The men turned their eyes away.

'What can be the matter with the old woman?' they asked again.

Kelara could feel the lump that had come up into her throat dissolving away as she went on weeping. When she felt it had disappeared she thanked the woman who had given her support. Then she stood on tiptoe to see into the courtyard where the march-past was now coming to an end. She saw her husband, his head gleaming in the sun, grin foolishly at the Chief of the white men. Something happened inside her which she could not understand. Meka seemed to her like someone she had never seen before. Could that be her husband who was grinning away over there? She looked down at the pair of old slippers wrapped up in a newspaper that she was holding under her arm. Then she stood up on her toes again. The man laughing over there had no connection with her. She felt frightened at herself. She rubbed her eyes and looked at Meka again. The corners of her mouth drooped in a grimace of contempt. She forced her way through the crowd till she reached a gawky youth whose hand she seized. He looked at her open-mouthed in astonishment.

'It is you who spoke just now,' she said to him. 'Thank you. The Holy Spirit spoke through your mouth.'

The young man was going to protest, then he changed his mind and passed his hand over his lips.

'Good God,' he said out loud. 'What was it I said then?' 'You want to know?' said his neighbour, a short young man who could easily have been taken for Chinese. 'It was you who made the old woman start crying just now . . .'

When the gawky young man turned round in his horror to apologize to Kelara she had disappeared.

'I don't understand,' he said. 'Was she the wife of the chap they've just given the medal to over there?' he asked his neighbour.

'She may well be, because she started crying when you said he ought to have been given lots of medals. How did you know that he had lost his land and his sons for the medal they gave him?'

'The Commandant was saying that last night to M. Pipiniakis when they were talking over dinner. You forget I am the Commandant's houseboy . . .'

The two young men fell silent

Ferdinand Oyono (Cameroon)
Excerpt from *The Old Man and the Medal*
Translated from the French by John Reed

The Trial

The audience in the union hall had listened to Tiémoko's story in total silence, and in telling it he had recovered some of his normal self-assurance. Before sitting down, he summed up the case against his uncle.

'Diara is a worker, like all the rest of us, and like the rest of us he voted for the strike – for an unlimited strike, until we won what we were asking for – but he has not kept his word. He got help from the union, enough to live on, as we all did, and he has used it, but he has not repaid any of it since he went back to work. But more than this, he has informed on the women who are supporting us so valiantly, and he has forced them to get off trains whenever they have tried to use them. That is why I wanted some of the women to be here today, although there were a lot of people who didn't agree with that idea.

'That is all I have to say, and now it is up to others to say what they think. But let no one forget that while we are talking here, many of our comrades are in prison.'

When Tiémoko sat down, the silence was so profound that it seemed almost as if the big meeting hall had suddenly emptied. Diara had drawn his legs back under his chair and sat so stiffly he might have been made of stone. Looking at his father, Sadio saw that his eyes were empty of all feeling, lost in a faraway past where there was no strike, no place of judgement, and no accused.

Suddenly a woman's voice was heard. 'I would like to say . . .'

Several irritated voices called, 'Quiet!'

'Who spoke down there at the back?' Konaté demanded.

'It's one of these silly women!' someone said.

'But I told the women to come,' Tiémoko said. 'They have important things to say. Come forward, Hadi Dia.'

A woman with heavily tattooed lips and a face crisscrossed with scars rose and walked to the front of the hall. For an occasion such as this, she had obviously thought it a good idea to put on all the best clothes she owned. Tiémoko made a place for her beside him on the bench.

'Hadi Dia,' he said, 'tell everyone now what you have already told your neighbours. You can speak here without fear and without shame.'

The woman had a hare lip, and when she opened her mouth to speak the people nearest her could see the gaps between her teeth. 'It was the other day . . . that is, it was about two weeks ago . . . I was with Coumba, her sister Dienka, and the third wife of . . . of . . .'

'The names are not important. Go on.'

'We took the "smoke of the savanna" to go to Kati. Diara asked us to show our tickets, and when we got to Kati he came back to us with a *toubab* soldier. He said something to him in the *toubab* language, and the soldier took away the tickets. We had to come back but he didn't give us back the money for them. I told the whole story to my husband when we got home.'

'Hadi Dia, is all of what you have said true?' Konaté asked.

'Ask Diara.'

'All right, Hadi Dia, you may return to your seat. And you, Diara, have you anything to say?'

The accused remained motionless and silent, while the woman went back to her own place. It was the first time she had ever spoken at a meeting of the men, and she was filled with pride. Another, older woman went up to speak, going this time directly to the stage. Her name was Sira, and she spoke rapidly and confidently.

'With us, it was on the way to Koulikoro – you all know the place where the train goes up a little rise between here and Koulikoro – he stopped the train and made us get off. Eight women alone, right in the middle of the brush! I tell you, he is nothing but a slave of the *toubabs!* Tiémoko is right – he should be crucified in the market-place!'

'Thank you, Sira,' Konaté said, 'but you should tell only what you have seen. Go back to your seat.'

Two more women came forward and told of happenings that were more or less similar to the first ones, and after that there was a heavy silence in the hall. The idea of women addressing a meeting as important as this was still unfamiliar and disturbing. The men gazed absently at the stage, waiting for something to happen, their glances wandering from Konaté to Diara, and then to the unhappy figure of Sadio.

Suddenly a masculine voice said, 'I would like to speak,' and a towering, muscular workman got to his feet. His head was curiously shaved so that his hair formed a ring around his skull, and he seemed uncomfortable in his feast-day clothing. Everyone recognized him immediately as the first man who stopped work after the strike was called, and there was a murmur of approval from the audience. He was sure to have something to say, and it was right that he should speak.

He began by giving an account of his own actions during the strike, and of those of the men in his group, and only when he had completed this did he come to the case of Diara.

'Diara has behaved badly towards all of us,' he said. 'Yes, as God is my witness, he has done wrong. I am as sure of that as I am that some day I will be alone in my grave. When I told the men who worked with me to put down their tools, they did it as if we were all one man; and here today we are all still agreed to go on with the strike. But you, Diara – you are one of our elders; you should have guided us and helped us. Instead, you took the side of our enemies, and after you had betrayed us you spied on our women. We are not ashamed to admit that it is the women who are supporting us now, and you have betrayed them, too. For my part, I say that we should put Diara in prison – yes, that is just what we should do – put him in prison.'

'Brother,' someone in the hall said, 'you know that the prison belongs to the white men.'

'I know that, but we can build one!'

'And where would we get the money? We don't even have enough to feed a prisoner – not to mention that the *toubabs* would never let us do it anyway.'

'Everything you say is true, man – I know as well as you that the *toubabs* have stolen all of our rights, even the right to have a prison of our own and punish our own; but that is no reason to defend a traitor! If we can't put Diara in prison, we can at least do what the Koran teaches us to do – we can have him scourged!'

The man had begun to shout, and the muscles of his face and neck were contorted with anger. 'We should decide right now how many lashes he will receive and who'll be appointed to carry out the judgement!'

He sat down again, still muttering aloud, 'You are a traitor, Diara, a traitor, a traitor!'

There was a turbulence of voices in the hall; everyone seemed to want to speak at once. Some were in favour of flogging, while others still thought that a means of imprisonment should be found, and one man said that Diara should be made to turn in all the money he had earned to the strike committee. Theories and ideas went from bench to bench, and all sorts of advice was hurled at the members of the jury. In the midst of the uproar, only the accused remained motionless, as if he were not even present in the room. Once or twice, as the hearing went on, he had asked himself, 'Why *did* I do it?' and the question disturbed him, because he could not provide an answer. Surely it had not been because he wanted money or jewels or fine clothes, richly embroidered and starched? Had his pride made him seek the stimulant that comes from holding power over others? He saw himself again, giving orders to the women, with the policeman at his side. Had it been the taste of flattery that had separated him from the others, or the sense of well-being that comes with a full stomach? Or had it been simply the cold emptiness of his own kitchen? The questions mingled and blurred in Diara's mind and then disappeared completely, leaving him alone again before the crowd in the hall, his eyes wide open but unseeing, his lower lip trembling.

Fa Keïta, the Old One, had been present throughout the trial, with Ad'jibid'ji sitting quietly beside him. He had been asked to be a member of the jury, but he had refused because he had not believed, until the last minute, that the young people would actually carry out such a plan. Now he rose slowly to his feet.

'I have a few grains of salt to contribute to the pot,' he said, and then added, glancing in Tiémoko's direction, 'if, that is, you are willing to accept my salt.'

Konaté said. 'Whatever you have to say, Old One, will be listened to with both ears.'

'A long time ago,' Fa Keïta said, 'before any of you were born, everything that happened happened within a framework, an order that was our own, and the existence of that order was of great importance in our lives. Today, no such framework exists. There are no castes among people, no difference in the quality of grain or of the bread that is made from the grain; there are no weavers, no artisans in metal, no makers of fine shoes.

'I think it is the machine which has ground everything together this way and brought everything to a single level. Ibrahim Bakayoko said to me, not long ago: "When we have succeeded in stirring up the people of this country, and making them one, we will go on and do the same thing between ourselves and the people on the other side of the ocean."

How all this will come about I do not know, but we can see it happening already, before our eyes. Now, for instance, Tiémoko has had this idea, which he took from a book written in the white man's language. I have seen more suns rise than any of you, but this is the first time in my life that I have seen a . . . a . . . What is it called, child?' he asked, leaning toward Ad'jibid'ji.

'Tribunal, Grandfather.'

'A tribunal,' Fa Keïta repeated tonelessly. 'And I think that Tiémoko has done well. We all wanted the strike; we voted for it, and Diara voted with us. But then Diara went back to work. You say that he is a traitor, and perhaps you are right. If we are all to win, then we should live as brothers, and no one should go back unless his brothers do.

'I have heard you calling for punishment, but I know that you will not kill Diara. Not because some of you would not have the courage or the will, but because others would not let you do it, and I would be the first of them. If you imitate the hirelings of your masters, you will become like them, hirelings and barbarians. For godly men, it is a sacrilege to kill, and I pray that God will forbid such a thought to take root in your minds.

'You have spoken also of flogging, of beating Diara. The child who is seated beside me is punished that way very seldom, although my father beat me often, and the same thing is probably true of most of you. But blows correct nothing. As for Diara, you have already beaten him – you have struck him where every human worthy of the name is most vulnerable. You have shamed him before his friends, and before the world, and in doing that you have hurt him far more than you could by any bodily punishment. I cannot know what tomorrow will bring, but in seeing this man before me I do not think that there is one among us who will be tempted to follow in his footsteps.'

In the stillness, some of the women could be heard sniffing, trying to hold back tears.

'And now,' Fa Keïta said, 'I apologize for having abused your kindness. Diara, lift up your head. You have been the instrument of destiny here – it was not you who was on trial; it was the owners of the machines. Thanks to you, no one of us now will give up the fight.'

The old man looked around him for a moment and then left the hall in silence. Ad'jibid'ji remained seated on the bench.

Tiémoko had listened avidly to Fa Keïta's words, but even as he told himself, 'This is what I should have said,' he was angry with the Old One. He had moved the crowd with his gentle words and the calmness of his voice. 'I should have struck harder,' Tiémoko thought, 'and answered him firmly. He has beaten me now, because I don't know enough about these things, but it will be different next time. I must write to Bakayoko tonight.'

All of the earlier heat of the argument seemed to have vanished from the hall. Men and women looked at each other furtively, and then one by one they began to walk silently toward the door.

While all of this was taking place, the eight members of the jury had not said a word. Now one of them rose and put on his cap, and two others followed his example. Konaté took the director of the Koulikoro committee by the arm, and the two men walked off together, conversing in lowered voices. Tiémoko himself started toward the door, and, as he passed the bench where Ad'jibid'ji sat, regarding him with a mixture of curiosity and dislike, he thought, 'There is more in that child's head than in all the rest of the hall.' His irritation with Fa Keïta had turned against himself, and the line of his jawbone hardened. 'It isn't a question of being right,' he muttered furiously, 'it's a question of winning!'

Soon after he had gone, there were just three people still in the meeting hall: Diara, his son Sadio, and Ad'jibid'ji, sitting quietly on her bench. Diara was unable to rid his mind of the thought of the woman Hadi Dia. He had held the votive lamb at her christening, and today she had denounced him; she had insulted him in public, and he knew that a wound like this would never heal. Sadio was still slumped in his chair. His fingers toyed mechanically with the papers scattered on the table, and tears ran down his cheeks. He was conscious that, from this day forward, his father could be reviled and insulted by anyone, perhaps even beaten, and he would have no defence. And he knew that wherever he himself went, people would look at him and say, 'Your father is a traitor.' Not one of the men in the hall, not one of his friends, had even spoken to him before he left. He was alone, desperately alone. He looked up toward the door and saw Ad'jibid'ji, who seemed to be following the silent drama on the stage with a kind of sadistic pleasure. Her eyes remained fixed on Sadio for a moment, and then turned to Diara, as if she were engraving the scene on her mind and wanted to be sure she missed nothing. From the intensity with which she regarded Diara, she might have been listening for the sound of his tears.

At last, Sadio got up and moved across the stage toward his father. A feverish trembling racked his slender body, and he seemed unnaturally tall beside the broken figure in the chair. He opened his lips to gulp in air, wanting to speak, and then he just fell to his knees at his father's side. Diara bent over the figure of his son and cried aloud, like a child who has just been punished.

Sembene Ousmane (Senegal)
Excerpt from *Gods Bits of Wood*
Translated from the French by Frances Price

In My Country

In my country they jail you
for what they think you think.
My uncle once said to me:
they'll implant a microchip
in our minds
to flash our thoughts and dreams
on to a screen at John Vorster Square.
I was scared:
by day I guard my tongue
by night my dreams.

Pitika Ntuli (Azania)

Getting off the Ride
(Excerpt)

I know this ride bloody well.
I'm from those squatted mothers
Those squatted mothers in the daylight air;
Those mothers selling handouts,
Those mothers selling fruits,

Those mothers selling vegetables,
Those mothers selling till dusk
in the dusty strees of Clermont, Thembisa,
Alex, Galeshewe, Dimbaza, Pietersburg.
Those mothers in dusty and tearful streets
that are found in Stanger, Mandeni, Empangeni
Hammarsdale, Mabopane, Machibisa, Soweto.
I'm one of the sons of those black mamas,
Was brought up in those dusty streets;
I'm the black mama's son who vomits
on the doorstep of his shack home, pissed with
concoction. Because his world and the world
in town are as separate as the mountain ranges
and the deep sea.
I'm the naked boy
running down a muddy road,
the rain pouring bleatingly
in Verulam's Mission Station;
With the removal trucks brawling for starts
Starts leading to some stifling redbricked
ghetto of four-roomed houses at Ntuzuma.
I'm the pipeskyf pulling cat
standing in the passage behind Ndlovu's barbershop
Making dreams and dreams
Dreaming makes and makes;
Dreaming, making and making, dreaming
with poetry and drama scripts
rotting under mats
or being eaten by the rats.
I'm the staggering cat on Saturday morning's
West Street. The cat whose shattered hopes
were bottled up in beers, cane, vodka;
Hopes shattered by a system that once offered
liquor to 'Exempted Natives' only.
I'm the bitter son leaning against the lamp post
Not wishing to go to school
where his elder brother spent years, wasted years

at school wanting to be white; only to end as
messenger boy.
I'm the skolly who's thrown himself
out of a fast-moving train
Just to avoid blows, kicks and the hole.
I'm one of the surviving children of Sharpeville
Whose black mothers spelled it out in blood.
I'm the skhotheni who confronts devileyed cops
down Durban's May Street . . .
Since he's got no way to go out.
I'm the young tsotsi found murdered in a donga
in the unlit streets of Edendale, Mdantsane.

. . .

I'm the puzzled student
burning to make head and tail of Aristotle
because he hasn't heard of the buried
Kingdom of Benin or the Zimbabwe Empire,
The student who is swotting himself to madness
striving for universal truths made untrue.
I'm the black South African exile who has come
across a coughing drunk nursing his tuberculosis
on a New York pavement and remembered
he's not free.
I'm the black newspaper vendor
standing on the street corner 2 o'clock
in the morning of Sunday,
Distributing news to those night-life-crazy
nice-timers who will one day come into knocks
with the real news
I'm the youthful Black with hopes of life
standing on file queue for a job
at the local chief's kraal,
This chief who has let himself and his people
into some confused Bantustan kaak
Where there's bare soil, rocks and cracking cakes
of rondavel mudbricks.
I'm the lonely poet

who trudges the township's ghetto passages
pursuing the light,
The light that can only come through a totality
of change:
Change in minds, change
Change in social standings, change
Change in means of living, change
Change in dreams and hopes, change
   Dreams and hopes that are Black
   Dreams and hopes where games end
   Dreams where there's end to man's
creation of gas chambers and concentration camps.
I'm the Africa Kwela instrumentalist whose notes
profess change.

                  Mafika Gwala (Azania)

Why, O Why, Lord?

You know, Lord, what is going on, this moment,
in the hearts of Toivo ya Toivo,
Nelson Mandela and Aaron Mushimba.
Certainly you know the hearts of my brethren,
their daily sufferings, far away on the vast
and lonely weald, among the sheep.
You see them despised and neglected,
paid a mere trifle; you read their thoughts
deep down in the pits, where they are slaving
for next to nothing.

Lord, the many new graves of the children from Soweto
are well known to you, and so are the tears
of their parents and comrades. You are undeceived
by the reasoning and hypocrisy of Turnhalle;
you have observed the hundreds of prisoners
maltreated in the camps of north Namibia.
They are cruelly struck with the butt ends of rifles;

cigarettes are put out against their naked bodies.
We are miserable and afflicted like the children
of Israel in Egypt. And you are aware of it all.

Why, O why, Lord?
Why do you seem deaf to our doleful cries?
Or have you turned your back upon us?
How long will you allow them to trample us underfoot?
Is our trust nothing to you, is our hope vain?
Why, why, why do you keep us waiting?

Why, O why, Lord?
Why did you create us? Did you make us only to be shot
like dogs infected with rabies? Did you make us to be
oppressed and put to scorn for ever? Why, Lord, why?
Are there limits to your love, and are we expelled?
Did you make us 'Kaffers', 'Bantus', 'Non-whites'?

Were we doomed to stand humbly at the back door of the 'Baas',
receiving a splash of water from a rusty marmalade tin?
Did you create us to live on 'Yea, Baas' and 'Yea, Missus'?
Did you make us the human caricatures of this world?
Why, O why, Lord, did you create us?

Why, O why, Lord?
Why did you tell us through your word that we were made
in your own image? Why this teaching that, regardless of language,
race and colour, all men are equal in your eyes,
and that we ought to treat and accept each other as such?
Why did you make us realize that our slavery is at an end,
that we are liberated men and women, bought at a high price
with the blood of your only Son? It might have been better
if you had let us alone in our blindness; it would have been
easier then to submit to our fate. It is impossible now.
We have been brought to see, for ourselves,
that we are incomparably more precious than all diamonds
from Oranjemund and all uranium from Rossing.
Why, O why, Lord, did you open our eyes?

Why, O why, Lord?
Why don't you answer when we cry out to you? How long
will you remain passive, looking silently at our agony
and our tears? The yoke has become unendurable,
we won't carry it one step farther.
Why do you allow iniquity and lies to rule over us,
you who redeemed us at the cost of your own life?
You are King of kings and they struck you with their
fists and cudgels; they spat upon you to show their
utter contempt! Cruel nails pierced your hands and feet,
and all this only because of your great and infinite
love for us. Why, O why then are you silent?

From the depths we call to you: Save us in our distress!
Guide us in the right way to Namibia, and not
to a neo-colonial Southwest Africa.
O Lord of the whole world,
refresh our souls and make them new; we are consumed
with thirst for release, righteousness, redemption,
Shalom. Fill our callous, empty hands with your good gifts.
Crush the copper gates and shatter the iron locks
of Robben Island. Break up the prison camps where
our brethren are captive and tortured, help them, Lord!
We call to you, save us in our deadly fear!
We are trembling and feeble. Take our destiny in your
strong right hand; through us let the world see your wonders!
Give us the Spirit of Life so that we may arise.
Then help us to raise, unwearyingly, under your guidance,
the beacons of your kingdom in this country! Amen.

Zephania Kameeta (Namibia)

NeHanda Nyakasikana

O NeHanda Nyakasikana
How long shall we, the VaNyai groan and suffer?
Holy tutelary spirit!

How long shall we the VaNyai suffer oppression?
We are weary of drinking our tears.
How long shall we have forbearance?
Even trees have a rest,
When their leaves are shed;
Then when spring comes,
New leaves and blossoms sprout to adorn them,
To attract wild beasts and bees by their scent.
As for us when will peace and plenty come our way?
The young ones our women bear, given us
By you, Great Spirit, who should be the inheritors
Of your hard-earned substance, all have uneasy time
In their own land, and grope for a period of calm
And happiness. Everywhere they stand as on hot ashes,
Their feet with blisters are covered through hot oppression
Of the forces of Pfumojena. How far will the tyrants go?
In every house and every village
Our people are being pulled out and punished;
In every place and every court
Where they are all accused, they are treated like flies
Killed without reason, without an honest trial.
Where is our freedom, NeHanda?
Won't you come down to help us?
Our old men are treated like children
In the land you gave them, merciful creator;
They no longer have human dignity
They possess nothing.
The great calamity has befallen them
Holy father, merciful mountain?
Won't you hear our cry?
What foul crime have we committed
That you should abandon us like this?
NeHanda Nyakasikana, how long shall it be
That we, the VaNyai must suffer?
Holy tutelary lion spirit! How long shall it be?

That we, the VaNyai must suffer oppression;
By this cursed Pfumojena who is devouring our land?

Solomon Mutswairo (Zimbabwe)
Translated from the Shona by Alec J. C. Pongweni

I Heard Small Children Ask*

i heard small children ask:
where's tiro
mdluli
mohapi
saloojee
haroon.
they asked where's
ahmed timol
biko
and the answer came from
the birds
the leaves of plants
and from the earth itself
they're gone
they are no more.
the hand that slays in the dark
has removed them
only from the face of the earth.

i heard children ask:
what happened to mandela
to sisulu
mbeki
gwala
the list was long
i lost count.
they asked about sobukwe
about mahlangu
they were asking about the heroes
of their times.

they wanted to know about mama ngoyi
and all the heroines
whose sweat had brought hope
for the young and old.
maybe they would have forgotten
had mxenge
not been added to the list.
but now they shall ask:
where's g.m.
when history books are rewritten
the answers to these questions
will be in
black on white . . .
no longer whispered in corridors
but spoken
openly.
and when the story is retold
about g.m.
it shall be said:
scavengers
murderers
beasts
masquerading under the dark of night
in cowardly manner
ambushed a lone warrior
slew him
and threw him into the dumps
trying to disguise their
dirty dastardly crime.
they may have smiled and joked
because they are beasts
with sick minds.
did they not start with the dogs . . .
sordid minds
poisoned the dogs
as a prelude to their macabre game.
as they cut him to shreds

they satisfied
their gruesome sense of humour.
and the son of the soil
lay on the soggy grounds
his blood
washed into the soil
in final enactment
of his belongingness to the earth
the final
marriage
and return in soul
and blood to the land he loved
so dearly
so totally
    . . . and his return to his roots
was made complete.
and as torments fell
the earth rejoiced,
plants swayed merrily
as their roots
for so long thirsting
drank their fill.
Where the drops of blood fell
a monument shall emerge
and a fountain
from which africa shall drink
shall open
and griffiths' blood shall not
have been shed in vain.

                    Ben J. Langa (Azania)

Azania is Tired*

Azania is tired of detentions,
Azania is tired of bullets from the enemy,

Azania is tired of holding gatherings,
Year after year without any success,
Azania is tired of working for you, white
    man in the cities,
Azania is tired to go deep down to dig
    gold for you,
Azania wants to dig gold for its own
    children.
Azania is tired, Azania is tired,
Azania is tired of crying.

Sons and daughters of Africa, this is where my poem ends, and I want to put it straight to you that I'm tired of coming into this big church and standing here rendering poems. From now on, I think there is a better solution: instead of standing here and talking, I should be doing something deep in the bushes of Africa!
Crowd: (Wild applause.)

> Unidentified Soweto poet at a 16 June commemoration at
> Regina Mundi Church, 1981
> (Azania)

The Call

There is no success without a struggle
What are you waiting for?
Where are you when the struggle for land is on,
What are you waiting for?

Chorus
What are you waiting for?
The moment has come,
What are you waiting for?

Have you not yet joined,
What are you waiting for?
Join our Mau Mau army,
What are you waiting for?

Even if you think you are rich,
What are you waiting for?
Land is truly our national wealth,
What are you waiting for?

What sort of man are you,
What are you waiting for?
Or are you one of the whites,
What are you waiting for?

And you, man of religion,
What are you waiting for?
Remember land is the source of national strength,
What are you waiting for?

Even if you think you are too important,
What are you waiting for?
Let us unite in struggle,
What are you waiting for?

Unity is strength,
What are you waiting for?
Mau Mau is the people's movement,
What are you waiting for?

We are struggling for our liberation,
What are you waiting for?
Don't you yourself like to be free,
What are you waiting for?

The Mau Mau (Kenya)
Translated from the Gikuyu by Maina Wa Kinyatti

The Song of a Child Who Survived Nyadzonia

We saw the soldiers come.
They came from the setting of the sun.
They came with armaments.
They came with fury.
They came painted black like black people.

But soon we got to know.
Soon we got to know who they were,
Soon the whole earth was a-thunder with bomb blasts,
Soon the whole earth was aflame with furious and frightening fire.

And with my child's eyes and child's mind
I saw a leg flying from a falling person.
I saw a human head bouncing like a bouncing ball.
With my child's eyes and child's mind
I saw a man fleeing for dear life walking on two legs without a head –
Listen man! A man walking on two legs without a head!

With my child's ear and child's mind
I heard a man painted black
Shouting, Fire! Fire! *Bulala zonke!* Fire!

With my child's ear and child's mind
I heard a crack, I heard a bang,
I heard a blast, the cracks split and the fire blazed.
The soldiers shelled and shelled and shelled.
They shelled until I was dead.
They shelled until I could no longer hear, see, think or feel.

I don't know how long I was dead, or unconscious as they say.
I woke up in a nightmare and opened my eyes.
I saw a pool of blood.
I saw blood flowing like a stream where we drank,
Mixing with the waters of the stream where we drank.

I looked at my mother.
She lay peacefully, quiet, not crying.
I called, I got no answer.
I looked at my mother again.
There were only holes where eyes should have been
And exposed flesh where nostrils should have been.

I looked for my father.
My father was not there and up to this day
I don't know where they buried my father.
I wiped the thick clots of blood

From my face and looked at myself:
What's this?
What's wrong with me? I asked.
What's wrong?
Then I saw there was something wrong:
I could not move because my leg,
My right leg, was no longer there.
And when those kind people took me to hospital,
They asked me where I came from,
I told them my mother, father, grandmother, brother and I
All fled from Rhodesia
To find this life, this death, this horror at
Nyadzonia.
These, they told me, were the doings of oppressors,
These, they told me, were the doings of racists,
These, they told me, were the massacres of Nyadzonia.

Emmanuel Ngara (Zimbabwe)

A False Hero of Independence*

Kenya regained her Uhuru from the British on 12 December 1963. A minute before midnight, lights were put out at the Nairobi stadium so that people from all over the country and the world who had gathered there for the midnight ceremony were swallowed by the darkness. In the dark, the Union Jack was quickly lowered. When next the lights came on the new Kenya flag was flying and fluttering, and waving, in the air. The Police band played the new National Anthem and the crowd cheered continuously when they saw the flag was black, and red and green. The cheering sounded like one intense cracking of many trees, falling on the thick mud in the stadium.

In our village and despite the drizzling rain, men and women and children, it seemed, had emptied themselves into the streets where they sang and danced in the mud. Because it was dark, they put oil-lamps at the doorsteps to light the streets. As usual, on such occasions, some young men walked in gangs, carrying torches, lurked and whispered in dark corners and the fringes, really looking for love-mates among the crowd. Mothers warned their daughters to take care not to be raped in the dark. The girls danced in the middle, thrusting out their buttocks provokingly, knowing that the men in corners watched them. Everybody waited for something to happen. The 'waiting' and the uncertainty that went with it – like a woman torn between fear and joy during birth-motions – was a taut cord beneath the screams and the shouts and the laughter. People moved from street to street singing. They praised Jomo and Kaggia and Oginga. They recalled Waiyaki, who even before 1900 had challenged the white people who had come to Dagoreti in the wake of Lugard. They remembered heroes from our village, too. They created words to describe the deeds of Kihika in the forest, deeds matched only by those of Mugo in the trench and detention camps. They mixed Christmas hymns with songs and dances only performed during initiation rites when boys and girls are circumcised into responsibility as men and women. And underneath it all was the chord that followed us from street to street. Somewhere, a woman suggested we go and sing to Mugo, the hermit, at his hut. The cry was taken up by the crowd, who, even before the decision was taken, had already started tearing through the drizzle and the dark to Mugo's hut. For more than an hour Mugo's hut was taken prisoner. His name was on everybody's lips. We wove new legends around his name and imagined deeds. We hoped that Mugo would come out and join us, but he did not open the door to our knocks. When the hour of midnight came, people broke into one long ululation. Then the women cried out the five Ngemi to welcome a son at birth or at circumcision. These they sang for Kihika and Mugo, the two heroes of deliverance, from our village. Soon after this, we all dispersed to our various huts to wait for the morning, when the Uhuru Celebrations would really begin.

Later in the night, the drizzle changed into a heavy downpour. Lightning, followed by thunder, would for a second or two red-white-light our huts, even though it only came through the cracks in the walls. The wind increased with the rain. A moaning sound, together with a continuous booming which went on all night, came from swaying and breaking trees and hedges as the wind and the rain beat the leaves and the branches. Some decaying thatched roofs freely let in rain, so that pools collected on the floor. To avoid being drenched, people kept on shifting their beds from spot to spot, only to be followed by a new leakage.

The wind and the rain were so strong that some trees were uprooted whole, while others broke by the stems, or lost their branches.

This we saw the following morning as we went into a field near Rung'ei, where the sports and dances to celebrate Uhuru were to take place. Crops on the valley slopes were badly damaged. Running water had grooved trenches that now zigzagged all along the sloping fields. Uprooted potato and bean crops lay everywhere on the valley floor. The leaves of the maize plants still standing were lacerated into numerous shreds.

The morning itself was so dull we feared the day would not break into life. But the rain had stopped. The air was soft and fresh, and an intimate warmth oozed from the pregnant earth to our hearts . . .

In the afternoon the sun appeared and brightened the sky. The mist which in the morning lingered in the air went. The earth smoked grey like freshly dropped cow-dung. The warming smoke spread and thinned upwards into the clear sky. The main ceremony to remember the dead sons and bless foundations for a new future was to be performed in the afternoon. It seemed that everybody had been waiting and making themselves ready for this occasion. Except for the old women and a few other people who were ill or lame, most people from our village came to the meeting. This was Kihika's day; it was Mugo's day; it was our day.

Other people from Ndeiya, Lari, Limuru, Ngeca, Kabete, Kerarapon, come in lorries and buses, and filed out into Rung'ei market-place. There were the schoolchildren in their khaki uniforms of green, red, yellow – of every colour in the rainbow; the village children in tattered clothes with flies massed around their sore eyes and mouths; women, dressed in Miengu and Mithuru, with beads around their necks; women in flower-patterned calicos that showed bare their left shoulders; women, in modern frocks; women, singing Christian hymns mixed with traditional and Uhuru songs. Men stood or talked in groups about the prospects opened up by Uhuru. There were those without jobs, who wore coats that had never come into contact with water or soap; would the government now become less stringent on those who could not pay tax? Would there be more jobs? Would there be more land? The well-to-do shopkeepers and traders and landowners discussed prospects for business now that we had political power; would something be done about the Indians?

We sat down. Githua, whom we playfully called our 'monolegged champion', freely wept with great joy.

The crowd made a harmony: there's something beautiful and moving in the spectacle of a large mass of people seated in an orderly disorder.

A tree was planted at the spot where Kihika once hung. Near it, and tied to a stone, were two black rams, without blemish, for the big sacrifice. Warui and two wizened old men from Kihingo village had been chosen to lead in the sacrifice after tributes to those who had died in the struggle had been concluded. Mbugua and Wanjiku occupied two prominent chairs near the platform. Chairs for the main speakers and leaders of the celebrations were arranged around the microphone that stood on the raised platform. Mumbi, who in the village heard about Gikonyo's broken arm, had gone to the hospital.

We waited.

Again there was the breathless expectation that had hung over our village since the night. It seemed that most people still expected that Mugo would speak. They wanted to see him in the flesh and hear his voice. Stories about Mugo's power had spread from mouth to mouth and were mainly responsible for the big turnout. It would have been impossible to deny the many conflicting reports that overnight turned into stimulating legends. In any case, nobody, especially from our village, would have taken any denial seriously. Some people said that in detention Mugo had been shot at and no bullet would touch his skin. Through these powers, Mugo had been responsible for many escapes from detention of men who later went to fight in the forest. And who but Mugo could have smuggled letters from the camps to Members of Parliament in England? There were those who suggested that he had even been at the battle of Mahee and had fought side by side with Kihika. All these stories were now freely circulating in the meeting. We sang song after song about Kihika and Mugo. A calm holiness united our hearts. Like those who had come from afar to see Mugo do miracles or even speak to God, we all vaguely expected that something extraordinary would happen. It was not exactly a happy feeling; it was more a disturbing sense of an inevitable doom.

The secretary of the Party stood in place of Gikonyo. Nyamu was a short man, heavily built, who during the Emergency was caught, redhanded, with bullets in his pockets. It is said that his rich uncles (they were loyalists) bribed the police, and this, together with his youth, for he was only seventeen, saved him from a death sentence, the way of all those caught with arms and ammunition. Instead, he was imprisoned for seven years. Nyamu now called upon the Revd Morris Kingori to open the meeting, with a prayer. Before 1952, Kingori was a renowned preacher in the Kikuyu Greek Orthodox Church, one of the many independent churches that had broken with the missionary establishment. When these churches were banned, Kingori went without a job for a long time, before he joined the Agriculture Department during land consolidation in the Central Province, as an instructor, a job he still holds to this day. As a preacher, he used to sing and dramatize his prayers; he raised his voice and eyes to heaven, then suddenly lowered them. Often, he would beat his breast and pull at his hair and clothes. Protest alternated with submission, meekness with anguish, warning with promise. Now, he stood on the platform, a bible in his hand.

Kingori: Let us pray. Lord, open thou our hearts.

Crowd: And our mouths shall show forth thy praise.

Kingori: God of Isaac and Jacob and Abraham, who also created Gikuyu and Mumbi, and gave us, your chidren, this land of Kenya, we, on this occasion ever to be remembered by all the nations of the earth as the day you delivered your children from Misri, do now ask you to let your tears stream down upon us, for your tears, oh Lord, are eternal blessings. Blood had been spilt for this day. Each post in our huts is smeared not with the blood from the ram, but blood from the veins and skins of our sons and daughters, who died, that we may live. And everywhere in our villages, in the market-place, in the shambas, nay, even in the air, we hear the widows and orphans cry, and we pass by, talking loudly to drown their moaning, for we can do nothing. Lord, we can do nothing. But the cry of Rachel in our midst cannot be drowned, can never be drowned. Oh God of Isaac and Abraham, the journey across the desert is long. We are without water, we are without food, and our enemies follow behind us, riding on chariots and on horseback, to take us back to Pharaoh. For they are loth to let your people go, are angered to the heart to see your people go. But with your help and guidance, Lord, we shall surely reach and walk on Canaan's shore. You who said that where two or three are gathered together, you will grant whatsoever they shall ask, we now beseech you with one voice, to bless the work of our hands as we till the soil and defend our freedom. For it is written: Ask and it shall be given unto you; knock and it shall be opened; seek and ye shall find. All this we ask in the name of Jesus Christ our Lord, Amen.

Crowd: Amen.

People started singing, led by the youth band with drums, guitars, flutes and tins. Again they recreated history, giving it life through the words and voices: land alienation, Waiyaki, Harry Thuku, taxation, conscription of labour into the whiteman's land, the break with the missions, and, oh, the terrible thirst and hunger for education. They sang of Jomo (he came, like a fiery spear among us), his stay in England (Moses sojourned in the land of Pharaoh) and his return (he came riding on a cloud of fire and smoke) to save his children. He was arrested, sent to Lodwar, and on the third day came home from Maralal. He came riding a chariot home. The gates of hell could not withhold him. Now angels trembled before him.

Nyamu read apologies from the M.P. for the area and from members of the Regional Assembly, all of whom had gone to Nairobi to represent Rung'ei area in the national celebrations. He did not mention Mugo's absence.

Next came the speeches. Most speakers recounted the sufferings of the Emergency, or else told of the growth of the Party. They were proud of Kihika, a son of the village, whose fight for freedom would never be forgotten. They recounted his qualities of courage, humility and love of the land. His death was a sacrifice for the nation.

At the end of each speaker, the crowd cheered or sang, even if the men and women had only repeated points already made. Githua's voice, as he cried, cheered and shouted, drowned that of those who sat near him. All the time most people expected Mugo to speak. Whenever a speaker sat down, they thought the next on the list would surely be

Mugo himself. But they waited patiently because the best dish was always reserved to the last.

In the end, Nyamu announced that General R., the man who had fought side by side with Kihika, would speak, in the place of Mugo. Circumstances outside anybody's control had prevented Mugo from coming to the meeting. This announcement was met with silence. Then from one corner, a man shouted for Mugo. The demand was immediately chorused from different parts of the field, until the meeting seethed with Mugo's name in a threatening unison. Then the unison broke into undisciplined shouting and movement; people stood up, groups formed, and they all argued, gesticulated, protested, as if they had been tricked into the meeting. Nyamu consulted the elders. They decided to make one last appeal to Mugo. It took time for Nyamu and the elders to bring the gathering back to order with a promise that a delegation of two would be dispatched immediately to fetch Mugo. The two elders were asked not to take 'No' for an answer. Meanwhile, would the people sit and hear General R's words? They settled down again with the song of the trench.

> And he jumped into the trench,
> The words he told the soldier pierced my heart like a spear;
> You will not beat the woman, he said,
> You will not beat a pregnant woman, he told the soldier.

Below the words was the sound of something like a twang of a cord, broken. After it, people became deathly quiet.

General R. stood by the microphone, and his red eyes tried to penetrate the faceless crowd. He cleared his throat, twice. He knew what he wanted to say. He had rehearsed this act, word for word, many times. But now, standing on the edge of the precipice, he found it difficult to jump or fix his eyes on the scene below. Compressed into a single picture, his life in the forest flashed through his mind. He saw the dark caves at Kinenie, the constant flights from bombs in Nyandarwa forest, thirst, hunger, raw meat and then their victory at Mahee. Tell them about this, a voice in him insisted. Tell them how you and Kihika planned it. This picture and the voice disappeared. Now it was the face of the Revd Jackson Kigondu that stood before him: Jackson had consistently preached against Mau Mau in churches and in public meetings convened by Tom Robson. He called on Christians to fight side by side with the white man, their brother in Christ, to restore order and the rule of the spirit. Three times had Jackson been warned to stop his activities against the people. 'In the name of Jesus, who stood against the Roman colonists and their Pharisee homeguards, we ask you to stop siding with British colonialism!' But Jackson became even more defiant. He had to be silenced. It was the same Jackson who now stood before him, mocking him, 'We are still here. We whom you called traitors and collaborators will never die!' And suddenly General R. recalled Lt Koina's recent misgivings. Koina talked of seeing the ghosts of the colonial past still haunting Independent Kenya. And it was true that those now marching in the streets of Nairobi were not the soldiers of the Kenya Land and Freedom Army but of the King's African Rifles, the very colonial forces who had been doing on the battlefield what Jackson was doing in churches. Kigondu's face was now transformed into that of Karanja and all the other traitors in all the communities in Kenya. The sensation of imminent betrayal was so strong that General R. trembled in his moment of triumph. He clutched the microphone to steady himself. He was suddenly aware that the crowd had stopped singing and were watching him. This threw General R. into a panic. Could everybody see the face or was it only in the mind? General R. wondered in his panic. He looked straight ahead, and addressed the face that mocked him.

'You ask why we fought, why we lived in the forest with wild beasts. You ask why we killed and spilt blood.

'The white man went in cars. He lived in a big house. His children went to school. But who tilled the soil on which grew coffee, tea, pyrethrum, and sisal? Who dug the roads and paid the taxes? The white man lived on our land. He ate what we grew and cooked. And even the crumbs from the table, he threw to his dogs. That is why we went into the forest. He who was not on our side, was against us. That is why we killed our black brothers. Because, inside, they were white men. And I know even now this war is not ended. We get Uhuru today. But what's the meaning of "Uhuru"? It is contained in the name of our Movement: Land and Freedom. Let the Party that now leads the country rededicate itself to all the ideals for which our people gave up their lives. The Party must never betray the Movement. The Party must never betray Uhuru.

It must never sell Kenya back to the Enemy! Tomorrow we shall ask: where is the land? Where is the food? Where are the schools? Let therefore these things be done now, for we do not want another war . . . no more blood in my . . . in these our hands . . .'

General R. found it difficult to continue. Looking at these people, his doubt fled, he knew they were behind him, that in asking for change he had spoken their word. The mocking face of the Revd Jackson disappeared. Now he resumed his speech in a calm, confident voice.

'We want a Kenya built on the heroic tradition of resistance of our people. We must revere our heroes and punish traitors and collaborators with the colonial enemy. Today we are here to honour one such hero! Not many years ago today, Kihika was strangled with a rope on a tree here. We have come to remember him, the man who died for truth and justice. We, his friends, would like to reveal before you all the truth about his death, so that justice may be done. It is said, I am sure this is the story you all know, that Kihika was captured by security forces. But have you ever stopped to ask yourselves a few questions? Was he captured in battle? Why was he alone? Why was he not armed? Shall I tell you? On that night Kihika was going to meet somebody who betrayed him.'

He paused to let his words sink. People looked at one another, and started murmuring. The drama was even more exciting than they had imagined.

'Go on!' someone shouted.

'We hear you,' several voices cried out.

General R. continued.

'Maybe he who betrayed Kihika is here, now, in this crowd. We ask him to come forward to this platform, to confess and repent before us all.'

People looked this way and that way to see if anybody would rise. General R. waited, enjoying the tension, the drama was now unfolding as he had envisaged. Though he could not see him, he knew where Karanja sat. He had told Mwaura and Lt Koina to keep him in sight.

'Let him not think he can hide,' General R. went on. 'For we know him. He was Kihika's friend. They used to eat and drink together.'

'Speak his name,' Githua stood up and shouted.

'Toboa! Toboa!' more people cried, severally, almost thirsty for revenge.

'I give him a last chance. Let him come forward as a sign of repentance.'

People suddenly stopped rumbling and shouting. They sat tensed up, eyes turned in the same direction, to see the man who was standing. He was tall, imposing, but those near him could see his face was agitated. Nobody had seen Mugo come to the scene. He wore a dirty coat and sandals made from an old lorry tyre. It is Mugo, somebody whispered. The whisper spread and became louder. People clapped. People shouted. At last, the hermit had come to speak. The other drama was forgotten. Women cried out the five Ngemi to a victorious son. General R. was angry with Mugo for ruining the climax of the other drama. Would Karanja escape? He did not show his anger, in fact, he immediately left the microphone to Mugo. People waited for Mugo to speak.

'You asked for Judas,' he started. 'You asked me for the man who led Kihika to this tree, here. That man stands before you, now. Kihika came to me by night. He put his life into my hands, and I sold it to the white man. And this thing has eaten into my life all these years.'

Throughout he spoke in a clear voice, pausing at the end of every sentence. When he came to the end, however, his voice broke and fell into a whisper. 'Now, you know.'

And still nobody said anything. Not even when he walked away from the platform. People without any apparent movement created a path for him. They bent down their heads and avoided his eyes. Wanjiku wept. ('It was his face, not the memory of my son that caused my tears,' she told Mumbi later.) Suddenly Githua rose from his corner and followed Mugo. He laughed and raised one of his crutches to point at Mugo, and shouted: 'A liar – a hyena in sheep's clothing.' He denounced Mugo as an impostor and challenged him to a fight. 'Look at him! Look at him – the man who thought he would be our Chief. Ha! ha! ha!' Githua's laughter and voice only sharpened the profound silence at the market-place. People sat on with bowed heads for a minute or so after Mugo and Githua had gone. Then they rose and started talking, moving away in different directions, as if the meeting ended with Mugo's confession.

The sun had faded; clouds were gathering in the sky. Nyamu, Warui,

General R., and a few other elders remained behind to complete the sacrifice before the storm.

Ngugi wa Thiong'o (Kenya)
Excerpt from *A Grain of Wheat*

Admonition to the Black World
(Excerpt)

PERSPECTIVE: For twenty-five centuries now, invaders and hegemonists from white lands (Iran, Greece, Rome, Arabia, Western Europe and Russia) have assaulted Africa. In 525 BC, black Egypt fell to white Persians, the ancestors of today's Iranians. After them Greeks (332 BC) and Romans (30 BC) also conquered Egypt. From the seventh century AD, Arabs overran North Africa, spread their imperial religion with sword and guile, and enslaved and sold Africans. And from about the tenth century AD Arabs and Shirazi-Persians did likewise on the East African coast.

From the sixteenth century AD, western Europeans carried off slaves from Africa before finally conquering the whole continent at the end of the nineteenth century. Thereafter, the millennia-long retreat of African peoples turned into a crusade against white power. Following the initial victories of political independence, the crusade has settled into a dog-fight to expel tenacious white settlers from the continent.

In the Sudan, John Garang leads a war against a relentless southward expansion by Arab settlers. In Southern Africa, the black population is in rebellion against white settler rule. In fortress Ethiopia, Mengistu Haile Mariam resists an Arab-financed dismemberment of Ethiopia.

But in all too many parts of Africa today, agents of a long-dormant Arab imperialism are bribing and preaching their way to fresh hegemony. So too are the agents of Russian might; so too are the agents and money-lenders of the West. And victory is far from assured to the Blacks.

I: SCATTERBRAINED LAND

Ah, this land
This black whore
This manacled bitch
Tied to a post and raped
By every passing white dog:

The dog of the crescent sword
The dog of the militant cross
The dog of the red star!
Listen! Listen to the pack
Of scavenger dogs from white heartlands
Snarling in their gang rape of Africa!

Black Lady
Forced to wear
A white turban of shame
And white shoes of shame
With the acid of humiliation
Burning in her eyes
As she suffers their gang rape!

Ah, this land
This scatterbrained land
For two and half millennia
Most unlucky in its rulers;
This continent
This father of sciences
For two and half thousand years
Wallowing in a murk of magic,
Like an eagle
Shot in soaring flight across the skies
Which dropped, wings cracked,
Into the lightless ooze
Of a mangrove ravine,
And is forever unable to scramble up;
O, unlucky land!

Ah, Africa
Birthplace of monotheism
Home of the Sun Disc of Aten –
That father to the Tablet of Moses,
And grand uncle to the Cross of Jesus,
And grandfather to the Crescent of Mohammed,
And great-grandfather to the Red Star of Marx!

For what are they –
Tablet, Cross, Crescent and Red Star –
But icons of latter-day cults
Fashioned by white imitators
Of that heretic theological line
Invented in the fourteenth century BC
By Akhenaten, King of Khemet?†
Yet, behold this venerable land,
Assaulted, dismembered,
In its supine, demented dotage,
By the mongrel progeny
Of a bastard it discarded!
Behold the white religions,
Their war banners flying high;
A trinity of alien icons:
Red Star, Cross and Crescent,
Competing for reverent kisses
From black auxiliaries.

O paragons of self-contempt
With a genius for suicide!
For two and a half millenia
Driven by brainwashed shame,
They have bleached their black identity,
Scraping it off like shit from their fine skin;
They have scrammed from their black identity
Like a man fleeing his menacing shadow!
And like whales
Demented by sea-borne infections in their brains,
They have beached themselves on white shores,
And are panting for white theologies
From St Peter's,
From the Ka'aba,

---

†Khemet was the indigenous name for the kingdom known to us as Egypt of the
Pharaohs. It meant the land of the Blacks, and is the root of the word Chemistry. All
names in this poem are given in their Khemetic originals where these have been
ascertained. The more familiar Hellenic and Arab versions are avoided.

From the Kremlin.
Like beached whales,
They have fled their habitat,
Fled their dark sea waters
Polluted by humiliations;
They are lusting for sacred waters
They hope will whiten their souls.

That one claims he is an Arab.
He now wears around his neck
A fake genealogical chain
Linking himself to the Quraish.
Look, look at him now!
Look at what airs he wears!
He feels his worth increased
In the sight of his alien god;
And when he bites off his African tongue,
And stutters in Arabic,
He is giddy with divine pride
At being able to address his fellows
In 'the language of God himself'!
And when he dons the Arab turban,
And nails Arab names to his brow,
And bows in obeisance to Mecca,
Five times a day like a lizard,
Dramatizing thereby his allegiance
To the Arabs and their homeland,
He feels the gates of heaven opening for him!
He hears the trumpet of angels
Blowing a fanfare to welcome him!

That other one,
At morning assembly each day,
Lustily chants
The identity of his desire:
'Our ancestors, the Gauls,
Were blond-haired and blue-eyed!'
But he was not taught to add:

'Were half-naked and lived in caves.'
Yet his face, this strange Gaul,
Has nothing blond,
Has nothing blue,
Is ebony black!

And the third,
Less crude, more cerebral
In his flight from his identity,
Declares with bright-eyed passion:
'I am deracialized;
And I am denationalized!
The God of the Dialectic, of Historical Materialism,
Is colour and nation blind.
From the mud of primitivism
He lifted me to astral planes,
And showed me the Universal Father!
I have done my dialectical ablutions,
I stand naked and purified,
All ready to approach his altar.
Do not taint me with black identity;
Taint me not with parochialism!
I must cross that grand threshold;
I must stand under the radiant gaze of Prophet Marx,
I must join the mass of assimilation
Into the Universal!'

And another of that sad lot,
Deranged by the world's contempt,
Grabbed a white boy by the collar
And sputtered into his face:
'I have bleached my face like yours;
I've adopted your white names;
I've defected to your white religion;
I've whitewashed my ancestral tree.
Why won't you treat me as your equal?
Why do you treat me like a dog?'
'O dear dear,' the white replied,

'If you spit on what you are,
Why should I not do so?
If you flee from what you are,
And crave to be what I am,
Doesn't that show that what you are
Is inferior to what I am?
Who would treat his mimic as an equal?
Do you think I am dotty like you?'

O terrible, terrible, terrible!
What meningitis of the soul
Has twisted their identity spines?
Like yam tendrils fleeing earth damp,
They grope for a stake to twine on
And lift their leaves to the light:
They grope, despairingly grope,
For any genealogical tree
With white bark.

II: THE ANGER OF ANCESTORS

And before this demented motley
Leaning its mammoth wretchedness
On the back of a burning horizon,
Behold the ancestors!
The volcanic anger of progenitors!
And their eyes,
Smarting at this circus of absurdities,
Are thirsting for the new black man
   the black man who would not be whipped;
   the black man who would not sell his kind;
   the black man shielded by ramparts of cunning,
   by parapets of reticence
   against beams of false self-knowledge
   aimed to char our heads;
   the black man who would not suffer his brains
     to be inflated with flattery,

    soaked in whiskey,
    shattered with nuances of contempt,
    scattered on a pavement before mocking faces,
    before mocking white compassions,
    and trampled by shined boots spiked with dollars.

But everywhere
    in bazaars of febrile desires
    a glitter of tinsel dreams,
    a delirium of cash and lace,
    elixirs of mad modernity
    sold by titillation;
    And on the podia of academia,
    catechists of aesthetica
    are hawking esoterica;
    And from minarets and pulpits,
    ecclesiastical gunners
    in turbans and dog collars
    are shooting into black souls
    bullet commandments from killjoy gods;
    And from pulsing electronic towers
    Intellectual acrobats
    Make somersaults of reason
    to lure us to cheer our destroyers.
Everywhere, everywhere,
    fat chefs of sophistries,
    lying mothers of invention,
    grand ineptitudes, perched high on saddles of power,
    conjure mirages of dancing waters
    to scald the thirst in our throats.
Everywhere, everywhere,
    from plazas of delirious power,
    razzle-dazzle magicians
    joyfully transmute our hopes
    to hot ash.

And they say, the ancestors say:
    the pinkcheeks conquered us,

raped our imaginations, fathered on us
bastard ambitions that will stuff our seed
down the gullet of their greed.
Behold what strange progeny our conquerors sired on us:
    Behold our new notables
    Evangelists of new disorders
    Black messengers of white gods
    Brown skins with blond souls
    Inebriate swooners before madonnas
    Crusaders for the European Cross
    Jihadeers for the Arab Crescent
    Militants of the Russian Star
    Trans-civilized idolators all
    Craving a white massage!
Behold what strange progeny
Our conquerors sired on us.

III: IF YOU LET THEM

O Blacks, hear and heed!
When the final war begins,
To drive white predators from your lands,
Across hot sands and burning seas,
The jackals of the white race,
Greed and reconquest in their hearts,
Will dash forth to exterminate you.
They will caress your ears with lovely lies,
Numb your minds with white religions,
Distract your eyes with flashing wonders,
And riddle your bodies with white-hot bullets.
They will dispatch their black auxiliaries –
Black satraps wielding white power,
Black bishops in white dogcollars,
Black mullahs in white turbans,
Black generals in uniforms of white armies –
Who will skin and send your carcasses to meat shops.

If you let them, if you let them,
These believers in the partnership
Of white rider on black ass,
They will drug you with delusions,
Mad, suicidal illusions,
With fairy-tales of good, white heavens,
With lies about white benevolence;
And with force, fraud and your own naive goodwill,
They will sweep your bones from veldt and forest,
Return your land to rack and ruin,
To their heartless despoliation.

If you let them, if you let them,
They will use your fears against you,
Your lack of daring against you,
Your respectability against you,
Your sweet reasonableness against you,
Your craving for trinkets against you,
Your thirst for their praise against you,
Your hunger for their world against you,
Your contempt for your own against you,
Your longing for world brotherhood against you,
Your sense of self-shame against you,
Your belief in their goodness against you,
Your legendary patience against you,
Your fairness fully against you,
Your restraint roughly against you,
Your sincerity sharply against you,
Your avarice, cowardice, ignorance, hates,
Your irresolution against you.
And they'll stuff your mouths once more
With glass shards of defeat,
And force you to swallow them.

Woe to them who forget their history
And drug their hearts with false memories.
Woe to them who put their faith
In the fairness of white foes;

Who embrace as brothers those jackals
Who swarmed in and grabbed our homeland,
Africa, land of Blacks,
And hacked our ancestral stalwarts to bloody deaths
On the abattoirs of the centuries.

Chinweizu (Nigeria)

II — POWER, WAR
AND AFFAIRS OF STATE

The God of the State

Furthermore, there was one of these gods which was called 'the god of the state' and it belonged to the government of this Rocky Town. This special title was given to it because it was the most powerful and terrible of all the rest of the gods and idols, except the god of thunder. The height of this 'god of the state' was just like that of a sternly looking giant. It was too terrible and fearful for the eyes of human beings to see, because it held above its head a very long and big spear by the right hand in such a fearful way as if it was preparing to stab to death without hesitation one who might go near it or stand at a short distance before it. This big and fearful spear which it held was so dazzling from its sharpness that it was hard to look at it for a half-twinkling or thirty seconds, without the eyes being hurt. (In the Yoruba language, 'twinkling' means minute.)

The body of this 'god of the state' was fearfully decorated with the skins of various kinds of animals such as lions, tigers, leopards, crocodiles, boar, forest lizards, etc. All of these skins were jointly woven into one huge garment of the Rocky Town's type. The huge garment reached only to its elbows, neck and a half of its thighs. On the left of this god, there was a complete skeleton of a man which it held tightly with the left hand. The platform on which it stood upright was about twenty metres above the ground. It was round but was flat at the top. Hundreds of skulls of men, women, animals, big birds of all kinds, etc. were stuck round the platform and so many were gathered round the feet of the god.

The neck of this terrible god was very huge and several thick veins were sprung out round it. Its eyes were just like those of an owl but bigger and more fearful. Each was moving sternly to different directions at one-twinkling intervals. Its nose was the same shape like that of a human but bigger. Each of the nostrils was so large that it could easily contain a big bottle. Its head had the shape of that of a human as well, but it was bigger than that of a human. The hair on this head weighed more than one ton of a load. All was muddled together from the rotten blood of the animals, humans, etc. which was pouring on it often and often. Each of its jaws was flat and thick beyond what a person could see and laugh at.

The upper lip of this 'god of the state' was spread on the lower one and it could not move up or down because of the large quantity of long hair which pressed it on one place. And the lower one was dropped towards its chest because of the very long and thick beard which overweighed it.

Furthermore, one of its jaws was painted with white and red paints, while the other was painted with white and yellow paints. So whenever the strong breeze started to blow, the garment of the various kinds of animal skins which were woven together would be making different kinds of fearful noises which the ears of the human beings could hear and be happy from. So for its fearful and ugly appearance both young men and women of the town feared it greatly. But they gave it much respect which they could not even give to the king.

As thousands of the gods, idols, etc. which belonged to the common people of the town were kept in the shrines at the bank of this river, as well as the 'god of the state', special ceremonies were performed for them in the tenth month of the year, for seventeen days and nights. The sacrifices which were given to each of the gods, idols, etc. were of different kinds. But the kinds of the sacrifices which were given to the 'god of the state' were almost all kinds of the bush animals and domestic animals, including kola nuts, bitter kola nuts, palm oil, etc. And this 'god of the state' was the imitation of the very powerful and most kind god or spirit of the river.

Special sacrifices were given to the god of the river once in a year. But many people were giving the god thank-offerings in addition. Of course, as he was kind, it was so he was cruel. Because sometimes he made the barren women to become mothers of children, and sometimes when he was cruel, he forced swimmers to drown and then dragged them to the place of his abode in the bottom of the river, and there he would detain them throughout their lives' time. So when sacrifices were ready to be given to him in the year, a very big canoe would be carved from a mighty tree. Several kinds of bold images would be carved right round its body. Each of the images would be painted with different colours of paints, and the canoe itself would be beautifully painted both inside and outside. Then after, all of the sacrifices including one young man and one young lady were put in the canoe. Then many animals and fowls would be slaughtered. Having cooked their flesh and every one of the people having eaten it to his or her satisfaction, they would start to sing and dance round the canoe and also the 'god of the state'.

Having sung, danced and drunk the palm-wine for a while, then one big ewe would be slaughtered in front of the 'god of the state'. So having poured some of its blood on the 'god of the state', they would pour the rest on the heads of the young man and the lady who were dressed in beautiful clothes, etc. After that, the whole people would pray greedily to the god of the river to accept their sacrifices and to send peace and good health to them in return. Having prayed greedily like that for about twenty twinklings, then the drummers would start to beat their drums, and as the whole people started to sing the song of the god of the river loudly, some of the strong men would push the canoe to the middle of the river. As the water started to carry the canoe away gently, the drummers would continue to beat the drums and the rest of the people would continue to sing, dance, etc. until the canoe would be lost to their view. But as soon as the canoe was lost to their view, the people would continue to sing and dance as they were going back to the town.

Amos Tutuola (Nigeria)
Excerpt from *The Witch Herbalist of the Remote Town*

The Killing of the Cowards

After Noliwa's death Chaka underwent a frightful change both in his external appearance and also in his inner being, in his very heart; and so did his aims and his deeds. Firstly, the last spark of humanity still remaining in him was utterly and finally extinguished in the terrible darkness of his heart; his ability to distinguish between war and wanton killing or murder vanished without a trace, so that to him all these things were the same, and he regarded them in the same light. Secondly, his human nature died totally and irretrievably, and a beast-like nature took possession of him; because although he had been a cruel person even before this, he had remained a human being, his cruelty but a human weakness. But a man who had spilt the blood of someone like Noliwa, would understandably regard the blood of his subjects exactly as if it were no different from that of mere animals which we slaughter at will. This was Chaka's act of greatest magnitude in preparing himself for the kingship he so much coveted; and with Noliwa's blood he had branded himself with an indelible mark which resembled that of the kings of Isanusi's home. We are unable to measure Nandi's grief when she heard the report of Noliwa's death, because she loved her very much, and regarded her as no less than her daughter-in-law.

After such preparations, Chaka attacked Buthelezi's and Qwabe's territories just to try out his own strength, and also to put his untried young warriors to the test and see how they would perform. He went out with armies which were more than twice the strength of Dingiswayo's. In the whole of Nguniland there was peace and prosperity, and the land was warm and the nations lived in great contentment when Chaka took to the road with his armies to go and bring that peace in the world to an end.

It is perfectly understandable that in those two battles some ran away, some lost their spears, some threw theirs, and some returned without having captured any from the enemy; that happens among all nations, people kill each other, people capture loot from each other. In these two battles Chaka attacked only with the new regiments and held back the older ones; and among those new regiments there was only one which stood its ground and continued fighting even as the others turned and fled. Even when the enemy was making a concerted assault on them, threatening to wipe them out, they stood firm without giving an inch, until Chaka sent reinforcements to help them push back the enemy. Some few others were in the habit of making a quick retreat when they felt the heat of battle, and then turning back quickly for a fresh assault; but this particular one remained unshaken.

There was a young man in that same regiment from whom Chaka never removed his eyes. When they were ordered into battle, this young man went with his eyes deep-set, way back in their sockets, and he held his spear high with a backward thrust, and grasped his shield by its handle, with his chest pushed out like that of a bird swimming. And as soon as they met the enemy, that young man who was of a lean physique became transformed and he held his shield close to him, grasping it by its thong handle, and his spear stabbed with an upward thrust rather than downward. His performance in those two battles was exactly like Chaka's when he was still a warrior. His name was Mzilikazi.

When Chaka returned home with his armies, he called all the grown up men and women to the royal place at Mgungundlovu; the armies comprising young boys were also summoned; which means that he called together his entire nation and assembled it outside the city walls.

When everyone had come, he went there ushered by Mbopha, leader of the king's courtiers, and followed by the young army which had acquitted itself so well in those two battles. Mbopha was reciting praises as he walked, telling about the profound wisdom of the king, and the justness of his verdicts. When Chaka reached the assembled multitude, he raised his little spear which contained medicines of witchcraft, and there was dead silence, then he called all the regiments which he had taken out to battle, and he ordered them to stand to one side. When they were there, he said that each warrior should produce his own spear as well as the one he had captured from the enemy warrior he had killed. Those who had them showed them, and those who did not were told to stand apart from the rest. Those whose spears were captured by the enemy were also told to stand by themselves apart from the others. After that he called those who ran away from the battle, and their spears and battle dresses were taken away from them, and they were also made to stand to one side. Those who had thrown their spears were also called and made to stand by themselves.

The commanders of the regiments stood near the king, crowding around him. Chaka looked at them and then he looked at the people he had commanded to stand to one side in the midst of the assembled crowd, and then he raised his spear which had killed nations of people, and there was dead silence; the commanders strained their ears in order to hear what the king's wish might be, and the king said: 'Let the Nkandle and Myozi regiments come to the front.' The commanders of these regiments ran at once and fetched them and made them stand in the centre of the crowd; and then Chaka raised his voice and said: 'All you who are present here, open your ears and hear me well; open your eyes and see, and be witness to the deed that I shall perform, and the law I am going to lay down by the example of these ones here. Do you see these people?'

The crowd: 'We see them, O King.'

Chaka: 'These are cowards who ran away from battle, and yet I had instructed them very strictly that no one in my armies should ever do such an ugly thing, because he who runs away disgraces our name, Mazulu, which means those who are invincible; besides this running away of theirs is already an indication that one day the Mazulu will be defeated. These are people who deserve a very heavy punishment.'

Malunga was suddenly heard from somewhere in the crowd saying: 'The king's command must be obeyed by each and every warrior, because he who does not obey the king's command is failing to obey the command of Nkulunkulu himself who sent the king here to come and teach his children, the Mazulu, the art of war, and thus deliver them from their enemies.' Chaka turned about often, looking on all sides, and the people trembled, because when he was angry he turned into a veritable wild beast. He looked at these two regiments which stood in the centre of the crowd, and then lifted his spear and pointed it at those who had run away. He did this without uttering a word. In the twinkling of an eye the warriors fell upon the condemned like wild dogs charging into a flock of sheep. Those thousands died and became food for the vultures right there at their home, not in battle, but within view of their parents, within view of the young women and the children, and they became exposed as cowards who surpassed all other cowards.

After they had been executed, there was dead silence. At that time Chaka was so angry that he was foaming at the mouth; and then the king's courtiers, the men appointed specially to advise the king, said: '*Ao*, how great his wisdom! This deed will ensure that there will never again be any cowards in Zulu's empire! No warrior will ever again turn his back on the enemy!' They spoke these words with their heads bowed to show how overwhelmed they were. About twenty of Zwide's people who were now under Chaka's rule cried when they saw these people killed, among whom were their own children and their brothers. Then Chaka ordered that they be brought to him, and he would comfort them in their grief.

When those killed had been carried to a place outside the crowd, Chaka once again raised his spear, and he instructed the commanders to summon forward the Dinare and Dilepe regiments. When those two regiments came, the people understood that the killing had not yet ended, and they were greatly frightened, because it was the first time that they had ever witnessed such a massacre. Ndlebe was moving about in the crowd, spotting those who were crying and bringing them to the king to be comforted for the death of their children.

'These whom you see here now are cowards just like the first group; they are the ones who threw away their spears which I had gone to great pains to have forged and strengthened with the potent medicines of Zululand.' Someone shouted in the midst of the crowd and said: 'It is obvious that they threw away those spears because they were running away.' Chaka paced this way and that, then he stopped and looked around; he raised his spear and pointed it at them while maintaining his silence, and at once the vultures swarmed up in flight above as the warriors brought them more food.

The king's men: 'How great his understanding! The spears of Zululand will no longer be lost, and the king's efforts will no longer be reduced to naught through people throwing away their spears on purpose as they run away.'

Chaka raised his spear a third time, and when the people saw it all things turned as dusty as the earth, they saw grey. He said: 'Those whom you see now are those who returned from battle without having captured any enemy spears; that is to say that they did not kill anyone.' A voice shot out of the crowd: 'If they did not kill, it is clear that they had gone there simply to increase the volume, but were afraid to go into the heat of battle, where warriors stabbed each other with their spears. They are cowards.' Two or three princes from nations which had been destroyed, said: 'O King, let the lion withdraw its claws and tread on its paws; your spear has killed, it is enough; have mercy on them, great master!' Chaka said he had heard them, and he bade them come to him; the spear nevertheless pointed to the very ones for whom the plea had been made, and the vultures rose again as more food was brought to them. They indeed were full already, and were leaving the rest for the scavenging hyena which, out of fear, never comes out to eat while the sun is shining.

The king's men: 'Oh, how great his understanding! It is a deep pool that goes down endlessly. Among the Zulu armies, no warrior will ever again go to war simply to increase the tumult!' They signalled to each other with their brows to prove to the king how overwhelmed they were by his unequalled wisdom.

Chaka once more lifted his spear, and passed word to the commanders, and two more regiments were brought into the midst of the crowd, and the people were dead with fright. 'These are the ones who threw Zulu's spear at the enemy whereas it was made to stab at close range, and that way they have thwarted the instructions that go with the medicines with which they were fortified. . . ' His mother, Nandi, came while he was speaking in that manner, and threw herself at her son's feet and said: 'I implore you, O King, do please hear me, I say, let the lion tread on its paws, O Zulu, it is the first time that they have wronged you, and they have seen the enormity of their crime. They will repent, and will fight your wars, O father.' Chaka was utterly silent. Nandi, for her part, remained prostrate. Then Chaka said: 'Just because of my mother, since she is my mother who bore me, who fetched me from Nkulunkulu and brought me into the world, I forgive you, don't do it again.' Chaka then told his mother to leave and go home, he had heard her prayer.

When Nandi had left, Chaka called out saying: 'The sentencing of the warriors is now over. I told you to open your ears and listen, and open your eyes and see; and you have heard, and you have seen. All of you who are present here, including you boys, be warned that the penalty for whomsoever shall do even a single one of these deeds, is death. I have called you so that you may hear for yourselves and see for yourselves. My law has to be obeyed completely, not outwardly only, but in the heart also, because I shall consign him who carries it out only because he is bound to do so, to that place over there (pointing to where the corpses had been thrown).

'I end by saying, open your ears once more and listen; open your eyes once more and see clearly. You saw these ones when they cried. That crying meant that I had done wrong in my judgements; and to say that I, Chaka, have erred is a great wrong. Besides, that crying will weaken the hearts of my warriors in battle when they die unmourned, and will make them run away. Now I am going to teach them the proper way to cry for their children, besides I have said that they should come to me for comfort, so that I can make them forget the death of those for whom they are mourning.' The commanders listened with great diligence, and then he said: 'You must gouge out these eyes of theirs which are overflowing fountains, and thus only will they forget their children who have done such great wrongs.' In the twinkling of an eye their eyes were gouged out, and they were let loose outside the crowd and it was said that if they knew how to find their way back to their homes, they were free to do so; if some should fall down the cliffs, then so be it.

The king's men: 'Not since the creation of all the nations has there been a man whose judgements equal those of this one! He testifies by his words, he testifies by his deeds too that he is one sent by Nkulunkulu.'

Chaka lifted his spear one more time and said: 'These ones you see here now are those who give free rein to their tongues. You heard them for yourselves. They will spoil my warriors by making them believe that there will always be someone to plead for them.' He paused, and then he said: 'You must pull out by their very roots these tongues of theirs which babble so much; you must not cut them for fear they might start sprouting again. Only that way will they stop meddling in the affairs of kings when they chastize their subjects.' In the twinkling of an eye, those people's tongues were pulled out, and they died.

The king's men: '*Siyakubonga, siyakudumisa*, Zulu (We thank you, we praise you, O Zulu)! Your judgements are just and they are without favour. Your eyes see deep into people's chests, they reveal things which are hidden to others! Your ears hear the plots which are hatched in people's hearts! All your deeds testify, O Zulu, that you are no mortal being, but the servant of Nkulunkulu, you are the Heaven which is towering over us all.' If any one of them had spoken in a manner which did not please Chaka, the penalty would have been death.

Chaka shouted for the last time: 'I hope you have seen for now and for always, I hope you have heard for now and for always!'

The regiment which had refused to retreat even when the battle was hot was given the entire loot which had been captured from Qwabe's and Buthelezi's; the cattle were given to them to become their property rather than for immediate feasting by the regiment. Chaka took not a single one of them even though they were so many. In addition to that, this regiment was promoted immediately to join the senior regiments who were called to active duty only when there was real danger, which meant that the time for them to qualify for marriage was very close. Mzilikazi was elevated to the rank of commander of that very regiment, and was also given the privilege to choose for himself one hundred cattle from the king's herds, and also select their bulls. That was how Chaka rewarded his braves.

On that one day the people who were killed were counted in tens of thousands. That is how cowardice was banished from Zulu's domain, and from that day the Zulu warriors went to war understanding in full the saying: 'A boy-child is an ox apportioned to the vultures.' They went to war understanding that they were not the children of their parents, but of the king; they went with the resolve to win or else die there rather than be killed like mere dogs, at home, before the eyes of the women. From that day on one Zulu warrior was equal to ten of the enemy, and could put them to flight. The day they went to the attack again Chaka's command to his armies was: 'Go, my children, and work with diligence and come back victorious, with a lot of war spoils; otherwise don't come back.'

This was only the beginning of Chaka's numerous massacres. Those who witnessed the events of that day had nightmares throughout that night. They grew thin because it was the first time that the people had ever witnessed such a deed.

Thomas Mofolo (Lesotho)
Chaka, Chapter Nineteen
Translated from the Sesotho by Daniel P. Kunene

Arrawelo: The Castrator of Men

Old Gallade had made such a mockery of the venerable authority vested in him that the score of chieftains convened after his death (which had been greeted with a universal sigh) were determined to wrest the leadership from the disreputable Rer-Kase and confer it upon the second prominent family in the powerful Harti nation. This wasn't an easy decision to make, because the only surviving direct descendant of the Calhighe was a young woman who went by the unprepossessing name, Arrawelo. Little was known about this lass except that she was a tomboy who loved riding wild ponies bare-back. Had it not been for the chronic ineptitude and outrageous conduct of the deceased Ugaas, who of late had insisted on eating nothing save the fresh marrow of gestating young she-goats and having a virgin in his bed every night, it would have been inconceivable to confer sovereignty upon a woman.

Forty years later, his successor, the dreaded Arrawelo, sat upon the threshold of the only water-hole in sight, insisting on a manicure while the thirsty herds waited. Forty years of sheer hell, of murder and mayhem, culminating in a nation of eunuchs and savage matrons. Within ten years of her ascension, Arrawelo had made the castration of all new-born male babies her official policy. The stalwarts who had hitherto carried on the losing resistance against the mad queen had been killed, castrated or driven into exile. Castrate, kill. Kill or castrate, it was all one to this cruel queen and her fanatical female legions. Those few matrons who appeared to waver were promptly eliminated alongside their men. There was no dilly-dallying about the way Arrawelo conducted her affairs of state. Some murderous plot or another was always in the making at her court whenever she wasn't away riding her spirited pony at the head of her shrieking furies, pursuing her enemies across the borders. And it was a rare occasion when she was not engaging one party or another in battle. The wild women clad in loincloths, their hair clipped close to their skulls and their bare bosoms heaving rhythmically as they rode impassioned across the land, were dreaded more than Azrail, the Angel of Death. They knew no mercy.

Arrawelo's methods were so effective that in time there were only three males, as far as it was known to her, who had been spared her henchwomen's dismembering knives. One of the three fortunate males was a mere youth, the queen's own grandson but for whom she harboured no tender feelings. Her magicians and astrologers had long ago prophesied that she would perish by the spear of a grandson. She would have got rid of the accursed boy had it not been for the frantic pleas of her only daughter. In any case, she had not set eyes on the boy since the day he was born. His mother had so far kept him out of the ageing queen's sight, a sound policy for all parties concerned. The second uncastrated male was a huge sort of fellow who, though known to be weak in the head, had for some time successfully catered to Arrawelo's abnormal erotic needs. The woman was a sexual beast. She was once overheard lamenting how she failed in achieving optimum gratification in intercourse. The male sexual organ, it was purported, was at peak condition in early morning while the female's became most receptive at noon when the sun reached its zenith. The timing was off. She had even once kept her brainless lover captive in a dark cave for the span of a day and night in an attempt to foil nature, but she failed because his manhood's pulse kept pace with the cycle of time. It was a mystery to anyone why a woman of Arrawelo's insatiable appetite would wish to have her male subjects unmanned.

There was a third man who had escaped mayhem at Arrawelo's hands. He was an old wizard who had proven too clever for all her cunning and often unpredictable tactics. Some said that this man had once been Arrawelo's own playmate long before she was a queen. In any case, the wily old fellow had managed to hide out nearly the entire reign of the mad queen. A freak of good fortune had made his task easier, for he had been born with retracted testes. At the height of Arrawelo's ravages, he had inflicted upon himself convincing scars by slicing up his vacant scrota; thus fooling the evil eyes of the queen's henchwomen.

It was rumoured that the mock-males at Arrawelo's court secretly aided him in his relentless struggle for dignity because he in turn helped them solve the queen's puzzling riddles. She often asked them to perform impossible tasks so that she could amuse herself at their expense as they failed one round after another. Arrawelo understood the nature of men perhaps better than any other woman. And she ruthlessly exploited their weaknesses. If her wish wasn't executed promptly and to her liking, many men would die. And often they did, for only Allah could satisfy her usually ridiculous demands. Luckily, these poor unfortunate weaklings had the wizard in hiding to assist them interpret her riddles.

Once she ordered them to lead one of her beasts of burden to a certain very steep-sided mountain and load the camel with gravel without the benefit of containers. This, they thought, was one of the most difficult assignments she had ever given them. They were confounded. Then someone remembered the old wizard and there seemed cause for hope yet.

After they had presented their case to him, the old man thought for a moment, then instructed them to do the following: first, they should bathe the camel with the sticky gum of the injir tree, then lead the beast to the pre-agreed mountain and, after scaling it, persuade the animal to roll over on its back until it was thoroughly covered with gravel. The troop of eunuchs followed the old man's instructions faithfully and were rewarded with success. But Arrawelo was far from being pleased. It rankled her that such a heap of non-persons could find the right solution for one of her more knotty riddles. She suspected the presence of uncastrated males in her court and ordered a thorough search. 'Humph! Whoever said the uncastrated are no more?' she cried in exasperation.

As her lieutenants searched in vain for the troublesome adversary, Arrawelo cast about for yet another riddle to confound her army of eunuchs. If their elusive mastermind failed to solve this one, she reasoned, they might be frightened into betraying him. One day, after all attempts at flushing out the mysterious ringleader had failed, she summoned her eunuchs to her presence and ordered them, without preliminaries, to go and measure the rainbow for her. The harried geldings did not believe that even the old wizard could see a way out of this one.

The old man's answer, however, came promptly and without much deliberation. He advised them to return to her ladyship and politely ask for something to measure the rainbow with. This, of course, infuriated Arrawelo so much so that she lost her temper and sent many of them to the gallows. 'Humph!' she gasped in exasperation, 'whoever said the uncastrated are no more?' The old man's plan was to wage a war of nerves with the cruel queen so as to discredit her in the eyes of her cohorts. On this score his plans seemed to be working. Arrawelo had been behaving erratically, neglecting the affairs of state and seeming wholly preoccupied with the war of wits which she was carrying on with her invisible adversary. Her behaviour on this very day was more irrational than usual. Whereas it was proper to water the herds first, she defiantly positioned herself on the edge of the well and ordered her servants to give her a bath and manicure before all else, insisting that every single one of her fingers and toes be washed separately, a task which would have required the better part of a day for its successful completion. This was the height of madness. Not even the most chauvinistic of her lieutenants could see any sense in it. The thirsty herds, without which her kingdom was of no consequence, had to be held at bay in the blistering noonday heat while the fat queen insisted on a manicure! It would have to be explained only in terms of infirmity due to extreme old age. The queen had grown senile. Something drastic had better be done. But who dared raise a finger against the dreaded Arrawelo? Her bodyguard, consisting of tall sinewy warriors clad in loincloths, stood erect and intimidating with their muscular arms folded across their heaving chests under firm out-thrust breasts which gave them an added aura of indomitable vigilance. They formed an impregnable circle under the great gnarled and arching bardeh tree, while their tall polished spears stood lined against the fig tree's deeply creased trunk. These haughty female warriors remained aloof and imperturbable as numerous eunuchs and female underlings bustled about the fat sulking queen. Those next in command wandered about, as if distracted, unsure of what ought to be done. The clamorous bleating and lowing of the thirsty herds was having its toll on their frayed nerves. The situation was growing desperate, yet they could not decide on a course of action.

It was a short while later that someone spied a company on horseback closing in fast from the direction of the settlement. It could be the usual patrol that one was wont to encounter at any given moment crisscrossing the country. But considering the purposeful manner in which they rode up, leaving behind a spectacular trail of dust, it was most probably Aourahla, the mad queen's only daughter. Someone had already sent for her, since she was the only person who had no fear of the dread old woman.

The party consisted of three riders, two swift and ominous, the third bringing up the rear at a leisurely pace. As the horsemen approached, there arose a sigh of relief among Arrawelo's entourage. Her bodyguard grew subdued and meek, though the queen herself remained unaffected by the sudden hush about her.

In a flash, the two forward riders were upon the main party. The valorous Aourahla scattered her mother's bodyguard abroad with her spirited mare while the other rider, a young man of robust bearing and as spirited as the fearless stallion he rode confronted the defiant queen who suddenly looked up in annoyance. 'Get out of the way, Grandma!' the youth commanded in a firm masculine voice the old man-hater wasn't used to. In his right hand, high above his head, he held poised a polished spear as tall as any that the queen's bodyguard could boast.

'Hah!' sneered Arrawelo, apparently quite oblivious to the imminent danger she was in. 'And who are you to address me like that?' cried she, looking him up and down. But those who stood close enough to see noticed an unfamiliar cloud of uncertainty creeping over her countenance. 'Guard!' she roared in her most authoritative manner, 'take him away!' But her guard's spirit had already been broken by the terrible Aourahla who had trampled them down under the iron hoofs of her fire-breathing warhorse. In any case, any aid would have come too late for the unfortunate queen. The tall spear which had been poised in the boy's hand tore through his grandmother's thickset neck and barely emerged out of the seat of her great back, through the convoluted folds of her purple dress of Persian weave. She was so big, a veritable fortress in brass rings and jingling bracelets, that it was doubted that a single spear, a toothpick in a stout leg of mutton, thrown by a mere youth could do her much harm. But there she lay motionless in a heap, her mouth agape, her turgid lips daubed with dark blood. The boy stood over the dead queen, like an enraged lion over a contested kill, wielding in his hand a second spear until his proud mother rode up to his side. 'Obey him!' she roared in a voice not unlike the late queen's. 'He is my son and I speak to you in my mother's name.'

Aourahla was not speaking from a position of utter weakness. The old wizard (the third rider in the attacking party) had quickly mustered a troop of emboldened eunuchs and their sympathizers and was preparing to take a final stand against the fallen queen's loyal forces. He no longer masqueraded as a spineless eunuch but dashed about conspicuously on horseback, exhorting his followers. Fortunately, it did not come to full-fledged civil strife. Arrawelo's cohorts had been dealt a stunning blow by her startling death. They saw no alternative to rallying to their dead queen's apparent heir.

After the herds were watered, Arrawelo was buried in the manner of the royal dead. Over her grave, which was dug not far from the waterhole, every one of her former subjects placed a stone, though there were those who cast their stones not so much out of a spirit of reverence but to make doubly sure that the fallen tyrant remained confined to her terrible grave.

It was after Arrawelo's death that the practice of performing clitoridectomy on pubescent girls was instituted to render them more tractable later in life. This was to be the legacy of her bloody reign. This and the rude pyramids scattered throughout the Nugaal; though no one ever explained how one woman's grave could be found in so many places all at once.

Abdi Sheik-Abdi (Somalia)

A Story of Our Times

In the middle of nowhere we saw a team of workmen dig something up. A few days later, we saw an earth-mover. A week later, a road. Three weeks later we saw a strip of tarmac. We knew then that Nomakhwezi had got herself a man with power. We knew he must be a minister. On a Sunday we saw a chauffeured black limousine cruising on the tarmac. It was the minister of finance.

Six weeks later we saw the same team of workers, digging, chanting. A week later the tarmac was gone. We knew then there was either a *coup* or the affair was over. Seeing Khwezi at the bus stop was enough to tell us.

A month later we saw the same team of workers. We knew the lovers had made up. We organized a demonstration. Placards flew: 'Don't waste public funds', 'Down with . . .'

The workers organized a counter-demonstration. They accused us of taking their jobs from them. The lovers agreed.

Pitika Ntuli (Azania)

Halfway to Nirvana

'Frankly,' he said through the electronic glass partition, 'it will be a sad day for some of us when this catastrophic drought is over. Fortunately,' he snapped a finger, 'it will go on. And on.'

I'd noticed the fellow at the last three conferences I'd covered for my magazine, the struggling satirical sheet *Sic Transit*. A lot of people writing to the editor spell the first part of our magazine's name *Sick*. The publisher normally owes the small staff three months' wages. Still,

I keep searching out the humorous vein hidden somewhere under life's jugular, writing pieces I hope are funny, but which in my heart I know are merely ridiculous. Besides, it's possible to earn short-order income at conferences doubling as a translator. That's how I came to develop such a keen interest in conferences. And that's how I met Christian Mohamed Tumbo.

Yes of course, I asked him how he came to possess such perfectly ecumenical names. Were they pseudonyms he'd chosen himself?

'No,' he answered readily. 'My mother was a good Christian, my father an equally good Muslim.'

'So you became . . .'

'A compromise.'

It was our first conversation. I knew at once I'd hit the hidden vein. In spite of everything, there was something likeable about this rotund fellow. His charm was indeterminate, but I knew it had something to do with the liveliness of his tiny eyes. They were like trapped sparks. There was also the incongruous smoothness of his baby cheeks. His teeth were ugly and uncared-for. But he bared them so often, and in such a pleased smile that in the end one got used to them, like frequent, affectionate visitors. He spoke a voluble, jovial French. It was he who said, right in the middle of a solemn-sounding speech about the present threat of famine, that conference sessions were excellent for working up a thirst, in preparation, come break-time, for the real objective of such gatherings: drinking. He'd aroused laughter that time, with his slightly dangerous sense of humour. He said it was all a technique, the technique of the griot: take a bantering attitude to truths others prefer to bury under taciturn official masks.

At least once, though, his humorous technique had backfired. In a moment of absent-mindedness, participants at the end of a development strategies conference had asked him to give the vote of thanks. He gave a honeyed speech, full of francophone marshmallows and admiration for the organizers' many superlative qualities. The last, but not the least of these super qualities, he concluded, was the Chairman's enviable ability to appear chronically overworked even while riding on the Nirvana line. After this joke I noticed conference officials and participants avoided him. I sought him out.

I found him exceedingly open, eager, in fact, to talk. He seemed to have had to keep to himself something he wanted to share – a huge joke. Finally he'd found a friendly female ear, mine. Still, I doubt if he'd ever have opened up so totally except for an accident.

Because we talked frequently during breaks, we often sat near each other during sessions. Conferences are not hard work, but they are tedious, and when poorly organized they can be exhausting in a wasteful way. I'd noticed that Christian Mohamed Tumbo never seemed crushed by the monotonous drudgery of all these speeches. At the end of each session, he could be seen far ahead of the others, bounding joyfully toward the cocktail bar, a manic spirit unchained.

The secret of his energy, when I discovered it, surprised me with the elegance of its sheer simplicity: during most conference sessions, Christian Mohamed Tumbo slept. He had the priceless political gift of being able to sleep with his eyes open; not wide open – that was the beauty of it – just a shade narrowed, like the eyes of an alert person paying receptive, benevolently critical attention to whatever was going on.

Participants were being asked when they wanted to go on a field trip to a disaster area: 1500 hours or 1700 hours. The usual practice at conferences is for the organizers to fix all important decisions. The participants endorse them by acclamation. This was an unimportant matter, however, and individual preferences were being canvassed. The Chairman called Christian Mohamed Tumbo twice, a third time. Tumbo sat there looking particularly intelligent and smart, but hearing nothing. I nudged him awake as the Chairman repeated the question. Christian Mohamed Tumbo said '1700 hours', then turned to ask me what it was all about. I knew why he trusted me: I was on the conference circuit, without being part of the conference establishment. He had nothing to fear from me. There may have been an additional, more frivolous reason. Perhaps he wished we'd get to be closer friends.

For a period Christian Mohamed Tumbo suffered no further embarrassment in his sleep. On at least three occasions, though, he came close. It was inevitable that catastrophe would strike one day. What floored me was the way it happened. I'd imagined Christian Mohamed Tumbo sleeping his way through a conference session and the Chairman, innocent soul, asking the usual earth-shaking question: What, in the opinion of your delegation, would be the implementational modalities for achieving the objective of the total eradication of poverty and injustice in Africa by, at the latest, the year Plus 4000? Instead, it was Christian Mohamed Tumbo himself who took the initiative, and spoke in his sleep. Loud and clear, as in a ringing peroration.

The conference, incidentally, was another one on the drought. The Chairman, a sombre fellow from the Cosmic Meteorological Organization, had gone through the part of his closing speech about the present drought being an unprecedented threat requiring unprecedented measures. He had come to the part about the urgent need for further conferences to promote reflection on the problem that had been discussed for the past ten years. The shout came, bold and clear: '*Vive la Sécheresse!*'

The Chairman, embarrassed by the interruption, wound up in a hurry. Two of the organizers leaned forward, apparently uncertain whether there was a heckler to be bounced, or a gaffe to be diplomatically ignored. But Christian Mohamed Tumbo had fallen quiet again.

We were so close together that I felt the eyes turned on him were glaring at me too. To cover my embarrassment, no doubt, but so spontaneously I was astonished at my presence of mind, I did Christian Mohamed Tumbo a service he claims he'll never forget. I rose, loudly applauding the Chairman's speech as if here at last was the international bureaucrat who had found the magic words for solving the world's problems.

The Chairman was sitting as I rose. One of the organizers pointed to me, thinking I was asking for the floor. In the intense confusion, the Chairman gave me the floor. I flew at the chance.

'*Comme notre collègue vient de le dire,*' I said, putting such a desperate roll on the francophone *r* in the next word that I bruised the lining of my throat, '*vivre la sécheresse, c'est notre problème numéro un. Monsieur le Président, nous vous félicitons vivement pour votre exposé.*'

The tension eased. A sigh of relief came from someone, probably a participant now convinced he had misheard the shout after all.

On the way down to the poolside restaurant for dinner, a couple of people came to congratulate me. At the cocktail bar just before the restaurant entrance, Christian Mohamed Tumbo was uncharacteristically morose.

'I spoke in my sleep, didn't I?' he asked me.

'Yes.'

He winced, but couldn't suppress his curiosity. 'What did I say?'

'*Vive la sécheresse.* You must have been having a nightmare.'

He smiled enigmatically: 'A nightmare first, then a dream. In the nightmare Africa's deserts became forests and gardens. It was frightening. Luckily, the nightmare ended. The deserts regained their dryness. Familiar signs of famine reappeared: skeletons in the Sahel sand. I recognized our continent. I suppose that's when I shouted '*Vive la sécheresse.*'

'Long live the drought?' I queried.

'I know what you're thinking,' he said, staring at me as at a beloved but retarded sibling. 'The man makes his living working for an anti-drought organization. But this same man thinks the end of the drought would be a disaster. Right?'

'More or less.'

He took a moment deciding whether I was worth his confidence. Then his eyes took on a 100-watt intensity. 'You're looking at a man who'd have died ten years ago if frustration could kill. I taught secondary-school Geography for fifteen years. Every year I earned starvation wages, and watched my students come back five years later with academic degrees and salaries that gave me a headache just to imagine. I was getting to be a sick man, bitter as a dwarf lemon.

'There's no better work than teaching, but in time I realized what I needed was not a better job but more money and a bit of respect from the swinish society.

' "Try Nirvana," a friend advised me. I thought Nirvana was some new version of Transcendental Meditation, or a drug to cure hypertension. A cure for frustrated greed. Green in every way, that's what I was. The friend explained Nirvana: the UN System in one seamless phrase: European salaries diplomatic status tax exemption duty free goodies travel galore clean paperwork cool hotels, per diems in dollars. A smooth talker, my friend.

'I tried the Nirvana Highway, and ran into a wall. The wall has secret holes in it, and only those already on the other side can pull you through. Besides, I don't even have a bachelor's degree. Everyone in Nirvana has to have that. At least.

'I'd practically given up on getting near Nirvana at all when the same friend told me about the NGO approach. Non-Governmental Organizations. Well, I found the NGO road open even if the Nirvana highway was blocked. My friend introduced me to a Swede with a permanent crease in his forehead and foundation money behind him, looking for an African assistant to help him set up an agency to Fight the Drought.

'I went to the Swede and listened to him for four hours. He could have been a regular missionary, if he'd been a shade less intelligent. I listened to his absurd litany of strategies and solutions. I know droughts and floods have been part of African history for thousands of years. But he kept saying The Drought was an unprecedented disaster. I agreed absolutely with him. Between this strange Swede and me, why shouldn't there be a perfect identity of views?

'The Swede found his African assistant, and I found my NGO, half-way to Nirvana. The Anti-Drought Organization. Nice acronym, ADO. Since that day, four years ago, I've changed from a man of problems into a man of solutions. I've forgotten what it feels like to be in debt. I have three villas. Two are embassy residences. Rent paid a year in advance. In dollars. The third I live in myself. ADO pays me a handsome rent for living in my own house. Every month I travel abroad. When I'm on the move my salary stays intact, while per diems compensate me for my dedicated suffering in hotels and night-clubs as I move from capital to capital, conference to seminar, fighting the drought.

'I didn't mean to shout. The words escaped me, but I know I'd live a lot less well if there were no drought or famine.'

We'd finished dinner, except for the liqueur. As I drained the small, sweet glass, it caught the light from the swimming-pool outside and broke it into a frail, momentary indoor rainbow. I put the tiny glass against the menu, propped up against a twin rose in a vase.

> *Langouste mayonnaise*
> *Potage de légumes*
> *Salade niçoise*
> *Entrecôte aux échalottes*
> *Plateau de fromage*
> *Coupe Mont Blanc*
> *Café Liégeois*

'Nice meal, eh?' Christian Mohamed Tumbo asked.

I nodded, then rose to go to the poolside area. He wanted to go up to his room. Perhaps he'd hoped, but he swallowed his regret as we shook hands, parting. He pressed mine like a tyro conspirator, winked into the bargain, and, as I walked towards the electronic glass partition, called out softly: '*Vive la sécheresse.*'

Ayi Kwei Armah (Ghana)

Jubilant Throng

A long convoy
Of black ants
Winds its way
Through the wilderness
Bearing their booty,
They return home
To feast . . .
The queen mother
Of the hillock
Weeps alone . . . !

  * * *

You young widow
In black,
How beautiful you are
With those beads of tears
Glittering on your cheeks,
How dignified
The bearing of your
Sorrow-ridden body!
Do not blame me
Sister,
Do not be angry with me,
Do not hate me
You true Daughter
Of the Land.

Your husband was
An obstacle blocking
The path of Our Progress,
He had to be urgently removed . . .

I had to kill him,
And I did it kindly,
He did not suffer long,
He died instantly!

He was arrogant
And your beauty spurred him on,
His words were swords,
Heads rolled when he spoke . . .

*   *   *

When you embraced
Your man
In your soft bed,
Other wives wept alone
Covered only by the blanket
Of bitter agony,
And taunted by the memories
Of past embraces.

When you sat around
The table
And joked with him,
Other wives sang red dirges
And beckoned the ghosts
Of their murdered husbands.

When you heard his voice
Through the telephone
And saw him on television,
Others played with
The distant echoes
Of dead men's voices.

When you walked hand in hand
By the Lakeside
And let the starlight
Dance on your white teeth
As you smiled and giggled,
Other wives cut
The veins of their neck
To let their black sorrows
Flow with their blood!

           *   *   *

My sister,
Do not be angry with me,
Show gratitude to me,
I have done a great thing
I have liberated
The People
And have made you
Famous!

Okot p'Bitek (Uganda)
Extract from *Song of a Prisoner*

The Old Man and the Census

I will not mourn with you
your lost populations, the silent
columns of your ancient fief
erased from the king's book of numbers

For in your house of stone
by the great road
you listened once to refugee voices
at dawn telling of plagues
in their land across seven rivers

A hornbill in flight
you tucked in your feet

from the threshold
out of our threatening gaze

But pestilence farther
than tales of dawn
may buy a seat on Ogun's reckless
chariot and knock by nightfall
on your iron gate

Take heart; decimation
by miscount however grievous
is a happy retreat from bolder uses
of the past. Take heart: these
scribal flourishes behind smudged
entries, these trophied returns
of titular head-hunters
can never match the quiet flow
of true blood

But if my grudging comfort fail
then take this long and even view to 1984
when the word is due
to go out again

and – depending on which Caesar
orders the count – new conurbations
may sprout in today's wastelands
and thriving cities dissolve
in sudden mirages

and the ready-reckoners at court
will calculate the gain
and the loss and make us
one hundred million strong

                    Chinua Achebe (Nigeria)

Elegy for Slit-drum
With rattles accompaniment

CONDOLENCES . . . from our swollen lips laden with condolences

The mythmaker accompanies us
The rattles are here with us

condolences from our split-tongue of the slit drum condolences

one tongue full of fire
one tongue full of stone—

condolences from the twin-lips of our drum parted in condolences:

the panther has delivered a hare
the hare is beginning to leap
the panther has delivered a hare
the panther is about to pounce—

condolences already in flight under the burden of this century:

parliament has gone on leave
the members are now on bail
parliament is now on sale
the voters are lying in wait—

condolences to caress the swollen eyelids of bleeding mourners,

the cabinet has gone to hell
the timbers are now on fire
the cabinet that sold itself
ministers are now in gaol—

condolences quivering before the iron throne of a new conqueror:

the mythmaker accompanies us (*the Egret had come and gone*)
Okigbo accompanies us the oracle enkindles us
the Hornbill is there again (*the Hornbill has had a bath*)
Okigbo accompanies us the rattles enlighten us—

condolences with the miracle of sunlight on our feathers:

The General is up . . . the General is up . . . commandments . . .
the General is up the General is up the General is up—

condolences from our twin-beaks and feathers of condolences:

the General is near the throne
an iron mask covers his face
the General has carried the day
the mortars are far away—

condolences to appease the fever of a wake among tumbled tombs

the elephant has fallen
the mortars have won the day
the elephant has fallen
does he deserve his fate
the elephant has fallen
can we remember the date—

Jungle tanks blast Britain's last stand—
the elephant ravages the jungle
the jungle is peopled with snakes
the snake says to the squirrel
I will swallow you
the mongoose says to the snake
I will mangle you
the elephant says to the mongoose
I will strangle you

thunder fells the trees cut a path
thunder smashes them all – condolences . . .

THUNDER that has struck the elephant
the same thunder should wear a plume – condolences

a roadmaker makes a road
the road becomes a throne
can we cane him for felling a tree – condolences . . .

THUNDER that has struck the elephant
the same thunder can make a bruise – condolences:

we should forget the names
we should bury the date
the dead should bury the dead – condolences

from our bruised lips of the drum empty of condolences:

trunk of the iron tree we cry *condolences* when we break,
shells of the open sea we cry *condolences* when we shake . . .

Christopher Okigbo (Nigeria)

The Battle of the Elephants

(For Christopher Okigbo)

(They called her a
demented old bitch
and listened not to
her song.)

They call her a demented old witch
She can see through the eye of the needle
And read the writings on the face of the cloud
With chalk painted on her brows
She can catch the breath of the wind
And give sense to their fury . . .

Today the old bitch lives alone
In a solitary hut in the open market
And sings with the winds and the rains
The song of the demented
Which some call the song of the spirits:–

There will be a battle of the elephants
The mighty husky elephants
With tusks reaching out into the sky

There will be a battle of the elephants . . .

Under the armpit of the daylight
Under the eyelash of nightfall

You can hear the battle in the distant mountains
The crying and shouting in the green valleys
The sing-song cacophony of frogs and toads
Clapping in merriment for the elephants.
The men in the village stand and watch;
Who can separate fighting elephants? They ask;
Who can separate the river from running into the ocean? . . .

And the villagers and the hunters
Stand and watch
Their fields and crops destroyed
Under the heavy feet of the elephants;
And the hunters refuse to shoot
And the elders refuse to counsel
And watch their fields and crops destroyed
Under the heavy feet of the elephants.

And the elephants destroyed the fields
And the elephants destroyed the crops
And the elephants pounded the earth
And the elephants destroyed the village.

For they said:—
Who can stop the river from running into the ocean?;
Who can tell the length of the mighty river?

Ihechukwu Madubuike (Nigeria)

Battle Hymn

We are poured on the enemy like a mighty torrent:
We are poured like a river in spate when the rain is in the mountains.
The water hisses down the sands, swirling, exultant, and the tree that
    stood in its path is torn up quivering.
It is tossed from eddy to eddy.
We are poured on the enemy and they are bewildered.
They look this way and that seeking escape, but our spears fall thickly
    about them.

Our spears cling to their bodies and they are routed.
They look this way and that for deliverance, but they cannot escape
    us, the avengers, the great killers.
God of our fathers, guide our spears, our spears which thy lilac has
    touched.
They are anointed with sacrifice, with the sacrifice of unblemished
    kids, consecrated and hallowed by the nightjar of good omen.
Help us, high Spirit. Slay with us.
Let death come to their ranks, let the villages mourn their lost warriors.
Let their villages be desolate, let them echo with the cry of mourning.
We shall return rejoicing; and the lowing of cattle is in our ears.
The lowing of innumerable cattle will make glad our hearts.

Acholi (Uganda)

A Warrior's Lament

Now on the battlefield
I know what faces me.
It is death; my death.
I do not hate those I fight;
It is their deeds I hate.
Those I am fighting for do not love me;
My death shall not grieve them,
Nor shall it bring them joy.
No law compels me to fight;
None has sent me out to fight
Except my deep love for my own.
My friends want me to desert the field,
That I may not perish in battle.
But they forget: A serpent
Does not attack a child before its mother's eyes.
It is true that my mother, my mother's offspring,
My friends, the beautiful girl I want to marry,
Are worrying themselves to death about me;
Still I shall not leave the battlefield

For the enemy to march them away before my eyes.
I have left home to live in the bush.
The hunting I do now is the shooting of fellow humans.
I have become a beast of the forest
That I may bring peace to my own.
I am in the midst of battle now.
Listen to what is resounding in the forest where I stand!
Kwaku-kwaku is our morning greeting;
Unudum! Unudum! the song of guns!
As it sounds and resounds I become uncaring about life,
And strum my gun like a guitar.
When all the gunfire stops
I lift up my head,
I laugh;
When I turn around
The companions of my morning meal
Have become corpses.
I know one day it will be my turn.
I have already seen my death.
One day I will lie like my friends who lie here.
Vultures, termites, and other creatures of the forest
Shall hold a conference on top of me.
My bones will lie scattered in the bush.
When some farmer clears the forest
He'll gather up my skull and bones;
When he burns the debris of the forest he'll burn me.
When crops grow they'll grow on my bones.
No maiden shall kiss my lips
For the earth, it is not kissed.
Thus my life shall come to an end.
And my companions and my kin,
They shall lift up their eyes forever,
Up the road at the horizon,
Looking for one that shall never return.
And the last we shall see of each other
Was before I departed for war.

The next time we set eyes on each other
Shall be in the land of rest.

Nnamdi Olebara (Nigeria)
Translated from the Igbo by Chinweizu

Colonel Chumah's War*

'It's very good to see you again, Charles,' the Chief of Def-Ops said, settling into his chair behind a vast table topped with telephones, situation reports, maps, diagrams and pens and pencils.

'Same here, Eme,' Colonel Chumah replied.

The Provost-Marshal had delivered him there and made his disappearance. The two were alone now in the big office and the Chief of Def-Ops had buzzed his assistants that he would receive no callers for the next hour.

The Chief of Defence Operations was a tall, fair-skinned career soldier in his early thirties. After a training stint in the United States before the war he had affected the close-cropped, crew-cut hair-style popular among American soliders. He smiled easily and wore a halo of perpetual unflappability. Though they were both colonels, Chumah was his senior in the pecking order.

The Chief of Defence Operations lifted his eyes from a sheaf of situation summaries and looked at the man before him.

The Chief of Defence Operations put the papers together carefully and pushed them to a corner beside his braided cap and slim polished baton. He shifted in his chair nervously.

'Now, Charles,' he began, not quite certain how to continue. 'I . . . I suppose . . . I think we better get back to where we were eleven months ago.'

The Chief's voice rumbled sombrely for nearly thirty minutes. He had missed out nothing. But he had decided to skip Port Harcourt for the time being. He had also skilfully skated over the matter of the Christian Brothers.

On the other hand, the Chief of Def-Ops thought, picking up and examining afresh the green message sheet lying face down at his elbow, the Colonel was going to join the 5 Commando soon. So might he not as well get on with it?

'Now, Charles, your orders,' the Chief said. 'The General has directed that you assume, with immediate effect, the deputy command of 5 Commando under Colonel Jacques Rudolf.' The Chief looked up from the message form.

Chumah uncrossed his legs, took the cigarette from his lips, and glared across the desk.

The Chief did not meet his eyes. He scanned the message form again. 'Colonel Rudolf is being informed this noon,' he added finally, and put aside the green paper.

'Listen, Eme,' Chumah was jabbing the stub of cigarette at the Chief of Defence Operations. 'Do you mean that the General wants me to join what you call the Christian Brothers?'

The Provost Marshal had told him about the white adventurers.

'That's the order, Charles.'

'Join mercenaries and fight alongside them, you mean that?'

'I suppose it means the same thing as the contents of the message, Charles,' Eme said, without meeting Chumah's eyes.

'Then I must demand an urgent meeting with the General.'

'Is it necessary, really?'

'Absolutely. I must have a word with him.'

'I doubt the chances of a meeting, Charles. The General has been very busy lately.' The Chief's eyes met Chumah's briefly. 'Besides, Charles, the subject of the Christian Brothers is not one he'll readily discuss just now. He thinks we ought to give them a chance to carry out their offensive plans . . .'

'You sound as if these chaps have just arrived here and are trying to find their feet. But I gather they have been here for nearly one year. One very costly year!

'Do you, for one moment, reckon that a soldier of fortune fighting for money will plan an offensive to win you a war and thus terminate his employment?'

'Now take it easy, Charles,' the Chief said. 'I understand your feelings very well.'

'I'm not accepting the General's orders,' he announced bluntly. 'I'm not prepared to fight alongside mercenaries who are making money at the expense of the lives of the people who are contributing the money. They will prolong the war as long as they can. And I'm not sure I want to help them do that,' Chumah broke off to light a fresh cigarette.

The Chief made no reply.

'Let me repeat what you'll tell the General,' Chumah resumed. 'Tell him I refuse to be led by a white mercenary commander. I'm a senior member of the High Command, not an under-officer!'

'But that, as you know, Charles, amounts to disobeying orders,' he tried not to sound threatening. 'Not my orders, hell, you are my senior in the hierarchy, but the General's orders. And he may not like it. I should stick to the old rule, Charles. Obey before protest.'

'I don't expect the General to like it. But neither do I like his orders.'

'I doubt that I can tell him that, Charles. Maybe I should try to wangle a meeting after all. But most of us would hate to see you back in detention, Charles. Truly.'

'Back in detention, yes,' Chumah replied. 'Frankly I would prefer that to being commanded by your Christian Brothers.'

'I told you earlier on Charles, that I understood your sentiments,' the Chief replied. 'It's genuine. But why don't we say you'll think it over for a day or two? That would sound reasonable,' the Chief suggested quietly.

'I shall indeed let you know if I do change my mind. In the meantime, I shall get down to Port Harcourt and look up my family. They are staying with my brother. I've got to see them first before I think of going off to be commanded by mercenaries.'

The moment the Chief of Defence Operations had dreaded most and avoided longest had descended without warning. His palms gripped the arms of his chair firmly as Colonel Chumah rose from his.

'Wait a moment, Charles,' the Chief held up a trembling hand.

Chumah sat back into his chair.

'You . . . you . . . can't go to Port Harcourt, I'm afraid,' the Chief began shakily.

'I can't what? Another arrest?'

'Not an arrest, Charles, but . . .' the Chief rubbed his eyes and his face uncomfortably.

'Port Harcourt,' he said with difficulty, 'fell five months ago. I couldn't tell you that at the beginning . . .'

'Five months ago?'

'Yes.'

'And where is my family? Where did they evacuate to?' Chumah asked in a strangely calm voice, rising to his feet at the same time. He fixed an inquiring gaze at the Chief, who was slumped back deflatedly, avoiding Chumah's eyes.

The continued silence began to forewarn Chumah of an unpleasant answer. His heart raced in panic.

'Where were they evacuated to then, Eme?' he repeated.

'We're still trying to locate them, Charles . . .'

'Locate them? What the devil do you mean?'

'Now sit down, Charles. Sit down and take it easy. Listen to me,' he pleaded desperately. 'I tell you, Charles, it's not easy.'

'I can listen just as well standing,' Chumah snapped. 'Forget about taking it easy. Just tell me where in the devil you say you're trying to locate my wife and child.'

'It is like this . . .'

'You know what the terrain there is like. Only two approaches to the city, a virtual cul-de-sac. The enemy burst out along the Aba road, a few miles to the city, cut off that outlet into the town and threatened the other, Owerri road. With a situation like that only a few people managed to evacuate the city. Most of them are still bottled up in there.'

'You only *hope* they are, don't you? The vandals have almost certainly massacred them for sport! My God, why are you all so naïve?'

'We believe your family will be found as soon as we clear the town of the enemy,' the Chief said without much truth.

He didn't mention the reports that confirmed the mutilation of his wife, child and younger brother by irate natives soon after the enemy's entry.

The Chief stopped, expecting the ultimate explosion that would submerge the room in the debris of Chumah's famous wrath. He held his breath and waited for it.

For three minutes that seemed like three hours, nothing happened. The Chief could hear his own heart thumping loudly in the reigning silence.

Slowly he raised his eyes at the man standing, frozen before his desk.

Tears were rolling down Colonel Charles Chumah's face, falling in droplets on to his beard. His clenched fists were rigid beside his body.

Chumah's lips moved. He licked them and raised his eyes at the Chief of Defence Operations.

'Who lost Port Harcourt, Eme?' It was a thick, subdued tone that didn't seem to come from the powerful man the Chief knew.

'It was an emergency unit assembled from all divisions,' he answered vaguely.

'Yes but who manned the main positions?'

'The Commando, Colonel Rudolf.'

'Thank you,' Chumah said. He fished out an over-used handkerchief and dabbed the tears from his face.

'Now you can tell the General I'm accepting his posting to 5 Commando,' Chumah said unexpectedly. 'And send a signal to Colonel Rudolf that I look forward to joining him.' He pocketed the handkerchief, brought out the pack of cigarettes and began to light one.

'I'm reporting to 5 Commando first light tomorrow. Now that I've got no family to look after, I suppose I've got time on my hands.' His voice was bitter.

'Charles for God's sake don't take it that way, you . . .'

'Thanks for your sympathy, Eme. It's appreciated.'

He was out of the door before the Chief could put in another word.

Eddie Iroh (Nigeria)
Forty-eight Guns for the General, Chapter Twenty-three

The Destruction of Sosso the Magnificent*

Sosso was a magnificent city. In the open plain her triple rampart with awe-inspiring towers reached the sky. The city comprised 188 fortresses and the palace of Soumaoro loomed above the whole city like a gigantic tower. Sosso had but one gate; colossal and made of iron, the work of the sons of fire. Noumounkeba hoped to tie Sundiata down outside of Sosso, for he had enough provisions to hold out for a year.

The sun was beginning to set when Sogolon-Djata appeared before

Sosso the Magnificent. From the top of a hill, Djata and his general staff gazed upon the fearsome city of the sorcerer-king. The army encamped in the plain opposite the great gate of the city and fires were lit in the camp. Djata resolved to take Sosso in the course of a morning. He fed his men a double ration and the tam-tams beat all night to stir up the victors of Krina.

At daybreak the towers of the ramparts were black with sofas. Other were positioned on the ramparts themselves. They were the archers. The Mandingoes were masters in the art of storming a town. In the front line Sundiata placed the sofas of Mali, while those who held the ladders were in the second line protected by the shields of the spearmen. The main body of the army was to attack the city gate. When all was ready, Djata gave the order to attack. The drums resounded, the horns blared and like a tide the Mandingo front line moved off, giving mighty shouts. With their shields raised above their heads the Mandingoes advanced up to the foot of the wall, then the Sossos began to rain large stones down on the assailants. From the rear, the bowmen of Wagadou shot arrows at the ramparts. The attack spread and the town was assaulted at all points. Sundiata had a murderous reserve; they were the bowmen whom the king of the Bobos had sent shortly before Krina. The archers of Bobo are the best in the world. On one knee the archers fired flaming arrows over the ramparts. Within the walls the thatched huts took fire and the smoke swirled up. The ladders stood against the curtain wall and the first Mandingo sofas were already at the top. Seized by panic through seeing the town on fire, the Sossos hesitated a moment. The huge tower surmounting the gate surrendered, for Fakoli's smiths had made themselves master of it. They got into the city where the screams of women and children brought the Sossos' panic to a head. They opened the gates to the main body of the army.

Then began the massacre. Women and children in the midst of fleeing Sossos implored mercy of the victors. Djata and his cavalry were now in front of the awesome tower palace of Soumaoro. Noumounkeba, conscious that he was lost, came out to fight. With his sword held aloft he bore down on Djata, but the latter dodged him and, catching hold of the Sosso's braced arm, forced him to his knees whilst the sword dropped to the ground. He did not kill him but delivered him into the hands of Manding Bory.

Soumaoro's palace was now at Sundiata's mercy. While everywhere the Sossos were begging for quarter, Sundiata, preceded by Balla Fasséké, entered Soumaoro's tower. The griot knew every nook and cranny of the palace from his captivity and he led Sundiata to Soumaoro's magic chamber.

When Balla Fasséké opened the door to the room it was found to have changed its appearance since Soumaoro had been touched by the fatal arrow. The inmates of the chamber had lost their power. The snake in the pitcher was in the throes of death, the owls from the perch were flapping pitifully about the ground. Everything was dying in the sorcerer's abode. It was all up with the power of Soumaoro. Sundiata had all Soumaoro's fetishes taken down and before the palace were gathered together all Soumaoro's wives, all princesses taken from their families by force. The prisoners, their hands tied behind their backs, were already herded together. Just as he had wished, Sundiata had taken Sosso in the course of a morning. When everything was outside of the town and all that there was to take had been taken out, Sundiata gave the order to complete its destruction. The last houses were set fire to and prisoners were employed in the razing of the walls. Thus, as Djata intended, Sosso was destroyed to its very foundations.

Yes, Sosso was razed to the ground. It has disappeared, the proud city of Soumaoro. A ghastly wilderness extends over the places where kings came and humbled themselves before the sorcerer-king. All traces of the houses have vanished and of Soumaoro's seven-storey palace there remains nothing more. A field of desolation, Sosso is now a spot where guinea-fowl and young partridges come to take their dust baths.

Many years have rolled by and many times the moon has traversed the heaven since these places lost their inhabitants. The bourein, the tree of desolation, spreads out its thorny undergrowth and insolently grows in Soumaoro's capital. Sosso the Proud is nothing but a memory in the mouths of griots. The hyenas come to wail there at night, the hare and the hind come and feed on the site of the palace of Soumaoro, the king who wore robes of human skin.

Sosso vanished from the earth and it was Sundiata, the son of the buffalo, who gave these places over to solitude. After the destruction of Soumaoro's capital the world knew no other master but Sundiata.

Mandingo (Guinea and Mali)
Excerpt from the epic *Sundiata* as recited by the griot Mamadou Kouyaté
Transcribed and translated into French by D. T. Niane
Translated from the French by G. D. Pickett

War Sweeps Umuchukwu*

The war had at least one healthy effect on Umuchukwu. The recruitment teams swept away the thieves and ne'er-do-wells as a sanitary worker sweeps off refuse from the market. One of them, who nicknamed himself King Kong, had been a terror to most people at Umuchukwu, especially to women and children. He could impound any jar of palm wine or any foodstuffs brought to the market for sale, without paying for them and without apology. He could walk into any maize farm and cut as many cobs of maize as he wanted, claiming that he was merely walking in the path of Jesus Christ who reaped where he did not sow. He bragged that he had a single bone in his lower right arm which more than doubled the strength and effectiveness of that arm, and claimed that any man he struck with the full strength of that arm would crawl about eating grass without knowing what he was doing. Secret representations had been made to the District Commissioner to extract some muscles from King Kong's right arm, but without success. At one time it was rumoured that even the white men feared King Kong. As soon as the recruitment drive began, every one daring enough to do so goaded King Kong into enlistment, flattering him by saying that all Britain needed was a handful of supermen like him to confound the Germans. His departure was celebrated widely, and there was no doubt that prayers were regularly offered in secret that he should not return from the war or that if he did, it should be with the proper number of bones!

The second man everyone was happy to see taken away in the 'Belly-never-full' lorry (as the monstrous-looking army lorry was described) was Uke, who could steal your shirt from your back in broad daylight without your knowledge. If he paid you a visit and began to compliment you on your well-fed goat or sheep you promptly warned him that you would hold him responsible for any goat or sheep missing from your house. He was believed to take the form of a leopard at will, if that appeared the only means of obtaining what he wanted. It was alleged that he concealed a scar on his left arm where he was shot one night carrying a goat and scaling a wall. The owner of the goat reported that he had fired at a leopard and hit its left fore-limb. Uke did not appear in public for a month after the leopard incident, and nobody knew his whereabouts; it was therefore easy to link him with the leopard.

Uke opted to join the army, to wipe off the public disgrace which came with his theft of the only goat of an aged woman fast losing her sight. He had been made to parade the village, his hands tied behind him and the pot in which the goat-meat had been found boiling, on his head. He had been cursed, spat on and flogged all the way. At the end of it he had joined the army after buying the old woman another goat.

The war seemed to have transformed Uke, judging from the letters he wrote from Burma. He said he had shed his bad ways as a snake discards its old skin, and planned to lead a decent life on his return from the war. He had written to the Church teacher to enter his name in the Church books, and sent some money as his initial payment. He had asked his age grade to find him land, preferably close to a main road, where he would build a decent house and open a shop on his return. In his letter to Mazi Laza, he expressed a strong desire to find a wife. Beautiful Indian and Burmese girls were pestering him for marriage, he wrote, but he was determined not to marry a foreign girl. His preference was for a girl from Umuchukwu; but knowing what problems might confront him at Umuchukwu he said he would consider a girl from any of the neighbouring towns. He enclosed a photograph of himself in army uniform, for presentation to the parents of any girl considered suitable for him. He urged that the photograph of whichever girl was selected be taken and air mailed to him. He would make some money available to Mazi Laza for the bride price as soon as this became necessary.

'If the war can transform people so easily, all of us should seek enlistment!' So remarked everyone as the news from Uke circulated round Umuchukwu.

Chukwuemeka Ike (Nigeria)
Excerpt from The Potter's Wheel

The President's Wife*

'If I may, I'd like to ask Mother a question . . . If you had to choose between a head of state whose wife is a non-African, and a couple in which the husband, the country's leader, is of casted birth, which of these couples would you prefer?'

The old woman remained silent for a moment, looking at her hands. The clock struck the half-hour.

'The First Lady of a country should have been born in that country. To be precise, I would be in favour of denying all men and women married to foreigners access to highly political positions.'

She had spoken without haste or excitement.

Kad glanced at the doyen. After a moment's silence, the old man said:

'I wouldn't be as extreme as my wife. However, I must acknowledge that for the sake of national pride, the presidential couple should be of native birth. Casted or not.'

'Aren't you afraid people might accuse you of racism?' objected Kad, to keep the discussion going.

Cheikh Tidiane folded his arms.

'Why should that be considered racism? And who are "people"?' asked the old woman. Receiving no answer, she continued:

'Would people in Washington accept a Negro as First Lady? A woman from an African country? Or in Moscow, Peking, London, Tokyo, Rome, Paris . . . The problem of castes is a live issue in Europe. Take the case of the Prince of Wales – Edward the . . . I forget which – who had a choice to make: a commoner, or the throne of England. The woman was of his race, but not of his aristocratic caste. He chose the woman. For a woman, the Prince's attitude is very flattering. More recently, take the case of President Bourguiba. No one can doubt his nationalism, nor the loyalty of the woman who was with him during his years of struggle. But the time came when for the sake of his fellow countrymen and their pride, he had to choose a wife from his own country, or resign. He chose to remain Tunisia's Head of State, and married a Tunisian woman. Even in France, a black West Indian could through a historical accident have become President temporarily. What happened? He simply vanished. Our Independence is of very recent date. And you men are very sensitive to "people". In view of the powerful influence a wife can have over her husband's actions, it seems to me that there's no doubt at all on this point.'

She paused. Djia Umrel Ba was merely voicing opinions she had long meditated. Joom Galle, startled, was gazing at his wife. She raised her head and continued without vehemence:

'Consider the question from another angle! We all know heads of state, men and women, who claim royal descent – great-grandchildren of a king, an emperor, a great warrior. These glorious names from the past cement our unity today. These links with legend lend present fame a lustre that extends to the clan, the tribe as a whole. There are still praise-singers to single out deeds and facts to feed our pride. A people needs these labels, these stamps of approval.'

'Maybe! Maybe, Umrel. But what you are saying is very dangerous,' interrupted Joom Galle.

'I am a narrow-minded woman, and set in my views . . . Fear of what "people" will say is a sign of weakness on the part of the elite, and of governments. We live like pebbles in a creek, tossed from one bank to the other. When the African side suits our needs of the moment, we cling to it. But as soon as it hinders us, we fling ourselves in the stream to cross to the modernity imported from Europe. We are forever fleeing our African realities. In the case of Senegal, this two-sidedness dates from a long way back, before you were born . . .'

'How's that?' asked Kad eagerly.

'How's that?' The old man became agitated. Behind the crystal clearness of his glasses, his old eyes, rimmed with silver, glanced at each of them in turn. 'How's that? Look at the inhabitants of the towns, Saint-Louis, Dakar, Rufisque, Gorée . . . Because of their long period of contact with Europeans, they thought themselves more "civilized" than the other bush Africans living in forest or savanna. This arrogance grew when they alone were given the vote and considered French citizens. People from these four communes, and their descendants, were proud of being the equals of Europeans. They began to parody them, and acquired a pretentious mentality . . . How many times have we heard a man from Dakar, Gorée, Rufisque or Ndar (Saint-Louis) say contemptuously to his country cousin: "I was civilized before you were." These alienated, rootless people, enslaved from within – of whom I was and still am one – were unconsciously the most faithful and devoted servants of the then prevailing system of occupation . . .'

The doyen paused to catch his breath. Behind his distant deep gaze, his thoughts were gathering momentum. He continued:

'In the years 1945–50, Léon Mignane would say during his election campaigns: "I will free you from the serfdom of 'native' status . . . I will make you . . . French citizens." That was why the peasants supported him. Twenty years after our Independence, our thinking still bears the marks of serfdom. When we talk of foreign goods . . . we never mean French cars or goods. The foreigners in our country are English, American, Japanese, Chinese, Russian.'

'Similarly, I've known Africans who were highly critical of certain regimes or ideologies, without realizing that their opinion was based on the European system, their gold standard,' concluded Kad.

'Exactly,' exclaimed Djia Umrel. 'What model of society are we offered through the media? We're made to swallow outdated values, no longer accepted in their countries of origin. Our television and radio programmes are stupid. And our leaders, instead of foreseeing and planning for the future, evade their duty. Russia, America, Europe and Asia are no longer examples or models for us.'

'It would be a dangerous step backwards, to revert to our traditions . . .'

'That's not what I'm saying, Joom Galle,' she interrupted. 'We must achieve a synthesis . . . Yes, a synthesis . . . I don't mean a step backwards . . . A new type of society,' she ended, blinking.

There followed a brief silence.

Kad was observing them. This elderly couple amazed him. He was full of admiration for them.

Sembene Ousmane (Senegal)
Excerpt from *The Last of the Empire*
Translated from the French by Adrian Adams

III — RULERS AND RULED

Admonition to a Chief*

Tell him that
We do not wish for greediness
We do not wish that he should curse us
We do not wish that his ears should be hard of hearing
We do not wish that he should call people fools
We do not wish that he should act on his own initiative
We do not wish things done as in Kumasi
We do not wish that it should ever be said
  'I have no time, I have no time'
We do not wish personal abuse
We do not wish personal violence.

Ashanti (Ghana)

Olorum Nimbe*

I am greeting you, Mayor of Lagos,
Mayor of Lagos, Olorum Nimbe,
Look after Lagos carefully.
As we pick up a yam pounder with care,
As we pick up a grinding stone with care,
As we pick up a child with care,
So may you handle Lagos with care.

Yoruba (Nigeria)

Refugee

A man running at dawn
A man fleeing at break o' new day
A woman screaming at dawn
A child running at break o' new day
A child fleeing at dawn
A black man
A black woman
A black child
Running, fleeing at break o' new day which is everyday
From
Black men
Black women
Black children

Stephen Ndichu (Kenya)

Adamu and His Beautiful Wife

In a certain town there lived an ascetic whose name was Adamu. Adamu was a man of exemplary character. He was so good that he possessed supernatural power. He could understand the languages of the animals, birds, insects, trees, and stones.

In the same town there was born a beautiful girl who was a few years younger than Adamu. Her parents belonged to the middle class. This girl was so beautiful that she was loved and desired by anyone who saw her. The ruler of the town began to court her with confidence that it was he and he alone that could marry such a beautiful girl. Although parents had full control and could control the destiny of their sons and daughters, the parents of that girl could not exercise such control over their daughter. Naturally they gave consideration to any of those important and rich people who were asking the hand of their daughter in marriage including the ruler of the town. The girl chose no one among her admirers but Adamu, the ascetic. The parents did not like to marry their daughter to Adamu because he was a poor man. Though they gave no consideration to anyone but the ruler, yet they were considering him under threat and compulsion. For they preferred marrying their daughter to a rich man, rather than either the ruler or the poor ascetic Adamu.

The girl was determined by all means to marry no one but Adamu. When her parents wanted to compel her to marry the ruler, in order to escape his threat, she stopped eating and drinking and preferred death to marrying anyone but her beloved Adamu, the ascetic. When the parents saw that they were going to lose her they explained the situation to the ruler. They begged him to allow their daughter to marry Adamu so that she might survive. They proposed a plan to him, suggesting that the ruler plan to kill Adamu after the marriage accidentally. The ruler accepted their proposition and allowed the girl to marry Adamu. When the girl heard that she could now marry Adamu, she began to eat again and soon regained her beauty. In the meantime the parents began to think of how to get rid of the ruler after the ruler had got rid of Adamu.

The girl, who was nicknamed 'Sonkowa', was married to Adamu. Both Adamu and Sonkowa were very happy together. Adamu then learned of the plan to kill him made by the ruler and the parents of his wife. He did so through his supernatural powers. When he learned this, he planned secretly to emigrate from the town with his wife.

It was at dawn on a certain day that Adamu and Sonkowa left the town without knowing exactly where they were going. When Adamu and his wife left the town, all the buildings, trees, and occupants of the town were crying and weeping in a language only he could understand. They did so because they knew that if Adamu went away, they would miss him bitterly.

As they left the town, they met a group of ants. The leader of the ants said to Adamu, 'Where are you going to at this time of the day?' Adamu said, 'My wife and I are leaving the town because the ruler is after my life, so we wish to go somewhere where we can live in peace.' The ant said. 'If you leave the town, we shall always be unhappy. Can we join you?' Adamu said, 'I am not leaving the town because I like doing so, but I am leaving because I am compelled to. If you like to join us, you can do so with pleasure.' So the ants joined Adamu and Sonkowa on their way to an unknown destination. As they advanced a little they met Slipperiness and Stumbling. Both asked Adamu for permission to join him. Adamu agreed. No sooner had they walked a little farther than they were met by two crown birds. They too joined Adamu's company with pleasure. Then came a frog and a snake and they both joined Adamu's company. Adamu, his wife Sonkowa, and their friends travelled day and night for many days before arriving at a big town which was surrounded by a high wall which had only one gate. They were all glad to arrive at a town at last. The name of the town was Danisa.

Danisa was a very, very big town. It was so big and so beautiful that it looked more than a town. It was a grand city. The king of that city was a very famous man and he was notorious for his love of beautiful women. The king was a very wise man and a very good and shrewd administrator. He had his police and bodyguard. He had detectives and spies. The chief of spies was a leper whom he chose because no one would dream of a leper being a spy. The office of the leper was at the gate of the town. He was always present at the gate. He left it only when it was closed. There was nothing that could go either in or out of the city without his knowledge. He was so capable in his work that the king had every confidence in him.

When Adamu, his wife Sonkowa, and their company arrived at the gate, the leper saw them and was perplexed by the beauty of Sonkowa. He could not believe his eyes and he was not sure if she was human or an angel. When Adamu saw the leper he understood his train of thought by his supernatural power. He said to himself, 'It looks as if I have jumped from the frying-pan into the fire.' When Adamu and company entered the city, he looked for accommodation and was lucky to find an abandoned old house.

When Adamu reached the house with his company, Slipperiness and Stumbling told Adamu that they would stay in front of the door of the hall of the house. Adamu made a hole for the snake, a small pond for the frog, and several small holes for the ants. The crown birds took the big tree in the house as their residence.

For the first time in his life the leper left the gate while still open in order to follow Adamu and see where he was going to live. As soon as he saw the house of Adamu, he ran to the palace and asked to see the king alone. He told him that he had brought him excellent news. He said to the king, 'Your Majesty, how many ears have you?' The king said, 'Naturally I have two ears, why?' The leper said, 'Add a third ear to your two ears even if it be an imaginary one, for the news is so enchanting that two ears are not enough to listen to it properly.' The king said, 'How can I add what God has not given me?' The leper insisted that the king should add the third ear, even if only an imaginary one. The king agreed and said, 'I have three ears.' The leper said, 'Your Majesty, today I have witnessed a beauty beyond expression. We have a stranger who has an angelic wife who matches no one on earth but you. She is so beautiful that you can never believe your eyes when you see her. If it is the last thing I do, I wish to see that delicate angel become your wife.' The king said to the leper, 'You have said that she is a wife, how can she be my wife then?' The leper said, 'Your Majesty, nothing on earth is beyond your reach. Anything in this city is yours. It will be a misuse of nature if such a beautiful angel is allowed to remain in the hands of such a poor man. You can call him and tell him that you love his wife. I am sure that he will be happy to do what your Majesty wishes.' The king said, 'I do not like to take his wife away from him by force. You should do something to persuade him to give me his wife. I leave everything to you and I shall be grateful if you succeed in making her my wife. Your position will be upgraded as a reward.'

Now that the leper was charged with the responsibility of taking away Sonkowa from Adamu, he began to think what trick he could use. He finally made up his mind to poison Adamu. He therefore put poison in some food. It could kill only male persons. He sent the food to Adamu. When the messenger reached the front of Adamu's house, Slipperiness made the feet of the messenger slip and then Stumbling made him stumble. He fell down on the ground and scattered the food on the ground. Another messenger was sent, he met the same fate. This was done several times without success. The leper at last gave up trying to poison Adamu.

The leper suggested another trick to the king. He asked the king to call Adamu and make him do an impossible thing, telling him that failure to do so would mean losing his wife. Adamu was called by the king. He was given two sacks, one of millet and one of corn. The two contents of the sacks were mixed together and Adamu was told to bring the two grains separate within two days or else he would lose his wife. Adamu took the grains and went away weeping. He came to his house and told his wife of the situation. They both wept. When the ants heard them weeping, their leader came and asked them what was the matter.

Adamu explained to them and the ants told them not to worry for God would help them. The ants took the grains, corn and millet, and within a day they had separated them into two sacks – one of corn and one of millet as requested by the king. Adamu went and informed the king that his order was carried out and that the grains were separated in a shorter time than the king had ordered. Both the king and the leper were surprised by the work of Adamu. Adamu was allowed to go. The king then asked the leper what would be done next. The leper suggested that the king's ring should be thrown into the middle of the city's big lake and that Adamu should be told to recover it within three days.

The king sent for Adamu in whose presence the king's ring was thrown into the middle of the city's largest lake. Adamu was told to recover that ring from the lake within three days or else he would have to surrender his wife. Adamu heard the king's order and he went back home weeping and wondering what to do. For everybody knew that it was impossible for any human being to swim on the surface of the lake, even more so to dive in it as the lake was full of hungry crocodiles and water poisonous to human beings. When Adamu reached home he explained the situation to his wife. They sat down weeping and wondering what on earth to do. When the frog heard them, he came and asked Adamu what was wrong. Adamu told the frog what the king had ordered him to do within three days. The frog told Adamu not to worry at all because God was on his side. The frog went to the lake and dived into it. Although he was a frog like other frogs in the lake, he had to fight his way through crocodiles, fish, and other frogs in order to look for the ring. He managed with the greatest difficulty to reach the middle of the lake, but could not find the ring. He could not find it because the largest and most senior crocodile had swallowed it as it was thrown into the lake. He almost lost hope when an idea came into his mind that he should provoke the crocodile to anger so that he might swallow him also. The frog preferred death to returning to Adamu a failure. The frog provoked the crocodile, who became infuriated and swallowed him. The senior crocodile was so large that his belly was like a huge room. When the frog reached the intestine of the crocodile he found the ring together with many other living things which had been swallowed earlier by the crocodile. When the frog found the ring, he began to think of how he could get out of the belly of the crocodile. He got the idea of

biting the crocodile and so bit the liver of the crocodile. The biting hurt
the crocodile so much that he vomited almost all that was in his stomach.
The frog was one of the things vomited. The frog ran quickly to Adamu
and took the ring to him. The frog explained to Adamu all the difficulties
that he had encountered in getting the ring out of the lake. Adamu was
very grateful to God and the frog.

It was now the second day after the order of the king to Adamu had
been issued. Adamu went to the palace and took the ring to the king.
The king and the leper were more than surprised to see the ring recovered
from the lake. The king began to fear that perhaps Adamu and his wife
were not human beings. So the king suggested to the leper that he should
leave Adamu and his wife alone. But the leper thought that his failure
to defeat Adamu and get his wife for the king might undermine his
position in the palace, so he did not give up. He started to contemplate
the most impossible thing Adamu might be ordered to do. He at last
formed the idea of asking Adamu to produce seven new stalks of millet
within one month. At this time, it was the winter season. It was
impossible to get new stalks of millet in that country or anywhere near.
The land was dry and the farmers expected to have rain in order to grow
their seeds within the next four months from the time when Adamu was
to be asked to produce the seven stalks of millet within one month.
When the king heard that idea, he too thought that Adamu would be
defeated this time because it looked impossible for anyone to produce
seven new stalks of millet within one month from that time. So the king
gave his approval to this idea.

The king sent for Adamu and told him to produce seven new stalks
of millet within one month or else divorce his wife so that the king might
marry her. When Adamu heard the king's order he was very much
perturbed for he knew that no miracle on earth could produce new
stalks of millet within one month or even within six months at that time
of the year. He went home unhappy as before. He informed his wife of
the king's order. Sonkowa was very sad because she realized that she
was the source of all the trouble to Adamu. They began to weep and
yell as before. When the crown birds heard them yelling and weeping
they came to them to see what was wrong. Adamu then explained
everything to the crown birds. The crown birds asked them to stop

weeping. They promised to do all they could to produce the required seven new stalks within the fixed time.

The crown birds then got ready to leave the city in order to fly to the country where they could get new stalks of millet. They bade farewell to Adamu and Sonkowa and went on their way towards the east. As they began to fly, they started to sing the following verses:

> To be or not to be is the will of God,
> To make impossible be possible is the will of God,
> To rain or not to rain, new stalk is of God,
> To find seven new stalks is simple for God
> To possess good faith is to submit to the will of God.

The crown birds continued to fly day and night singing their songs until they reached a place where it was the rainy season and the people had started to sow their seeds. They went on and on and within seven days they reached a place where millet was ripe for the harvest. When they reached a certain farm where the young farmers were harvesting their millet, they stopped at a small stream. They drank water. After they had drunk water, they were transformed into two beautiful girls. They walked and passed by the young farmers. When the young farmers saw how beautiful they were, they were attracted by them. The young farmers approached them and asked them where they were going in the hot sun. The girls answered that they were visiting some relatives of theirs and that they would soon get back. The young farmers offered to escort them but the girls asked them not to bother because they would get back anyway. So the girls went away as if they were going to a definite place. They went away and stayed for some time and then came back. They found the young farmers still busy with harvesting their millet. The young farmers invited the young, beautiful girls to rest a little in their farm-hut. They sat there and conversed with one another. The farmers asked the girls where they came from. The girls told them lies as they were not human beings but crown birds. After they had finished their conversation, the young girls said that they would like to start moving towards home. The farmers promised to visit them in their homes. The farmers made two bundles of millet for the two girls and carried them while escorting them. They escorted them a long distance and when the girls saw that they were near the small stream at which they had changed into human beings, they asked the farmers to go back from there and they thanked them very much for their kindness. The farmers made an appointment to visit the girls after two days. The farmers returned to their farms astonished by the beauty of the two girls. The girls walked a little farther until they reached the small stream. It was there that they changed into crown birds. Each of them carried fourteen stalks of millet in their wings. They began to fly home singing as before. They arrived back home within seven days. Altogether they spent fourteen days to and fro. They brought the new stalks of millet to Adamu, who was so delighted that he fainted. He was ordered to produce seven new stalks of millet within one month but within fourteen days he had twenty-eight new stalks of millet. So Adamu took a bath and went to the king with fourteen new stalks of millet. He said to the king, 'Your Majesty, your order has been carried out. I have brought with me fourteen new stalks of millet within fourteen days and not seven within one month as you had ordered me to do. I have brought an additional seven stalks so that you may give them to some of your noble ones. May God save your Majesty. I wish to retire now after carrying out your order.' The king and the leper were very much astonished. The king told Adamu to go away in peace. He further told the leper that he should not have any further new ideas. He blamed the leper very much for making Adamu humiliate him (the king). The leper observed that the king was very angry with him. He did not say anything to the king but left.

The leper went home and began to think of what to do. An idea came to him that he should cause the execution of Adamu. Now, in that city the penalty for stealing is death. The death penalty for stealing was started at the time when the thieves disturbed the people of the city. From then on the penalty continued to stand and anyone who stole was executed. So the leper conspired with the lady of the king's chamber, who stole some properties of the king, and with the police, who threw the property into Adamu's house. When the king realized his property was missing, he ordered a search in the houses of the city. The police, who conspired with the leper, went straight to Adamu's house. They searched the house and found the missing property. Adamu was arrested and taken to prison. The verdict was the death penalty, especially as the property was the king's. The king did not know that this had happened through the conspiracy of the leper, the king's chamber lady, and some of the police. He was in any case pleased that this time he had the means of getting rid of Adamu in order to marry his beautiful wife. The leper, in order to raise his dignity once more with the king, told the king that it was through his idea that this happened. Although the king was not pleased to hear that Adamu was to be executed through a conspiracy, there was nothing he could do, as he wanted very much to have Adamu's wife as his own and this was the only opportunity of getting Adamu out of the way.

Previous to the arrest of Adamu, the snake which Adamu took to the city told him that he would be arrested and that an attempt at his life would be made. The snake told Adamu that when the execution was about to take place he would come and bite the prince, the eldest son of the king, that the prince would faint, and that the only medicine to get the prince to recover would be to rub the liver of a leper on to the bite.

So the king ordered an announcement to be made of the execution of Adamu, the thief of the property of the king. When the day of the execution came, almost all the people of the city were present to witness the execution of the man who dared to steal the property of the king. The wife of Adamu was brought to the place of execution so that as soon as it took place, the king might take Sonkowa, who was to be his wife. The leper regarded the day of execution as a red-letter day for him. He had been waiting for that day for so long because of a number of set-backs. At the place of execution all the nobles of the city were present. Chairs were arranged and the king and the prince, the king's cabinet set in the middle. They all sat down in an air of festivity and then the hour of the execution arrived. As the king ordered the execution to proceed, there appeared a large serpent in the middle of the arena. The serpent went straight and bit the prince and disappeared. The prince fainted. All attention was now given to the prince. All the doctors and learned men tried all they could to save his life but they failed. Whenever one doctor after another gave his medicine the condition of the prince, far from improving, became worse. When all the doctors gave up hope, Adamu, who was about to be executed, asked to be allowed to give his medicine. The leper intervened and condemned any suggestion that

Adamu might give regarding medicine for the prince. But the king allowed Adamu to give the medicine. Adamu said that the medicine he had was simple and that was that the liver of a leper should be rubbed on the bite. There was no leper present except the leper who was the chief detective of the king and who had all the time been planning to take away Adamu's wife for the king and through whose conspiracy his very execution was about to take place. The king, realizing that his son was far dearer to him than the leper, ordered that the leper should be slaughtered, that his liver might be used to make his son recover. The leper started to run, saying that there was a leper near by and that it would be unfair for the king to slaughter him. The leper was caught and slaughtered. The liver was rubbed on the bite and the prince recovered and asked the people what was happening. It looked to him as if he had been dreaming.

The king was very grateful to Adamu. He released him and he was very pleased to let him go free. Furthermore, the king invited Adamu to be his grand vizier. Adamu did not accept that offer because he believed in being an ascetic. He felt that he could not combine the post of grand vizier and the state of being an ascetic. So the king gave Adamu and his wife a new house and promised to provide them with food throughout the rest of their lives. He accepted a post of legal and moral adviser to the king.

Though Adamu and Sonkowa were now free to live peacefully, he still continued to live with his sincere friends who had helped him throughout his struggle against the intrigues of the leper. He also sent for the parents of his wife and also his own parents. They all came and they lived happily together. He had several sons and daughters, who grew up and helped in raising the standard of education of the country.

Hausa (Nigeria)
Retold and translated by Bashir Sambo

At the Hospital*

At that period, the township had not yet completely lost all recollection of the customs of the colonial regime which, if nothing else, had been a great provider of medical care and had welcomed all patients without discrimination. The time had not yet come when, as soon as someone said that they were going to the hospital in the town for medical attention, they would find scorn and derision poured upon them. When Perpetua told her about her plan, Anna-Maria, far from discouraging her, congratulated her on her initiative and wanted to take her to the hospital herself, claiming she knew the place well.

Walking down the road, bordered on the right by waste ground and on the left running beside the hospital made up of long, single-storey buildings with narrow porches, the two women found themselves at last in front of the maternity section, where the gynaecological unit was. The way in was through a large gap made in the hibiscus hedge and across an uneven stretch of ground enclosed on all sides by this hedge or by the wall of the maternity hospital and covered with a dirty gravel which under the sun burnt the soles of their bare feet.

They wanted to be among the first, so the two women from Zombo-town had hurried. But when they reached the hospital towards half-past eight, the odd-shaped area in front was already swarming with women wearing their best clothes. Many carried before them bellies distended like over-full waterskins. Anna-Maria and Perpetua, one leading the other by the hand, tried to pick their way through, making towards some steps leading up to a narrow door. The other patients already formed a dense crowd around this, barring the progress of the two friends. They were anxious, the look on their faces cross, and at the same time resigned, each woman carrying a little wooden stool and a sunshade. They seemed to be waiting for a signal to scale the curved wall of the maternity wing which backed on to the place where they were standing. It was easy to imagine the front of the building, inside the hospital, with male nurses in white coats hurrying by, overworked doctors and perhaps mothers and patients hobbling painfully.

Then the crowd dissolved. One after the other they moved gently back from the steps. The patients sat down on their stools, their legs stretched out in front of them, almost level with the dirty gravel, the sunshades open above their heads. It must be because they had not brought a sunshade and a stool, evidently indispensable accessories in this place, that the two women from Zombotown felt they were being picked out, at first, only by subtle smiles of ironic commiseration. Even

Anna-Maria was confused. She had not been here since she brought a relative shortly before Independence.

After whispered consultations in little groups among the women, the looks Perpetua and Anna-Maria received were from faces set in an expression of envy.

'You're a lucky wife,' said a young woman dressed in pink suddenly in a bland voice. She was staring at Perpetua's poor little steel wedding ring.

'Why is that?' said Perpetua, surprised.

'Why? Don't pretend you don't know. You know very well what I mean. You haven't brought a stool or a sunshade because you know you're going straight in to see the doctor, without having to wait like the rest of us. Everyone can't be married to an army man or a policeman, can they? But we didn't see much of them in the struggle for Independence, did we, the army and the police?'

'I'm not married to a policeman or an army man!' protested Perpetua.

'You are!'

'I promise you I'm not,' said Perpetua, excited.

'Well then, my dear, you ought to have brought a stool and a sunshade. Because if you really aren't married to a policeman or an army man you may have a long time to wait. You may even have to come back tomorrow – and the day after that. Do you know what? It seems the government's medicine chests are bare, all the medicines are used up. So that means no medicines, no medical care, no medical advice – at least not for us. They say that Baba Tura and his friend Langelot are always going round the world begging for medicines that are supposed to help the poor Africans. And they get given them, it seems. Tonnes and tonnes and more tonnes. But once they get back here, instead of giving them out, they sell them. And at a price!'

'Langelot,' screamed another woman from the same group as the one in the pink dress. 'Langelot, what a curse he is. When will God get rid of him for us? Why must the poor Africans always find that one in the way? Against Ruben, it was Langelot. Today, four years after Ruben, it's still Langelot.'

'But who exactly is this Langelot?' asked Perpetua, more out of politeness than because she did not know.

'What! You don't know who Langelot is?' said the young woman in pink with a snort of laughter. 'What kind of bush do you come from? Perhaps you've never heard of Papa Baba either?'

But Anna-Maria had already taken Perpetua gently by the arm and was drawing her away from the woman in pink, and speaking in her ear.

'Be careful, my little Perpetua,' she whispered. 'They say the town is swarming with informers and trouble-makers. They will worm something out of you and then go and tell the police that you are a secret Rubenist, as you know, my child. While times are so hard, it's a very profitable business that. Don't talk politics in public with people you don't know.'

It must have been about eleven o'clock. A crack opened in the little door at the top of the round steps. Immediately the patients leapt to their feet and rushed up to a man who had come out from the consulting room. He had a white coat, bare legs and wore plastic sandals on his feet. He said a few words in a low voice, presumably in French. Then, while some of the patients waved under his nose a piece of paper that they had been feverishly uncrumpling, others were trying to break through the crowd by convulsive wriggling of their shoulders and bottoms, arms raised, fists clenched on what was no doubt also a medical pass. Unconcerned, rising above the surge of patients pressed around him and swaying now to the left, now to the right, the man let in, one after the other, about twenty women, looking carefully at the note which each one showed him. Then to the great bewilderment of Perpetua and Anna-Maria, who could not believe their eyes, the man in the white coat followed them inside and shut the door behind him.

'Come on then,' shouted the young woman in pink with bitter gaiety. 'The policemen and the army men are inside getting their helpings. Out here, we can whistle for it. There's only enough for them nowadays and the rest have to lump it.'

The fact is that the tiny number that had been tapped off had not appreciably thinned the crowd of patients. Undiscouraged, they settled down again in the courtyard and began to wait. You could tell the mothers-to-be, apart from the size of their bellies, from their appetites when soon, towards midday, they began to nibble roast peanuts, while the ones who had come provided unpacked their scanty meals and set themselves unceremoniously to the task of building up their wasted energy.

'Don't move from here, my little Perpetua,' said Anna-Maria. 'If you can get examined today, whatever you do, don't lose your chance. I'll have to nip back to Zombotown. Don't worry about Edward. He can have dinner with my husband. And I'll bring you something back here. It won't be too long, you'll see. I'll take a taxi for once. Oh, and I'll fetch you something to sit on. It looks as if it might go on until it gets dark.'

When Anna-Maria got back from Zombotown, some kind soul, upset at seeing Perpetua on her feet ever since she arrived, had lent her own stool to her for a few minutes so that she could rest her legs. Perpetua had gone to sit down against the hibiscus hedge, in the shade. She was doubled over, her face buried in her arms crossed over her knees, as if she had dozed off.

'Come on, sit up, Pet,' said Anna-Maria, giving her a shake. 'You mustn't give up, my girl. Here, have something to eat and drink. I've brought some things for you. Edward has been very good, yes, very good, and understanding and everything. Have they called anyone else while I've been gone?'

'No one,' said Perpetua, with a sigh. She was so tired, her eyes red.

The male nurses and other employees at the hospital who had closed up the consultation room, apparently to go and have lunch, came back. They could be heard moving about in the corridors again, their plastic sandals flapping softly on the cement floor. They could see them opening the windows, flinging the shutters back against the concrete walls. The women got to their feet again, though this time with no excitement, and once more crowded round the steps, trembling, evidently expecting the man in the white coat to come out. But the minutes passed and then hours. The women went back and sat on their stools. The sun, which had been scorching as always during the first three hours of the afternoon, suddenly grew cool and began to drop, vaguely drawing the shadows of the palm trees across the dirty laterite-coloured gravel. One or two of the patients, without indignation, even with a certain grace of gesture, got ready to go away, putting on the canvas shoes they had taken off for a while, folding their sunshades, picking up a stool or a bag, exchanging polite remarks with an acquaintance they had made.

The young woman in the pink dress signalled to Perpetua with her hand and shouted: 'No hope today, *sita*, my sister. See you tomorrow?'

In fact, half an hour after this gloomy prediction, the man in the white coat opened the narrow door, came down the steps and announced, not to the women but to some invisible audience, his face detached and distant: 'We haven't received the medical supplies we were expecting. We can't let you into the consulting room. Same as yesterday. Same as tomorrow perhaps. But come back and see. We can't promise anything. Please believe me, there's nothing we can do about it.'

There was no shout of anger, no word of surprise.

On the way back Anna-Maria was worried at the strangely heavy steps of her young friend. They were broken and uncoordinated. Such lethargy seemed to her excessive for the disappointment Perpetua had suffered. Back at Zombotown, in her house, she brought up bile several times and began to shiver. Anna-Maria suggested she should go to bed and stayed with her all the evening, afraid that something might happen, perhaps a miscarriage.

Fortunately Perpetua was much better in the morning, though there was still a very bitter taste in her mouth; her eyes were clouded and her limbs felt weak. She had got over the shock but she had been deeply shaken, perhaps not physically but certainly in her spirit.

Apart from the hospital, there was no doctor in Oyolo – not even at the Catholic Mission, though it was a large one and well off.

According to Anna-Maria, there were a hospital and doctors at the Foe-Minsili Protestant Mission between Oyolo and Ntermelen, but off the main road, nearly twenty kilometres deep in the forest. That distance would have to be covered on foot, or by taxi which would cost a fortune. Then when you got there, you would still have to pay for the consultation and treatment. It was an American mission, in fact; the treatment was excellent, provided you had the money.

But in the end Perpetua wanted to hear no more about hospitals and doctors and tried to find comfort in work and creativity while she waited for her child to be born.

Mongo Beti (Cameroon)
Excerpt from *Perpetua and the Habit of Unhappiness*
Translated from the French by John Reed and Clive Wake

Song Composed under a Tyrannical King

I'll buy myself an ugly old woman.
Why, don't you see?
Every beautiful woman is for the King,
And *young* ugly women are for the Chiefs!

Baganda (Uganda)

Protest against Councillors

Let word go to the councillors at Aboh:
The governing of this world is it done with guns?
Is it done with swords?
Even when they have no licence
They jump into cars and drive about.
When you get to Afo Oru market,
They block the road with cars.
And look! A young man comes to the market,
They beat him up and toss him into a van.
Councillors!
Are you saying we should leave off trading?
Are you saying we should go off and make bullets?
Government made a promise at the beginning:
If a man in a ditch holds out his hand
A share of government services shall reach his hand.
Ezinihitte, a king among towns, has held out his hand;
A share of government services is now due.
Don't we belong to the party at Enugu?
No big road leads to our market;
No piped water touches our lips.
Alas!
This census count isn't clear to us.

Igbo (Nigeria)
Translated by Chinweizu

Peasants

'The Masters of the Dew' – Jacques Roumain

The agony: I say their agony!

the agony of imagining their squalor but never knowing it
the agony of cramping them in roach-infested shacks
the agony of treating them like chattel slaves
the agony of feeding them abstract theories they do not understand
the agony of their lugubrious eyes and bartered souls
the agony of giving them party cards but never party support
the agony of marshalling them on election day but never on banquet
    nights
the agony of giving them melliferous words but mildewed bread
the agony of their cooking hearths dampened with unuse
the agony of their naked feet on the hot burning tarmac
the agony of their children with projectile bellies
the agony of long miserable nights
the agony of their thatched houses with too many holes
the agony of erecting hotels but being barred from them
the agony of watching the cavalcade of limousines
the agony of grand state balls for God know who
the agony of those who study meaningless 'isms in incomprehensible
    languages
the agony of intolerable fees for schools but with no jobs in sight
the agony of it all I say the agony of it all
but above all the damn agony of appealing to their patience
Africa beware! their patience is running out!

Syl Cheney-Coker (Sierra Leone)

A Shortage of Beggars*

'Is it much further?' Mour asked, seething with impatience.

'When the tarred road gives out', the chauffeur replied, 'there is a long sandy track that we must follow for about five miles before reaching the new Slum-Clearance Resettlement Area.'

As soon as the tarred road was out of sight Mour had the impression that the car was lost in a wilderness which seemed to stretch to infinity: a dreary, bare landscape, lifeless, swept by a wind of such violence that its howls mingled with the clouds of dust whipped up from the sand-dunes and with the fierce moans of the sea that foamed in fury.

Mour has never set foot in these parts, he only knew of their existence from maps on which they are marked in red; that indicated vacant zones in which a good part of the population could be accommodated. He is also discovering other realities, without even being aware of it: neither the skilful manoeuvres of his chauffeur, nor the swaying of the car from side to side, nor the murky atmosphere that he tries to penetrate from behind his dark glasses, can hold his attention; what intrigues him is that he has not yet glimpsed any houses.

'Sally, are you sure this is the right place? You haven't made a mistake?'

Sally turns round slightly towards the back seat. 'We'll soon be there, sir.'

The chauffeur confirms this. 'This is the right place. Those buses we're passing are all coming from there . . .'

Mour is reassured and can once more follow the drift of his own thoughts. Seated in the right corner of the back seat of the car, dressed in a simple boubou and slippers, to put the beggars at ease, he cannot imagine that his errand can fail. 'I'll pay whatever is necessary.'

'One week later . . . Is it fitting that such a simple thing as a shortage of beggars should make me miss the part in the national destiny that I am called upon to play? A bull, twenty-one yards of material, seven hundred cola-nuts, that's enough to make an unforgettable feast . . . Since they've taken refuge in this wilderness, the paupers must be hungry . . . No, they will never have seen so much munificence in one day . . .'

The chauffeur parked the car in front of a house surrounded by a green-painted fence, and turned to his employer, 'We're here, sir. This is the beggars' house.'

'Oh! So you knew it . . .'

'Yes, yes, sir. Everyone knows this place, sir!'

'*Assalamu alleikum!*'

'*Malikum salam.*'

No one has moved, nobody is interested in knowing the identity of the visitor who has just parked such a large car in front of the house. They are used now to this type of visit. Nguirane Sarr, in his suit and tie, continues to draw plaintive melodies from his guitar; he sings the song of friendship that a little girl composed in far-off times to immortalize her play-mate, the hippopotamus, who was shot by a cruel hunter.

Salla Niang is seated on her mat playing with some cowrie-shells; her head-scarf is tied in a peak on top of her head, her legs stretched out and crossed in front of her, and a long toothpick is stuck in the corner of her mouth. And then there is this crowd of beggars moving about, chatting, or lying asleep or scratching themselves amidst the continual squalling of the babies who are playing in the sand in the courtyard.

Mour is struck by the sight. Astonishment rather than compassion. He has never seen, as if simultaneously projected on to a screen, the image of so many physical defects, so much physical decrepitude and human disintegration from which, it is true, some patches of light stand out, like this Salla Niang whose face gleams like a bronze bust, fashioned by a master sculptor. By spontaneous association of ideas he begins to think of certain insalubrious districts of the City, certain slums in the middle of which stand a few buildings in ostentatiously luxurious style, like castles standing in solitary state.

'*Mba jamm ngeen am?* Are you in peace?'

'*Tabarak Allah!* We give thanks to God!'

'Who is the master of this house?'

Only now does Salla Niang raise her eyes to look at the visitor.

'What do you want?'

'I'd like to speak to the master of the house.'

'I'm in charge here.'

A clarion-call of a voice, clear and crystalline like a stream of molten silver. Mour is silent for a moment, then begins to wonder what kind of links there might be between this lady and these beggars.

'I've come about a matter concerning the beggars . . .'

'Ah . . .'

Mour would have felt more at ease if he had been invited to sit down, but Salla makes no move in this direction. She asks Nguirane to approach and the others to listen to 'the visitor who wishes to speak to us'.

Since his arrival Mour has noticed frequent comings and goings: he has seen people making donations to the first beggar they meet; he has seen others going the rounds of the *bàttu*-bearers, examining them closely without being in the least shocked, and finally making their gift to the chosen one. He thinks to himself that these people are possibly not as wretched as one might have imagined. 'But then, how do they make use of everything they receive? Why don't certain ones of them aspire to more cleanliness, more decency? Could they possibly have taken on the identity of the mask that they had been obliged to wear in order to arouse people's pity, to such a point that now that their situation is visibly improved, they continue to play the game of poverty and starvation?'

'This is the reason for my visit to these parts: I have a very, very important sacrifice to make. You are the ones I am going to offer it to, but I cannot bring it to you here. It is essential that tomorrow morning – tomorrow morning only – it will only be for a few hours – it is essential that tomorrow you go to take up your regular vantage points. You must take up your stands in every part of the City! Just as you used to do before; in front of the markets, at the entrance to the hospitals, at the traffic-lights, in front of offices, clinics, banks, shops, throughout the City, in every part of the City. You will receive offerings from me, offerings that will make it worth your while having taken the trouble to travel from here. And besides, you've been huddled together here for such a long time, as if you were scarcely human. For once in a while get out and about, at least to stretch your legs a bit!'

If it had not been for the laughter that greeted him from every side, Mour would have continued his speech; he had been trapped, without realizing it, by the demon of eloquence by which he stirred up and magnetized the crowds in political arenas.

'Go out into the streets, can you be serious?'

'Now that we are here in peace, to expose ourselves to harassment again!'

'Such an action would be to return voluntarily to a hell from which the Lord has delivered us!'

'May the Lord preserve us from that! May he preserve us! *Yalla Tere!* May the Lord preserve us!'

'You don't risk anything, absolutely nothing! I guarantee that nothing will happen to you. It will simply be a matter of going to get what I shall be giving you, and you won't regret it!'

Mour has deliberately tried to arouse the greed of certain of the beggars, but he does not seem to have succeeded.

'Besides,' says Nguirane Sarr, 'who are you, to talk to us like this and guarantee our safety?'

'I am the Director of the Public Health Service. I am in charge of all the people who might cause you any trouble.'

'Ah! . . . So you are Mour Ndiaye, who they talk about on the radio every day?'

Mour's heart swelled with pride as he replied to Nguirane, 'Yes, that's me. You have nothing to fear.'

The news is immediately shouted throughout the gathering: 'It's Mour Ndiaye!'; 'Mour Ndiaye has come to talk to us'; '*Ngoor si nyeu*, the gentleman who's here, Mour Ndiaye, here . . .'

Salla has not yet opened her mouth. She has simply watched the scene. Nguirane Sarr has got up, placed his guitar on the chair that he had been sitting on, straightened his jacket and tie and says in a voice that seemed to Mour mocking and disrespectful.

'So, governor, you drove us away and now you're the one who comes to fetch us back! What may be the reason for this, if I may ask?'

Salla smiles in complicity.

Mour is astonished at the impertinence of this beggar; he could never have imagined that so much effrontery in voice and manner could be found in a blind man who depends on others for his existence. 'So they start cheeking us now!' Mour almost gives way to the temptation to put this fellow in his place, but he speedily remembers that he is obliged to contain his irritation and to try to establish a peaceful dialogue with these people. Haunted by the idea of failure and bedevilled by the obsession of the sacrifice – 'a week later, the Vice-Presidency' – he deliberately chooses to play his last card, that of dishonesty.

'We don't have to misunderstand each other, chaps. Have you ever seen me intervening directly, in person, in the war waged against you?'

General silence.

'We bosses, we're in an awkward position; we're made responsible for everything, and God only knows that we haven't the slightest idea of half the actions that our inspectors commit; they do as they like and then people say that it's the chief.'

Mour realizes that his attempts to justify himself have fallen flat, so he changes his tactics. 'You've got radio sets, haven't you? You listen to the radio every day, so you must have heard all last week programmes broadcasting information to citizens and particularly those who are eligible for pensions . . . You've heard what's happened, haven't you?'

No one replied to Mour's questions. He tries to detect some reaction in the silent crowd; then he turns to Salla Niang and Nguirane Sarr, but neither of them seems to have heard what he has just said. He continues: 'You know that some contemptible individuals were depriving widows of their just dues, which is contrary to our religion and to what is right. In order to get someone to see to their papers, these poor women were paying considerable sums in advance to government inspectors, who are paid by the Government to do this work. Do you think that their chiefs knew what was going on? – Certainly not, since they were severely punished as soon as the administration became aware of the inhuman transactions that they were involved in. Can you imagine that these widows, who hadn't the means to pay in advance, were being put in touch with 'money-lenders' who advanced them the sums demanded with huge interest and against papers that they had to sign, to prove that they owed money! And then after making hundreds of applications, going from one office to another, going backwards and forwards in vain, and receiving hundreds of promises, these poor widows finally reached the right department to find themselves faced with creditors who sometimes took their whole pension. All that is the fault of unscrupulous employees, acting contrary to their superiors' directives . . . You can see that this business is far more serious than yours . . . yes, more serious, inasmuch as you, at least, you are here and you manage to find enough to live on. But a widow, a woman all alone, who often has no work, who has no support, with her whole family! Their sufferings only ceased on the day that the heads of departments realized what had been going on.'

The heavy silence which greets Mour's flight of oratory deeply disappoints him. His story has neither convinced nor moved the beggars. So, then, Mour decides to put his cards on the table.

'Can I count on you tomorrow? I'm prepared to satisfy all your demands!'

Thereupon he hears on all sides a murmur which gives him a little hope. He looks again at Nguirane Sarr who has already resumed his seat and placed his guitar on his lap. Mour decides to address him familiarly. 'You fellow with the guitar, what do you say?'

'You're asking us to return to the same places that you yourself drove us away from!'

Mour is worried. Very worried. On the brink of despair. But he must not give in, he must win the battle . . . 'One week later . . . And they are there, in front of me, on them my destiny depends . . . But this blind beggar, what pigheadedness! . . . God is the Creator of all things, He alone knows why he has ordered the world as He has done . . . For if this blind man had his sight, he would have been a phenomenon!'

'Guitar-player, you have not understood what I have just said to you! It is my men who went too far!'

'They weren't satisfied with driving us away, they tracked us down, flogged us, beat us like dogs!

'They are men who act without thought; they are inhuman! I have never been informed of this savage behaviour! Go back on the streets tomorrow, and you'll see if they lay a hand on you!'

'You drove us away!'

Now Salla Niang finds the scene amusing. Mour's appearance of being outmanoeuvred, Nguirane's grave countenance. The crowd's indifference. She bursts into peals of laughter: 'What a liar, what a damned liar! . . . If my former employer's countless marabouts had challenged him when he was waging such a heated campaign against marabouts, he'd have denied that he was the main person responsible for the anti-marabout campaign . . . But why do they wear a reversible boubou! Why don't they remain what they are, and show their real face! . . . *Nii noo seu!* How petty they are! They'll go anywhere to follow their ambition or if it's in their own interests, even if they go to the devil.'

She has made up her mind to get rid of Mour. He is visibly at the end of his tether. She is pitiless; her humour turns to derision; the sight of him irritates her.

'Monsieur Ndiaye, you can go. Tomorrow, if it please the Creator, all the beggars will be back at their old posts.'

Mour feels an enormous weight lifted from his chest. He can finally breathe again!

'They will be back at their posts?'

'Certainly', Salla replied, 'they will go . . .'

'Thank you, sister. You see, we are all equal, we are all of the same condition, for we are all human; so we should find grounds for agreement on every occasion. Thank you, sister.'

When he has once more passed through the gate of the property, Salla hastens to say to her fellow beggars, 'Don't budge from here. No one is to budge from here ever again! Tomorrow, we shall see that he bites the dust!'

Nguirane Sarr is seized with uncontrollable laughter, so uncontrollable and so infectious that all the beggars join in the general hilarity. When everyone has rejoiced at what they call Mour's 'madness' – 'it's because he's mad that he dared to come here to seek us out' – Nguirane Sarr, acting the buffoon this time, imitates blows being most energetically administered, saying, 'Salla, you have the knack of plying the whip without even raising your little finger. Swi-i-sh-sh! Swi-i-sh-sh! Swi-i-sh-sh! Poor fellow, he'll be none the worse for it – just a bruised back. Nothing serious.'

Aminata Sow Fall (Senegal)
The Beggar's Strike, Chapter Thirteen

PART TWO

The Local and Intimate Turf

IV — BIRTH AND CHILDHOOD

Mate

Dedicated to the Family Planning Clinic

Don't smile at me staff nurse
I gatecrashed into this life
You did not want me to be born
I beat the barricades of your birth-control scheme
I swallowed the pill
In her womb
I diluted the solution you distribute
I was a tiny spermatozoon
Wagging my tail
Invisible invincible
I glided past your loop
Dashed straight to the ovule
To mate you
Check!

Bicca Maseko (Azania)

Ritual Song by Parents of Twins*

SHE: Salongo's big penis digs
Deep into my womb;
Spits the seeds so hot,
Tickles and crushes the path.
My Salongo, Father, come,
Come and fuck me more

HE: Nalongo's vagina is deep;
         My penis searches its corners,
         Swims across to the end
         Finds the place for my seeds.
         Come, my Nalongo, come
         Mother, I'll fuck you more

                         Bonnie Lubega (Uganda)
                         From *Outcasts*

A Mother Praises Her Baby

You son of a clear-eyed mother,
You far-sighted one,
How you will see game one day,
You, who have strong arms and legs,
You strong-limbed one,
How surely you will shoot, plunder the Herreros,
And bring your mother their fat cattle to eat,
You child of a strong-thighed father,
How you will subdue strong oxen between your thighs one day,
You who have a mighty penis,
How many and what mighty children you will beget!

                         Khoikhoi (Azania)

A Mother to Her First-born

Speak to me, child of my heart.
Speak to me with your eyes, your round, laughing eyes,
Wet and shining as Lupeyo's bull-calf.

Speak to me, little one,
Clutching my breast with your hand,
So strong and firm for all its littleness.
It will be the hand of a warrior, my son,
A hand that will gladden your father.
See how eagerly it fastens on me:

It thinks already of a spear:
It quivers as at the throwing of a spear.
O son, you will have a warrior's name and be a leader of men.
And your sons, and your sons' sons, will remember you long after you
    have slipped into the darkness.
But I, I shall always remember your hand clutching me so.
I shall recall how you lay in my arms,
And looked at me so, and so,
And how your tiny hands played with my bosom.
And when they name you great warrior, then will my eyes be wet with
    remembering.

And how shall we name you, little warrior?
See, let us play at naming.
It will not be a name of despisal, for you are my first-born.
Not as Nawal's son is named will you be named.
Our gods will be kinder to you than theirs.
Must we call you 'Insolence' or 'Worthless One'?
Shall you be named, like a child of ill fortune, after the dung of cattle?
Our gods need no cheating, my child:
They wish you no ill.
They have washed your body and clothed it with beauty.
They have set a fire in your eyes.
And the little, puckering ridges of your brow—
Are they not the seal of their finger-prints when they fashioned you?
They have given you beauty and strength, child of my heart,
And wisdom is already shining in your eyes,
And laughter.

So how shall we name you, little one?
Are you your father's father, or his brother, or yet another?
Whose spirit is it that is in you, little warrior?
Whose spear-hand tightens round my breast?
Who lives in you and quickens to life, like last year's melon seed?
Are you silent, then?
But your eyes are thinking, thinking, and glowing like the eyes of a
    leopard in a thicket.
Well, let be.
At the day of naming you will tell us.

O my child, now indeed I am happy.
Now indeed I am a wife –
No more a bride, but a Mother-of-one.
Be splendid and magnificent, child of desire.
Be proud, as I am proud.
Be happy, as I am happy.
Be loved, as now I am loved.
Child, child, child, love I have had from my man.
But now, only now, have I the fullness of love.
Now, only now, am I his wife and the mother of his first-born.
His soul is safe in your keeping, my child, and it was I, I, I, who have
    made you.
Therefore am I loved.
Therefore am I happy.
Therefore am I a wife.
Therefore have I great honour.

You will tend his shrine when he is gone.
With sacrifice and oblation you will recall his name year by year.
He will live in your prayers, my child,
And there will be no more death for him, but everlasting life springing
    from your loins.
You are his shield and spear, his hope and redemption from the dead.
Through you he will be reborn, as the saplings in the spring.
And I, I am the mother of his first-born.
Sleep, child of beauty and courage and fulfilment, sleep.
I am content.

Didinga or *Lango* (Uganda)

Lull-a-Dirge

Don't cry, baby,
Sleep, little baby;
Father will nurse you,
Sleep, baby, sleep.

Lonely bird flitting away to the forest so fast,
Gold-speckled finch, your feathers wet all fading,
Tell me, shivering bird, have you seen her—
Have you seen my crying baby's mother?

> She went to the river at early dew,
> A pot upon her head;
> But down the water floats her pot,
> And the path from the river is empty.

Shall I take him under the palm
Where the green shade rests at noon?
> Oh no, no, no,
> For the thorns will prick my baby.

Shall I take him under the giant bombax
Where the silk-cotton plays with the wind?
> Oh no, no, no,
> For the termite-eaten bough will break
> And crush my little baby,
> My little sleeping baby.

The day is long and the sun grows hot,
So sleep, my little baby, sleep;
For mother is gone to a far, far land – alas!
She is gone beyond the river!

Joe de Graft (Ghana)

Song of a Hungry Child*

> Hunger is beating me.
> The soapseller hawks her goods about.
> But if I cannot wash my inside,
> How can I wash my outside?

Yoruba (Nigeria)

Bird Riddle

Challenger. What bird do you know?
Proposer. I know the white-necked raven.
Challenger. What about him?
Proposer. That he is a missionary.
Challenger. Why so?
Proposer. Because he wears a white collar and a black cassock, and
is always looking for dead bodies to bury.

(Azania)

Boy on a Swing

Slowly he moves
to and fro, to and fro,
then faster and faster
he swishes up and down.

His blue shirt
billows in the breeze
like a tattered kite.

The world whirls by:
east becomes west,
north turns to south;
the four cardinal points
meet in his head.

Mother!
Where did I come from?
When will I wear long trousers?
Why was my father jailed?

Oswald Mtshali (Azania)

The Guns of Langalanga*

The guns of Langalanga
Who fires them?
We fire them, we fire them, we fire them, bang, bang;
The guns of Langalanga
Who fires them?
We fire them, we fire them, we fire them, bang, bang;
Bang, bang, bang, bang,
Big bang;
Bang, bang, bang, bang,
Big bang.

Acholi (Uganda)
Translated by Okot p'Bitek

Misra and Askar*

To make the picture more complete, one must talk about your paternal uncle, namely Uncle Qorrax. The truth is, he too had designs on Misra and you suspected he had his way with her many times. It was no secret that you didn't like Uncle Qorrax or his numerous wives: numerous because he divorced and married such a number of them that you lost count of how many there were at any given time, and at times you weren't sure to whom he was married – until one day a woman you nicknamed 'Shahrawello' arrived on the scene and she *stayed* (as Scheherazade of the *One Thousand Nights* did). But neither did you like his children.

He was a ruthless man, your uncle was, and you were understandably frightened of him. You often remember him beating one of his wives or one of his children. Naturally, you didn't take his apparent little kindnesses nor did you accept the gentle hand he invariably extended to you. You shunned any bodily contact with him. It was said you cried a great deal if he so much as touched you, although he never gave you a beating and could hardly have justified himself in scolding you. You were an orphan and you had a 'stare' with which to protect yourself. He didn't want the 'stare' focused on him, his wives or his children.

When you were a little older and in Mogadiscio, living in the more enlightened world of Uncle Hilaal and Salaado, you began to reason thus: you didn't like Uncle Qorrax's children because they behaved as children always do, no more, no less; they insisted on owning toys if they were boys, or on making dolls and dressing them if they were girls. His sons enjoyed being rough with one another, they took sadistic pleasure in annoying or hurting one another, whereas his daughters busied themselves nursing or breast-feeding dolls or clothing bones, not as though they were women caring for infants with broken hearts but as though they were little girls. In retrospect, you would admit there was a part of you which admired these girls when they jumped ropes, challenged the boys, or took part in daredevil games – not when they chanted childish rhymes which small girls always did at any rate. And you admired the boys, from a distance anyway, when they dislodged fatal shots from catapults, cutting short the life of a gecko climbing up a wall or a lizard basking in the sun. It was the life-giving and life-taking aspects of their activities which interested you.

You once said to Misra that if there was anything you shared with adults, it was the visceral dislike of children's babble or the infantile rattle of their mechanical contrivances and the noise of their demands, 'I want this', 'I want that'. You concluded your remarks to the surprise of those listening to you (there was a woman neighbour, married to an invalid, a man who lay on his back all the time, suffering from some spinal complaint you had no name for), by saying, 'When will children stop wanting, when will they *be*, when will they do a job, as Karin's husband says, when will they accomplish something – not as children but as *beings*?'

She commented, 'But you are an adult.'

Karin agreed, 'He is. Surely.'

What you didn't say, although it crossed your mind, was that you *were* an adult, and, for whatever it was worth, you believed you were *present* at your birth. But no one said anything. Perhaps because you knew that when windows of bedrooms closed on the sleeping lids of children's heads nodding with drowsiness; when their snores filled the empty spaces of the rooms they were in; when their tongues tasted of the staleness of slumber in their mouths; when their parents surrendered themselves to their dreams, pushing out of their way the daylight inhibitions of who enjoyed the company of whom, in bed; when thoughts were unharnessed and allowed to roam freely in the open spaces of the uncensored mind: it was then, you knew, that Misra and you could tell each other stories no one else was listening to. And in the privacy of the late hour, in the secrecy of the night's darkness, you could afford to allow the adult in you to emerge and express adult thoughts, just as Misra could permit the child in her to express its mind.

And then the two of you would gossip. Like adults, you would exchange secrets each had gathered during the previous day, you would condemn and pass judgements. You would talk about people, talk about Shahrawello whose daily blood-letting of Qorrax was said to have kept him in good check. You also gossiped meanly and unpardonably about a neighbour's son who ate ten times as much as you and who, at four and a half, didn't utter a single word save 'food'; a boy who weighed 'a ton' and whose open mouth had to be stuffed with victuals of one sort or another. You nicknamed him 'Monster' following your overhearng his mother say, 'Oh Lord, why have you made me give birth to a monster?' Misra would feign interest in hearing you tell the story but suddenly her features would change expression, suggesting you were overdoing it, and she would say, 'That's enough, Askar', and would immediately change the subject to something less trivial, less controversial; or she would tell you a story until your breathing was slow, then shallow, as if you were wading through a pond where the water was muddy and knee-high. Misra was an expert at handling your moods. And she was different from your uncle's wives. As mothers, these were generally indulgent for the first two or three years. Then they became ruthlessly rigid with their children, who were expected to behave according to strict codes and norms of behaviour with which they had not been made familiar. You imagined these women to be in season all the time, what with their constant loss of temper with their children and their caning them whenever they didn't leave the room the moment they were instructed to do so.

Misra would say, 'To these women, when in their best moods, children are like passing royalty. Don't you notice how everything comes to a standstill when they totter past them and how they are admired?'

And you asked, 'But why do people love children?'

'Some because they can afford to lavish a moment's indulgence on a child that didn't keep them awake the previous night; some because they see angels in the infants they spy and marvel at God's generosity; some because they have no children themselves and envy those who are thus blessed. There are as many reasons why adults admire children as there are adults who admire them.'

'And why is it that they don't like me?' you said.

She answered, 'Because you are no child. That's why.'

In your mind, the memory door opened and you saw visiting relatives of Uncle Qorrax's and they were giving his children cash with which to buy sweets or footballs; you also saw that these same relatives caned them if they caught them misbehaving in public. But when it came to you, they asked after your health, although they did so with extreme caution, speaking articulately to Misra in the manner of one who was talking to a foreigner who didn't understand the nuances of one's language. And these relations never took liberties with you, no, they didn't. You wondered if it was 'guilt' that made them act the way they did, 'guilt' that made them look away when you 'stared'. Or were they uneasy because yours was the 'stare' of a parentless child?

'I want you to think of it like this,' said Misra to you one night. 'You are a blind man and I am your stick, and it is I who leads you into the centre of human activities. Your appearance makes everyone fall silent, it makes them lower the volume of their chatter. And you too become conscious and you interpret their silence as a ploy to exclude you, and you feel you're being watched and that you're being denied entry into their world. From then on, you hold on to the stick, both as guide and protector. Since you cannot sense sympathy in their silences, you think it is hate. You, the blind man, and I, the stick. And together we pierce the sore – that's their conscience.'

You said, 'No wonder they don't like me!'

Again, Misra changed the subject to less demanding topics, topics that were less burdensome than the notions of 'guilt' or 'conscience'. And she lulled you to and led you to sleep: gently, slowly, with a voice that changed rhythms and a lullaby sung in a language that wasn't your own. Some of the tales she told you had plenty of blood in them, there was no denying that. In a couple of these, there were even human-eating types – with Dhegdheer dying not and the heavens raining not! On occasion, she would give, in outline, the moral of the tale before she narrated it to you and at times, she would let you retell it so you had the opportunity of offering your own interpretation. Years later, you discovered (it was Karin who gave you the information) that Misra used to have these tales told to her when you were away from the compound so she could feed your fantasies on them when you returned. Admittedly, this endeared her to you.

Unlike Uncle Qorrax's children, you never stole things from anyone. You mentioned your needs – and Misra met them. If she couldn't, she told you why. And she trained you not to value money or possessions. Also, no visiting relation unfolded secretly on to your outstretched palm a coin a parent might not have given you. Uncle Qorrax's children, you knew, stole from their father. They conspired to do so – one of them would keep an eye on him, say, when he was in the lavatory and the others would rummage his pockets and take away a small sum that he wouldn't notice and share it among themselves. Often, they timed it so it coincided with the arrival of nomads, who had come to buy provisions from his shop, pitching their tents in their compounds, when there was a great deal of movement. They knew he dared not put embarrassing questions to these guest-clients. His sons knew he would never offer them or their mothers anything they could do without. It was his 'public' persona that insisted on being generous at times. He could be kind to his children and wives when 'others' were there; he could even be generous. When alone with them, he was a miser. So, they stole from him when he wasn't there.

Misra had a public and a private persona too. She was warmer and kinder when alone with you, calling you all kinds of endearments, sharing with you secrets no other soul knew about. And in any case, you needn't have stolen anything from Misra or from yourself. It was when she wore the mask of the public persona that you 'stole' from her time a few moments of tenderness which you exchanged surreptitiously.

And when Misra was in season and therefore nervous, you were entrusted to Karin, who was equally kind, equally generous – and who treated you, not as a child, but as a grandchild. Because you were two generations apart, Karin indulged you in a way which didn't meet Misra's patent of approval. The two women were the best of friends – the one with an ailing husband who had lain on his back for years and who was confined to a mattress on the floor from where he saw, whenever he looked up at the ceiling, a portrait of Ernest Bevin; the other, a woman who, by virtue of her foreignness, felt she had access to the Somali cosmos – if there is anything like that – only through you. Karin baby-minded for her. Likewise, when she was indisposed, Misra looked after the old man. Conveniently for the three of you, Karin and her husband's compound lay between yours and Uncle Qorrax's. And so you were content to go from one compound to the other without ever needing to touch the fringes of the third – namely Qorrax's.

But Qorrax called at yours when he chose, preferably when you began breathing shallowly through your nose, almost asleep. He would wait until your dream had taken you to a watery destination – where it was moist, green and all your own – your Eden. Then he would come into bed with Misra.

Oh, how you hated him!

Nuruddin Farah (Somalia)
Excerpt from *Maps*

Simangele and Vusi*

The veranda of Simangele's home was very popular with the boys of Mayaba Street. Simangele's parents had done all they could to chase the boys away. But then, it was the only veranda in the neighbourhood that was walled round. To most boys, its low front wall came up to their shoulders, so that anyone looking at them from the street would see many little heads just appearing above the wall. The boys loved to climb on that wall, run on it, chasing one another. There had been many broken teeth, broken arms, and slashed tongues. Yet the boys, with the memory of chickens, would be back not long after each accident.

Once, Simangele's parents decided to lock the gate leading into the yard. But the boys of Mayaba Street, led by none other than Simangele himself, simply scaled the fence. Then it became a game to race over it: either from the street into the yard, or from the yard into the street. The fence gave in. By the time it was decided to unlock the gate, it was too late. People either walked in through the gate, or walked over the flattened fence. Simangele's father then tried to surprise the boys by sneaking up on them with a whip. But it did not take long for them to enjoy being surprised and then chased down the street. He gave up.

Thoba, who was never allowed to play too long in the street, always felt honoured to be on that veranda. He was feeling exactly this way when, as he looked at the rain, he gave way to an inner glow of exultation.

'Oh!' he exclaimed, 'it's so nice during the holidays. We just play soccer all day.' He spoke to no one in particular. And nobody answered him. The others, with the exception of Mpiyakhe, really did not share Thoba's enthusiasm. They were always free, always playing in the street. Just whenever they wanted. Thoba envied these boys. They seemed not to have demanding mothers who issued endless orders, inspected chores given and done, and sent their children on endless errands. Thoba smiled, savouring the thrill of being with them, and the joy of having followed the moment's inclination to join them on the veranda.

'How many goals did we score?' asked Mpiyakhe.

'Seven,' replied Vusi.

'Naw!' protested Simangele. 'It was six.'

'Seven!' insisted Vusi.

'Six!' shouted Simangele.

The two boys glared at each other for the second time. Thoba noticed that Nana had raised his head and was looking fixedly at the brewing conflict.

The rain poured gently now; it registered without much intrusion in the boys' minds as a distant background to the brief but charged silence.

'It doesn't matter, anyway,' said Vusi with some finality. 'We beat you.'

'Naw!' retorted Simangele. 'You haven't beaten us yet. The game was stopped by the rain. We are carrying on after the rain.'

'Who said we'll want to play after the rain?' asked Vusi.

'That's how you are,' said Simangele. 'I've long seen what kind you are. You never want to lose.'

'Of course! Who likes to lose, anyway,' said Vusi triumphantly.

There followed a tense silence, longer this time. All the boys looked at the rain, and as it faded back into their consciousness, the tension seemed to dissolve away into its sound. They crossed their arms over their chests, clutching at their shoulders firmly against the cold. They seemed lost in thought as they listened to the sound of the rain on the corrugated roofs of the township houses. It was loudest on the roof of the A.M.E. church which stood some fifty yards away, at the corner of Mayaba and Thelejane Streets. The sound on this roof was a sustained, heavy patter which reverberated with the emptiness of a building that was made entirely of corrugated iron. Even when the rain was a light shower, the roar it made on the church roof gave the impression of hail. Occasionally, there would be a great gust of wind, and the noise of the rain on the roofs would increase, and a gust of sound would flow away in ripples from house to house in the direction of the wind, leaving behind the quiet, regular patter.

'If there was a service in there,' said Thoba breaking the silence, and pointing towards the church with his head, 'would the people hear the sermon?'

'Reverend Mkhabela has a big voice,' said Mpiyakhe, demonstrating the size of the voice with his hands and his blown up cheeks.

'No voice can be bigger than thunder,' said Vusi matter-of-factly.

'Who talked about thunder?' asked Simangele, and then declared emphatically, 'There's no thunder out there. It's only rain out there.'

'Well,' said Vusi who probably had not meant his observation to be scrutinized, 'it seems like thunder.'

'Either there is thunder, or there is no thunder,' declared Simangele.

'Exactly what do you want from me?' asked Vusi desperately. 'I wasn't even talking to you.'

'It's everybody's discussion,' said Simangele. 'So you don't have to be talking to me. But if I talk about what you have said, I will talk to you directly. So, I'm saying it again: either there is thunder there, or there is not thunder out there. And right now there is no thunder out there.'

Vusi stepped away from the wall and faced Simangele, who also stepped away from the wall, faced Vusi, and waited. There was only Thoba between them. A fight seemed inevitable, and Thoba trembled, out of fear, and then also from the cold, which he could now feel even more, because it again reasserted both itself and the rain as the reasons he should have gone home in order to avoid a silly fight. He should have gone home. His mother was right. Now, he could be caught in the middle. He felt responsible for the coming danger, because he had said something that had now gone out of control.

Mpiyakhe moved away from the wall and squatted next to Nana, who was also looking at the conflict. But a fight did not occur. Vusi stepped towards the wall, rested his hands on it, and looked out at the rain. Simangele made a click of annoyance and then turned towards the wall. Mpiyakhe sprang to his feet, and everybody looked at the rain once more. Thoba desperately tried to think of something pleasant to say; something harmless.

Then he saw two horses that were nibbling at the grass that loved to grow along the fence that surrounded the church. Horses loved to nibble at that grass, thought Thoba. And when they were not nibbling at the grass, they would be rubbing themselves against the fence. They loved that too. Horses were strange creatures. They just stood in the rain, eating grass as if there was no rain at all.

'Does a horse ever catch cold?' asked Thoba, again to no one in particular. It had been just an articulated thought. But Vusi took it up with some enthusiasm.

'Ho, boy! A horse?' exclaimed Vusi. 'A horse? It's got an iron skin. Hard. Tough.' He demonstrated with two black bony fists. 'They just don't get to coughing like people.'

'Now you want to tell us that a horse can cough,' said Simangele.

Nobody took that one up. The others looked at the two horses. Thoba considered Vusi's explanation, while at the same time frantically trying to find something to say before Simangele pressed his antagonism any further. An iron skin? thought Thoba, and then spoke again.

'What sound does the rain make when it falls on the back of a horse?' But Vusi ignored the question and made another contentious statement.

'Me,' said Vusi, 'I don't just catch cold. Not me!' he declared.

'Now you are telling us a lie,' said Simangele. 'And you know that very well.'

'Now, don't ever say I tell lies,' shouted Vusi.

'There's no person in this world who never gets ill,' insisted Simangele.

'I never said "never",' Vusi defended himself. 'I said, "don't just".'

Simangele did not pursue the matter. He had made his point. He was a year or two older than the other boys, and by far the tallest. The wall of the veranda came up to his chest. He had a lean but strong body. It was said he was like that because he was from the farms, and on the farms people are always running around and working hard all day, and they have no chance to get fat. So they become lean and strong. And when they get to the towns they become stubborn and arrogant because they don't understand things, and people laugh at them; and when people laugh at them they start fighting back. Then people say, 'Beware of those from the farms, they will stab with a broad smile on their faces.'

Simangele had lived in the township for two years now, but he was still known as the boy from the farms. And he could be deadly. Whenever there were street fights between the boys of Mayaba Street and those of Thipe Street, Simangele would be out there in front, leading the boys of Mayaba Street and throwing stones at the enemy with legendary accuracy. Sometimes Simangele would retreat during a fight, and then watch the boys of Mayaba Street being forced to retreat. Then he would run to the front again, and the enemy would retreat. And everybody would have seen the difference. Few boys ever took any chances with Simangele.

Vusi, on the other hand, was one of those boys who were good at many things. He was very inventive. He made the best bird traps, the best slings, the best wire cars; and four-three, and six-one, and five-two, always came his way in a game of dice. But it was in soccer that he was most famous. He was known to all the boys in the township, and everybody wanted to be on his side. He was nicknamed after Sandlane, Charterston Rovers' great dribbling wizard, who had a deformed right hand that was perpetually bent at the wrist, with the fingers stretched out firmly. And Vusi would always bend his wrist whenever the ball was in his possession. And his team mates would cheer 'Sandla-a-a-ne-e-e-!' And they would be looking at his deformed hand and its outstretched fingers, dry and dusty on the outside like the foot of a hen when it has raised its leg. And Vusi would go into a frenzy of dribbling, scoring goals with that sudden, unexpected shot.

Vusi was the only boy in Mayaba Street who could stand up to Simangele. The two had never actually fought, but they had been on the brink of fighting many times. The general speculation was that Simangele really did not want to take a chance; for who knew what would happen? Vusi was known to have outbraved many boys, even those acknowledged to be stronger than he. The problem with Vusi was that he fought to the death. All the boys knew he was a dangerous person to fight with, because you would be hitting and hitting him, but Vusi would keep coming and coming at you, and you would begin to lose hope. And then he might defeat you not because he was stronger, but because he kept coming at you, and you lost all hope. That is why it was thought Simangele never wanted to go all the way. In any case, there was really nothing awesome about Simangele's bravery. He had to be brave: he was older. But Vusi? He was a wonder.

It was for this reason that Thoba was busy considering Vusi's claim that he never got ill. It sounded familiar. Vusi was like Thoba's father. He was just that kind of person. Thoba's father was not the sick type; and Thoba's mother had always told visitors that her husband was a very strong man. And since Thoba felt instinctively on Vusi's side, he felt a pressing need to bear witness, if only to establish the truthfulness of Vusi's claim.

'My own father doesn't just get ill,' he declared. There was a brief silence after this and then the others began to laugh. And Thoba felt how terrible it was to be young and have no power. Whatever you said was laughed at. It was a deeply indulgent laugh that helped to blow away all the tension that had existed just before. They just laughed. It was always the case when you are not very strong, and you have to say something.

'What is he telling us, this one?' said Mpiyakhe in the middle of a guffaw. 'Your family gets knocked down with all kinds of diseases. Everybody knows that. Softies, all of you. You're too higher-up. That's your problem. Instead of eating *papa* and beans, you have too many sandwiches.'

'Now, that is a lot of shit you are saying' said Thoba trying to work up anger to counter the laughter.

'Don't ever say that about what I'm saying,' threatened Mpiyakhe.

'And what if I say it?' retorted Thoba.

'Take him on, boy, take him on,' said Simangele nudging Mpiyakhe in the stomach with an elbow.

Thoba began to feel uneasy. It was strange how the conflict had suddenly shifted down to him and Mpiyakhe who were at the lower end of the pecking order among the boys of Mayaba Street. He had fought Mpiyakhe a few times, and it was never clear who was stronger. Today he would win, tomorrow he would lose. That was how it was among the weak; a constant, unresolved struggle. Why should a simple truth about one's father lead to ridicule and then to a fight? Thoba looked at Mpiyakhe and had the impulse to rush him. Should he? What would be the result of it? But the uncertainty of the outcome made Thoba look away towards the rain. He squeezed his shoulders, and felt deeply ashamed that he could not prove his worth before Vusi and Simangele. He had to find a way to deal with his rival.

Mpiyakhe's father was a prosperous man who ran a flourishing taxi service. His house, a famous landmark, was one of the biggest in the township. If a stranger was looking for some house in that neighbour-hood, he was told: 'Go right down Mayaba Street until you see a big, green house. That will be Nzima's house. Once there, ask again . . .'

Screwed on to the front gate of the big, green house was a wooden board on which was painted 'Love Your Wife' in white paint. And when-ever a man got into Mpiyakhe's father's taxi, he was always asked: 'Do you love your wife?' Thus, Mpiyakhe's father was known through-out the township as 'Love Your Wife'. As a result, Mpiyakhe was always teased about his father by the boys of Mayaba Street. And when-ever that happened, he would let out steam on Thoba, trying to trans-fer the ridicule. After all, both their families were 'higher-ups' and if one family was a laughing-stock the same should be applied to the other.

Thoba and Mpiyakhe were prevented from fighting by Nana, who suddenly began to cough violently. They all turned towards him. The cough was a long one, and it shook his frail body until he seemed to be having convulsions. Thoba wondered if Nana was going to die. And what would Nana's grandmother do to them if Nana died in their presence? If she healed people, surely she could also kill them. Nana continued to cough. And the boys could see his head go up and down. They looked at each other anxiously as if wondering what to do. But the cough finally ceased; and when Nana looked up, there were tears in his eyes and much mucus flowing down in two lines over his lips. He swept his lower arm over his lips and nose and then rubbed it against the side of his shirt.

'You should go home,' said Vusi to Nana.

'How can he go home in this rain?' said Simangele, taking advantage of Nana's refusal. Vusi turned away indignantly. Thoba wondered if he should take off his shirt and give it to Nana. But he quickly decided against it. He himself could die. He turned away to look at the rain. He saw that Vusi was looking at the horses eating grass in the rain. He saw the concentration on Vusi's face. He watched as a sudden gleam came to Vusi's eye, and Vusi slowly turned his face away from the rain to fix an ominously excited gaze on Simangele. He looked at the rain again, and then his look took on a determined intensity. He turned to Simangele again.

'Simangele,' called Vusi. 'How would you like to be a horse in the rain?'

'A horse in the rain?' said Simangele tentatively. He looked at Thoba and Mpiyakhe, and seemed embarrassed, as if there was something he could not understand.

'Yes, a horse in the rain,' said Vusi. There was a look of triumph in his face. 'Look at the horses. They are in the rain. Yet they have nothing on them. I bet you can never go into the rain without your shirt.'

Simangele laughed. 'That is foolishness,' he said.

'No,' said Vusi. 'It is not foolishness.' And as he spoke, Vusi was slowly pulling out his shirt without loosening the belt that held it tightly round the waist where it was tucked into the trousers. All the while he was looking steadily at Simangele.

Simangele stopped laughing and began to look uneasy. Once more he looked at Vusi and Mpiyakhe. And then he looked at Nana on the floor. Their eyes met, and Simangele looked away quickly. Meanwhile, his jaws tightened, Vusi was unbuttoning his shirt from the rumpled bottom upwards. Then he took off his shirt slowly, exposing a thin, shining, black body, taut with strength. Thoba felt a tremor of iciness through his body as if it was his body that had been exposed. Vusi had thrust his chest out and arched his arms back so that his shirt dangled from his right hand. Soon his body was looking like a plucked chicken.

'I'm a horse now,' said Vusi. 'Let's see if you too can be a horse.' He did not wait for an answer. Dropping his shirt with a flourish, Vusi flung himself into the rain. He braced his head against the rain and ran up Thelejane Street, which was directly opposite Simangele's home and formed a T-junction with Mayaba Street. Thelejane Street went right up and disappeared in the distance. Vusi ran so fast, he seemed to have grown shorter. Soon he was a tiny black speck in the rain; and the far distance of the street seemed to swallow him up. Not once did he look back.

It had all happened so suddenly, Thoba thought. Just like the day a formation of military jets had suddenly come from nowhere and flown low round the township a number of times, deafening the place with noise. And then they were gone, leaving behind a petrifying, stunned silence which totally blocked thinking until many minutes later.

Simangele looked like someone who thought he had enough time, but when he got to the station found that the train was already pulling out, and that he had to suffer the indignity of running after it. He looked at Thoba and Mpiyakhe. They looked back. Then a wave of anger and frustration crossed his face.

'What are you doing here on my veranda?' he yelled at the two boys. They moved towards a corner away from him. There was silence. Then Simangele looked at Nana.

'I didn't mean you,' he said with a faint plea in his voice. Then he looked at the small figure in the rain. It was so far now that it did not even seem to be moving. He looked at the sky. It was grey, and the rain was grey. He looked at the two boys, again. Thoba cringed, and looked well into Simangele's eyes. And then suddenly Thoba did not feel afraid any more. As he looked into Simangele's eyes, he felt a strange sense of power over Simangele. Simangele did not want to go into the rain, but he would go, because Thoba was looking at him. Mpiyakhe was looking at him. Nana was looking at him with those large eyes. And they had all been there when Simangele was challenged. He would have to go.

Slowly, and seemingly with much pain, Simangele fingered the buttons of his shirt. He unbuttoned only the three upper buttons and pulled the shirt over his head. Just then, a gust of wind swept the rain, making it sound harder on the roofs of houses. Simangele shuddered. He threw his shirt on the floor and then stretched his leg out into the rain and watched his gray, dry skin turn brown and wet. Then he eased himself into the rain. He shivered, and that made him seem to decide he had better run. He was out there now, running in the street, following Vusi. But his strides were much less confident than Vusi's magnanimous strides. Simangele jumped over puddles where his challenger had just waded in and out of them like a galloping horse. Thoba and Mpiyakhe watched him in silence until he vanished into the distance.

Njabulo Ndebele (Azania)
Excerpt from 'The Test'

Obu's Classroom*

The Lord is my shepherd; I shall not want.
He maketh me to lie down in green pastures!
He leadeth me beside still waters.
He restoreth my soul . . .

The class listened to Obu with envy, admiration, hatred as he rattled through Psalm 23, hardly pausing for breath and without missing out a single word. The whole class had been given one week to memorize the psalm in English, so that each pupil could recite it accurately even if knocked up from sleep. At the end of the week, 'We shall see', the class teacher, inquired whether each pupil had done his homework.

'Yessir!' the class had intoned in unison, with the stress on the sir.

'Tell me what the mouth cannot accomplish!'

'Nothing!'

The teacher went on: 'I can cut a broad road through the winding Milliken hill in one day. By what means?'

'With the mouth!' the class echoed.

'I will pass London Matriculation tomorrow and get a degree from Fourah Bay College the day after. By what means?'

'With the mouth!' Cromwell's voice drowned most other voices. He had no illusions about his academic ability; he hung on at school simply because his elder brother had warned him that he could not obtain a commercial driver's licence unless he passed or at least read Standard 3. Psalm 23 would simply not stick to his small round head (barbered that week in the style appropriately designated 'sahara'). He prayed that 'We shall see' would take up more time cracking jokes so that the recitation of Psalm 23 could be put off till another day.

'What's impossible for the mouth to accomplish?'

'Nothing!'

'We shall see' pursed his lips and nodded affirmatively like a wine connoisseur. 'We shall see how many of you have actually memorized Psalm 23 and how many merely say so with their upper lips . . .'

Cromwell cut him short: 'One question has been puzzling me since last night . . .'

'It can puzzle you one more night, Cromwell. Today is for Psalm 23.

And if you can only recite that psalm, you may find your puzzle gone because "The Lord is my . . ." Go on from there, Cromwell.'

Cromwell was totally unprepared for the first shot, and the little he knew quickly evaporated in his confusion: 'De Lord is my shee-p . . . my sheep . . . De Lord is . . . is . . . not want . . .'

The smile on the teacher's face dried up as he waited for Cromwell to stop. He removed his handkerchief from his stool, spread it on the table and sat on it, making sure he had prevented his wide-rimmed shorts from creasing. 'Is that how you think you will pass Standard 2 this year?'

'Excuse, Sir, please don't predict that my pitcher will break even before I get to the stream,' replied Cromwell, looking at his desk rather than at the teacher to whom he spoke, and vibrating his right leg as if to keep down his temperature.

'Who is predicting that your pitcher will break?' The teacher's voice rose shrilly, and the pupils observed an involuntary movement of his nose – the sign that he was on the verge of losing his temper. 'I'm only warning you that if you can't memorize even the first verse of such a simple and popular psalm, you shouldn't blame anybody if you fail Standard 2 again.'

'If you fail me again, will my mother's soup pot fail me, too?'

The teacher's nose moved again, this time with the up and down movement of a piston. He, however, smothered his anger when he remembered his humiliating experience early in the previous year, after which he had decided never again to allow himself to get worked up over Cromwell. It was a scene such as this that had driven him into challenging Cromwell to a wrestling contest. Although Cromwell was clearly not an infant, judging from the hairs he kept pulling off his chin during classes, yet there was nothing in his appearance to suggest physical prowess. He might have been 5 feet 9 but for a stoop which reduced his height by about two inches and made him resemble a giant semi-colon, but height was not always synonymous with strength.

On Cromwell's part, he had accepted the challenge, not because he was sure he could throw 'We shall see', but because he knew the contest would burn up the remainder of the period for arithmetic and probably erode into the period for geography. He had never seen the teacher wrestle or fight so there was no way of assessing his strength. Somehow he felt the teacher would not throw him; a man who fed on a diet of cow peas and African spinach and who drank clean spring water in preference to the vitalizing brown water from ponds could not be strong. Even if the teacher threw him, what about it? The teacher who throws his pupil could not expect an eagle's feather for doing so: a teacher should throw his pupil just as it is a dog which should bite a man and not vice versa. If on the other hand he could throw his teacher, that would be great news. So he had hopes of gain and nothing to lose.

The eagle's feather had gone to Cromwell. He had lost the first bout to his teacher, but quickly made up for lost ground by throwing his teacher in the two succeeding bouts. The last bout was watched by at least half the school, and won Cromwell a thunderous ovation, especially when for a brief second he put his right foot on the vanquished teacher's chest the way a hunter would pose for a photograph with his foot on the body of the elephant he had killed. That was nearly a year ago but its memory remained very fresh in the teacher's mind. He had authorized the headmaster to cut off his arm, his leg, even his private parts if he was ever again caught wrestling or fighting with any pupil.

'We shall see' swallowed his anger: 'Sometimes I wonder why you don't stay beside your mother's soup pot instead of wasting precious time and money coming to school.' To avoid giving Cromwell the chance to retort, the teacher asked the boy sitting at one end of the front row to recite the psalm.

The boy recited two verses without difficulty, and a smile was already lighting up the teacher's face when the tap was turned off and the boy dried up. No amount of prompting could help him. The teacher went through the front row, pupil by pupil. None of them could recite the entire psalm.

'Is there any pupil who can recite the whole psalm?' he inquired, angry and disappointed.

A boy and a girl shot up their hands. Neither of them could make it.

'Is this the kind of class I've been saddled with this year?' Surprisingly the teacher's nose did not twitch. He lowered himself from the table where he sat and walked over to the corner of the room where the class monitor generally kept his work basket, to pick up his cane. 'If there are some of you who think that Standard 2 is the class for eating *akara* and playing *koso*, I will soon flog you out of it. We shall see!'

He bent his cane this way and that, to test its reliability. The more cowardly pupils could no longer sit on their benches. Margaret, the girl who sat next to Obu, drifted closer to him as if she needed someone to steady her vibrating nerves. The pathetic appeal on her face was obvious; she looked up to Obu to intervene and save her from the impending catastrophe. Obu stared at the blackboard in front of him, without seeing much. He knew the whole psalm off by heart, but he feared he would incur the collective ire of the class if he pushed himself forward. Then Margaret's pathetic appeal did it. It reminded 'We shall see' of the presence of the little genius at a time he earnestly wished that at least one pupil would save him from flogging the whole class.

'What about you, Obuechina?'

Obu rose from the bench, oblivious of the prayer Margaret was silently saying for him. He avoided all eyes by focusing his own on his desk. Without missing one word, and hardly pausing for breath, he rattled through the entire psalm.

'Ek – ce – llent! Ek – ce – llent!' shouted 'We shall see', proud and happy as he would have been if he had scored three-nil over Cromwell in their wrestling contest. He did not know when the cane dropped from his hand as he jumped down from the table where he sat, rushed to Obu, shook hands with him and led him by the hand to the platform. As if he were not certain the whole class could see Obu clearly where he stood by the side of the teacher's table, he asked Obu to stand on the table.

'I hope everybody can see him clearly?' he asked.

The reply was obvious. Some pupils nodded; nobody spoke. Cromwell swore he would smash the precocious monkey's head if he thought he could put the whole class to shame whenever he chose; how much better it would have been if nobody in the class had recited the psalm. Margaret felt as if a very close friend had just emerged victorious from a gruelling wrestling contest. Unfortunately the victor was too shy to acknowledge her ear-to-ear congratulatory grin; the eyes of the class – hostile, envious, passive – were too many for him so he avoided them by looking at his toes.

'Give him the special hand clap!' ordered the teacher, 'One – two – three four five – six! Again–' he sang, 'One – two – three four five – six!

And the third time – One – two – three four five – six! And one for
"*jara*": One – two – three four five – six!'

An excited teacher helped Obu down from the table. 'Here is at least
one boy who takes his homework seriously. Some of you care more for
your mothers' soup pots.' The teacher deliberately kept his eyes away
from Cromwell, for whom the jibe had been intended. 'I tell you, watch
this boy. Watch him in five years' time, in ten years' time. We shall see
where he will be, and where some of you here will be. We shall then see
whether it is important to do your homework . . .'

The teacher was interrupted by the shooting up of three impatient
little hands.

'Yes,' the teacher invited the boy who could recite only two verses;
he had been bobbing up and down like a tadpole in quick motion, in
his anxiety to attract the teacher's attention.

'I want to try again, Sir,' pleaded the boy, looking forward to sharing
in some of Obu's glory.

'You've had your chance for today.'

'Sir, but I know it. I don't know what happened to me when I stood
up . . .'

'The Lord will not ask you what happened to you if you are absent
when He calls,' interrupted the teacher, swinging his eyes away to
another pupil in a manner that brought it clearly to the first boy that
his chapter was closed.

'I want to recite it, Sir,' offered another boy. The offer was rather
reluctant. The boy was not sure he could recite the whole psalm. He
had raised his hand so as to be counted among those who had done
their homework, hoping that the teacher would not call on him. It was
a technique that had often worked. You put up your hand when you
do not know the answer. The teacher counts you among the brilliant
pupils and leaves you to invite the less brilliant pupils – those whose
hands are not up – to answer the question. He hoped the technique
would work this time, but when he saw the teacher's eyes swinging in
his direction, he lowered the outstretched hand unobtrusively as if it
had never been raised, using it to support his head.

'No more for today,' announced the teacher, to the intense relief of
the boy. 'I can't jump from eating yam foofoo and bitterleaf soup to
chewing raw *garri*. I give the rest of you three more days to memorize

the psalm. After that time, if there is still any one of you who can't recite it as if you were reciting Our Lord's Prayer, I'll teach that person from where water gets into the fluted pumpkin! Is that all right?'

'Yessir,' chorused a jubilant class. The boy at the front row shuffled his feet and wriggled on his bench to demonstrate his unhappiness at the postponement.

'What is there the mouth cannot accomplish?'

This time the class did not respond.

Obu felt something force its way into the left pocket of his brown khaki shorts. The bell for the midday recess had sounded gbo-gom, gbo-gom, gbo-gom from the headmaster's office, to the relief of most pupils, and he was putting back an exercise book into his brown raffia satchel. He promptly grabbed the pocket to catch red-handed whoever the thief was.

'I put something there for you,' whispered Margaret, smiling shyly as she bent over the long desk to escape the teacher's inquisitive eyes. 'Wait until we go out for recess before opening it.'

Obu released his hold on the bulging pocket. Before he had time to imagine what it was, the teacher had begun the marching song and the class began to march out, row by row, singing with the teacher:

> Good morning, mister Joe.
> Good morning to you all.
> I'm coming to ask you about a famous war.
> The people of that city, they had no sense.
> When a rocket was falling, they shouted mewo! mewo!
> Mewo! Mewo! Mewo mewo mewo!
> When a rocket was falling, they shouted mewo! mewo!

The school rules required every pupil to vacate the classroom blocks during recess, to ensure that no pupil stayed back to work when he should be having a break for relaxation. The responsibility for enforcing this regulation was entrusted to Teacher, someone no pupil dared disobey; therefore every pupil left the classrooms every recess.

As soon as he ambled out of the classroom, Obu ran towards the school farm. Cromwell had looked at him threateningly as he marched out of the room. Fortunately Cromwell sat on the last row, three rows away from Obu; by the time the last row would march out Obu reckoned he would have disappeared from Cromwell's sight.

Giant *ukwa*, fried without being burnt, and nicely shelled ready for the mouth. The palm kernels were the special variety, called *aku okukoro* at Umuchukwu – white, soft to chew, and more juicy than the ordinary palm kernel. Obu's mouth watered as he decided whether to pour the entire package into his mouth at one go or to spread out the enjoyment by taking the ukwa and kernels one at a time, after prolonged intervals. Then suddenly his mouth dried up as the water was transferred to his eyes. It was the special kernels that did it. They rang a bell somewhere inside his memory box, and he bit his lips to hold back the tears. He found he could not. He closed the used bottle of petroleum jelly in which the gift had come, threw it into the nearby cassava plot and let loose his bottled-up emotions. He was sitting on a tree-stump sobbing hard when Cromwell materialized in front of him.

'No matter how many rivers the crab may ford, it will end up in an old woman's soup pot!' shouted Cromwell, panting but visibly pleased that his frantic search for Obu had not ended in vain. 'Bowl up that thing your girlfriend, Margaret, gave you quickly before I shatter your jaw. Before you tell me any lies, I saw what it was very . . .'

'Get out of here now or I'll break your head!'

Cromwell was taken aback, and spontaneously took two steps back. Until Obu rose to his feet angrily and spoke, Cromwell did not know he had been sobbing.

Obu bent low to blow each running nostril in turn and also to arm himself with a cassava stem. Cromwell took quick stock of the situation and decided that discretion was the better part of valour. Did not the proverb say that a man who wakes up in the morning and finds himself being pursued by a chicken should run for his life, for who knows whether the chicken grew teeth overnight? Moreover his eyes had scanned Obu's pockets and the ground on which he stood without alighting on any trace of Margaret's gift.

'Do you know it's me, Cromwell, you are addressing like that?'

'Go away, even if you are giant Alakuku, or I'll break your head with this!' Obu advanced two steps, determined to execute his threat if Cromwell did not have the good sense to leave him to his sorrow.

'I see Margaret gave you a scorpion and you are looking for somebody else to say he beat you.' Cromwell had to make his withdrawal graceful and honourable. 'Count Cromwell out of it. The day I'll feed your mouth with sand, I'll need no helper.'

Before Obu returned to the class, he hid the bottle where he could find it after school. That bottle of ukwa and aku okukoro had developed tremendous emotional value for him. It carried special memories of the pleasant world he had left behind at Umuchukwu.

Chukwuemeka Ike (Nigeria)
The Potter's Wheel, Chapter Fifteen

On the Brink of Manhood*

Awake and washed, handsome, shaven and seventeen years old, he now stood behind a window in a house in Mogadiscio – Uncle Hilaal's house. To his right, a writing-desk on which lay, not as yet filled out, a form from the Somali National University Admissions Committee, a form he hadn't had the peace of mind to look at, because he didn't know whether he would, after all, choose to go to university although he had passed his school certificate examination with distinction and was within his rights to say which course or faculty he wanted. There were, besides the unfilled-out form, two other notes – one from Uncle Hilaal, in whose charge he lived, telling him that Misra had been seen in town and that she had been looking for the whereabouts of Askar and was likely to turn up any day at this doorstep; the other from the Western Liberation Front Headquarters, in Mogadiscio, requesting that he appear before the recruitment board for an interview. He stood behind the window, contemplative and very still – resembling a man who has come to a new, alien land. Presently, he left the window and picked up the forms and the notes in turn. He realized that he couldn't depersonalize his worries as he had believed he might. It occurred to him, as an afterthought, that on reading the note from Uncle Hilaal last night when he got back (he had spent a most pleasant evening out in the company of Riyo, his girl-friend), his soul, out of despair, had shrunk in size while his body became massive and overblown. He wondered why.

Misra was here, in Mogadiscio!

Askar was now big, tall, clean as grown-ups generally are, and healthy. What would she make of him? he asked himself. He remembered how she used to lavish limitless love on him when sick; how she took care of him with the attentiveness of a child mending a broken toy. She would wash him, she would oil his body twice daily and her fingers would run over his smooth skin, stopping, probing, asking questions when they encountered a small scratch, a badly attended-to sore or a black spot. Boils were altogether something else. They never worried her. 'Boys have them when and as they grow up,' she said, repeating the old wives' notion about boils. 'They are a result of undischarged sperm.'

But how would she react to him and to his being a grown man, maybe taller than she, who knows; maybe stronger and more muscular than she? Would absurd ideas cross her mind: that she would like to give him a bath? Or would she offer to give him a wash or help him soap his back, or, why not?, sponge those parts of his body his hands can't reach, would she? Whose look would be earth-bound, his or hers? Would he be able, in other words, to outstare her?

Standing between them, now that he had turned seventeen and she forty-something, were ten years, each year as prominent as a referee stopping a fight – ten years in which he shed his childish skin and grew that of an adult, under the supervision of Uncle Hilaal. He was virtually a different person. Perhaps he wasn't even a person when she last saw him. He was only a seven-year-old boy and her ward and, sometimes he thought to himself, her toy too. Anyway, the ten years which separated them were crucial in a number of ways.

The world Uncle Hilaal and Salaado had introduced him to, his living in Mogadiscio with them, his schooling there and the world which these had opened up for him, was a universe apart from the one the war in the Ogaden imposed on Misra's thinking. But how did she fare in war? Why did she become a traitor? For there was a certain consistency in one story – that she had sold her soul in order to save her body – but was this true? Was it true that she had betrayed a trust and set a trap in which 100 Kallafo warriors lost their lives? Or did she surrender her body in order to save her soul? He then remembered that living with Misra wasn't always full of exhilaration and happiness, that there were moments of sadness, that it wasn't always fun. It had its pains, its agonies, its ups and downs, especially when the cavity of her womb overflowed with blood once every month. When this occurred, she was fierce to look at, she was ugly, her hair uncombed, her spirit low, and she was short-tempered, beating him often, losing her temper with him. She was depressive, suicidal, no, homicidal.

That was how Karin entered his life.

Nuruddin Farah (Somalia)
Excerpt from *Maps*

V – INSTRUCTIONS, MORALITY AND SOCIAL CONTROL

How the Leopard Got His Claws

In the beginning . . . all the animals in the forest lived as friends. Their king was the leopard. He was strong, but gentle and wise. He ruled the animals well, and they all liked him.

At that time the animals did not fight one another. Most of them had no sharp teeth or claws. They did not need them. Even King Leopard had only small teeth. He had no claws at all.

Only the dog had big, sharp teeth. The other animls said he was ugly, and they laughed at him.

'It is foolish to carry sharp things in the mouth,' said the tortoise.

'I think so too,' said the goat.

The monkey jumped in and began to tease the dog.

'Don't worry, my dear friend,' said the monkey. 'You need your teeth to clear your farm.'

The animals laughed at the monkey's joke.

When the farming season came round, King Leopard led the animals to their farmland. They all worked hard to prepare their plots. At the end of the day they returned home tired. They sat on log benches in the village square. As they rested they told stories and drank palm wine.

But soon it would be the rainy season, and the animals would have no shelter from the rain.

The deer took this problem to King Leopard. They talked about it for a long time. King Leopard decided to call the animals together to discuss it.

One bright morning . . . King Leopard beat his royal drum. When the animals heard the drum, they gathered at the village square. The tortoise was there. The goat was there too. The sheep, the grass-cutter, the monkey, the hedgehog, the baboon, the dog and many others were there.

King Leopard greeted them and said, 'I have called you together to plan how we can make ourselves a common shelter.'

'This is a good idea,' said the giraffe.

'Yes, a very good idea,' said many other animals.

'But why do we need a common house?' said the dog. He had never liked King Leopard.

'The dog has asked a good question,' said the duck. 'Why do we need a common shelter?'

'We do need somewhere to rest when we return from our farms,' replied King Leopard.

'And besides,' said the goat, 'we need a shelter from the rain.'

'I don't mind being wet,' said the duck. 'In fact I like it. I know that the goat does not like water on his body. Let him go and build a shelter.'

'We need a shelter,' said the monkey, jumping up and down in excitement.

'Perhaps we need one, perhaps we don't,' said the lazy baboon sitting on the low fence of the square.

The dog spoke again. 'We are wasting our time. Those who need a shelter should build it. I live in a cave, and it is enough for me.' Then he walked away. The duck followed him out.

'Does anyone else want to leave?' asked King Leopard. No one answered or made a move to go.

'Very well,' said King Leopard. 'Let the rest of us build the village hall.'

The animals soon scattered about to find building materials. The tortoise copied the pattern on his back, and made the plan of the roof. The giant rat and mouse dug the foundation. Some animals brought sticks, some ropes, others made roof-mats.

As they built the house, they sang many happy songs. They also told many jokes. Although they worked very hard everyone was merry.

After many weeks they finished the building.

It was a fine building. The animals were pleased with it. They agreed to open it with a very special meeting.

On the opening day the animals, their wives and children gathered in the hall. King Leopard then made a short speech. He said: 'This hall is yours to enjoy. You worked very hard together to build it. I am proud of you.'

The animals clapped their hands and gave three cheers to their king.

From that day, they rested in their new hall whenever they returned from their farm.

But the dog and the duck kept away from the hall.

One morning the animals went to their farms as usual. King Leopard went to visit a chief in another village.

At first the sun was shining. Then strong winds began to blow. Dark clouds hid the sun. The first rain was coming. The song-birds stopped their singing. The humming insects became quiet. Lightning flashed across the dark clouds. Claps of thunder sounded. The rain poured and poured.

The animals in their farms saw the rain coming and began to hurry to the village hall.

The dog also saw the rain coming and returned to his cave. But it was a very, very heavy rain. Water began to enter the cave. Soon it was flooded.

The dog ran from one end of his cave to the other. But the water followed him everywhere. At last he ran out of the cave altogether and made straight for the hall of the animals.

The deer was already there. He was surprised to see the dog enter the hall.

'What do you want here?' said the deer to the dog.

'It is none of your business,' replied the dog.

'It is my business,' said the deer. 'Please go out, this hall is for those who built it.'

Then the dog attacked the deer and bit him with his big, sharp teeth. The deer cried with pain. The dog seized him by the neck and threw him out into the rain.

The other animals came in one after the other.

The dog barked and threw each of them out. They stood together shivering and crying in the rain. The dog kept barking and showing his teeth.

Then the deer cried out:

O Leopard our noble king,
Where are you?
Spotted king of the forest,
Where are you?
Even if you are far away
Come, hurry home:
The worst has happened to us
The worst has happened to us . . .
The house the animals built
The cruel dog keeps us from it,
The common shelter we built
The cruel dog keeps us from it,
The worst has happened to us
The worst has happened to us . . .

The cry of the deer rang out loud and clear. It was carried by the wind. King Leopard heard it on his way back from his journey and began to run towards the village hall.

As he got near, he saw the animals, wet and sheltering under a tree. They were all crying. As he got nearer still, he could see the dog walking up and down inside the hall.

King Leopard was very angry. 'Come out of the hall at once,' he said to the dog. The dog barked and rushed at him. They began to fight. The dog bit the leopard and tore his skin with his claws. King Leopard was covered with blood. The dog went back to the hall. He stood at the door barking and barking. 'Who is next? Who! Who!' he barked.

King Leopard turned to the animals and said: 'Let us go in together and drive out the enemy. He is strong, but he is alone. We are many. Together we can drive him out of our house.'

But the goat said: 'We cannot face him. Look at his strong teeth! He will only tear us to pieces!'

'The goat is right,' said the animals. 'He is too strong for us.'

The tortoise stood up and said: 'I am sure we are all sorry about what has happened to the leopard. But he was foolish to talk to the dog the way he did. It is foolish to annoy such a powerful person as the dog. Let us make peace with him. I don't know what you others think. But I think he should have been our king all along. He is strong; he is handsome. Let us go on our knees and salute him.'

'Hear! Hear!' said all the animals. 'Hail the dog!'

Tears began to roll down the face of the leopard. His heart was heavy. He loved the animals greatly. But they had turned their backs on him. Now he knew they were cowards. So he turned his back on them and went away. Because of his many wounds he was weak and tired. So he lay down after a while to rest under a tree, far from the village.

The animals saw him go. But they did not care. They were too busy praising their new king, the dog. The tortoise carved a new staff for him. The toad made a new song in his praise:

> The dog is great
> The dog is good
> The dog gives us our daily food.
> We love his head, we love his jaws
> We love his feet and all his claws.

The dog looked round the circle of animals and asked, 'Where is the leopard?'

'We think he has gone away, O King,' said the goat.

'Why? He has no right to go away,' said the dog. 'Nobody has a right to leave our village and its beautiful hall. We must all stay together.'

'Indeed,' shouted the animals, 'We must stay together! The leopard must return to the village! Our wise king has spoken! It is good to have a wise king!'

The dog then called out the names of six strong animals and said to them: 'Go at once and bring back the leopard. If he should refuse to follow you, you must drag him along. If we let him go, others may soon follow his wicked example until there is no one left in our village. That would be a very bad thing indeed. It is my duty as your king to make sure that we all live together. The leopard is a wicked animal. That is why he wants to go away and live by himself. It is our duty to stop him. Nobody has a right to go away from our village and our beautiful hall.'

'Nobody has a right to go away from the village,' sang all the animals as the six messengers went to look for the leopard.

They found him resting under the tree beyond the village. Although he was wounded and weak he still looked like a king. So the six messengers stood at a little distance and spoke to him.

'Our new king, the dog, has ordered you to return to the village,' they said.

'He says that no one has a right to leave the village,' said the pig.

'Yes, no one has a right to leave our village and its beautiful hall,' said the others.

The leopard looked at them with contempt. Then he got up slowly. The six animals fell back. But the leopard did not go towards them. He turned his back on them and began to go away – slowly and painfully. One of the animals picked up a stone and threw it at him. Then all the others immediately picked up stones and began to throw. As they threw they chanted: 'No one has a right to leave our village! No one has a right to leave our village!'

Although some of the stones hit the leopard and hurt him, he did not turn round even once. He continued walking until he no longer heard the noise of the animals.

The leopard travelled seven days and seven nights. Then he came to the house of the blacksmith. The old man was sitting at his forge. The leopard said to him: 'I want the strongest teeth you can make from iron. And I want the most deadly claws you can make from bronze.'

The blacksmith said: 'Why do you need such terrible things?' The leopard told his story. Then the blacksmith said: 'I do not blame you.'

The blacksmith worked a whole day on the teeth, and another full day on the claws. The leopard was pleased with them. He put them on and thanked the blacksmith. Then he left and went to the house of Thunder.

The leopard knocked at the door and Thunder roared across the sky.

'I want some of your sound in my voice,' said the leopard. 'Even a little bit.'

'Why do you want my sound in your voice?' asked Thunder. 'And why have you got those terrible teeth and claws?'

The leopard told his story. 'I do not blame you,' said Thunder. He gave the sound to the leopard. 'Thank you for the gift,' said the leopard. And he began his journey home.

The leopard journeyed for seven days and seven nights and returned to the village of the animals. There he found the animals dancing in a circle round the dog. He stood for a while watching them with contempt and great anger. They were too busy to notice his presence. He made a deep, terrifying roar. At the same time he sprang into the centre of the circle. The animals stopped their song. The dog dropped his staff. The leopard seized him and bit and clawed him without mercy. Then he threw him out of the circle.

All the animals TREMBLED.

But they were too afraid to run. The leopard turned to them and said:

'You miserable worms. You shameless cowards. I was a kind and gentle king, but you turned against me. From today I shall rule the forest with terror. The life of our village is ended.'

'What about our hall?' asked the tortoise with a trembling voice.

'Let everyone take from the hall what he put into it,' said the leopard.

The animals began to weep as they had wept long ago in the rain. 'Please forgive us, O Leopard,' they cried.

'Let everyone take from the hall what he put into it,' repeated the leopard. 'And hurry up!' he thundered.

So the animals pulled their hall apart. Some carried away the wood, and some took the roof-mats. Others took away doors and windows. The toad brought his talking drum and began to beat it to the leopard and to sing:

> Alive or dead the leopard is king.
> Beware my friend, don't twist his tail.

But the leopard roared like thunder and the toad dropped his drum and the animals scattered in the forest.

The dog had already run a long way when the leopard roared. Now he ran faster and faster. His body was covered with blood, and he was very, very weak. He wanted to stop and rest a little. But the fear of the leopard was greater than his weakness. So he staggered and fell and got up and staggered on and on and on . . .

After many days the dog came to the house of the hunter.

'Please protect me from the leopard,' he cried.

'What will you do for me in return?' asked the hunter.

'I will be your slave,' said the dog. 'Any day you are hungry for meat I shall show you the way to the forest. There we can hunt together and kill my fellow animals.'

'All right, come in,' said the hunter.

Today the animals are no longer friends, but enemies. The strong among them attack and kill the weak. The leopard, full of anger, eats up anyone he can lay his hands on. The hunter, led by the dog, goes to the forest from time to time and shoots any animals he can find. Perhaps the animals will make peace among themselves some day and live together again. Then they can keep away the hunter who is their common enemy.

Chinua Achebe and John Iroaganachi, with 'The Lament of the Deer'
by Christopher Okigbo
(Nigeria)

The 'Wraith-Island'

Then we started our journey in another bush, of course, it was full of Islands and swamps and the creatures of the Islands were very kind, because as soon as we reached there, they received us with kindness and gave us a lovely house in their town to live in. The name of the Island was called 'Wraith-Island', it was very high and it was entirely surrounded by water; all the people of the Island were very kind and they loved themselves, their work was only to plant their food, after that, they had no other work more than to play music and dance. They were the most beautiful creatures in the world of the curious creatures and also the most wonderful dancers and musicians, they were playing music and dancing throughout the day and night. But as the weather of the Island was suitable for us and when we saw that we should not leave there at once, we were dancing with them and doing as they were doing there. Whenever these Island creatures dress, you would be thinking they were human beings and their children were performing always the stage plays. As we were living with them I became a farmer and planted many kinds of crops. But one day, as the crops had ripened enough there, I saw a terrible animal coming to the farm and eating the crops, but one morning I met him there, so I started to drive him away from the farm, of course I could not approach him as he was as big as an elephant. His fingernails were long to about two feet, his head was bigger than his body ten times. He had a large mouth which was full of long teeth, these teeth were about one foot long and as thick as a cow's horns, his body was almost covered with black long hair like a horse's tail-hair. He was very dirty. There were five horns on his head and curved and levelled to the head, his four feet were as big as a log of wood. But as I could not go near him, I stoned him at a long distance, but before the stone could reach him, he had reached where I stood and got ready to fight me.

Then I thought over that how could I escape from this fearful animal. Not knowing that he was the owner of the land on which I planted the crops, by that critical time, he was angry that I did not sacrifice to him before I planted crops there, but when I understood what he wanted from me, then I cut some of the crops and gave him, so when he saw what I gave him, then he made a sign that I should mount his back and I mounted his back, and by that time I did not hear him any more, then he took me to his house which was not so far from the farm. When we reached there, he bent down and I dismounted from his back, after that he entered his house and brought out four grains of corn, four grains of rice and four seeds of okra and gave them to me, then I went back to the farm and planted them all at the same time. But to my surprise, these grains and the seeds germinated at once, before five minutes they became full-grown crops and before ten minutes again, they had produced fruits and ripened at the same moment too, so I plucked them and went back to the town (the Wraith-Island).

But after the crops had produced the last fruits and when dried, I cut them and kept their seeds as a reference as we were travelling about in the bush.

'Not Too Small To Be Chosen'

There were many wonderful creatures in the olden days. One day, the king of the 'Wraith-Island' town chose all the people, spirits and terrible creatures of the Island to help him to clear his corn-field which was about two miles square. Then one fine morning, we gathered together and went to the corn-field, and cleared it away, after that, we returned to the king and told him that we had cleared his corn-field, he thanked us, and gave us food and drink.

But as a matter of fact none of the creatures is too small to choose for a help. We did not know that immediately we left the field, a tiny creature who was not chosen with us by the king went to the field and

commanded all the weeds that we had cleared to grow up as if they were
not cleared.

He was saying thus: 'THE KING OF THE "WRAITH-ISLAND" BEGGED
ALL THE CREATURES OF THE "WRAITH-ISLAND" AND LEFT HIM OUT, SO
THAT, ALL THE CLEARED WEEDS RISE UP; AND LET US GO AND DANCE TO
A BAND AT THE "WRAITH-ISLAND"; IF BAND COULD NOT SOUND, WE
SHOULD DANCE WITH MELODIOUS MUSIC.'

But at the same time that the tiny creature commanded the weeds, all
rose up as if the field was not cleared for two years. Then early in the
morning of the second day that we had cleared it, the king went to the
field to visit his corn, but to his surprise, he met the field uncleared, then
he returned to the town and called the whole of us and asked that why
did we not clear his field? We replied that we had cleared it yesterday,
but the king said no, we did not clear it. Then the whole of us went to
the field to witness it, but we saw the field as if it was not cleared as the
king said. After that we gathered together and went to clear it as before,
then we returned to the king again and told him that we had cleared it.
But when he went there, he found it uncleared as before and came back
to the town and told us again that we did not clear his field, then the
whole of us ran to the field and found it uncleared. So we gathered
together for the third time and went to clear it, after we had cleared it,
we told one of us to hide himself inside a bush which was very close to
the field, but before thirty minutes that he was watching the field, he
saw a very tiny creature who was just a baby of one day of age and he
commanded the weeds to rise up as he was commanding before. Then
that one of us who hid himself inside the bush and was watching him
tried all his efforts and caught him, then he brought him to the king;
when the king saw the tiny creature, he called the whole of us to his
palace.

After that, the king asked him who was commanding the cleared
weeds of his field to rise up after the field had been cleared: The tiny
creature replied that he was commanding all the weeds to rise up,
because the king chose all the creatures of the 'Wraith-Island' town but
left him out, although he was the smallest among all, but he had the
power to command weeds etc. which had been cleared to grow up as if
it was not cleared at all. But the king said that he had just forgotten to
choose him with the rest and not because of his small appearance.

Then the king made excuses to him, after that he went away. This was a very wonderful tiny creature.

After we (my wife and I) had completed a period of eighteen months in this 'Wraith-Island', then I told them that we wished to continue our journey, because we were not reaching our destination at all. But as the creatures of this Island were very kind, they gave my wife many expensive articles as gifts then we packed all our loads and when it was early in the morning, the whole people of the 'Wraith-Island' led us with a big canoe and they were singing the song of 'goodbye' as they were paddling along on the river. When they accompanied us to their boundary, they stopped, but when we went down from their canoe, then they returned to their town with a lovely song and music and bade us goodbye. If it was in their power, they would have led us to our destination, but they were forbidden to touch another creature's land or bush.

Amos Tutuola (Nigeria)
Excerpt from *The Palm-Wine Drinkard*

Justice

A woman one day went out to look for her goats that had wandered away from the herd. She walked back and forth over the fields for a long time without finding them. She came at last to a place by the side of the road where a deaf man sat before a fire brewing himself a cup of coffee. Not realizing he was deaf, the woman asked:

'Have you seen my herd of goats come this way?'

The deaf man thought she was asking for the water-hole, so he pointed vaguely toward the river.

The woman thanked him and went to the river. And there, by coincidence, she found the goats. But a young kid had fallen among the rocks and broken its foot.

She picked it up to carry it home. As she passed the place where the deaf man sat drinking his coffee, she stopped to thank him for his help. And in gratitude she offered him the kid.

But the deaf man didn't understand a word she was saying. When she held the kid toward him he thought she was accusing him of the animal's misfortune, and he became very angry.

'I had nothing to do with it!' he shouted.

'But you pointed the way,' the woman said.

'It happens all the time with goats!' the man shouted.

'I found them right where you said they would be,' the woman replied.

'Go away and leave me alone, I never saw him before in my life!' the man shouted.

People who came along the road stopped to hear the argument.

The woman explained to them:

'I was looking for the goats and he pointed toward the river. Now I wish to give him this kid.'

'Do not insult me in this way!' the man shouted loudly. 'I am not a leg-breaker!' And in his anger he struck the woman with his hand.

'Ah, did you see? He struck me with his hand!' the woman said to the people. 'I will take him before the judge!'

So the woman with the kid in her arms, the deaf man, and the spectators went to the house of the judge. The judge came out before his house to listen to their complaint. First, the woman talked, then the man talked, then people in the crowd talked. The judge sat nodding his head. But that meant very little, for the judge, like the man before him, was very deaf. Moreover, he was also very near-sighted.

At last, he put up his hand and the talking stopped. He gave them his judgement.

'Such family rows are a disgrace to the Emperor and an affront to the Church,' he said solemnly. He turned to the man.

'From this time forward, stop mistreating your wife,' he said.

He turned to the woman with the young goat in her arms.

'As for you, do not be so lazy. Hereafter do not be late with your husband's meals.'

He looked at the baby goat tenderly.

'And as for the beautiful infant, may she have a long life and grow to be a joy to you both!'

The crowd broke up and the people went their various ways.

'Ah, how good it is!' they said to each other. 'How did we ever get along before justice was given to us?'

(Ethiopia)

How a Woman Tamed Her Husband*

Once there was a woman who was greatly troubled by her husband. He no longer loved her. He neglected her and seemed to care little whether she was happy or sad.

So the woman took her troubles to the local witch-doctor. She told him her story, full of pity for herself and her sad plight. 'Can you give me a charm to make him love me again?' she asked anxiously.

The witch-doctor thought for a moment and replied. 'I will help you, but first you must bring to me three hairs from the mane of a living lion. These I must have before I can make the charm for you.'

The woman thanked the witch-doctor and went away. When she came near to her home she sat down on a rock and began to think, 'How shall I do this thing? There is a lion who comes often near to my village, it is true. But he is fierce and roars fearfully.' Then she thought again and at last she knew what she would do.

And so, rising early next morning she took a young lamb and went to the place where the lion was accustomed to stroll about. She waited anxiously. At last she saw the lion approaching. Now was the time. Quickly she rose and, leaving the lamb in the path of the lion, she went home. And so it was that every day early in the morning the woman would arise and take a young lamb to the lion. Soon the lion came to know the woman, for she was always in the same place at the same time every day with a young and tender lamb, which she brought for his pleasure. She was indeed a kind and attentive woman.

It was not long before the lion began to wag his tail each time he saw her and coming close to her he would let her stroke his head and soothe his back. And each day the woman would stay quietly stroking the lion, gently and lovingly. Then one day when she knew that the lion trusted her she carefully pulled three hairs from his mane and happily set out for the witch-doctor's dwelling.

'See,' she said triumphantly as she entered, 'here they are!' And she gave him the three hairs from the lion's mane.

'How is it you have been so clever?' asked the witch-doctor in amazement.

And so the woman told him the story of how she had patiently won the hairs from the lion.

A smile spread over the face of the witch-doctor and, leaning forward, he said, 'In the same way that you have tamed the lion, so may you tame your husband.'

(Ethiopia)
Retold by Professor Murad Kamel

Truth and Falsehood

Fène-Falsehood had grown big and learnt much. But there were many things that he still did not know, amongst others that man – and woman even less – bears no resemblance to the good Lord. So he took umbrage, and thought himself hard done by, every time he heard anyone say, 'The good Lord loves Truth!' And he heard it very often. It is true that some people said that Truth and Falsehood were as like as two peas, but the majority stated that Truth and Falsehood were like night and day. That is why, when one day he set out on a journey with Deug-Truth, Fène-Falsehood said to his travelling companion:

'You are the one whom the Lord loves, you are the one whom people no doubt prefer, so it is you who must do the talking wherever we go. For if I were recognized we should be very badly received.'

They set out early one morning and walked for a long time. At midday they entered the first house in the village which they had reached. After the exchange of greetings they had to ask before being given anything to drink. Then the mistress of the house gave them some lukewarm water, which would have made an ostrich vomit, in a calabash of doubtful cleanliness. She showed no signs of giving them anything to eat, although a pot full of rice was boiling at the entrance to the hut. The travellers lay down in the shade of a baobab in the middle of the courtyard and waited for the good Lord, that is to say luck and the return of the master of the house. The latter came back at twilight and asked for food for himself and the strangers.

'I've nothing ready yet,' said the woman, who could not have devoured the contents of the pot unaided.

The husband flew into a great rage, not only on his own account, although he was famished after spending the whole day working in the fields under the blazing sun, but because of his unknown guests, who had been left with empty bellies, and whom he had not been able to honour as any self-respecting master of a house should do. He asked:

'Is this the action of a good wife? Is this the action of a generous woman? Is this a good housewife?'

Fène-Falsehood, as agreed, prudently said nothing, but Deug-Truth could not keep silent. She answered frankly that a woman worthy of the name of mistress of the house might have been more hospitable to strangers, and ought always to have food prepared for her husband's return.

Then the woman flew into a furious rage and, threatening to arouse the whole village, ordered her husband to throw out of her house these impertinent strangers, who interfered with the way she ran her home and took it upon themselves to give her advice; otherwise she would return to her parents on the spot. So the poor husband, who could not see himself managing without a wife (even a bad housekeeper) and without any cooking, all on account of two passing strangers, whom he had never seen before and whom he would probably never see again in his life, was forced to tell the travellers to be on their way. Did they not remember that even if life was not all *couscous* it did nevertheless need some softening? Did they have to be so ill-bred as to say things so crudely?

So Deug and Fène continued their journey which had begun so inauspiciously. They walked for a long time till they reached a village where they found some children busy sharing out a fat bull which they had just slaughtered. On entering the house of the village headman, they saw some children saying to him,

'Here is your share,' and they gave him the head and the feet of the animal.

Now, since time immemorial, since N'Diadiane n'Diaye, in every village inhabited by man, it is the headman who distributes the meat, and chooses his own share – the best.

'Who do you think commands here, in this village?' the headman asked the travellers.

Fène-Falsehood prudently kept silent and did not open his mouth; Deug-Truth was obliged, as agreed, to give her opinion:

'To all appearances,' she said, 'it is these children.'

'You are most insolent!' cried the old man in a fury. 'Leave this village! Go, go immediately, or you will never leave it again! Begone, begone!'

As they went, Fène said to Deug:

'The results have not been brilliant so far, and I am not sure that they will be any better if I leave you in charge of our affairs any longer. So from now on I am going to look after both of us. I am beginning to think that even if the good Lord loves you, man does not appreciate you very much.'

Not knowing how they would be received in the village they were now approaching, from which came cries and lamentations, Deug and Fène stopped at the well before calling at any dwelling, and were quenching their thirst when a woman came along, all in tears.

'What is the meaning of these cries and tears?' asked Deug-Truth.

'Alas!' said the woman (who was a slave), 'our favourite queen, the youngest of the king's wives, died yesterday, and the king is so heart-sore that he wants to kill himself so that he may join the woman who was the fairest and most gracious of his wives.'

'And is that the sole cause of so much lamentation?' asked Fène-Falsehood. 'Go and tell the king that there is at the well a stranger who can bring back to life people who have even been dead for a long time.'

The slave went off and returned a minute later accompanied by an old man who led the travellers into a fine hut, where they found a whole roasted sheep and two calabashes full of couscous.

'My master brings you here,' said the old man, 'and bids you rest after your long journey. He bids you wait and he will send for you before long.'

The next day an even more copious meal was brought before the strangers and the day after the same thing happened. But Fène pretended to be angry and impatient; he said to the messengers:

'Go, tell your king that I have no time to waste here, and that I shall continue on my way if he has no need of me.'

An old man returned to say:

'The king is asking for you.' Fène followed him, leaving Deug in the hut.

'First, what do you desire as a reward for what you are about to do?' asked the king, when he came before him.

'What can you offer me?' replied Fène-Falsehood.

'I will give you one hundred things from all that I possess in this land.'

'That will not satisfy me,' Fène reckoned.

'Then you yourself say what you desire,' suggested the king.

'I desire the half of all that you possess.'

The king agreed.

Fène had a hut built above the grave of the favourite and went in alone, armed with a hoe. He could be heard puffing and panting; then, after a long time, he began to talk, softly at first, then in a loud voice as if he were arguing with several persons. At length he came out of the hut and stood with his back pressed firmly against the door.

'Things are getting very complicated,' he said to the king. 'I have dug up the grave, and woken up your wife, but scarcely had she returned to life and was about to emerge from beneath the ground, than your father woke up too and seized her by the feet, saying to me, "Leave this woman alone. What can she give you? Whereas if *I* return to earth, I will give you my son's whole fortune." He had barely finished making me this proposition, than *his* father emerged in his turn and offered me all his goods and half the property of his son. Your grandfather was elbowed out of the way by your father's grandfather, who offered me your property, your father's property, his son's property and the half of his own fortune. Scarcely had he finished speaking than *his* father arrived, so that your ancestors and the forebears of your ancestors are all now at the exit of your wife's grave.'

King Bour looked at his advisers, and the notables looked at the king. The stranger was quite right when he'd said that things were in a mess. Bour gazed at Fène-Falsehood, and the old men looked at him. What was to be done?

'To help you out of your dilemma, and to avoid too difficult a choice,' said Fène-Falsehood, 'just give me an idea of whom I should bring back, your wife or your father?'

'My wife!' cried the king, who loved the favourite more than ever. He had always been afraid of the late king, and had in fact precipitated his death with the assistance of the notables of the land.

'Naturally, naturally!' replied Fène-Falsehood. 'Only you see, your father did offer me double what you promised me just now.'

Bour turned towards his advisers, and the advisers gazed at him and at the stranger. The price was high, and what good would it do the king to see his beloved wife again if he were deprived of all his goods? Would he still be king? Fène guessed the thoughts of the king and of his notables.

'Unless,' he said, 'unless you give me, for leaving your wife where she is at present, what you promised me to bring her back.'

'That is certainly the best and most reasonable thing to do!' replied the notables in chorus, remembering how they had helped to get rid of the old king.

'What do you say, Bour?' asked Fène-Falsehood.

'Oh well, let my father, my father's father, and their fathers' fathers remain where they are, and my wife likewise,' said the king.

And so it was that Fène-Falsehood received half the king's goods for bringing no one back from the other world, while the king himself soon forgot his favourite and took another wife.

Wolof (Senegal)
Retold by Amadou Koumba; rendered in French by Birago Diop
Translated from the French by Dorothy S. Blair

Madam Universe Sent Man

As all kids and grown-ups well know, the Universe is made up of all sorts of objects, from the smallest sub-atomic particles to the mightiest stars. A very long time ago, well before grand, grand, grand, grand, grand Ma was born, and even before that time, the Universe was already in existence. That makes the Universe the oldest person around today.

The Universe was the only daughter of her parents and she grew up pampered and spoilt. By the time she was old enough to get married, she had gotten too fat from eating too much candies. Her tummy, in particular, was so out of shape that she looked forever pregnant.

She used to fill her huge bowl of a stomach with all sorts of dregs, because she was always hungry. The parents spent so much money feeding her that they soon were as poor as a church rat.

Her marriage was a great relief to her parents somehow, although they madly loved their only daughter. They were glad to have assistance with the feeding of their ever hungry daughter. The husband could not do much either. Every kobo of his monthly wages went into feeding Madam Universe and yet she kept complaining of hunger.

To try to keep her hunger pangs under control, she began to devour what ever looked chewable, no matter its food content and before long she had, floating in her tummy, substances ranging from gas and dust to small particles of stone and iron.

Several of these floating things quite often got stuck to each other, and some condensed to become the lumps of indigestible junk which today go by the names of Sun, Mercury, Venus, Earth, Mars, Jupiter, Saturn, Uranus, Neptune and Pluto.

Apart from these debris, which some people call planets, Madam Universe has, floating in her bottomless pit of a stomach, numerous chunks of rock which experts refer to as asteroids. The largest of these rocks is the one called Ceres.

Madam Universe's belly also contains millions of stars, many of which are as colourful, bright, old and large as the Sun.

It is all of the stars and planets and rocks and dust and iron and gas combined that cause Madam Universe to have the chronic belly-aches that she always has. The last time she had such pains, she screamed thunder and lightning for days, frightening all of us to death, but she does not seem to care. As soon as she recovers from one belly-ache, she is busy again, munching all the trash she can lay her hands on.

Because of all the garbage in her tummy, satellites continue to collide and explode, causing more fireworks and clouds and dust and gas and millions of flying missiles.

The stars are in perpetual motion, and have, floating around them, a collection of dust, gas, clouds and millions of other celestial bodies in a seemingly predetermined pattern. There are millions of stars in the Universe, some large, some very tiny compared to the size of the Earth. They form numerous clusters known as galaxies, the most well-known being the Andromeda Nebula and, of course, our own Milky Way.

The Milky Way formation is only visible from the Earth through a powerful telescope and it is like many millions of satellites swimming in a cluster, in Madam Universe's stomach. This cluster of stars and particles of stone and iron is connected by a gravitational force like a thread, and the entire arrangement looks like a flat wheel with spiral arms. The rather not-too-noticeable star, near the edge of the wheel of the Milky Way, is our very own dear Sun.

The Sun is the most exciting lump of junk in the belly of Madam Universe as far as we are concerned. This is because the Sun is the nearest of all the big bright stars to the Earth, and it gives us life.

The Sun itself is made up of a dense mass of glowing matter. It is roughly spherical in shape and it is some 1,392,000 kilometres across. At the Sun's centre, its temperature is about 13 million degrees Centigrade (a coal fire is about 800 degrees Centigrade). Under such severe heat, all substances near it boil or melt or crack up.

Mercury, Venus, Earth, Mars, Jupiter, Saturn, Uranus, Neptune and Pluto all revolve around the Sun. The planets are near the Sun in the order they are listed, with Mercury the nearest to the Sun of the nine planets.

The planet Earth is the third nearest to the Sun, and so far appears to be the only one with life as we know it.

Besides having us humans, the Earth is a very interesting bit of junk. In shape, it looks like a slightly flattened sphere and it has an equatorial radius of 6,378 kilometres and a polar radius of 6,357 kilometres. It has its own satellite called Moon which is 3,476 kilometres in diameter and only 384,400 kilometres distant from the Earth. The Moon rotates in the same amount of time as it takes to revolve round the Earth: 27 days, 7 hours and 43 minutes. The Moon reflects light from the Sun and, of course, it is a very poor reflector at that, so we have developed electricity to assist the Moon and brighten up our nights.

The Earth's structure is in three main units. The core or the centre is, in radius, half that of Earth. Outside this core is the unit known as the mantle and outside the mantle we have the crust. The crust varies in thickness from 35 kilometres, under the continents, to 5 kilometres under the oceans.

The centre of the Earth is considered to be made up of iron-nickel alloy. The mantle is of magnesium-rich silicates. Volcanic lava is formed in the mantle of Earth, so, much of the mantle is soft and liquid. The continental crust developed from thousands of millions of years of welding together of mountain belts of different ages. The oceanic crust consists of what is called basalt lava, and is thought by scientists to be only 250 million years old.

What all of these statistics add up to is that the Earth is very very old indeed. In fact, it is over 5,000 million years old and it is very rich in minerals, particularly in parts of it.

Other parts are almost entirely barren, while others still are very volcanic in nature. By and large, the Earth is a sweet bit of junk to own and preserve and to do this job, Madam Universe sent Man.

Madam Universe told Man, look here my kid, I am sending you to Earth to be master of all its gold and diamonds and silver and iron, and animals that crawl or walk and mangoes and oranges and stuff. Madam Universe told Man that everything on Earth is his to manage, enjoy and where possible improve upon. And Man said, me, you mean all these are for me, and Madam Universe said yes my boy. But Madam Universe gave Man just one condition and that was that Man was to multiply.

Now, that baffled Man for a while because he thought Madam Universe was trying to set him arithmetic, and he didn't like arithmetic. So Madam Universe came to Man's aid by providing him with a woman, who, with the help of the Man, was to fill the whole Earth with babies. Well, Madam Universe did this because she did not want vacancies to occur in the management of the Earth's resources. She did not want to have to advertise for such vacancies because advertising costs too much and causes delays. Madam Universe arranged things so that the management of the Earth would pass directly from parents to their children.

Man saw that the arrangement was clever and he worked hard with his Mrs to produce helpers for their increasingly difficult occupation of food-gathering, hunting and looking after their cave.

A few months after they got married, Mrs Man's stomach began to swell like a balloon and this got her really worried. At first, they tried to press the stomach down with their hands, it did not work. Then, they used ropes and herbs and yet the stomach got bigger and bigger, so they gave up.

Just as Mrs Man was beginning to feel like she was going to burst open, she started to have labour pains, resulting in the birth of a beautiful bouncing baby boy. It was the first baby to be born on Earth and he was dark brown in colour with rich curly Afro hair like the parents. The parents were delighted that they could reproduce themselves. They called the baby Dudu, meaning dark and beautiful. The parents showered the child with love and affection, being their first child, and the child grew up strong, healthy, tall, lively, quick to learn and full of smiles. A very happy child. The parents were so satisfied with the way Dudu was developing that they were soon busy again trying to make another baby.

Three years after the birth of Dudu, the parents had a baby girl they called Asia, because of the way the child sneezed as soon as she was born. Asia too, was beautiful but not as dark as her parents or Dudu. She was rather on the small side, but she had a crown of luxuriously straight dark hair on her head. To the parents, she was simply a precious jewel.

Four years after Asia was born, Mrs Man gave birth to their third child, who eventually turned out to be their last. The child was a boy, but this time, he had rich long straight hair on his head and almost transparent skin. The parents were worried about his transparent pale colour and feared that he might not live. They called him Ebo, meaning the delicate and transparent one. Every member of the family devoted time and effort to keep Ebo alive.

Mr and Mrs Man used most of their spare moments on the education of their three kids, teaching them to respect their parents and each other and to always work as a family. Every night mother and father took turns to formulate and tell the children stories and sing them nursery rhymes.

As the children became old enough, they were gradually introduced to the hazardous life of trying to fend for themselves. The boys would follow their father out on hunting and food-gathering trips while Asia stayed home to help mother with domestic chores.

The family stayed close for many years enjoying and suffering good and bad times together while the children gained confidence in their individual abilities.

From the age of fifteen, however, Ebo was already itching to break away from the family and be on his own. He kept nagging the parents about this until the parents called the family together to share out the Earth among the three children. The parents insisted, though, that none of the children was to leave home until both of them, the parents, were dead.

Mr Man was the first to die and the speculation was that he lived for nearly one hundred and fifty years. The wife died eight years after him at the ripe old age of a hundred and fifty-four years.

Within two weeks of burying their mother, Ebo left to set up a new home on his property which he named Europe.

Asia was a little reluctant to be separated from her senior brother so soon. Besides, she was scared to venture so far out by herself because she had never been alone before.

As for Dudu, he did not have to pack and move because he had inherited the parents' old hut and land. Dudu's land was considered poor for food-gathering and hunting because the family had exploited the land for over 150 years. Dudu called his property Africa.

Ebo was supposed to have the best land bargain of the three children, followed by Asia. In fact, while Asia was slowly preparing to move to her property she offered Dudu the opportunity of moving with her. All that Dudu would say at the time was that he might take Asia up on her offer later, depending on how soon life started getting too tough for him in Africa.

The morning that Asia was to finally leave home, Madam Universe suddenly appeared, full of apologies for neglecting the children for so long. Asia was the first to complain that she needed a companion now that she was going to be so far away from her brothers. Dudu too suggested that he could do with a helper, and Madam Universe said she would do better than that. Madam Universe provided Dudu with a wife, Asia with a husband and arranged for Ebo's wife to join him in Europe. With that settled, the children were ready to live their separate lives, independent of each other.

Asia and her husband moved to their new world which she called Asia. Dudu and wife changed location from North to West Africa and Dudu renamed his parents' old settlement the 'Sahara desert'.

For several years, the three families lived happily on their separate properties. They all prospered and raised very large families. As their children became old enough, they got married and moved to other parts of their individual parents' properties to set up home and raise their own families.

The children named their new settlements mostly after themselves. In Europe they settled Germany, Austria, Britain, France, Portugal, Spain,

Italy and so on. Ebo's children even spread as far afield as Sweden and Russia.

Asia's children settled China, India, Japan, Mongolia, Tibet, and Dudu's children moved into areas they called Zululand, Congo, Sudan, Ethiopia, Zimbabwe, Somalia, Egypt and so on.

Ebo's children, like their father, were very aggressive by nature and were soon fighting and grabbing territories from each other. With increased fighting between them, Ebo's children gradually perfected their weapons of intimidation and death.

In the meantime, Dudu's children, in Africa, were basking in their infinite sunshine, very much at peace with one another. As for Asia's children, although they had had minor skirmishes, by and large, they, like Dudu's children, had not really progressed from the bow and arrow age.

It was only a matter of time before Ebo's children started turning their attention from fighting each other in Europe to fighting each other in Africa.

At first, Dudu's children welcomed their cousins from Europe with open arms as is the African tradition. They treated their guests to endearing melodies and food and encouraged them to share in their abundant wealth and warm weather.

Very soon, Ebo's children were feeling comfortable enough to fight each other over who had first landed on what bits of Africa. Then they started fighting over who was to have the lion's share of Africa's flourishing minerals and people.

Ebo's children captured Africans with trickery and superior weapons to enslave them in the new worlds of North and South America. The Africans who resisted capture, they killed, and it is estimated that over 100 million Africans were murdered by Ebo's children during the slave trade alone.

The Africans that were too fast on their feet to be captured or killed, and those that were not captured because they were too young or old or sick, were enticed with strange religions and articles of no value and assembled in political prisons in Africa, which Ebo's children proudly proclaimed dominions and colonies.

While those Africans who survived the torture of the middle passage across the Atlantic Ocean were watering arid sands with their sweat to build America, millions of their kin were being massacred in Africa by Ebo's children. The rest were slaving for Ebo's children to loot and plunder Africa's plentiful gold, silver and diamonds to build London, Paris, Hamburg, Lisbon, Moscow and so on.

Right now, Ebo's children are still busy at it, robbing Africa, even though they have reluctantly granted some of their colonies paper independence.

No African country has yet regained her economic independence. Madam Universe has said she is hoping that one day soon, Dudu's children in America, West Indies, Africa and wherever they may be in the world, would begin to work together as a family, to rescue the left-overs, if any, of Ebo's children's spoliation of mineral-rich Africa.

Naiwu Osahon (Nigeria)

The Song of a Twin Brother

(To Kofi Awoonor)

Stand unshod upon the terrazzo floor of your balcony.
Look over the barricade
    to the savannah grasslands of your countryside.
Silence the stereo sound of your radiogram.
Open your soul
    to the mellow tones of your rustic brother's xylophone;
    so many moons ago,
    before our world grew old,
    I had a twin brother
    We sucked the same breast,
        walked the same earth
    but dreamt of worlds apart.
Here I am today, holding on to grandfather's sinking boat
    while Atsu, my twin brother,
    floats on air in a jumbo jet
        and stares into the skies
        and dreams of foreign ports.

Atsu e e e !
Atsu e e e ! !
>   Do not forget the back, without which there is no front.
>   Dada is still alive, but grown silent
>   and full of songs sung in a voice
>   that hints of a heart overstrained
>   with the burdens of a clan without elders.

>   Our roof is now a sieve, Atsu,
>   The rains beat us, and beat us.
>   Even in our dreams.
>   And the gods, they say, are not to blame
>   The State farms have burnt the thatch and dug its roots
>   They grow rice and cane sugar,

But Oh! Atsu.
My twin brother Atsu!
>   Our bowels are not made for the tasty things of life
>   The sugar and rice all go to Accra
>   for people with clean stomachs and silver teeth
>   to eat and expand in their borrowed glory.

Atsu e e !
Atsu lee ! !

>   I shall give your name to the winds.
>   They will roam the world for you.
You forget,
>   Atsu my father's former son,
>   You forget the back, without which there is no front.
Papa has lost his war against hernia.
Seven Keta market-days ago, we gave him back to the soil.
And Dada is full of Nyayito songs,
>   sorrowing songs sung in a voice whose echoes
>   float into the mourning chambers of your soul.

Danyevi lee ! !
>   Dada says,
>   the tasty things of life are good
>   but

do not chase fortune beyond the point
where old sky bends down to have a word with Earth,
do not bury your arm in a fortune-hole.

There have been others before,
                                          Atsu,
There have been others before you.
Armattoe went away,
        came and went again,
        and then he never came.
Katako too went away,
        came and went again
        and then he came – but without his soul.
Atsu,
        I sit under this oak, where you and I once sat
        and cast cowries in the sand.
        I close my eyes and give your name to the winds.

        They will roam and roam and find your ears.
Ffonyevi lee ! !
        Papa has gone to Tsiefe,
        Dada is full of Nyayito songs
        and I, Etse, your twin brother,
        my heart overflows with unsung dirges.

        Many many moons ago,
        Before the silence came,
        I had a twin brother.
                We shared the same mat
                But parted in our dreams.

                                Kofi Anyidoho (Ghana)

The Guest in Your House

The first day in your house,
You more than welcome your guest,
You roast him some fish, you brew him some beer,
You offer him all that is best.

The second day still
You are willing to give
Some milk and some bread,
And so let him live.

On the third day, the food
Becomes somewhat rare—
He may have some rice,
If with you he will share.

On the fourth day, you send him
Out into the fields;
Then after a little bite,
You make him shine up your shields.

The fifth day, your guest
Is as thin as a cricket.
You whisper to your wife,
You've never acted so wicked.

On the sixth day, you hide
So he can't see you;
If you want to eat,
In secret, you so do . . .

On the seventh day, really,
You have had enough!
You throw him out with your fists:
You had to get tough!

You are really not
An unkindly man—
But sometimes one has to
Defend his own stand!

(Tanzania)

The Day of Treachery

Do not be like the people of Ngoneni
Who rushed with warm arms
To embrace a man at the gates
And did likewise on the day of treachery
Embracing the sharp end of the short spears.

                              Mazisi Kunene (Azania)

An Old Politician to a Novice

This old game to which we are committed—
We must play it
Watching each step
As men do that walk
Sheer mountain paths:

Hitch not your hope to others,
That when they slip
They may tumble to their death
Alone,
While you climb on.

Watch!

                              Joe de Graft (Ghana)

Laugh with Happiness

E, you, in sorrow, pay heed to what
    I say,
This world is full of perplexity,
    if you have to continue to live in it.
Till the day you depart, let your
    sorrow turn into laughter.
Laugh I say for laughing is happiness,
    leave behind your sorrows,

Laugh to heal your wounds, laugh to
    send away your troubles,
Laugh to allow the body to grow in
    health and vigour,
Laugh in order to rise should you fall.
Rise and rise again, roll not on the ground,
Rise and laugh, laugh and continue to
    play.
Continue to laugh and in a big way
    you should celebrate.
Let yourself laugh to your heart's
    content, let your face light up
    as you laugh.
God, the creator of this world,
    happiness was His own thing,
Sorrow will perish, laughter is its
    sure cure.
Make it a habit to laugh every day.

Night and day, let happiness have
    its way,
Let no doubt of an impending calamity
    coming your way, forbid that,
    I say,
Laugh with people when it dawns,
    and laugh again when night falls,
Laugh when the sun goes down, and
    be forever resolute,
Your sorrows to ignore for sorrows
    are damaging.
Laugh now with delight in the face
    of distress,
Distress is like a joke, to him who
    laughs.
Laugh ha! ha! ha! it is the way of
    the world,

Laugh, you son and daughter of Adam,
   laugh for the mortal is born to
   laugh,
Laughter is his and her companion
   as sorrow is their enemy.

Sorrows age even when the mortal
   is still young,
Sorrows act as poison to life,
   so avoid sorrows, I say,
Sorrows are corrosive, they bring an
   early death,
So laugh to arrest an early end.

Happiness is a gift bestowed upon
   the mortal,
Even stars as they twinkle
   remind us that this is so.
When clouds clear away, the stars
   in Heaven smile at us,
Light is shed upon the earth,
   bringing waves of happiness,
To the big and small, that happiness
   is both destined.
Laugh, for laughter is tonic to the
   body nourishing it with strength
   and vigour,
The heart looks to better times,
That, to the mortal, is most satisfying.

So I say, laugh kwa! kwa!
   to purify your heart,
Laugh with the beautiful angels in
   heaven where they reside,
Laugh, for doubt not, your turn
   will come.

Shabaan Roberts (Tanzania)
Translated from the Swahili by Ali A. Jahadhmy

On the Eve of Krina*

The great battle was for the next day.

In the evening, to raise the men's spirits, Djata gave a great feast, for he was anxious that his men should wake up happy in the morning. Several oxen were slaughtered and that evening Balla Fasséké, in front of the whole army, called to mind the history of old Mali. He praised Sundiata, seated amidst his lieutenants, in this manner:

'Now I address myself to you, Maghan Sundiata, I speak to you king of Mali, to whom dethroned monarchs flock. The time foretold to you by the jinn is now coming. Sundiata, kingdoms and empires are in the likeness of man; like him they are born, they grow and disappear. Each sovereign embodies one moment of that life. Formerly, the kings of Ghana extended their kingdom over all the lands inhabited by the black man, but the circle has closed and the Cissés of Wagadou are nothing more than petty princes in a desolate land. Today, another kingdom looms up, powerful, the kingdom of Sosso. Humbled kings have borne their tribute to Sosso, Soumaoro's arrogance knows no more bounds and his cruelty is equal to his ambition. But will Soumaoro dominate the world? Are we, the griots of Mali, condemned to pass on to future generations the humiliations which the king of Sosso cares to inflict on our country? No, you may be glad, children of the "Bright Country", for the kingship of Sosso is but the growth of yesterday, whereas that of Mali dates from the time of Bilali. Each kingdom has its childhood, but Soumaoro wants to force the pace, and so Sosso will collapse under him like a horse worn out beneath its rider.

'You, Maghan, you are Mali. It has had a long and difficult childhood like you. Sixteen kings have preceded you on the throne of Niani, sixteen kings have reigned with varying fortunes, but from being village chiefs the Keitas have become tribal chiefs and then kings. Sixteen generations have consolidated their power. You are the outgrowth of Mali just as the silk-cotton tree is the growth of the earth, born of deep and mighty roots. To face the tempest the tree must have long roots and gnarled branches. Maghan Sundiata, has not the tree grown?

'I would have you know, son of Sogolon, that there is not room for two kings around the same calabash of rice. When a new cock comes to the poultry run the old cock picks a quarrel with him and the docile hens wait to see if the new arrival asserts himself or yields. You have come to Mali. Very well, then, assert yourself. Strength makes a law of its own self and power allows no division.

'But listen to what your ancestors did, so that you will know what you have to do.

'Bilali, the second of the name, conquered old Mali. Latal Kalabi conquered the country between the Niger and the Sankarani. By going to Mecca, Lahibatoul Kalabi, of illustrious memory, brought divine blessing upon Mali. Mamadi Kani made warriors out of hunters and bestowed armed strength upon Mali. His son Bamari Tagnokelin, the vindictive king, terrorized Mali with his army, but Maghan Kon Fatta, also called Naré Maghan, to whom you owe your being, made peace prevail and happy mothers yielded Mali a populous youth.

'You are the son of Naré Maghan, but you are also the son of your mother Sogolon, the buffalo-woman, before whom powerless sorcerers shrank in fear. You have the strength and majesty of the lion, you have the might of the buffalo.

'I have told you what future generations will learn about your ancestors, but what will we be able to relate to our sons so that your memory will stay alive, what will we have to teach our sons about you? What unprecedented exploits, what unheard-of feats? By what distinguished actions will our sons be brought to regret not having lived in the time of Sundiata?

'Griots are men of the spoken word, and by the spoken word we give life to the gestures of kings. But words are nothing but words; power lies in deeds. Be a man of action; do not answer me any more with your mouth, but tomorrow, on the plain of Krina, show me what you would have me recount to coming generations. Tomorrow allow me to sing the "Song of the Vultures" over the bodies of the thousands of Sossos whom your sword will have laid low before evening.'

It was on the eve of Krina. In this way Balla Fasséké reminded Sundiata of the history of Mali so that, in the morning, he would show himself worthy of his ancestors.

Mandingo (Guinea and Mali)
Excerpt from the epic *Sundiata* as recited by the griot Mamadou Kouyaté
Transcribed and translated into French by D. T. Niane
Translated from the French by G. D. Pickett

VI — WORK AND PLAY

Children's Planting Song*

Mother, give me peas, I am
   going to sow.
I go, I go, I go, I go to sow,
If it had not been for kitiezo,
   the wild vegetable, hunger
   would have killed us.
When you have meat, you grind
   with a smile on your face.
I go, I go, I go, I go to sow.

Luhya (Kenya)

Fire Song at an Expiation Ceremony

Fire, fire, fire of the hearth below, fire of the hearth above,
Light that shines in the moon, light that shines in the sun,
Star that sparkles at night, star that cleaves the light,
Spirit of the thunder, shining eye of the storm,
Fire of the sun that gives us light,
I summon you for expiation, fire, fire,
Fire that passes, and everything dies behind your track,
Fire that passes, and everything lives behind you,
The trees are burned, ashes and ashes,
The grasses have grown up, the grasses have set seed.
Fire friend to man, I summon you, fire, for expiation.
Fire, I summon you, fire guardian of the hearth,
You pass, they are conquered, none overcomes you,
Fire of the hearth, I summon you for expiation

Fang (Cameroon and Gabon)

214

The Rain-man's Praise-song of Himself

No house is ever too thick-built
To keep me, the rain, from getting in.
I am well known to huts and roofs,
A grandson of Never-Been-There.
I am mother of the finest grasses,
Father of green fields everywhere.
My arrows do not miss their aim,
They strike the owner of huts.
I am a terror to clay walls and the architecture of termites,
Fear-inspiring above and below.
When I pour in the morning, people say:
'He has cut off our lips and stopped our mouths,
He is giving us juicy fruits.
He has rained and brought mushrooms,
White as ivory.'

Aandonga (Angola and Azania)

Girls' Song for the Game of 'Pots'

Leader:
We mould a pot as our mothers did.
The pot, where is the pot?

Chorus:
The pot it is here.
We mould the pot as our mothers did.
First, the base of the pot.

Leader:
Strip by strip and layer by layer,
Supple fingers kneading the clay,
Long fingers moulding the clay,
Stiff thumbs shaping the clay,
Layer by layer and strip by strip,
We build up the pot of our mother.

Chorus:
We build up the pot of our mother,
Strip by strip and layer by layer.
Its belly swells like the paunch of a hyena,
Of a hyena which has eaten a whole sheep.
Its belly swells like a mother of twins.
It is a beautiful pot, the pot of our mother.
It swells like a mother of twins.

Leader:
Oh, clay of the river, bend to our hands,
Curve delicately.
See the strong shoulder and narrow neck.
(In, children, in)
Strip by strip and layer by layer,
Supple fingers kneading,
Long fingers moulding,
Stiff thumbs shaping,
The beautiful pot, the pot of our mother.

All:
The pot, the pot of our mother

Didinga (Uganda)

The *Ogbanje* Healer*

Mama Obu recounted the different incidents which strengthened her suspicion that Obu was an *ogbanje* (a child who is born into the world over and over again). More than one knowledgeable person had said the same thing about the scar on Obu's left cheek. It was a short vertical line which appeared to have been deliberately carved. It was suggested that it had been carved on him by the last family to which he had been born over and over again, when they found him out. With that mark accompanying him to the grave, he could not return to the same family or the mark would expose him. A family desperately in need of a son

was bound to lavish kindness on him, so he had chosen to be born to
Mazi Laza and his wife.

'I had ignored all such suggestions, knowing that it is not unusual for
children to be born with natural marks. Yesterday I changed my mind.'

'Why?' inquired Mazi Laza, fully awake.

'On the advice of Nwakaku, that woman who had such ill luck with
ogbanje children, I called Obiano into my room after lunch to question
him about the mark. As soon as my eyes went to the mark, his eyes lost
their sparkle. By the time I had ended my question, he had developed a
high temperature and begun to shiver as if he would have convulsions.
I had to apply coconut oil on him to lower his temperature.'

'Hm . . . And what do your *ogbanje* experts advise you to do?'

'You ask as if you were a stranger to Umuchukwu, or as if you were
born yesterday!' she retorted.

'Will you keep your voice down?' chided Mazi Laza.

'Why must I keep my voice down?'

'If you can't keep it down, leave my room or I'll leave it for you! I'm
sure I can still catch one bout of sleep before day breaks.'

'All right, I'll keep my voice down,' Mama Obu conceded, speaking
softly. 'But I must say that I'm tired of being treated as if I don't know
what I'm doing or saying. If Obiano doesn't mean anything to you, he
means the whole world to me. I know what I suffered before God sent
him to me; I know all the insults I received. I will not fold my arms and
see anyone snatch him away from me because I know what my condition
will be if he is no more. So when I fret about his welfare, everyone
should recognize that a mad man is not without some common sense.'

'You don't need to tell me what Onyibo means to you as well as to
me,' remarked Mazi Laza, anxious to get to the meat of the matter now
that his wife had released the pent-up steam.

'If he means that much to you, show it!'

'You think I don't?'

'I don't know,' Mama Obu replied.

'Maybe because I don't walk on my head, or because I don't agree to
feed him on eggs and to insulate him from housework. However, that's
another matter which I'll take up with you on another occasion.' After
a brief pause, Mazi Laza went on: 'With regard to the *ogbanje* discussion,
do you now insist on calling that Awa woman to examine him?'

'Yes, unless you know a better method of handling the matter.'

'I don't know what the Catechist will say if he hears that Laza brought a pagan woman to . . .'

'Don't annoy me with that stale story of yours about the Catechist,' cut in Mama Obu. 'The Catechist should not push his mouth into something he knows nothing about. If he chooses to do so, that is his own look-out. If he can remove *ogbanje*, let him tell us; if he cannot, he should shut his mouth and stop interfering with those to whom God has given the power to do so.'

Mazi Laza yielded, but wanted to be given prior notice of the date when the Awa woman would come; that would enable him to arrange an alibi for himself to escape the Catechist's certain query when he got to learn about the visit.

The day the woman came, Mazi Laza left home on his Eagle bicycle early in the morning to collect money from his several debtors. It was only two days before Christmas and he needed the money badly before schools reopened.

Nwomiko, the Awa woman, was the leading *ogbanje* expert for miles around, and she had a hard time keeping her several engagements. She was pint-sized, nothwithstanding the innumerable cocks she received as part of her professional fees. Her little feet alternated so rapidly as she walked that people wondered whether they ever hit the ground before taking off again. She had a pair of sharp, penetrating eyes which saw you before you saw them. She was accompanied by a young girl carrying a long market basket for the fruits of her labour.

As soon as Nwomiko arrived, Mama Obu took her to the kitchen veranda facing the back wall of the compound where they shared a cola nut. Nwomiko threw a lobe into her mouth and her teeth went to work at terrific speed; she was always in a hurry. Mama Obu presented the sacrificial gifts to her – a raffia mat on which the gifts would be displayed, a comb, twelve large coconuts, three large yams, two bars of soap, six yards of white shirting, six yards of *jioji* cloth, and one cock. The sacrifice was imperative if the other *ogbanje* were to release Obu. Nwomiko readily agreed not to offer the sacrifice close to the compound so as not to embarrass Mazi Laza. Since sacrifices for the *ogbanje* must be placed on ant-hills if they are to be accepted, she would deposit the sacrifice on one of the ant-hills she had spotted far from Mazi Laza's house. Her attendant collected the offertory with practised hands.

'Obiano!' Mama Obu called. There was no reply.

'Obuechina!' she repeated. Still no reply.

It looked like a miracle. Obu had disappeared within the short time she took Nwomiko to the kitchen veranda. His mother saw in this conclusive proof that he was an *ogbanje*, otherwise how did he recognize Nwomiko when her visit had been a closely guarded secret?

'When and where does he usually visit?' inquired Nwomiko.

Mama Obu named a few persons whose houses he normally visited, pointing out that they did not bring him up to visit people's homes. 'He is in Oti's house,' Nwomiko announced. 'Send for him there.'

Mama Obu chose to go herself to avoid further obstacles. Nwomiko was right; there Obu was, fidgeting with the wheels of the okwe tree cut for Oti by his father. Obu walked up to her silently and she led him home. As soon as he saw Nwomiko, he burst into tears. His mother swallowed hard.

'This looks an obvious case,' Nwomiko observed. 'Howbeit, let me see your left palm.'

'And the right,' she continued, after examining Obu's left palm. At the end of the examination, she turned to Mama Obu and nodded: 'Yes, he certainly is!'

'It is not true, Ma,' Obu shouted, sobbing. His mother went over to console him.

'Leave him alone,' Nwomiko admonished her. 'It's women like you who encourage the *ogbanje* by pampering them all the time. Do you know that the boy you fondle that way has signed to leave you the day he attains his ninth birthday?'

Mama Obu's heart flew off and her hands dropped from Obu as if his body had suddenly been charged with electricity.

'What did you say?'

'He signed up that he would live with you for nine years only, after which you would have had a corpse on your hands.'

Mama Obu looked at her son who had stopped sobbing. Nwomiko asked Obu to take her to the place where he had buried his *ogbanje* stone, the mysterious stone which determined how long the *ogbanje* would live. He did not utter a word. Nwomiko went out, followed by

Mama Obu who dragged Obu by the arm. They trotted after Nwomiko as the fleet-footed woman surveyed the compound, shaking her head at the end of the tour. She could not find any clue. She stole a momentary glance at Obu, paused for a while and made for the door leading out of the compound. She did not take much time outside the compound before she stopped with finality by one of the orange trees in front of the compound.

'It's here,' she pronounced.

Mama Obu felt great relief that the spot had been located, hoping that the woman was right. Since Nwomiko mentioned that Obu planned to die on his ninth birthday, her blood pressure had soared sharply. She feared that the hour glass might run out even before they could discover the spot where Obu buried his *ogbanje* stone.

'Someone should fetch me a hoe,' Nwomiko instructed. Ogechukwu who had worked her way into the group ran inside the compound to bring the hoe. Obu could be heard trying to restrain his running nose.

Nwomiko did not dig deeper than a foot before she plunged her hand into the hole with lightning speed, fingered the earth beneath, and produced a small object.

'Here it is,' she announced, presenting the *ogbanje* to Mama Obu. 'He had buried it much deeper than this initially, but it rises nearer to the surface as the end of his present life approaches.'

Mama Obu looked at the mysterious object. It looked like the kind of pebble one would find at the bed of a river or at the sea-shore, white and smooth. 'Does it mean that everything is all right now?' she asked as she returned the stone and the group returned to the house. 'Can he now remain with us all the time?'

'Yes,' pronounced the woman with that air of authority and finality which comes only with years of successful practice. 'Now that I have impounded his stone, he ceases to be an *ogbanje*.'

Mama Obu's superabundant love for her only son gushed back as if it had been held in check by a powerful dam. She bent down to clasp Obu warmly to her chest as she would welcome a prodigal son, thankful to God and Nwomiko that her days of anxiety were over, and that she could not have acted more promptly. Had she succumbed to her husband's reservations, she would have lost her most treasured earthly possession in two weeks' time. All the Catechist could have contributed would have been to bury the child and tell his parents that the dead are blessed . . . She would keep all that until Papa Obu returned from his meaningless journey.

Nwomiko left as soon as she had collected much more than her professional fee from an excited Mama Obu. She had another child to save at Obuchie before returning home that same day, and so could not afford to wait for a meal. As soon as she left, Mama Obu went to see her son. He was fast asleep on her bed. Although Nwomiko had told her that Obu would go into a long sleep lasting several hours, she bent close to make sure that he was breathing and alive. He was, so she let him sleep, deeply relieved and happy that she now had a son born to stay.

Could Nwomiko be right in speculating that she might yet bear more sons, now that the *ogbanje* who had blocked her womb to keep back any rival had lost his powers?

How wonderful it would be if it could come true; to have an only son is to leave yourself too much at the mercy of the gods. But Nwomiko had been reluctant to stake her reputation on it, and age was creeping in, so . . .

5 January 1943 passed without incident. It was Obu's ninth birthday on which, according to Nwomiko the *ogbanje* expert, Obu was to have died if he had remained an *ogbanje*.

Mazi Laza had not resumed his trading; he still had seed yams to tie in his barn and heaps of grass to cut for repairing the roof of his compound walls.

That morning, however, he announced that he was too weak to work; the truth, which he did not wish to disclose even to his wife, was that he had been apprehensive of what Obu's ninth birthday would bring. When he dissociated himself from the *ogbanje* ritual, he did so only to establish an alibi in case the Church teacher or someone else took him to task for being a member of the Church Committee and yet presiding over a pagan *ogbanje* ceremony in his house. He had seen enough evidence to convince him that the *ogbanje* existed, but since the Church preached against it he had no option but to dissociate himself openly from the ritual. He was happy that his wife had ignored his objections, and he had no doubts about the efficacy of Nwomiko's work. However, as Obu's ninth birthday drew nearer, he found himself getting more and more jittery, praying that Obu would not turn out to be Nwomiko's lone mistake. He could not afford to lose his only son.

All through the night, Mama Obu hardly slept a wink. Each time she stirred, she listened to Obu's breathing to make sure that he was still alive. The little sleep she could have had was abruptly ruined by a horrible nightmare. When the day finally broke, she roused Obu from sleep and decided to spend the rest of the day keeping vigil over him to make sure nobody snatched him away from her.

'Missus, thanks be to God that Obuechina is still with us,' Mazi Laza addressed his wife, three days after Obu's ninth birthday. 'There is now no question as to whether or not he is an *ogbanje*.'

'When you thank God, you should also thank me,' Mama Obu reminded him. 'It is easy to disappear from your house and leave someone else to carry your responsibility. When you return you thank God!'

'I said what I said deliberately. I know you invited Nwomiko, and she claimed to have removed the boy's *ogbanje*. Whether she did or not, or whether or not the boy was ever an *ogbanje*, neither you nor I know. That is why I said we should thank God that the boy is alive. He knows what is what.'

'I have been watching the way you shape your mouth to discuss a major lump inside the body as if it were mere craw-craw on the skin. I wish – no; I could not wish that anything had happened to Obiano. Let me accept that I was the daughter of a sheep, as you've always regarded me.'

'Let that point go with the wind.'

Chukwuemeka Ike (Nigeria)
Excerpt from *The Potter's Wheel*

I Spoil Everything*

I spoil everything!
They all laugh at me!
I go to the lake – I draw muddy water,
I go to the gardens – I gather grass,

I make porridge – it is all watery.
I brew beer – it is all lumpy.
　　They all laugh at me!
　　I spoil everything.

　　　　　　　　　　Vandau (Mozambique)

The Goldsmith*

Of all the different kinds of work my father performed, none fascinated me so much as his skill with gold. No other occupation was so noble, no other needed such a delicate touch; and, moreover, this sort of work was always a kind of festival: it was a real festival that broke the monotony of ordinary working days.

So if a woman, accompanied by a go-between, crossed the threshold of the workshop, I would follow her in at once. I knew what she wanted: she had brought some gold and wanted to ask my father to transform it into a trinket. The woman would have collected the gold in the placers of Siguiri, where, for months on end, she would have crouched over the river, washing the mud and patiently extracting from it the grains of gold. These women never came alone: they were well aware that my father had other things to do than to make trinkets for all and sundry; and even if the making of jewellery had been his main occupation, they would have realized that they were not his first or his only customers, and that their wants could not be immediately attended to.

Generally these women required the trinket for a certain date, either for the festival of Ramadan or for the Tabaski; or for some other family festival, or for a dance ceremony.

Thereupon, to better their chance of being quickly served, and the more easily to persuade my father to interrupt the work he had in hand, they would request the services of an official praise-singer, a go-between, and would arrange with him in advance what fee they would pay for his good offices.

The praise-singer would install himself in the workshop, tune up his cora, which is our harp, and would begin to sing my father's praises. This was always a great event for me. I would hear recalled the lofty deeds of my father's ancestors, and the names of these ancestors from the earliest times; as the couplets were reeled off, it was like watching the growth of a great genealogical tree that spread its branches far and wide and flourished its boughs and twigs before my mind's eye. The harp played an accompaniment to this vast utterance of names, expanding it and punctuating it with notes that were now soft, now shrill. Where did the praise-singer get his information from? He must certainly have developed a very retentive memory stored with facts handed down to him by his predecessors, for this is the basis of all our oral traditions. Did he embellish the truth? It is very likely: flattery is the praise-singer's stock-in-trade! Nevertheless, he was not allowed to take too many liberties with tradition, for it is part of the praise-singer's task to preserve it. But in those days such considerations did not enter my head, which I would hold high and proud; for I used to feel quite drunk with so much praise, which seemed to reflect some of its effulgence upon my own small person.

I could tell that my father's vanity was being inflamed, and I already knew that after having sipped this milk-and-honey he would lend a favourable ear to the woman's request. But I was not alone in my knowledge; the woman also had seen my father's eyes gleaming with contented pride; and she would hold out her grains of gold as if the whole thing was settled: my father, taking up his scales, would weigh the gold.

'What sort of trinket do you desire?' he would ask.

'I want . . .'

And often it would happen that the woman did not know really what she wanted, because she would be so torn by desire, because she would have liked to have many, many trinkets, all out of the same small quantity of gold: but she would have had to have much more than she had brought with her to satisfy such a desire, and eventually she would have to content herself with some more modest wish.

'When do you want it for?' my father would ask.

And she would always want it at once.

'Why are you in such a hurry? How do you expect me to find the time?'

'It's very urgent, I can assure you,' the woman would reply.

'That's what all women say, when they want an ornament. Well, I'll see what I can do. Now are you happy?'

Then he would take the clay pot that was kept specially for the smelting of gold and pour in the grains; thereupon he would cover the gold with powdered charcoal, a charcoal which he obtained by the use of plant juices of exceptional purity; finally he would place a large lump of the same kind of charcoal over the whole thing.

Then, having seen the work duly undertaken, the woman, by now quite satisfied, would go back to her household tasks, leaving her go-between to carry on with the praise-singing which had already proved so advantageous to her.

On a sign from my father, the apprentices would start working the two pairs of sheepskin bellows which were placed on the ground at each side of the forge and linked to it by earthen pipes. These apprentices remained seated all the time, with crossed legs, in front of the bellows; at least the younger did, for the elder would sometimes be allowed to take part in the craftsmen's work and the younger – in those days it was Sidafa – only had to work the bellows and watch the proceedings while awaiting his turn to be elevated to less rudimentary tasks. For a whole hour they would both be working the levers of the bellows till the fire in the forge leapt into flame, becoming a living thing, a lively and merciless spirit.

Then my father, using long pincers, would lift the clay pot and place it on the flames.

Immediately all work would more or less stop in the workshop: actually while the gold is being melted and while it is cooling all work with copper or aluminium is supposed to stop, for fear that some fraction of these less noble metals might fall among the gold. It is only steel that can still be worked at such times. But workmen who had some piece of steel work in hand would either hasten to finish it or would openly stop work to join the other apprentices gathered round the forge. In fact, there were often so many of them at these times pressing round my father that I, the smallest, would have to get up and push my way in among them, so as not to miss any of the operation.

It might happen that, feeling he had too little room to work in, my father would make his apprentices stand well away from him. He would merely raise his hand in a simple gesture: at that particular moment he would never utter a word, and no one else would, no one was allowed to utter a word, even the go-between's voice would no longer be raised in song; the silence would be broken only by the panting of the bellows and by the faint hissing of the gold. But if my father never used to utter actual words at this time, I know that he was uttering them in his mind; I could see it by his lips that kept working while he bent over the pot and kept stirring the gold and the charcoal with a bit of wood that would keep bursting into flame, and so had to be constantly replaced by a fresh bit.

What were the words my father's lips were forming? I do not know; I do not know for certain: I was never told what they were. But what else could they have been, if not magical incantations? Were they not the spirits of fire and gold, of fire and air, air breathed through the earthen pipes, of fire born of air, of gold married with fire – were not these the spirits he was invoking? Was it not their help and their friendship he was calling upon in this marriage of elemental things? Yes, it was almost certainly those spirits he was calling upon, for they are the most elemental of all spirits, and their presence is essential at the melting of gold.

The operation that was going on before my eyes was simply the smelting of gold; but it was something more than that: a magical operation that the guiding spirits could look upon with favour or disfavour; and that is why there would be all round my father that absolute silence and that anxious expectancy. I could understand, though I was just a child, that there was no craft greater than the goldsmith's. I expected a ceremony, I had come to be present at a ceremony, and it really was one, though very protracted. I was still too young to be able to understand why it was so protracted; nevertheless, I had an inkling, beholding the almost religious concentration of all those present as they watched the mixing process.

When finally the gold began to melt, I used to feel like shouting, and perhaps we would all have shouted if we had not been forbidden to make a sound: I would be trembling, and certainly everyone else would be trembling as we sat watching my father stirring the mixture, still a heavy paste in which the charcoal was gradually being consumed. The next stage followed swiftly; the gold now had the fluidity of water. The guiding spirits had smiled on the operation!

'Bring me the brick!' my father would say, thus lifting the ban that until then had kept us all silent.

The brick, which an apprentice would place beside the fire, was hollowed out, generously greased with Galam butter. My father would take the pot off the fire, tilt it carefully, and I would watch the gold flowing into the brick, flowing like liquid fire. True, it was only a very sparse trickle of fire, but oh, how vivid, how brilliant! As the gold flowed into the brick, the grease would splutter and flame and give off a thick smoke that caught in the throat and stung the eyes, leaving us all weeping and coughing.

It occurred to me later on that my father could easily have relinquished all the work of smelting the gold to one or other of his assistants: they were not without experience in these matters; they had taken part hundreds of times in the same preparations and they would certainly have brought the work to a successful conclusion. But as I have told you, my father kept moving his lips! We could not hear those words, those secret words, those incantations which he addressed to powers that we should not, that we could not hear or see: this was essential. Only my father was versed in the science of conjuring the spirits of fire, air and gold, and conjuring evil spirits, and that is why he alone conducted the whole operation.

By now the gold would have cooled in the hollow of the brick, and my father would begin to hammer and stretch it. This was the moment when his work as a goldsmith really began. I noticed that before embarking on it he never failed to stroke stealthily the little snake coiled up under the sheepskin; one can only assume that this was his way of gathering strength for what remained to be done, and which was the most difficult.

But was it not extraordinary, was it not miraculous that on these occasions the little black serpent always coiled up under the sheepskin? He was not always there, he did not visit my father every day, but he was always present whenever there was gold to be worked.

Moreover, it is our custom to keep apart from the working of gold all influences outside those of the jeweller himself. And indeed it is precisely because the jeweller alone possesses the secret of his incantations; but also because the working of gold, besides being a task of the greatest skill, is a matter of confidence, of conscience, a task which is not undertaken excepting after due reflection and experiment. Finally, I do not think that any jeweller would renounce the opportunity of performing such a task – I ought to say, such a spectacle – in which he can display his abilities with a virtuosity that his work as a blacksmith or a mechanic or even as a sculptor is never invested with; even though in these more humble tasks his skill is no less wonderful, even though the statues which he carves in wood with his adze are not insignificant works!

The snake's presence came as no surprise to me; ever since that evening when my father had talked to me about the guiding spirit of our race, it had ceased to surprise me; it was quite natural that the snake should be there: he had knowledge of the future. Did he impart any of that knowledge to my father? It seemed to me quite obvious that he did: did he not always warn him of what was going to happen? But I had another reason for believing implicitly in the powers of the little snake.

The craftsman who works in gold must first of all purify himself, that is, he must wash himself all over and, of course, abstain from all sexual relationships during the whole time. Great respecter of ceremony as he was, it would have been impossible for my father to ignore these rules. Now I never saw him make these preparations; I would see him address himself to his work without any apparent preliminaries. But from that moment it was obvious that, forewarned by his black guiding spirit in a dream of the task that would await him in the morning, my father must have prepared for it as soon as he arose, and had entered his workshop in a state of purity, his body smeared with the magical substances hidden in his numerous pots full of secret potions. So I believe my father never entered his workshop except in a state of ritual purity; and that is not because I want to make him out as being better than he is – he is a man like any other, and has a man's weaknesses – but always when it was a matter of ritual he was uncompromisingly strict.

The woman for whom the trinket was being made, and who would often have looked in to see how the work was getting on, would come for the final time, not wanting to miss anything of the marvellous sight as the gold wire, which my father had succeeded in spinning, was transformed into a trinket. She was here now, devouring with her eyes the fragile golden wire, following its tranquil and inevitable spirals round the little metal cone which gave the trinket its shape. My father would be watching her out of the corner of his eye, and sometimes I would see the corners of his mouth twitch into a smile: the woman's avid attentiveness amused him.

'Are you trembling?' he would say to her.

'*Am* I trembling?' she would ask.

And we would all burst out laughing at her. For she *was* trembling! She was trembling with covetousness for the spiral pyramid in which my father was inserting, among the convolutions, tiny grains of gold. When finally he terminated the work by placing at the summit the largest grain of gold, the woman would jump excitedly to her feet.

Then, while my father was slowly turning the trinket round in his fingers, smoothing it into perfect shape, no one could have displayed such utter happiness as the native woman, not even the praise-singer, whose trade it was to do so, and who, during the whole process of transformation, had kept on singing his praises, accelerating his rhythm, increasing his flatteries as the trinket took shape, and praising my father's talents to the skies.

Indeed, the praise-singer participated in a curious – I was going to say direct, effective – way in the work. He, too, was intoxicated with the joy of creation; he declaimed his rapture, and plucked his harp like a man inspired; he warmed to the task as if he had been the craftsman himself, as if the trinket had been made by his own hands. He was no longer a paid thurifer; he was no longer just the man whose services each and anyone could hire: he had become a man who creates his song under the influence of some very personal, interior necessity.

When my father, after having soldered the large grain of gold that crowned the summit, held out his work to be admired, the go-between would no longer be able to contain himself, and would intone the douga – the great chant which is only sung for celebrated men, and which is danced to only for them.

But the douga is a tremendous chant, a provocative chant, a chant that the go-between would not venture to sing, and that the man for whom it is sung would not venture to dance to, without certain precautions.

My father, forewarned in a dream, had been able to take these precautions as soon as he got up; the praise-singer had taken them as a matter of course when he had made his bargain with the woman. Just as my father had done, he had smeared his body with magic lotions and so had rendered himself invulnerable to the bad spirits which the douga would undoubtedly stir into activity, invulnerable also even to his fellow praise-singers who, jealous perhaps, were only waiting to hear the chant, the note of exaltation and the loss of control which that exaltation entails, to cast their evil spells upon him.

At the first notes of the douga, my father would rise and utter a cry in which happiness and triumph were equally mingled; and brandishing in his right hand the hammer that was the symbol of his profession, and in his left a ram's horn filled with magic substances, he would dance the glorious dance.

No sooner had he finished than workmen and apprentices, friends and customers in their turn, not forgetting the woman for whom the trinket had been created, would flock round him, congratulating him, showering praises on him, and complimenting at the same time the go-between, who found himself laden with gifts, gifts that are almost the only resources he has in his wandering life, that he leads after the fashion of the troubadours of old. Beaming, aglow with dancing and the praises he had received, my father would offer cola nuts, that small change of Guinean civility.

All that now remained to be done was to redden the trinket in a little water mixed with chlorine and sea-salt. I could go now: the ceremony was over! But often, as I was leaving the workshop, my mother, who might be in the yard pounding millet or rice, would call me.

'Where have you been?' she would ask, although she knew very well where I had been.

'In the workshop.'

'Oh, yes, your father was making something out of gold. Gold! It's always gold!'

And she would pound furiously the helpless bowl of rice or millet. 'Your father's ruining his health! You see what he's doing.'

'He's been dancing the douga,' I would reply.

'The douga! The douga won't stop him ruining his eyesight! And you would be better off playing here in the yard instead of going and breathing the dust and smoke in the workshop!'

My mother did not like my father to work with gold. She knew how harmful the soldering of gold can be: a jeweller can wear his lungs out, puffing at his blowpipe, and his eyes suffer by being so close to the intense heat of the forge; and even more perhaps from the microscopic delicacy of the work. But even if there had been no danger in it, my mother still would have disliked this sort of work: she held it in suspicion, for you cannot solder gold without the help of other metals, and my mother used to think that it was not strictly honest to keep the gold which was saved by its alloys, although this was the accepted thing; and she, too, was quite prepared, whenever she took cotton to be woven, to receive in return a piece of cloth of only half the original weight.

Camara Laye (Guinea)
The Dark Child, Chapter Two

Keep It Dark

Keep it dark!
          Don't tell your wife,
          For your wife is a log
          That is smouldering surely!
Keep it dark!

Keep it dark!
          Don't tell your wife,
          For your wife is a pot
          That resounds to the breeze.
          And then 'Bang'!
          It's all out and about!
Keep it dark!

Zezuru (Zimbabwe)
Translated by High Tracey

The Song of the Bottle

Let us sing the song of the bottle, aaa!
Its belly is clear like water,
But you can't see its heart.

Its mouth is on the top of its head, aaa!
Listen, listen, o men!
To lift it, you take it by the neck.
Its fathers laid on it a nasty 'fadi';
You cannot knock one against another,
For their bellies would be cut
To punish them.
Who touches their wounds
Will be torn by a sharp tooth.
When put in water, a bottle breathes quickly,
Like a drowning man.
The white men fill it with rum
Up to its shoulders
And then bring it to us.
This is the song of the bottle, aaa!

Malagasy (Madagascar)

As Beer Has Made Me Drunk

As beer has made me drunk
I too have made him drunk;
Though my homeward way I miss
He has caused me so much bliss.

Luo (Kenya)

The Apprentice

Ogunmola survived the ordeal of his apprenticeship, thanks to his having a past. A past that traced back to Oba. Oba, his great-grandfather. Oba, the illustrious. The wise ruler.

Ogunmola had the choice of going to school, but he would not. He had witnessed the fate of his grandfather and this had decided his position once and for all.

He was a mere child at the time. His grandfather was at the height of his glorious rule. Life was moving on meaningfully. Just as it had during the reign of the illustrious Oba, his father. He enjoyed the love and respect of his subjects. Peace and quiet dominated. Contentedness and accord prevailed . . .

Then suddenly they came. Uninvited. As if that was not enough, they said his grandfather did not know how to rule. His grandfather! The offspring of the illustrious Oba! One whose ability to rule in the time of poverty and riches, sedition and peace, pestilence and health had become a legend!

And that was not all. Life, they claimed, was being led not altogether the way it should. Everything had to be overhauled. A new beginning was necessary . . .

And indeed they immediately started to effect the changes. With inhuman speed and haste. Ogunmola, a mere child, saw it all. He was confused by it. But he had no difficulty in understanding the cause of the premature death of his grandfather. He was horrified to realize that his father could not become king after his grandfather. No one would continue the rule of Oba, his illustrious great-grandfather! He himself could have no pretensions . . .

In spite of this they wanted him to go to school! To put his stamp on those changes and proclaim them God-sent and just! Him, Ogunmola, the great-grandchild of Oba, the wise ruler! Never. Never, never, never. His royal blood revolted vehemently against the suggestion to succumb to an inglorious domination, to the worship of a false god. And he was a mere child.

But he had to do something. He had been born. What did it matter that the times were like this? Was that not the purpose of his birth? To make meaning of a life like this?

Ogunmola took up the challenge. He decided to become a master blacksmith. His years of apprenticeship began. Life was going to be meaningful from now on. So he thought.

He was mistaken. It was only then that his troubles actually began. It was hardly a year since he had been with Omotaiye, his master, when the latter called him aside:

'Ogunmola,' he began in his gentle, humane voice, 'you know I love you like a son, and that I have the highest respect for you as an apprentice. I believe you will make my name great yet. And that is why I'm grieved at what I see in your works lately.'

Ogunmola loved and respected his master. So it was with deep concern he heard these words. Emotions choked his voice as he said:

'May I know what grieves you, master? If it is within my power I will do everything to alleviate it.'

'When I look at the hoes, cutlasses, knives and other implements you forge,' the master continued, 'they show no definite character, they are amorphous. However minutely I scrutinize them, they fail to reflect the lessons I have been at pains to teach you. I have repeatedly said that your aim should be to forge a hoe that is both practical and cheap. What's the use of a beautiful hoe if everybody, everybody cannot afford it? As things are going now, people will soon begin to say that you are the apprentice of Omotola.' Thus concluded the master in a tone of the deepest regret.

For Omotaiye to say that the work of his apprentice resembled that from Omotola's workshop was the most serious criticism that Omotaiye could ever make against anyone that studied under him. Ogunmola knew this and was troubled. He agreed essentially with his master, but he felt within himself the existence of something. Something exclusively his own which he could bring to the forging of a hoe that would make that hoe more practical, more cheap, more attainable and more beautiful. For this reason he experimented endlessly. Little by little he approached his goal. But the closer he got to this goal, the more the hoes he forged differed from those of his master. He had noticed this and was worried, but he had hoped that his master would not perceive the difference. But alas . . .

'Master,' Ogunmola began excusing himself, 'you know I'm not imitating Omotola. I'm only trying to forge hoes my own way.'

'You're talking nonsense, my boy. That's an old story. It's all they say when they are actually turning against you. But for you to do that! You, whom I love so! You, who is . . .' The master was overpowered with emotions and could not continue. In a moment, however, he straightened up and added in a stern, uncompromising voice: 'Remember, if you choose to be my enemy, don't forget: an enemy is an enemy.'

Ogunmola was frightened, but he managed to say:

'I'm not your enemy, master.'

He was not believed. Life subsequently became difficult for him in his master's workshop. He tried to kill his initiative. All the same, anything he forged bore a quality that was not his master's. Something unmistakably his own. In the eyes of his master, however, this something showed increasing resemblance to products from Omotola's workshop. His love for his apprentice changed into dislike, and soon it matured into enmity. Explanations didn't help. They only made things worse.

During this trying period Ogunmola sought to survive the cruel reality of his apprenticeship by escaping into his past. He recollected the stories of his illustrious family as they were narrated to him by his mother. It was as if he had witnessed the events with his own eyes. Every night he dreamt of Oba, his great-grandfather, the wise ruler. He thrilled with joy in his sleep as he relived the last heroic deed of Oba.

'The plague came suddenly,' his mother had told him. 'Oba was ruling at the time. There was plenty. People were contented. Life was simple and meaningful. Then suddenly the plague!

'The effects were swift and disastrous. People died in hundreds. Soon it became evident that the population would be wiped out. It was then the wise men consulted the oracles.

'The Spirit of the land had been offended. An unusual atonement demanded. A man must sacrifice himself in expiation. No influence exerted. The choice completely voluntary. Sole motivation – the individual's love for the people. Otherwise the Spirit would not be appeased. Thus spoke all the oracles.

'For a long time nobody volunteered. People began dying in thousands. It was then, early one morning, that Oba, the wise ruler, the beloved of his subjects, called his family together. He hugged everyone with tender emotions and then announced his intentions.

'Word spread like a wild fire. Dissuasions increased every second. The population consulted together and sent a delegation. "Is it not enough that we should die like chickens? Must we also be left without a ruler? And a ruler like you? We would all die rather than lose you." These and many more were the words spoken. But Oba would not be dissuaded.

'It was a gloomy afternoon. Sorrow was in every heart. Fear written on every face. Oba, the illustrious, the wise ruler, walked calmly towards the Hill. Absolute silence reigned in the crowd of grieving subjects escorting their beloved ruler on his last journey. The gloomy silence was frequently pierced by heart-rending wailings that gushed forth from the desolate houses on the route. The bereaved mourned their dead. Almost at every step someone from the procession, who only a moment ago had been most actively alive, would suddenly stiffen and drop stone dead. Like a rotten dry wood blown down by the wind. Sorrow in every heart. Fear on every face.

'Oba hastened his steps. Soon he was at the edge of the precipice. Unspeakable fear gripped everyone as the wise ruler jumped the Hill. He vanished without a trace into the bottomless abyss.

'The Spirit of the land was pacified. A new life began. Your grandfather assumed the throne. He followed in the footsteps of Oba, his illustrious father, your great-grandfather, the pride of the land. Once again the land knew splendour, subjects enjoyed plenty and comfort, life was simple and meaningful . . .

'And suddenly they came. Uninvited . . . You know the rest of the story, my son.' Thus concluded his mother. Her voice sad.

His mother had died seven years ago, but the recollection of this story made him feel as if she was once again alive; as if he himself was once more a six-year-old carefree child. He was happy, relieved by the knowledge that life had once been meaningful, that once there had been a king who knew how to rule, that one day there might yet be another . . .

These thoughts were Ogunmola's succour in the trying days of his apprenticeship. Omotaiye soon got to hate him bitterly, and before long the master asked his apprentice to leave. Without a certificate testifying to the completion of his apprenticeship, Ogunmola could not practise. This even though he felt he had acquired enough of the basics on which he could build to become a great master himself. Thus he found himself on the other side of the river, knocking on Omotola's door.

'Eh, see who is here! Come in. Come right in. Haven't I always said you're welcome in my house? Yes . . . Really! . . . I'm not actually surprised. Isn't it common knowledge that Omotaiye is mad? I'm happy it happened, though. I have always dreamt of having an apprentice like you. With me it will be completely different. You'll be free to forge any kinds of hoes, cutlasses, knives and other implements exactly the way you like. Absolutely free. Of course, who would think of forging a hoe that is not durable as well as being beautiful? People know they are buying quality and, naturally, they're prepared to pay something extra. Why worry about every Tom, Dick and Harry? Where is the guarantee that even if their Dick could afford our hoe that he'll make good use of it? So, you see, you're welcome. Come right in.'

This was how Ogunmola was received by Omotola, the arch-enemy of Omotaiye, his former master. Ogunmola understood the condition of his acceptance, but he also knew that he had been promised freedom. However, a year had hardly gone by when Omotola called him for an explanation.

'I have given you sufficient time to get rid of all that nonsense with which Omotaiye had stuffed your head. Apparently, you're not in a hurry. Perhaps you don't even intend to . . . Yes, yes I quite understand. Far more than you suppose. You all say that even at the very moment you're going against one. But it's an old game, my boy, and the answer is as old as the Bible. You cannot serve two masters. So you're either for me or against me. And it's time you declared your stand.'

Again life became bitter for Ogunmola. What was he to do? He had sought to safeguard his honour by refusing to go to school but had ended up making things more difficult. And all because in this cruel time it was enough to be caught in the family quarrels of strangers to be denied one's dignity, one's rights.

Omotaiye and Omotola, as rumour had it, were twins. Identical twins. One was as tall and athletic as the other, as healthy and boisterous as the other, as courageous and ambitious as the other, as talented and hard-working as the other, as tempered and diplomatic as the other, as good a master as the other, as . . .

One could go on for ever enumerating the points of similarity. Yet these twins would be the very first to deny the existence of any such similarities, of any kind of relationship. They had never known each other from Adam. Didn't you study geography? How could you possibly confuse someone who lives on this side of the river with the one on the other side? Can't you recognize the signs of the time? Then, why won't you differentiate between the road that leads forward into the future from the one that goes backward into the past? . . .

The arguments were inexhaustible.

Ogunmola heard it all and was at a loss to explain that it was his least desire to serve as an arbiter in a family quarrel, that he did not want to be caught in the crossfire between two brothers, that his sole desire was to be a smith; a simple smith, forging hoes his own way and dreaming of Oba, the wise ruler, his great-grandfather when the going was tough.

Was that asking too much? Ogunmola could not tell. He knew only that this was a trying time and he wished he would survive it.

Odum Balogun (Nigeria)

Originality?

He who must do
Something altogether new
Let him swallow his own head.

Chinweizu (Nigeria)

Two Worlds

My elegant sculptures
moved in their stillness
champagne and wine flowed
flashlights and cameras click
forming a long line of uncomfortable sounds.

His eye flits over my work for ten seconds
then this fat American comes over to me
'Beautiful! Did you do it yourself?' he bellowed.
Without waiting for an answer
'Are you familiar with the works of Giacometti,
Picasso, Braque, Gaudier-Brzeska?'
Nothing about Africa, Asia or Latin America.
'How much? My wife will like this!'

An old Swazi woman comes smiling
smiling under her beehive hairstyle
'Whoever did this is crazy

so many people on one block of wood
some rising, others falling
just like life itself!'
She turns to me
'Who's your father? Your mother?
Grandparents?
From what tree of what roots?
What branch are you?'
I tell her as much as I know.
'Me too have a Mbonani in my tree
you must therefore be my nephew!'

Where we fit into the matrix of life
is that important.
I look at her
I look at him puffing his Havana cigar
Two worlds.

                              Pitika Ntuli (Azania)

VII — MEN AND WOMEN

Desire for a Woman*

Desire for a woman took hold of me in the night oo like madness,
desire for a woman took hold of me in the night oo like madness.

Azande (Zaïre)

Akosua 'Nowa

They say the guinea-fowl lays her treasure
Where only she can find it.
Akosua 'Nowa is a guinea-fowl:
Go tell her, red ant upon the tree.

I met Akosua 'Nowa this morning;
I greeted:
    Akosua, how is your treasure?
She looked me slowly up and down,
She sneered:
    The man is not yet here who'll find it!

Akosua 'Nowa has touched my manhood;
Tell her, red ant upon the tree:
If she passes this way I am gone,
I am gone to load my gun.

No matter how hidden deep her treasure,
By my father's coffin I swear
I'll shoot my way to it this day;
Son of the hunter king
    There is liquid fire in my gun!

Joe de Graft (Ghana)

When I Make Love*

When I make love with my lover, it is as if I were cleaning grain to feed myself: I eat and eat, a whole field full, yet my heart is not satisfied.

Berber (Morocco)

Konni and Uta*

Soon after three that afternoon, Konni again stood before her mirror, dabbing her lips to a bright red, and painting her cheeks. She put on a transparent scarf over her face, hiding the bruises.

She called on Anna – one of her friends who lived near the loco sheds, and when the clock was pointing to four, and the siren was howling in Lokotown and the men were coming home from work, she and Anna came out into the open.

They stood at a prominent junction in Lokotown so that all the men passing would see them. Meantime, their conversation became a kind of stage performance. They gestured and paraded. They laughed noisily, holding their sides. A few seconds listening would have revealed the truth. They were talking about nothing. Absolutely nothing.

Loco men who passed by looked back – as they were meant to do. Some of them whistled and passed on. The older men recognized these two women as baits they must avoid and walked faster towards their wives and children.

'We fight for bonus, wage increase, and all the rest,' they muttered. 'We go on strike. They give us more money – and what happens? These women take all we get. You see the dress she wears? Go to her house, and see the food she eats. In one day that woman spends what it takes a man one month to earn!'

A Lokotown man looked down at his grease-stained khaki and shook his head sadly.

'If you go now and talk to her, she will damn you,' another said. 'But you know? Everything she wears there was brought by you and me! Men of Lokotown! God save us!' He hurried away, pulling his partner after him. But there was one man who fell into the trap because he looked at the two women too long. His name was Uta. He was a short man and he went to work in a white shirt. You could see that he did not do any of the greasy jobs. He made a note of the girl, and asked the loco men around him a lot of questions.

In the evening, he found the address at Skylark Avenue and knocked at Konni's door.

'Come in,' she said. It really did pay to advertise.

Uta shuffled in, and sat down. He looked at the mirror which formed one side of the wall, and tried not to be scared. He could not gaze into his own eyes. It made him angry to detect an unsteadiness in his voice when he spoke.

'I – I saw you this afternoon,' he began. 'You were standing with another woman –'

'Myself?' said Konni, surprised. She bent her head patiently to hear more.

'I used to see you always.' He puffed. She was still looking at him as if he were some curious object.

He went on speaking and she kept listening. From time to time, a girl from the sewing-room came in with a piece of material and showed it to her. Without taking her eyes off Uta she would say 'excuse me' and follow the girl to the sewing section of her flat. During her absence Uta bit his nails, and cursed himself. This was a good time to leave, before he implicated himself.

When he finally left the flat he was not quite sure that he had achieved the impossible. Could he believe that she had actually meant he should come and take her to the Midnight Oil Club?

Promptly at nine he came back, dressed for the evening in a glossy costume. When she appeared his breath caught in his throat. The dress she had put on made him look like a servant beside her. He walked slightly behind her, but when they got to the entrance to the Midnight Oil he gladly paid the fee, chose a table, summoned the 'Service' and paid for the beer.

The 'Service' placed six bottles on the table for a start.

'What of cigarettes?' she said.

'D'you smoke?'

'I don't,' she lied. 'Only ah like am with beer.'

He could not dance. He sat there, and men came and took her out to the floor, talking volubly as they danced with her. He sat on alone till they brought her back to his table. He felt more like a servant than an escort. He still sipped slowly at his first bottle when he noticed that four of her bottles were empty. The fifth was already half gone.

This was the middle of the month, with pay-day at least two Saturdays away. His allowance was running low. The sacrifice of taking her out was already leaving a big hole in his pocket, but he believed that somehow things would come right. The girl was worth it. He swallowed and faced it bravely.

'No more beer?' she said suddenly. She drained her glass and bottle, and said, 'I tire for beer. Give me brandy.' At that point she excused herself and walked with her handbag to the ladies' room.

On her way she called out: 'Service! Where's de Service? Service!' And when a waiter came she directed him to Uta's table.

Uta felt his throat contract. He winked at the waiter, trying to make him say there was no brandy, but Uta was new in the Midnight Oil society and the waiter did not get him. He was still arguing with the waiter when he saw Konni sitting opposite.

She turned to him.

'You want some brandy too?'

'No!'

'What of beer?' she said. 'Or you will just sit down, no drink, no dance, no nothing.'

By the time he had paid for her six shots, it was still about ten-thirty, and he said he would be going home, that he had to be up early to go to work next day.

'Let's go, now,' he said.

She smiled. 'Remain small,' she said.

She was looking at the doorway, and he followed her gaze. Four or five men had just entered the club. They were definitely distinguished visitors looking at Lagos night life. Uta was asking her who they were, did she know them? But she was not listening. There was a fixed smile on her face put on for the benefit of the new arrivals. Her artificial eyebrows rose in recognition, and without so much as 'excuse me', she had left him for the newcomers.

Uta was raving mad. He could not go back home. He had spent all his money, and could not buy a drink to drown his sorrows. She had just fleeced him of the best part of his remaining allowance for the month and although it was nothing to her, to him it was the difference between starvation and survival. He must have some compensation for his pains.

He saw with disgust the way she was helping herself out of the strangers' tin of cigarettes and he knew he had lost her. He decided to stay and watch.

She danced with one man after the other, laughed too loud, chain-smoked and drank heavily and went to the ladies' room frequently. She must have a wonderful head for alcohol for she did not once behave drunkenly.

Midnight came and passed by and she had danced and flirted with everyone in the club. Uta could not get himself to leave. She disappeared once – he could not tell when. He searched and searched for her. It was during the heat of the dancing and she was away for about an hour. When next he saw her, she was in a new dress. She must have gone home to change. Uta hung about the place until he became an eyesore. His heart was only hurting him the more at what he saw. Towards three in the morning, he saw her rise, and she and the strangers left the club. Not a word to him – no thank you, no goodbye. He too came out, and saw Konni and the men get into a taxi and drive off.

He swallowed his grief and anger and disappointment. He was a railway clerk. He earned a regular salary. The men were visitors with plenty of money to spend. He did not sleep that night. There was a hole in his budget, and he had obtained no consolation for creating that hole. This girl Konni was cute as they said, but he would see to it that she did not get away with it, just like that. She was a parasite of Lokotown who despised the very men on whom she fed.

At the office next day, his eyes were sunken from lack of sleep and misery. He yawned now and again, and he looked out of his window at the engine which was shunting in the yard. He wanted to curse the driver for sounding his whistle so loud. What did he need to whistle for anyway?

He called on Konni in the afternoon. He was told she was out, but he knew she was inside. Those girls at the sewing-machines had given away the secret by laughing.

'I want to see her,' he insisted.

'She done go out,' they lied.

They were big girls. He looked about them, but there was none of them he knew. One of them looked like a housewife.

'I want to see her,' he said, irritated.

He was hungry and sore, and he had not reached home.

He sat on the steps, doggedly, determined to make a scene. Looking at her door, he suddenly saw it open. She came out in a dressing-gown.

'Mr Uta,' she said. 'I nor well. Go, till tomorrow!'

She went inside and banged the door and he heard the key turn in the lock. The girls giggled. They were giggling at him. They couldn't hide it. He knew. A lump of anger rose in his throat. To be treated like a dog! But why had he suddenly fallen into the clutches of this heartless woman?

He sat at her doorway for about an hour, unable to move. Then a friend of his hailed him from the street and determined him. He joined the man and went back home, but he still felt sore, and only answered the man's questions with 'I don't know . . . Yes . . .' and 'No'. He could not concentrate on his usual routine of living.

He returned to Konni's room at seven in the evening and sat on the steps. Somehow, he had become a dog, running after Konni, hanging on wherever she was. Or just waiting.

Cyprian Ekwensi (Nigeria)
Excerpt from 'Lokotown'

I am the Child without Friends*

I am the child without friends
Who plays alone with the dust,
I am the chick fallen into the ditch:
If it calls, its voice is small,
If it flies, its wings are weak,
If it waits, it fears the wildcat.
Do not make our love a love of stone
Whose pieces cannot come together;

Make it a love of lips,
Even angry, they draw close and meet.

Merina (Madagascar)

Love Song

A javelin without blood is not a javelin!
Love without kisses is not love!

Galla (Ethiopia)

Yoruba Love

When they smile and they smile
and then begin to say
with pain on their brows
and songs in their voice:
'the nose is a cruel organ
and the heart without bone
for were the bone not cruel,
it would smell love for you
and the heart if not boneless,
would feel my pain for you
and the throat, o, has not roots
or it would root to flower my love' –
run for shelter, friend,
run for shelter.

Molara Ogundipe-Leslie (Nigeria)

Lament of a Woman Separated from Her Lover

O merchant of merchandise
Who is at mount Burê!

The eyes have no axe;
The mind has no sickle
To cut down mountains.

Galla (Ethiopia)

Letter from a Contract Worker

I wanted to write you a letter
my love
a letter to tell
of this longing
to see you
and this fear
of losing you
of this thing which deeper than I want, I feel
a nameless pain which pursues me
a sorrow wrapped about my life.

I wanted to write you a letter
my love
a letter of intimate secrets
a letter of memories of you
of you
your lips as red as the tacula fruit
your hair black as the dark diloa fish
your eyes gentle as the macongue
your breasts hard as young maboque fruit
your light walk
your caresses
better than any that I find down here.

I wanted to write you a letter
my love
to bring back our days together in our secret haunts
nights lost in the long grass
to bring back the shadow of your legs

and the moonlight filtering through the endless
palms,
to bring back the madness of our passion
and the bitterness of separation.

I wanted to write you a letter
my love
which you could not read without crying
which you would hide from your father Bombo
and conceal from your mother Kieza
which you would read without the indifference
of forgetfulness,
a letter which would make any other
in all Kilombo worthless.

I wanted to write you a letter
my love
a letter which the passing wind would take
a letter which the cashew and the coffee trees,
the hyenas and the buffalo,
the caymans and the river fish
could hear
the plants and the animals
pitying our sharp sorrow
from song to song
lament to lament
breath to caught breath
would leave to you, pure and hot,
the burning
the sorrowful words of the letter
I wanted to write you

I wanted to write you a letter
But my love, I don't know why it is,
why, why, why it is, my love,
but you can't read
and I – oh the hopelessness – I can't write.

Antonio Jacinto (Angola)

Translated from the Portuguese by Margaret Dickinson

On being Told that the Girl of His Desire is a Blood Relative*

I go there, I find a relative
I go there, I find a relative!
I go here, I find a piece of stone
And I smash my testicles!
Tik! Tik! Tik! Tik! Tik!

Acholi (Uganda)
Translated by Okot p'Bitek

Girl's Rejection of a Poor Suitor*

'You want to marry me, but what can you give me? A nice field?'
'No, I have only a house.'
'What? You have nothing but a house? How would we live? Go
    to Bukavu; there you can earn plenty of money. You can buy
    food and other things.'

'No, I won't go. I don't know the people there. I have always lived
    here, and I know the people and want to stay here.'
'You are a stupid man. You want to marry me but you have
    nothing. If you don't go to Bukavu and earn money to buy me
    things then I won't marry you.'

Bashi (Zaïre)

Anowa and Kofi*

IN YEBI

*Lower Stage. Early evening village noises, for example, the pounding
of fufu or millet, a goat bleats loudly, a woman calls her child, etc.
ANOWA enters from lower right, carrying an empty water-pot. She walks
to the centre of the lower stage, stops, and looks behind her. Then she*

overturns the water-pot and sits on it facing the audience. She is wearing her cloth wrapped around her. The upper part of her breasts is visible, and also all of her legs. She is slim and slight of build. She turns her face momentarily towards lower left. During a moment when she is looking at her feet, KOFI AKO enters from the lower right. He is a tall, broad, young man, and very good-looking. The village noises die down.

He is in work clothes and carrying a fish trap and a bundle of baits. He steals quietly up to her and cries, 'Hei!' She is startled but regains her composure immediately. They smile at each other. Just then, a WOMAN comes in from the lower left, carrying a wooden tray which is filled with farm produce — cassava, yam, plantain, pepper, tomatoes, etc. Close behind her is a MAN, presumably her husband, also in work clothes, with a gun on his shoulder and a matchet under his arm. They pass by ANOWA and KOFI and walk on towards lower right. The woman turns round at every step to stare at the boy and girl who continue looking shyly at each other. Finally, the WOMAN misses a step or kicks against the block of wood. She falls, her tray crashing down.

ANOWA and KOFI burst into loud uncontrollable laughter. Assisted by her MAN, the WOMAN begins to collect her things together. Having got her load back on her head, she disappears, followed by her MAN. Meanwhile, ANOWA and KOFI continue laughing and go on doing so a little while after the lights have been removed from them.

Upper Stage. The courtyard of Maami BADUA and Papa OSAM's cottage. Village noises as in previous scene. Standing in the centre is an earthen hearth with tripod cooking pot. There are a couple of small household stools standing around. By the right wall is a lie-in chair which belongs exclusively to Papa OSAM. Whenever he sits down, he sits in this. By the chair is a small table. The Lower Stage here represents a section of a village side street from which there is an open entrance into the courtyard. In the background, upper left and upper right are doors connecting the courtyard to the inner rooms of the house.

In the pot something is cooking which throughout the scene Maami BADUA will go and stir. By the hearth is a small vessel into which she puts the ladle after each stirring.

BADUA *enters from upper right, goes to the hearth, picks up the ladle and stirs the soup. She is talking loudly to herself.*

BADUA: Any mother would be concerned if her daughter refused to get married six years after her puberty. If I do not worry about this, what shall I worry about?

(OSAM *enters from upper left smoking his pipe.*)

Besides, a woman is not a stone but a human being; she grows.

OSAM: Woman, (BADUA *turns to look at him.*) that does not mean you should break my ears with your complaints. (*He looks very composed.*)

BADUA: What did you say, Osam?

OSAM: I say you complain too much

(*He goes to occupy the lie-in chair, and exclaims, 'Ah!' with satisfaction.*)

BADUA: (*Seriously*) Are you trying to send me insane?

OSAM: Will that shut you up?

BADUA: Kofi Sam! (*Now she really is angry.*)

OSAM: Yes, my wife.

(BADUA *breathes audibly with exasperation. She begins pacing up and down the courtyard, with the ladle in her hand.*)

BADUA: (*Moving quickly up to* OSAM) So it is nothing at a-a-l-l (*Stretching the utterance of the last word*) to you that your child is not married and goes round wild, making everyone talk about her?

OSAM: Which is your headache, that she is not yet married, or that she is wild?

BADUA: Hmm!

OSAM: You know that I am a man and getting daughters married is not one of my duties. Getting them born, aha! But not finding them husbands.

BADUA: Hmm! (*Paces up and down.*)

OSAM: And may the ancestral spirits help me, but what man would I order from the heavens to please the difficult eye of my daughter Anowa?

BADUA: Hmm! (*She goes and stirs the soup and this time remembers to put the ladle down. She stands musing by the hearth.*)

OSAM: As for her wildness, what do you want me to say again about that? I have always asked you to apprentice her to a priestess to quieten her down. But . . .

(*Roused again,* BADUA *moves quickly back to where he is and meanwhile, corks both her ears with two fingers and shakes her head to make sure he notices what she is doing.*)

OSAM: (*Chuckles*) Hmm, play children's games with me, my wife. One day you will click your fingers with regret that you did not listen to me.

BADUA: (*She removes her fingers from her ears.*) I have said it and I will say it again and again and again! I am not going to turn my only daughter into a dancer priestess.

OSAM: What is wrong with priestesses?

BADUA: I don't say there is anything wrong with them.

OSAM: Did you not consult them over and over again when you could not get a single child from your womb to live beyond one day?

BADUA: (*Reflectively*) O Yes. I respect them, I honour them . . . I fear them. Yes, my husband, I fear them. But my only daughter shall not be a priestess.

OSAM: They have so much glory and dignity . . .

BADUA: But in the end, they are not people. They become too much like the gods they interpret. (*As she enumerates the attributes of priesthood, her voice grows hysterical and her face terror-stricken.* OSAM *removes his pipe, and stares at her, his mouth open with amazement.*)

They counsel with spirits;
They read into other men's souls;
They swallow dogs' eyes
Jump fires
Drink goats' blood
Sheep milk
Without flinching
Or vomiting
They do not feel
As you or I,
They have no shame.

(*She relaxes, and* OSAM *does too, the latter sighing audibly.* BADUA *continues, her face slightly turned away from both her husband and the audience.*)

BADUA: I want my child
  To be a human woman
  Marry a man
  Tend a farm
  And be happy to see her
  Peppers and her onions grow.
  A woman like her
  Should bear children
  Many children
  So she can afford to have
  One or two die.
  Should she not take
  Her place at meetings
  Among the men and women of the clan?
  And sit on my chair when
  I am gone? And a captainship in the army,
  Should not be beyond her
  When the time is ripe!

(OSAM *nods his head and exclaims, Oh . . . oh!*)

BADUA: But a priestess lives too much in her own and other people's minds, my husband.

OSAM: (*Sighing again*) My wife, people with better vision than yours or mine have seen that Anowa is not like you or me. And a prophet with a locked mouth is neither a prophet nor a man. Besides, the yam that will burn, shall burn, boiled or roasted.

BADUA: (*She picks up the ladle but does not stir the pot. She throws her arms about.*) Since you want to see Nkomfo and Nsofo, seers and dancers . . .

ANOWA: (*From the distance*) Mother!

BADUA: That is her coming.

ANOWA: Father!

OSAM: O yes. Well let us keep quiet about her affairs then. You know what heart lies in her chest.

ANOWA: Mother, Father . . . Father, Mother . . . Mother . . . (OSAM *jumps up and confused, he and* BADUA *keep bumping into each other*

as each moves without knowing why or where he or she is moving.
BADUA *still has the ladle in her hands.*)

BADUA: Why do you keep hitting at me?

ANOWA: Mother!

OSAM: Sorry, I did not mean to. But you watch your step too.

ANOWA: Father!

BADUA: And where is she?

(ANOWA *runs in, lower right, with her empty water-pot.*)

BADUA: *Hei.* Why do you frighten me so? And where is the water?

ANOWA: O Mother. (*She stops running and stays on the lower stage.*)

OSAM: What is it?

ANOWA: (*Her eyes swerving from the face of one to the other*) O Father!

OSAM: Say whatever you have got to say and stop behaving like a child.

BADUA: Calling us from the street!

OSAM: What have you got to tell us that couldn't wait until you reached here?

ANOWA: O Father.

BADUA: And look at her. See here, it is time you realized you have grown up.

ANOWA: Mother . . . (*Moving a step or two forward.*)

BADUA: And now what is it? Besides, where is the water? I am sure this household will go to bed to count the beams tonight since there is no water to cook with.

ANOWA: Mother, Father, I have met the man I want to marry.

BADUA: What is she saying?

ANOWA: I say I have found the man I would like to marry.

OSAM:
BADUA: }Eh?

(*Long pause during which* BADUA *stares at* ANOWA *with her head tilted to one side.*)

ANOWA: Kofi Ako asked me to marry him and I said I will, too.

BADUA: Eh?

OSAM: Eh?

BADUA: Eh?

OSAM: Eh?

BADUA: Eh?

OSAM:
BADUA: }Eh – eh!

(*Light dies on all three and comes on again almost immediately.* OSAM *is sitting in his chair.* ANOWA *hovers around and she has a chewing-stick in her mouth with which she scrapes her teeth when she is not speaking.* BADUA *is sitting by the hearth doing nothing.*)

ANOWA: Mother, you have been at me for a long time to get married. And now that I have found someone I like very much . . .

BADUA: Anowa, shut up. Shut up! Push your tongue into your mouth and close it. Shut up because I never counted Kofi Ako among my sons-in-law. Anowa, why Kofi Ako? Of all the mothers that are here in Yebi, should I be the one whose daughter would want to marry this fool, this good-for-nothing cassava-man, this watery male of all watery males? This—I-am-the-handsome-one-with-a-stick-between-my-teeth-in-the-market-place . . . This . . . this . . .

ANOWA: O Mother . . .

BADUA: (*Quietly*) I say Anowa, why did you not wait for a day when I was cooking *banku* and your father was drinking palm wine in the market-place with his friends? When you could have snatched the ladle from my hands and hit me with it and taken your father's wine from his hands and thrown it into his face? Anowa, why did you not wait for a day like that, since you want to behave like the girl in the folk tale?

ANOWA: But what are you talking about, Mother?

BADUA: And you, Kobina Sam, will you not say anything?

OSAM: Abena Badua, leave me out of this. You know that if I so much as whisper anything to do with Anowa, you and your brothers and your uncles will tell me to go and straighten out the lives of my nieces. This is your family drum; beat it, my wife.

BADUA: I did not ask you for riddles.

OSAM: Mm . . . just remember I was smoking my pipe.

BADUA: If you had been any other father, you would have known what to do and what not to do.

OSAM: Perhaps; but that does not mean I would have *done* anything. The way you used to talk, I thought if Anowa came to tell you she was going to get married to Kweku Ananse, or indeed the devil himself, you would spread rich cloth before her to walk on. And probably sacrifice an elephant.

BADUA: And do you not know what this Kofi Ako is like?

ANOWA: What is he like?

BADUA: My lady, I have not asked you a question. (ANOWA *retires into sullenness. She scrapes her teeth noisily.*)

OSAM: How would I know what he is like? Does he not come from Nsona House? And is not that one of the best Houses that are here in Yebi? Has he an ancestor who unclothed himself to nakedness, had the Unmentionable, killed himself or another man?

BADUA: And if all that there is to a young man is that his family has an unspoiled name, then what kind of a man is he? Are he and his wife going to feed on stones when he will not put a blow into a thicket or at least learn a trade?

OSAM: Anyway, I said long ago that I was removing my mouth from my daughter Anowa's marriage. Did I not say that? She would not allow herself to be married to any man who came to ask for her hand from us and of whom we approved. Did you not know then that when she chose a man, it might be one of whom we would disapprove?

BADUA: But why should she want to do a thing like that?

OSAM: My wife, do remember I am a man, the son of a woman who also has five sisters. It is a long time since I gave up trying to understand the human female. Besides, if you think well of it, I am not the one to decide finally whom Anowa can marry. Her uncle, your brother is there, is he not? You'd better consult him. Because I know your family: they will say I deliberately married Anowa to a fool to spite them.

ANOWA: Father, Kofi Ako is not a fool.

OSAM: My daughter, please forgive me, I am sure you know him very well. And it was only by way of speaking. Kwame! Kwame! I thought the boy was around somewhere. (*Moves towards lower stage and looks around.*)

BADUA: What are you calling him here for?

OSAM: To go and call us her uncle and your brother.

BADUA: Could we not have waited until this evening or dawn tomorrow?

OSAM: For what shall we wait for the dawn?

BADUA: To settle the case.

OSAM: What case? Who says I want to settle cases? If there is any case to settle, that is between you and your people. It is not everything one chooses to forget, Badua. Certainly, I remember what happened in connection with Anowa's dancing. That is, if you don't. Did they not say in the end that it was I who had prevented her from going into apprenticeship with a priestess?

(*Light dies on them and comes on a little later.* ANOWA *is seen dressed in a two-piece cloth. She darts in and out of upper right, with very quick movements. She is packing her belongings into a little basket. Every now and then, she pauses, looks at her mother and sucks her teeth.* BADUA *complains as before, but this time, tearfully.* OSAM *is lying in his chair smoking.*)

BADUA: I am in disgrace so suck your teeth at me. (*Silence*) Other women certainly have happier tales to tell about motherhood. (*Silence*) I think I am just an unlucky woman.

ANOWA: Mother, I do not know what is wrong with you.

BADUA: And how would you know what is wrong with me? Look here Anowa, marriage is like a piece of cloth . . .

ANOWA: I like mine and it is none of your business.

BADUA: And like cloth, its beauty passes with wear and tear.

ANOWA: I do not care, Mother. Have I not told you that this is to be my marriage and not yours?

BADUA: My marriage! Why should it be my daughter who would want to marry that good-for-nothing cassava-man?

ANOWA: He is mine and I like him.

BADUA: If you like him, do like him. The men of his house do not make good husbands; ask older women who are married to Nsona men.

OSAM: You know what you are saying is not true. Indeed from the beginning of time Nsona men have been known to make the best of husbands. (BADUA *glares at him.*)

ANOWA: That does not even worry me and it should not worry you, Mother.

BADUA: It's up to you, my mistress who knows everything. But remember, my lady – when I am too old to move, I shall still be sitting by these walls waiting for you to come back with your rags and nakedness.

ANOWA: You do not have to wait because we shall not be coming back here to Yebi. Not for a long long time, Mother, not for a long long time.

BADUA: Of course, if I were you I wouldn't want to come back with my shame either.

ANOWA: You will be surprised to know that I am going to help him do something with his life.

BADUA: A-a-h, I wish I could turn into a bird and come and stand on your roof-top watching you make something of that husband of yours. What was he able to make of the plantation of palm trees his grandfather gave him? And the virgin land his uncles gave him, what did he do with that?

ANOWA: Please, Mother, remove your witch's mouth from our marriage. (OSAM *jumps up and from now on hovers between the two, trying to make peace.*)

OSAM: *Hei* Anowa, what is wrong with you? Are you mad? How can you speak like that to your mother?

ANOWA: But Father, Mother does not treat me like her daughter.

BADUA: And so you call me a witch? The thing is, I wish I were a witch so that I could protect you from your folly.

ANOWA: I do not need your protection, Mother.

OSAM: The spirits of my fathers! Anowa, what daughter talks like this to her mother?

ANOWA: But Father, what mother talks to her daughter the way mother talks to me? And now, Mother, I am going, so take your witchery to eat in the sea.

OSAM: *Ei* Anowa?

BADUA: Thank you my daughter. (BADUA *and* ANOWA *try to jump on each other.* BADUA *attempts to hit* ANOWA *but* OSAM *quickly intervenes.*)

OSAM: What has come over this household? Tell me what has come over this household? And you too Badua. What has come over you?

BADUA: You leave me alone, Osam. Why don't you speak to Anowa? She is your daughter, I am not.

OSAM: Well, she is not mature.

BADUA: That one makes me laugh. Who is not mature? Has she not been mature enough to divine me out and discover I am a witch? Did she not choose her husband single-handed? And isn't she leaving home to make a better success of her marriage?

OSAM: Anowa, have you made up your mind to leave?

ANOWA: But Father, Mother is driving me away.

BADUA: Who is driving you away?

ANOWA: You! Who does not know here in Yebi that from the day I came to tell you that Kofi and I were getting married you have been drumming into my ears what a disgrace this marriage is going to be for you? Didn't you say that your friends were laughing at you? And they were saying that very soon I shall be sharing your clothes because my husband will never buy me any? Father, I am leaving this place. (*She picks up her basket, puts it on her head and moves down towards lower left.*)

BADUA: Yes, go.

ANOWA: I am on my way, Mother.

OSAM: And where is your husband?

ANOWA: I am going to look for him.

OSAM: Anowa, stop! (*But* ANOWA *behaves as if she has not heard him.*) Anowa, you must not leave in this manner.

BADUA: Let her go. And may she walk well.

ANOWA: Mother, I shall walk so well that I will not find my feet back here again.

(*She exits lower left.* OSAM *spits with disdain, then stares at* BADUA *for a long time. She slowly bows her head in the folds of her cloth and begins to weep quietly as the lights die on them.* Enter THE-MOUTH-THAT-EATS-SALT-AND-PEPPER.*)

OLD WOMAN: *Hei, hei, hei!* And what do the children of today want? Eh, what would the children of today have us do? Parenthood was always a very expensive affair. But it seems that now there is no man or woman created in nature who is endowed with enough powers to be a mother or a father.

(OLD MAN *enters and walks up to the middle of the lower stage passing* OLD WOMAN *on the way.*)

Listen, listen. The days when children obeyed their elders have run out. If you tell a child to go forward, he will surely step backwards. And if you asked him to move back a pace, he would run ten leagues.

OLD MAN: But what makes your heart race itself in anger so? What disturbs you? Some of us feel that the best way to sharpen a knife is not to whet one side of it only. And neither can you solve a riddle by considering only one end of it. We know too well how difficult children of today are. But who begot them? Is a man a father for sleeping with a woman and making her pregnant? And does bearing the child after nine months make her a mother? Or is she the best potter who knows her clay and how it breathes?

OLD WOMAN: Are you saying that the good parent would not tell his child what should and should not be done?

OLD MAN: How can I say a thing like that?

OLD WOMAN: And must we lie down and have our children play jumping games on our bellies if this is what they want? (*She spits.*)

OLD MAN: Oh no. No one in his rightful mind would say that babies should be free to do what they please. But Abena Badua should have known that Anowa wanted to be something else which she herself had not been . . . They say from a very small age, she had the hot eyes and nimble feet of one born to dance for the gods.

OLD WOMAN: Hmm. Our ears are breaking with that one. Who heard the Creator tell Anowa what she was coming to do with her life here? And is that why, after all her 'I don't like this' and 'I don't like that', she has gone and married Kofi Ako?

OLD MAN: Tell me what is wrong in that?

OLD WOMAN: Certainly. Some of us thought she had ordered a completely new man from the heavens.

OLD MAN: Are people angry because she chose her own husband; or is there something wrong with the boy?

OLD WOMAN: As for that Kofi Ako, they say he combs his hair too often and stays too long at the Nteh games.

OLD MAN: Who judges a man of name by his humble beginnings?

OLD WOMAN: Don't ask me. They say Badua does not want him for a son-in-law.

OLD MAN: She should thank her god that Anowa has decided to settle down at all. But then, we all talk too much about those two. And yet this is not the first time since the world began that a man and a woman have decided to be together against the advice of grey-haired crows.

OLD WOMAN: What foolish words! Some people babble as though they borrowed their grey hairs and did not grow them on their own heads! Badua should have told her daughter that the infant which tries its milk teeth on every bone and stone, grows up with nothing to eat dried meat with. (*She exits noisily.*)

OLD MAN: I'm certainly a foolish old man. But I think there is no need to behave as though Kofi Ako and Anowa have brought an evil concoction here. Perhaps it is good for them that they have left Yebi to go and try to make their lives somewhere else.

(*As lights go out, a blending of the* atentenben *with any ordinary drum.*)

Ama Ata Aidoo (Ghana)
Excerpt from *Anowa*

Bride Price

You must pay the price
Of wanting to marry
A university graduate,
A Ph.D. at that!
She's worth every bit
Of six thousand naira;
We must uphold tradition.

Agreed, but then
Can you give a guarantee
She's not shop-soiled–
All those years on the campus,
Swotting and sweating,
Sucking up to lecturers
For all those degrees?

Shop-soiled, you ask?
What do you mean 'shop-soiled'?
Our daughter's not old clothes,
She's not old books
That get soiled in the shop;
She's old wine, matured over the years
For the discerning taste.

Shop-soiled she may not be,

Matured no doubt she is;
But then is she untouched?
Has nobody removed the cork,
All those years in the varsity?

That we cannot tell you,
That's your business to find out
On your nuptial night
In the privacy of your bedroom.

In that case, in-laws, dear,
Can I return her then
And obtain a refund
According to tradition
If I should discover
Someone has sipped the wine
Before I got there?

Mabel Segun (Nigeria)

Song of a Bridegroom in Praise of His Bride
(Excerpt)

Namujezi, you flower from Jinkono's garden,
You plant too high to be reached!
Her noble figure is something to marvel at,
Her beauty turns the heads of the Aalombe,
The people of Jikokola are ravished too.
They run in their eagerness to give Namujezi gifts.
Namujezi's beauty is indescribable.
Jinkono's flower shines like a star.
I saw her from far away, before she came to us.
Namujezi, your eyes – how fresh-new they are!
And your teeth – as if you had gotten them only yesterday!
And your eyes – like those of a hornless cow!
Namujezi, open your eyes, clear as water;
Your teeth – just laugh, laugh out,
So that we may see them all and marvel at them.

We will let our game sleep
Until the morning star appears.
I will not leave the playground so long as Namujezi is there.
Where she is, the moon becomes the sun,
Night becomes bright day.
We are favourites of glorious night,
We are court servants of the moon.
Where you, Star-Namujezi, shine,
I will follow you, no matter where you go.
Well I know the signs of your passing.
Anyone knows Namujezi, even among many women.
She shines like the spring sun rising.
You say: 'No one can eat beauty.'
Yet I feed on Namujezi's.

Aandonga (Angola and Azania)

Bride's Complaint*

Father when I was a child, you promised me
We never would be separated.
Mother when I was a child, you promised me
We never would be separated.
But what of today?
Have you not broken your word?
Am I not leaving now?

Bini (Nigeria)

Bride's Farewell Song*

Oh, I am gone,
Oh, I am gone,
Call my father that I may say farewell to him,
Oh, I am gone.
Father has already sold me,

Mother has received a high price for me,
Oh, I am gone.

Baganda (Uganda)

Song of the Bridesmaids

Oh beautiful bride, don't cry,
Your marriage will be happy.
Console yourself, your husband will be good.
And like your mother and your aunt,
You will have many children in your life:
Two children, three children, four . . .

Resign yourself, do like all others.
A man is not a leopard,
A husband is not a thunder-stroke,
Your mother was your father's wife;
It will not kill you to work.

It will not kill you to grind the grain,
Nor will it kill you to wash the pots.
Nobody dies from gathering firewood
Nor from washing clothes.

We did not do it to you,
We did not want to see you go;
We love you too much for that.
It's your beauty that did it,
Because you are so gorgeous . . .
Ah, we see you laugh beneath your tears!

Goodbye, your husband is here
And already you don't seem
To need our consolations . . .

Rwanda (Rwanda)

Mola My Husband*

Mola my husband is great like my father.
Mola my master, a lion in the hills.
When he is away, I scan the hill slopes.
His strength crushes me like the eagle crushing a buck's shoulderblade.
I am the field for his hoe, the soil waiting for the first rains.
I hang like a liana from the mighty branches of a forest-giant.
I find shelter in his presence like the velvet monkey in the thick foliage
    of the mahogany tree.
I am my Mola's *mola*, I fit round his strong arm.
I am like the bats hanging from the ceiling of the caves in the rocks.
He is the rock that no spear can kill . . .

Alur (Zaïre)

Song of a Woman Whose Husband Had Gone to the Coast to Earn Money

Whenever I go out of the village
and see a stone
or a tree in the distance,
I think:
It is my husband.

Baule (Côte d'Ivoire)

A Woman's Complaint to Her Dance Group

I was going about my business
When I saw my husband out of the corner of my eye
Walking hand in hand with a girl O
I asked my husband: What are you doing with this one O?
He told me: Shut up, close your mouth!
That she's his housemaid O!
Umu Chi La Edu Uwa!

That she's his housemaid O!
I told my mother-in-law: Look, one of these days
That housemaid will become his wife O
That housemaid will become his wife O
Then he'll take that little farm and share it in two O
Then he'll take that little palm grove and share it in two O!

Then I rushed down to the village centre
To the house of our Headmaster O
To the house of our Headmaster O
Our Headmaster said: Do not cry, my child
That he would make him do penance
That for one married in church
It was not right to marry two wives
That it was against the law of the Church O.

Igbo (Nigeria)
Translated by Onwuchekwa Jemie and Ihechukwu Madubuike

Tirenje or Monde?*

'You drive yourself too hard, Chimba,' Tirenje said one day. 'Even a python grows old and weak. It is the man who goes under, not the work. There is always work.'

My house had become by now a regular meeting-place. Men and women, old and young, came round any time. Not for anything in particular. I bought a radiogram and had an electrician fit a loudspeaker above the veranda. People flocked round the house to hear the news three times a day. Often Tirenje served them tea, especially the elderly.

Since the day I had said No, she had not brought up the subject of assisting me with paper-work again. She continued her old amiable self.

'You do not hold me like a python any longer,' she said teasingly one morning. 'Your mind is too busy with other people, eh?'

I took her with a ferocity that surprised even me. As we lay panting side by side she said, 'That was not a python, it was a leopard!'

Another child was on the way.

About three months before Tirenje teased me I had met Monde in the big city. We had to visit the city in the south frequently for committee meetings and campaigning. She was serving tea at one of these meetings, as one of the administrative secretaries in the Ministry of Commerce and Industries. Tall, slender as a buck. Her eyes were narrow, almost Chinese: they would not stay long on whatever object she looked at. I had observed enough about women in the Copperbelt to know that eyes that refuse you are really seeking you out; those that open up for you have nothing to promise you.

Thus it was I said to myself, 'Chimba, here she is. Go get her.' I did. To me it was not even conquest. I always felt the drive to achieve something and simply took it for granted that I was going to own it. What people say – that you value something you have worked for – is true, but what you did not work hard for is not necessarily worthless. Monde took to me like that. I told her right from the beginning that I was married, had one child, that another was on the way, that I had lost the first-born.

'I have seen you come and go in the city,' Monde said. 'I have marked you as a man I would like to have. So your married life does not interest me. Not now. Because I couldn't do anything about it anyhow, could I? If you want to keep me and your wife, it is all right by me.'

'Would you rather take a man who can give you security as a legal husband?'

'It does not matter at present. When I want such a man, I will tell you. And if you don't want to be that man, you will tell me.'

What common sense! What a woman! I never stopped to brood over whether I should keep the one or the other – Tirenje or Monde. It was not important. I loved both very much. Each one fulfilled some part of me. And yet I could not bring myself to telling Tirenje about Monde, although I tried on the morning Tirenje talked about the python and the leopard. I felt I loved her more deeply when I had been to see Monde, who often came to the Copperbelt.

Again I felt rich, increased, to be loved by two women. Yes, that was it: to be loved by two women. More than that, I loved them both; each in a different way. To tell Tirenje would make me feel guilty of hurting her. Thinking back on it later, I remembered how the Hackett incident had rankled in me. So that I felt happier still that I could virtually say to the angels that were spying on me on his behalf: 'Tell him, go tell him that I'm free of his institutions!' But this was never in the forefront of my consciousness. It was only a soft voice, if even that, an awareness that Hackett never forgave me and that I needed no forgiveness anyhow.

The soft voice. I had to acknowledge at the same time, much as I hated to, a twinge of guilt. Not anything to deter me. Simply a soft voice that told me Tirenje would not like my relationship with Monde. Mornings as I lay in bed beside Monde, I would look up into the ceiling, thinking about Tirenje. Yes, there were nights when I did not enjoy Monde at all, because I dreaded the possibility that Tirenje might track me down to her lodgings. Sometimes I heard a voice outside in the yard which sounded like Tirenje, and my heart would kick me in the ribcage. Some days when I was in the big city, I would decide the very next day to drive back to Luanshya, longing to see Tirenje, to speak to her and the children, to hold her in my arms, to reassure her that I loved her. But always I would go to Monde with an aching hunger, a zest that seized me by the throat. I refused to contemplate giving up either one. I told myself, too, I was destined for great things. I just knew it . . .

I had seen more passionately demonstrative women than Tirenje. The woman who can pace the village or township, announcing publicly that she had caught another woman in bed with her husband; the one who can dig her nails into a rival and tear her clothes; the female who runs down the street crying and telling everybody that her husband has beaten her; the messy town female who wants to be seen with you in broad daylight for show-off. I say 'town' because in village life a woman would seldom do that. The injured wife will call the husband's relatives to discuss it. She will have received the teachings from the elders that you sit on family disagreements no matter how irksome, and solve them with your people. Came the preacher and gave us the idea from the pulpit that adultery must be publicly denounced, everything short of stoning the 'sinner'.

'How can I share my man with another woman!' Tirenje once said before we were married. 'Am I not enough to care for, feed, clothe, love and give you children? Look at us all here, we are all poor, we have to scratch for dirt to eat like chickens.'

'Suppose I earn enough to keep more than one?'

'I'm not an illiterate woman.'

'Why should an illiterate woman be able to handle one or two other wives of her man and you can't?'

'It is not a matter of *cannot*, it is that I would not have it.'

'Why? What is it that literacy has done that limits your capacity?'

'Because I know more.'

'Why?'

'Because I am literate. I selected you among many men. I have pegged my piece of land. No woman but me is going to graze in that land. When you know more – when you're literate, I think – I think – how can I say? – I think you become aware that there are certain things that should belong to you alone – a man, for instance.'

'Because you know more, because you are literate because you know more . . .'

We laughed the whole thing off.

Years later I puzzled over it. What is it in the printed word that, in expanding a woman's mental capacity, limits her capacity to tolerate others' claims on her husband's affections? If Monde had dramatized her demands in public I would have left her. She did not. Life was cosy for me that way. . .

I was sure that we were in for another exchange when I had a third letter from my father asking me to come home. Tirenje and the children were staying with him. I was sure because I hadn't had time to visit them in Shimoni. Moyo drove me to Shimoni. I would make official visits to the transport depots in the area at the same time.

'Your wife and children have gone home to Musoro,' my father said in a subdued voice. 'They waited and waited and then Tirenje said, she said, father you live on the little money Chimba sends you and I do not want to eat up all your food. She said, I must take the children to my father's house. I will be able to help him with that garden. She told me you had stopped sending money for four months.'

I did not feel in the mood to reply. Indeed I had failed to send them money. I was busy buying land in the city on which to build a house of my own. I could not bear the thought of being a government tenant any longer. Who knew, I might be fired one day, a coup might break upon us. Who knew? Who knows even now? That demotion had shaken me. Just that time. I knew I was destined for great things. I came to see the demotion as an event that should draw out the best in me for the climb that lay ahead.

'You know best,' my father said, as if to reply to my silence. 'You know best how to run your family, it is not for me to judge you. But it is a sin in God's eyes to abandon your children while you live as a big man in the city. It is a sin.'

'I will go to Musoro,' I said abruptly as if by reflex.

His face told me there was a thought bothering him, but it was a great effort to verbalize it. Bang it came as a question that made my heart miss a beat.

'Chimba,' he said, running his large sinewy hand over his whole face which was working, as if to steady it. 'Chimba, do you have someone living with you in the big city? Someone who has taken Tirenje's place?'

It was obvious throughout this meeting that he was trying desperately hard to subdue his emotions. I decided I should maintain that key.

I chuckled and paused and chuckled. I felt I was making myself a fool with this kind of response.

'How could I?'

He snorted and spat into a trash bucket at his side and snorted. 'You are not answering my question.'

'I do not have to. Did Tirenje tell you this?'

'What difference would it make who told me? The matter lies with your conscience. You are not answerable to me but to God. But I realize my God is not yours. I do not know you any more, Chimba, God forgive me! Go and comfort that good woman. She is married to a man not a government. Do you hear me? She needs a man. Even if she were starving it would not matter as long as she had her man by her side, not a – not a–' He took a deep breath and expelled it in exasperation.

'What about my two mothers?' I retorted, not without a little malice.

'They found other husbands, and I have prayed all these years that they have a better life than I could give them. God in the heavens is my judge.'

Yes, they did remarry. He was right. I could not tell whether he was feeling pity for me, in which case he must have felt superior. The speculation caused a constriction in my throat.

What did my father mean by *What difference would it make who told me? – The matter lies with your conscience?* I asked myself this question over and over again as we drove to Musoro. There was a regular bus service between the capital and the Copperbelt; lots of people made the distance by car – 200 miles or so. People talk. Could Tirenje . . . ? I made up my mind to deny it if I were confronted with the question, not to broach the subject on my own initiative.

It was evening when we arrived at the little farming town of Musoro, near the eastern border. They had had rain, and the smell of cow manure and savanna grass came on strong. The cry of crickets and cicadas pierced the cool air.

The children saw the car approach the house and I heard them yell to their mother. I had not seen them for four months and they ran toward me as I approached. Tirenje's face beamed with joy and surprise. That gave me a lift: the apprehension that was knotting up inside me, mixed with indignation, was coming under control.

'Who is that? *Moyo!*' she shouted as he came up to greet her. 'Oh we are so happy to see you again, Chimba! Has he not grown since I last saw him! We are so glad the gods have cared for you during your long journey. Papa, go and catch two of those fat chickens and make them ready for the pot.'

We always called our eldest son Papa because he was named for Tirenje's father.

'The rains were late,' she said as we went into the mud house, 'but the chickens are still thriving.' She looked thinner, but still carried herself well.

Her father came in from the garden. He was almost the living antithesis of my father. Shorter, slightly built, almost self-effacing. He had a lively face where my father's was grim. The ten years' difference between their ages was evident (he was seventy). He was more approachable without evoking pity, like my father after he had got religion. Tirenje's father's Christianity was not loud-mouthed: he did not allow it to be a ruling passion. He was cynical about it at times, without acting so. He had hauled the fat Baptist preacher over the coals for writing the letter that precipitated the Hackett incident. Told him, as Tirenje reported with great amusement, 'No more chicken and fried eggs and tea in my house, you hear me preacher man! No more! You hear me too, Tirenje, no more I say. You go pushing your belly from house to house peddling lies, spreading them all over like seed, badmouthing people who have done you or God no harm at all – in broad daylight when other men have gone to do an honest day's work. Why did you have to write to the white man? Is he your god also? Can you not ask your own ancestors to find out for you what the Almighty God wants you to do? Are you so muddle-headed you have lost your way to the ancestors? I am ashamed to be in your pants. The ancestors would have reminded you of the teachings of our elders – that a child is a human being whether he is born before or after marriage. Children are born and there is no sane law that will tell people when their children should be born. Even if Chimba does not in the end make my daughter a wife, the child is ours to cherish.' If I needed any moral support for what I had said to Hackett, this incident served me well. Tirenje's father had told the preacher not to visit his house again until he, the older man, would have asked his ancestors what to do about the preacher. 'No more,' he stressed.

Needless to say, the old man could not survive impeachment in the church council of elders. The American superintendent ordered his expulsion from the council. He told them they were free to do that but they were not going to drive him out of the church. They tried to do that but relented. From then onwards he sat with the other elderly men and women on the floor right at the back. As is customary in country churches where benches are few, the older people, like the children, sit on the floor, but at the back. They are thus saved the trouble of standing to sing or kneeling for prayer.

My father-in-law's helpers who lived nearby filled up drums with water and made open fires to heat it for our baths. It was a memorable night. Four months is nothing in a politician's life. But somehow as I went into Tirenje that night, it seemed like a long long time since my last visit at Luanshya. She was warm, responsive, receptive as ever, but it felt as if she was giving more than ever before. A few tremulous seconds I felt as if it might be the last. The very last . . .

'Tonight,' she whispered as we played around, 'hold me like a python, like in the old days.'

'A python does not spare the lungs of its victim.'

'I am a victim. Rather crush me than leave me again.' Indeed my arms seemed to take in the whole frame of her body.

In the morning Tirenje woke me up with breakfast.

'Moyo is up already,' she said, 'he is out in the field.' After she removed the tray and things, she came to sit on the bed, facing the wall.

'You are leaving me,' Tirenje said, looking alternately at the fingers she was wringing and at the wall. 'I have not told my father what is wrong.'

'I am not leaving you, Tirenje,' I said, 'what makes you think that?'

'I know it somehow, Chimba. I could feel you last night, I knew then that you are going to leave me. You are leaving me.' I knew she was crying softly. I sat up. I halfway stretched my arm to touch her shoulder. Then I could not, or would not. She turned round to face me, wiping her eyes with her gown.

'Take me with you then.'

'Let me go back to the city, and I swear I'll send a car to fetch you.'

'Chimba, you have said that so many times for three years now, and I cannot take it any more. Take us with you now.'

Silence. Then again, 'You are leaving me, Chimba, you are leaving me.' She was crying aloud now.

'Not now, Tirenje, hear me, I will send for you, I swear I will.'

She looked at her hands. Then she stiffened. 'I have heard that you are living with someone. I do not want to believe it. But hear me, Chimba, please hear me, I will not mind living in the city, as long as you let me and my children live in a separate house.'

I was stunned. I couldn't be hearing that from her own lips!

'You do not believe that I will not make trouble for you. But hear me my husband, I will not. Let us come. These children need a father, a real father, not a guardian. I need a man to live with, not a caretaker. After last night I may carry a baby in me. I need to be where you are. Hear me my husband.'

I told her I believed her. Impulsively I said, 'You have heard right. I have a woman living in the house. You must have known that I could not be content with one wife.'

'Have you married her?'

'How can I when I am also married to you?'

'By customary law?'

'No.'

'Will you take us?'

'Yes. Pack your things and let us go.' I cannot remember how I came to say that, or even what my voice sounded like. Looking back on it now I think it was her mention of the children. The last three years when I agonized about the separation it was more the image of the children that gave me a sense of loss. I had full confidence that Tirenje had immense resources inside her. Only later did it occur to me how impulsive my answer was at the time. Her tears did not make things easier. Her words *you are leaving me* cut through me because they found me out, they infuriated me because they demanded of me a decision which I had postponed for three years. Postponed until it felt as if I had decided not to make a positive move. Throughout the three years something kept telling me if Tirenje loved me and cared passionately enough, she would fight for her rights. I mean she would want to find out what was going on in my private life in the capital city. And when she found Monde she would rave and want to tear her apart in order to establish her claim. By the same token I would also ascertain if Monde's love for me could absorb a confrontation and thereby prove to me its weight – both in tears and resilience. And every time I thought like this I was reminded that Tirenje was not demonstrative in those terms. But why, I asked myself, should she take me so much for granted? Doesn't she know a husband has to be fought for just as much as a woman has to be fought for? Men have killed for women . . . I had proven my love for both by keeping both . . . The debate would become more and more futile and unimportant. Futile, partly because a man has a special kind of relationship with a woman who has borne him children, which is itself the supreme demonstration.

I took the children out to the stream. For the first time that morning I felt what it would be like to be separated from them forever or indefinitely. I wanted to hold them to me with bands of iron. It is possible, I said to myself. It is possible. If this thing did not work out, I'd still want to keep the children. All the more reason why time and again to myself I rejected the idea of divorce.

Back in the capital, Moyo asked Ankhazi, as he called his aunt Tirenje in Tumbuka, and the children to come and stay with him in Kolomo Camp, while I sorted things out for better accommodation. Old Mutiso and Moyo slept in the front 'room' and Tirenje and the children in the only other one, with a crude cloth partition between them. I would have preferred to put them in a hotel but Tirenje would have none of it. Good humouredly she said, 'I have never been in a hotel in all my life and I would not know how to conduct myself.' She had been all excitement on the road, as if she was not travelling into the unknown.

I visited them every evening. I found them an apartment on the edge of the town and insisted they move out of Moyo's as they were too cramped. She relented.

Moyo came to tell me about it. 'Asibweni, I am sorry very sorry about what happened. I should have asked you before. I was stupid. Asibweni!'

'Will you make some sense?'

'Mai wamung'ono asked me not to tell you.'

'Tell me what?'

'She asked me to take her to your house during the day. So I took her there during my lunch break. It is so near. We found Miss Lundia. I introduced them. Oh I am so foolish, asibweni.' When Moyo did not use the Tumbuka *ankbazi* for aunt, he called Tirenje *mai wamung'ono* in Chinyanja. He called me *asibweni* – uncle in Chinyanja. It irritated me that he never addressed Monde as aunt or even sister. I regarded this as a value judgement, which said a lot about his idea of himself.

'Get to the point, Moyo, I've no time to be wasting here!' Anger pushed up my gullet.

'Yes, I'm sorry, asibweni, sorry! They quarrelled. Bitterly. I don't know who started exactly but it must have been mai wamung'ono because, I do not know why, Miss Lundia could easily have started it. The gardener had to come in because they were going to rough each other up any moment.'

I postponed talking to both Monde and Tirenje about the incident beyond the preliminary 'I hear there was trouble here during the day . . . What happened? . . . Sorry to hear that . . .' Both were uncommunicative anyway that evening, and the next day I was going out to a dam site 200-odd miles south to examine transport plans for workers who would be engaged in the project. In the morning as we drove down, I told Moyo that he shouldn't worry about the incident any more. I was glad it had happened in my absence. I had not consciously created the setting for it either. And it wasn't as if I had paid to watch a cockfight. Something was bound to give.

Tirenje and the children were gone when I returned the following day. A letter awaited me at the apartment. The furniture was intact, the interior quite orderly. It was the kind of letter people write who forget most of what they learned about punctuation. Or, when they write in their native tongue, they find punctuation tedious, a nuisance in the flow of their thoughts. Tirenje always wrote to me in Chinyanja.

Beloved husband,

We have gone back to my father. I went to your house a house I would have been happy even thankful to call my own. I would have been happy Chimba I wanted to see with both eyes I saw with my own eyes I did not quarrel with your girl-friend she tells me with her own mouth that you are not married by law your girl-friend is not the fighting woman what pierces my heart like a spear is when she says to me she says when are you returning home? I ask which home? She says Musoro. I stand up on my two legs I shout to her I say are you married to my husband by law? She says no I say by the white man's law? She says no I ask again I say by the law of the Bemba? She says it is not my place to ask such questions I tell her Chimba is my husband did he not tell you that? She says you told her why are you keeping him? I ask she says Chimba is keeping me I say we were not born yesterday you know my meaning I am not here to play house like you I want my man give me back my man she says I should tell you that Chimba I should tell you that I want you back she says tell Chimba that and hear his own words. Chimba knows I love him you tell him and hear the words from his own lips. I know my man my own man I asked her questions as if I had not said to you that I would live in the city as your wife even if you had another woman. I got angry I shouted like a mad woman I wanted to tear my clothes off my body and tell her how cheap she was but the man working outside comes in and asks us not to fight I say to him I say I am not going to soil my hands with dirt like her does she think because she is a city woman she is clever and I am stupid? She rushes me but the man keeps her away these are my words husband. Do not say bad words to Moyo he does not know what to do when older people quarrel and fight these are my words I swear by Mirimba's and Chirundu's ancestors they are true. When I was back with the children I say to myself I say Tirenje daughter of Mirimba go back to the house of your father there

*is no life here. I was wrong to think that I could do it Chimba I was
wrong you know your own heart you must do what you think I have
this to say from my heart I asked you at Musoro I said do you have
another woman? Deep inside my heart I told you a lie to say that I could
live in the city even if you have another woman deep inside my heart I
wanted to hear from your own mouth hear you say you have another
woman what I have heard friends and enemies tell me in Luanshya you
said it but I still hoped my ancestors hear me truly Chimba I hoped that
my heart would turn round and I would see things your way. It is not
possible. Tell me what to do tell me what to do I will listen. For three
years now we have not talked Chimba my husband let us talk even by
letter but come to Musoro let us talk that is what people must do they
must talk with their elders with parents uncles aunts friends and heart
and mind will settle down. Tell me what to do tell me what to do.*

I am your wife Tirenje.

Why did she have to spoil the whole thing! I muttered to myself in
the centre of the apartment lounge. Why? Foolish woman! How foolish
women can be! When they are not trampled underfoot they put up
stupid meaningless fights! So you drew the confession out of me by a
trick! You couldn't even wait to see if the thing would work . . . if I had
taken you to the house there wouldn't have been this stupid quarrel . . .
But you couldn't wait to muck it all up, no, not you . . . You knew all
along you didn't have it in you to make it work and yet you let me go
to all this trouble and then almost precipitated a scandal. As if I didn't
have enough enemies in my line of work! I've tried, you know I did try
and you mucked it up . . .

Es'kia Mphahlele (Azania)
Excerpt from *Chirundu*

Not Even God is Ripe Enough to
Catch a Woman in Love

Once there was a man who was too fond of watching his wife. Day and
night he worried that she might see another man and fall in love with
him. But the wife grew tired of this habit and one day she told him:

'Husband of my head, husband of my breast, husband of my front, husband of my back! Why are you behaving like this? I have become tired of this terrible war!'

Then the husband asked: 'What kind of war?'

And she replied: 'The war of don't piss and don't shit.'

Then the husband said: 'Who asked you not to shit?' And the wife said: 'It is your attitude. Every time I go to shit or piss you suspect me of going to see a man.' 'But is it not my right as a husband to be watching my wife?' 'Well, let me warn you then,' said the wife: 'Even God is not ripe enough to watch me and catch me if I really want to love another man. What is wrong with falling in love with others anyway? I was not born to hate people.'

Then the man got even more frightened and he built a special upstairs house to keep his wife in and every morning when he went to his farm, he locked the seven doors of the house and he pocketed the keys.

One day the woman looked out of the window and took a liking to a man who was passing by. And she called out to him: 'Will you come up here?' The man looked up and saw that her neck was long and her eyes shone. 'I will come,' he said, 'if I can return from there in safety.'

'I will teach you to climb a tree,' the woman said, 'but you must know how to descend yourself. Are you not brave enough to come?'

The man said: 'I am brave, but remember war kills the captain and the river kills the swimmer and the cutlass kills the goat. Everyone has his own death prepared for him.'

'Then which kind of death will kill a lover?'

'The lover should die through woman. I will risk everything for you. For as I arrived in this world through a woman, so it is fair that I might depart from it through another.'

Then the woman threw him a piece of soap, on which she had made an impression of one of the keys to the house. And she instructed him to have a key cast by the blacksmith and return the following day. The key was marvellously made and the lover made an easy entrance to the thirsty woman.

This was how the man dipped his mouth into another man's soup and he came to enjoy her every day.

One day the husband returned and was surprised to find one of the doors of the house unlocked, for the lover had left so satisfied that he forgot all about locking the door.

The husband grew suspicious immediately and he started such palaver that the woman said in the end: 'Your jealousy is spoiling my good name. Let us go to the divine rock outside the town and let me swear on it, to settle this matter once and for all.' Now the husband was quite content with this, because it was generally known and proved that anyone who took a false oath on the rock would perspire, swell up and die. And they fixed the seventh day for the ordeal.

Now the woman began to wonder how to get out of her troubles and her mind grappled with the problem like a leper's hand trying to grasp a needle. In the end she had an idea and when the lover came the next day the woman told him the whole story and worry crumbled his brow and sweat bathed his face and he said: 'Is there any way in which I can help you in this trouble?' The woman said: 'All you have to do is to find a donkey and feed it on the way to the divine mountain in six days' time. You may leave the rest of the tricks to me.'

The day of the ordeal came and husband and wife set out for the mountain. Now the wife pretended to get more and more tired and when she noticed her lover in the distance with the donkey she pretended that she could go on no further and she sat down to rest. The husband thought that she was frightened of taking the oath and that she was trying to get out of things. Then he said to her: 'If you cannot walk then I will hire this donkey, on which you can ride to the mountain.' He called the lover who had put on some ragged clothes and they agreed on a fee of five shillings. The lover helped the woman on to the donkey and led the way.

Then the woman drew her husband near, and she said: 'A terrible thing has happened; for as I was climbing the donkey this ragged man could see what he was not supposed to see.' 'How could that be?' said the husband. And the woman replied. 'As I was hastily preparing for this oathtaking in the morning, I forgot to put on my knickers and as I was lifting my foot now, to climb the donkey, this ragged man here could see my nakedness.'

'Well,' said the husband, 'The beggar may have set eyes on my soup, but I don't mind that, as long as I am the one who is eating it.' And he hurried them on their way to the mountain.

When they reached the shrine of the rock the woman knelt down and she brought a sacrifice of cola and yam and she touched the rock with her forehead and she said:

> You, Oke, divine rock!
> You have been here to see our forefathers
> And you will be here to see our grandchildren.
> You lived to see the beginning of this town
> And you shall live to see its end.
> As I am praying to you today,
> So may I live to pray to you in the next dry season.
> Oke, divine rock,
> Witness my words,
> And punish me if I lie.
> I swear by your age and divine power
> That no man has ever seen my nakedness
> Except only my husband
> And this ragged donkey man here.
> If I do not speak the truth—
> Let my body swell up and die,
> Let me not see another sunrise
> Let me not even live to see the moon tonight.

The husband was surprised and happy to find that nothing happened to her at all. They returned home and the woman continued to enjoy her lover.

Thus she proved once again the old saying:

Not even God is ripe enough to catch a woman in love.

Yoruba (Nigeria)

Retold by Bakare Gbadamosi and Ulli Beier

Dialogue

> *Man*: May I perish, lady!
> I passed by your husband's house.
> I greeted him, he did not answer;
> I asked him the way, he did not speak.
> What does it mean?

Woman: Do not be disturbed.
I will keep day and night apart.
The night will be his,
Daylight will be yours.

Merina (Madagascar)

Lightning, Strike My Husband*

Lightning, strike my husband,
Strike my husband,
Leave my lover;
Ee, leave my lover.
Snake, bite my husband,
Bite my husband,
Leave my lover;
Ee, leave my lover.
See him walking,
How beautifully he walks;
See him dancing,
How beautifully he dances;
See him smiling,
How beautifully he smiles;
Listen to the tune of his horn,
How beautifully it sounds;
Listen to him speaking,
How beautifully he speaks;
See him performing the mock fight,
How beautifully he does it;
The sight of my lover
Is most pleasing.
Lightning, strike my husband,
Strike my husband,
Leave my lover;
Ee, leave my lover.

Acholi (Uganda)
Translated by Okot p'Bitek

Love Strikes Queen Saran*

Douga's wife looked at Da Monzon.
She was overwhelmed by his manly splendour;
the immediate love and desire she experienced
took away all control over her actions.
She spent a restless night and
her body was racked with a desire difficult to satisfy.
Her head was full of wicked ideas.
She forgot all Douga's generosity;
she forgot that she was first queen
of a country famous for the courage of its warriors
and the wealth of its people.
One idea obsessed her:
to possess Da, hold him in her arms;
to give herself to him entirely.
She was lost without realizing it.
Her frantic mind plunged into the darkness and
she forgot the rest of the world.
She had to have Da at any price.
She was prepared to commit any folly
and would even betray the man
who had never refused her anything.
She began to wonder how
she could declare her love to Da and convince him
that she was ready to leave everything,
give up everything,
as long as she could be his.

She called her seven house-servants,
her trusted confidantes,
the keepers of the secrets of her soul
who were ready to make any sacrifice for her.
She said to them: 'I am dangerously ill,
and I shall not survive my sickness.'
'How can you, mistress, since yesterday
have caught such an illness

that you are afraid you will die?'
'The illness penetrated my eyes.
It has taken root in my heart
and has drained away the waters of tranquillity
in which my soul bathed.
My heart is as dry as a *balanza* in winter;
the *balanza* which withers in spite of the rains
and becomes white, dead wood.
In spite of my gold and silver, servants and slaves,
in spite of the fields full of cattle,
the granaries full of corn,
in spite of the greatness of my husband
the hawk who pounces on the enemy
and takes him as if he were a chicken – yes, alas!
I am unhappy amidst all this!
and I shall die if no remedy can be found for the illness!'

'What can this strange sickness be
which makes you so unhappy,
oh beautiful and kind mistress?'
exclaimed one of the servants.
'I am suffering from a love
which burns more than fire,
which wounds more than an arrow,
which cuts more than a razor-edge.'

'You! in love!
You, who only had to jump over a sick horse
to cure it of its colic;
You, the precious pearl
whom only the eyes of Douga
alone have beheld?
No, mistress, you cannot make us believe
that you have ever loved any other than Douga
and never will you love anybody else.'

'If you do not believe my words
and will not help me to quench my desire,

then make ready to warm the water
which you will use to wash my corpse.
If tomorrow at sunrise
I have no hope of possessing my loved one
who kept me from sleep last night,
I shall die before the day is out, I swear it!'

The seven servants opened wide their eyes
and looked at each other in silence.
'Has not a wicked spirit,' they asked themselves,
'entered the soul of our queen
and taken away all control and reason?'
One said: 'Our duty must be
to try to cure our mistress
and do everything to preserve her health.'
Kounadi, the eldest of the servants,
said to the queen, going against the rule
forbidding anyone to pronounce her name:
'Saran, good, kind Saran, with whom are you in love?
with a spirit of the palace of King Solomon
or an heir to the throne of the Pharaohs of Misra?'

'No,' replied Saran. 'The one I love
is not a spirit of the elements, nor a prince of Misra.
He is born of a Bambara woman.
He grew up on the banks of the Dioliba
and played under the *balanzas* of Ségou.
I am in love with the prince Da.'

'Da Monzon! He who has come
to besiege Koré Douga?'

'Yes, him. I cannot prevent myself loving him.
It is something too powerful for me.
I am ashamed of myself,
but I can neither resist it nor remain silent.
That is why I am telling you this mortal secret.
The choice is yours: either you help me to reach Da
or you go and denounce me to Koré Douga.

If you choose the second solution
know then that Douga will have my head shaved;
he will dress me in rough bark
and will weigh me down with ignoble chains
as before he weighed me down
with gold and silver and pearls.
You will see me collapse under the whip
and then my head will be cut off
and thrown to the crows.
But before the end, when my mouth is bleeding,
my teeth broken, when I am dying of thirst,
I shall refuse the water offered me by a kind soul.
Give me Da, I shall say, I am thirsting for him;
water cannot quench my soul!'

Kounadi looked at her companions:
they were all weeping sincere tears . . .

Bambara (Mali)
Excerpt from 'Monzon and the King of Kore'
Translated by A. Hampate Ba

The Suit

Five-thirty in the morning, and the candlewick bedspread frowned as
the man under it stirred. He did not like to wake his wife lying by his
side – as yet – so he crawled up and out by careful peristalsis. But before
he tiptoed out of his room with shoes and socks under his arm, he leaned
over and peered at the sleeping serenity of his wife: to him a daily
matutinal miracle.

He grinned and yawned simultaneously, offering his wordless *Te
Deum* to whatever gods for the goodness of life; for the pure beauty of
his wife; for the strength surging through his willing body; for the even,
unperturbed rhythms of his passage through days and months and years
– it must be – to heaven.

Then he slipped soundlessly into the kitchen. He flipped aside the
curtain of the kitchen window, and saw outside a thin drizzle, the type

that can soak one to the skin, and that could go on for days and days. He wondered, head aslant, why the rain in Sophiatown always came in the morning when workers had to creep out of their burrows; and then at how blistering heatwaves came during the day when messengers had to run errands all over; and then at how the rain came back when workers knocked off and had to scurry home.

He smiled at the odd caprice of the heavens, and tossed his head at the naughty incongruity, as if, 'Ai, but the gods!'

From behind the kitchen door he removed an old rain cape, peeling off in places, and swung it over his head. He dashed for the lavatory, nearly slipping in a pool of muddy water, but he reached the door. Aw, blast, someone had made it before him. Well, that is the toll of staying in a yard where twenty . . . thirty other people have to share the same lean-to. He was dancing and burning in that climactic moment when trousers-fly will not come wide soon enough. He stepped round the lavatory and watched the streamlets of rainwater quickly wash away the jet of tension that spouted from him. That infinite after-relief. Then he dashed back to his kitchen. He grabbed the old baby bathtub hanging on a nail under the slight shelter of the gutterless roof-edge. He opened a large wooden box and quickly filled the bathtub with coal. Then he inched his way back to the kitchen door and hurried inside.

He was huh-huh-huhing one of those fugitive tunes that cannot be hidden, but that often just occur and linger naggingly in the head. The fire he was making soon licked up cheerfully, in mood with his contentment.

He had a trick for these morning chores. While the fire in the old stove warmed up, the kettle humming on it, he gathered and laid ready the things he would need for the day: briefcase and the files that go with it; the book that he was currently reading; the letters of his lawyer boss which he usually posted before he reached the office; his wife's and his own dry-cleaning slips for the Sixty-Minutes; his lunch tin solicitously prepared the night before by his attentive wife; and today, the battered rain cape. When the kettle on the stove began to sing (before it actually boiled), he poured water into a wash basin, refilled and replaced it on the stove. Then he washed himself carefully: across the eyes, under, in and out the armpits, down the torso and in between the legs. This ritual was thorough, though no white man a-complaining of the smell of wogs, knows anything about it. Then he dressed himself fastidiously. By this time he was ready to prepare breakfast.

Breakfast! How he enjoyed taking in a tray of warm breakfast to his wife, cuddled in bed. To appear there in his supreme immaculacy, tray in hand when his wife came out of ether to behold him. These things we blacks want to do for our own . . . not fawningly for the whites for whom we bloody well got to do it. He denied that he was one of those who believed in putting your wife in her place even if she was a good wife. Not he.

Matilda, too, appreciated her husband's kindness, and only put her foot down when he would offer to wash up.

'Off with you,' she would scold him on his way.

At the bus-stop he was a little sorry to see that jovial old Maphikela was in a queue for a bus ahead of him. Today he would miss Maphikela's raucous laughter and uninhibited, bawdy conversations in fortissimo. Maphikela hailed him nevertheless. He thought he noticed hesitation in the old man, and a slight clouding of his countenance, but the old man shouted back at him, saying that he would wait for him at the terminus in town.

Philemon considered this morning trip to town with garrulous old Maphikela as his daily bulletin. All the township news was generously reported by loudmouthed heralds, and spiritedly discussed by the bus at large. Of course, 'news' included views on bosses (scurrilous), the Government (rude), Ghana and Russia (idolatrous), America and the West (sympathetically ridiculing), and boxing (bloodthirsty). But it was always stimulating and surprisingly comprehensive for so short a trip. And there was no law of libel.

Maphikela was standing under one of those token bus-stop shelters that keep out neither rain nor wind nor sun-heat. Philemon easily located him by his noisy ribbing of some office boys in their khaki-green uniforms. They walked together into town, but from Maphikela's suddenly subdued manner, Philemon gathered that there was something serious coming up. Maybe a loan.

Eventually, Maphikela came out with it.

'Son,' he said sadly, 'if I could've avoided this, believe you me I would, but my wife is nagging the spice out of my life for not talking to you about it.'

It just did not become blustering old Maphikela to sound so grave and Philemon took compassion upon him.

'Go ahead, dad,' he said generously. 'You know you can talk to me about anything.'

The old man gave a pathetic smile. 'We-e-e-ll, it's not really any of our business . . . er . . . but my wife felt . . . you see. Damn it all I wish these women would not snoop around so much.' Then he rushed it. 'Anyway, it seems there's a young man who's going to visit your wife every morning . . . ah . . . for these last bloomin' three months. And that wife of mine swears by her heathen gods you don't know a thing about it.'

It was not like the explosion of a devastating bomb. It was more like the critical breakdown in an infinitely delicate piece of mechanism. From outside the machine just seemed to have gone dead. But deep in its innermost recesses, menacing electrical flashes were leaping from coil to coil, and hot, viscous molten metal was creeping upon the fuel tanks . . .

Philemon heard gears grinding and screaming in his head . . .

'Dad,' he said hoarsely, 'I . . . I have to go back home.'

He turned around and did not hear old Maphikela's anxious, 'Steady, son. Steady, son.'

The bus ride home was a torture of numb dread and suffocating despair. Though the bus was now emptier Philemon suffered crushing claustrophobia. There were immense washerwomen whose immense bundles of soiled laundry seemed to baulk and menace him. From those bundles crept miasmata of sweaty intimacies that sent nauseous waves up and down from his viscera. The wild swaying of the bus as it negotiated Mayfair Circle hurtled him sickeningly from side to side. Some of the younger women shrieked delightedly to the driver, '*Fuduga!* . . . Stir the pot!' as he swung his steering wheel this way and that. Normally, the crazy tilting of the bus gave him a prickling exhilaration. But now . . .

He felt like getting out of there, screamingly, elbowing everything out of his way. He wished this insane trip were over, and then again, he recoiled at the thought of getting home. He made a tremendous resolve to gather in all the torn, tingling threads of his nerves contorting in the raw. By a merciless act of will, he kept them in subjugation as he stepped from the bus back in the Victoria Road terminus, Sophiatown.

The calm he achieved was tense . . . but he could think now . . . he could take a decision . . .

With almost boyishly innocent urgency, he rushed through his kitchen into his bedroom. In the lightning flash that the eye can whip, he saw it all . . . the man beside his wife . . . the chestnut arm around her neck . . . the ruffled candlewick bedspread . . . the suit across the chair. But he affected not to see.

He opened the wardrobe door, and as he dug into it, he cheerfully spoke to his wife. 'Fancy, Tilly, I forgot to take my pass. I had already reached town, and was going to walk up to the office, if it hadn't been for wonderful old Mr Maphikela . . . '

A swooshing noise of violent retreat and the clap of his bedroom window stopped him. He came from behind the wardrobe door and looked out from the open window. A man clad only in vest and underpants was running down the street. Slowly, he turned round and contemplated . . . the suit.

Philemon lifted it gingerly under his arm and looked at the stark horror in Matilda's eyes. She was now sitting up in bed. Her mouth twitched, but her throat raised no words.

'Ha,' he said. 'I see we have a visitor,' indicating the blue suit. 'We really must show some of our hospitality. But first, I must phone my boss to tell him that I can't come to work today . . . mmmm-er, my wife's not well. Be back in a moment, then we can make arrangements.' He took the suit along.

When he returned he found Matilda weeping on the bed. He dropped the suit beside her, pulled up the chair, turned it round so that its back came in front of him, sat down, brought down his chin on to his folded arms before him, and waited for her.

After a while the convulsions of her shoulders ceased. She saw a smug man with an odd smile and meaningless inscrutability in his eyes. He spoke to her with very little noticeable emotion; if anything, with a flutter of humour.

'We have a visitor, Tilly.' His mouth curved ever so slightly. 'I'd like him to be treated with the greatest of consideration. He will eat every meal with us and share all we have. Since we have no spare room, he'd better sleep in here. But the point is, Tilly, that you will meticulously look after him. If he vanishes or anything else happens to him . . .' a shaft of evil shot from his eye . . . 'Matilda, I'll kill you.'

He rose from the chair and looked with incongruous supplication at her. He told her to put the fellow in the wardrobe for the time being. As she passed him to get the suit, he turned to go. She ducked frantically, and he stopped.

'You don't seem to understand me, Matilda. There's to be no violence in this house if you and I can help it. So just look after that suit.' He went out.

He made his way to the Sophiatown Post Office, which is placed exactly on the line between Sophiatown and the white man's surly Westdene. He posted his boss's letters and walked to the beerhall at the tail end of Western Native Township. He had never been inside it before, but somehow the thunderous din laved his bruised spirit. He stayed there all day.

He returned home for supper . . . and surprises. His dingy little home had been transformed, and the air of stern masculinity it had hitherto contained had been wiped away to be replaced by anxious feminine touches here and there. There were even gay, colourful curtains swirling in the kitchen window. The old-fashioned coal stove gleamed in its blackness. A clean, chequered oilcloth on the table. Supper ready.

Then she appeared in the doorway of the bedroom. Heavens! here was the woman he had married; the young, fresh, cocoa-coloured maid who had sent rushes of emotion shuddering through him. And the dress she wore brought out all the girlishness of her, hidden so long beneath German print. But no hint of coquettishness, although she stood in the doorway and slid her arm up the jamb, and shyly slanted her head to the other shoulder. She smiled weakly.

'What makes a woman like this experiment with adultery?' he wondered.

Philemon closed his eyes and gripped the seat of his chair on both sides as some overwhelming, undisciplined force sought to catapult him towards her. For a moment some essence glowed fiercely within him, then sank back into itself and died . . .

He sighed and smiled sadly back at her. 'I'm hungry, Tilly.'

The spell snapped, and she was galvanized into action. She prepared supper with dextrous hands that trembled a little when they hesitated in mid-air. She took her seat opposite him, regarded him curiously, clasped her hands waiting for his prayer, but in her heart she murmured some other, much more urgent prayer of her own.

'Matilda!' he barked. 'Our visitor!' The sheer savagery with which he cracked at her jerked her up, but only when she saw the brute cruelty in his face did she run out of the room, toppling the chair behind her.

She returned with the suit on a hanger, and stood there quivering like a feather. She looked at him with helpless dismay. The demoniacal rage in his face was evaporating, but his heavy breathing still rocked his thorax above the table, to and fro.

'Put a chair there,' he indicated with a languid gesture of his arm. She moved like a ghost as she drew a chair to the table.

'Now seat our friend at the table . . . no, no, not like that. Put him in front of the chair, and place him on the seat so that he becomes indeed the third person.'

Philemon went on relentlessly. 'Dish up for him. Generously. I imagine he hasn't had a morsel all day, the poor devil.'

Now, as consciousness and thought seeped back into her, her movements revolved so that always she faced this man who had changed so spectacularly. She started when he rose to open the window and let in some air.

She served the suit. The act was so ridiculous that she carried it out with a bitter sense of humiliation. He came back to sit down and plunged into his meal. No grace was said for the first time in this house. With his mouth full, he indicated by a toss of his head that she should sit down in her place. She did so. Glancing at her plate, the thought occurred to her that someone, after a long famine, was served a sumptuous supper, but as the food reached her mouth it turned to sawdust. Where had she heard it?

Matilda could not eat. She suddenly broke into tears.

Philemon took no notice of her weeping. After supper he casually gathered the dishes and started washing up. He flung a dry cloth at her without saying a word. She rose and went to stand by his side drying up. But for their wordlessness, they seemed a very devoted couple.

After washing up, he took the suit and turned to her. 'That's how I want it every meal, every day.' Then he walked into the bedroom.

So it was. After that first breakdown, Matilda began to feel that her punishment was not too severe, considering the heinousness of the crime. She tried to put a joke into it, but by slow, unconscious degrees, the strain nibbled at her. Philemon did not harass her much more, so long as the ritual with the confounded suit was conscientiously followed.

Only once, he got one of his malevolent brainwaves. He got it into his head that 'our visitor' needed an outing. Accordingly the suit was taken to the dry-cleaners during the week, and, come Sunday, they had to take it out for a walk. Both Philemon and Matilda dressed for the occasion. Matilda had to carry the suit on its hanger over her back and the three of them strolled leisurely along Ray Street. They passed the church crowd in front of the famous Anglican Mission of Christ the King. Though the worshippers saw nothing unusual in them, Matilda felt, searing through her, red-hot needles of embarrassment, and every needle-point was a public eye piercing into her degradation.

But Philemon walked casually on. He led her down Ray Street and turned into Main Road. He stopped often to look into shop windows or to greet a friend passing by. They went up Toby Street, turned into Edward Road, and back home. To Philemon the outing was free of incident, but to Matilda it was one long excruciating experience.

At home, he grabbed a book on abnormal psychology, flung himself into a chair and calmly said to her, 'Give the old chap a rest, will you, Tilly?'

In the bedroom, Matilda said to herself that things could not go on like this. She thought of how she could bring the matter to a head with Philemon; have it out with him once and for all. But the memory of his face, that first day she had forgotten to entertain the suit, stayed with her. She thought of running away, but where to? Home? What could she tell her old-fashioned mother had happened between Philemon and her? All right, run away clean then. She thought of many young married girls who were divorcees now, who had won their freedom.

What had happened to Staff Nurse Kakile? The woman drank heavily now, and when she got drunk, the boys of Solphiatown passed her around and called her the Cesspot.

Matilda shuddered.

An idea struck her. There were still decent, married women around Sophiatown. She remembered how after the private schools had been

forced to close with the introduction of Bantu Education, Father
Harringay of the Anglican Mission had organized cultural clubs. One,
she seemed to remember, was for married women. If only she could lose
herself in some cultural activity, find absolution for her conscience in
some club doing good, that would blur her blasted home life, would
restore her self-respect. After all, Philemon had not broadcast her
disgrace abroad . . . nobody knew; not one of Sophiatown's slander-
mongers suspected how vulnerable she was. She must go and see Mrs
Montjane about joining a cultural club. She must ask Philemon now if
she might . . . she must ask him nicely.

She got up and walked into the other room where Philemon was
reading quietly. She dreaded disturbing him, did not know how to begin
talking to him . . . they had talked so little for so long. She went and
stood in front of him, looking silently upon his deep concentration.
Presently he looked up with a frown on his face.

Then she dared. 'Phil, I'd like to join one of those cultural clubs for
married women. Would you mind?'

He wrinkled his nose and rubbed it between thumb and index finger
as he considered the request. But he had caught the note of anxiety in
her voice and thought he knew what it meant.

'Mmmmm,' he said, nodding. 'I think that's a good idea. You can't
be moping around here all day. Yes, you may, Tilly.' Then he returned
to his book.

The cultural club idea was wonderful. She found women like herself,
with time (if not with tragedy) on their hands, engaged in wholesome,
refreshing activities. The atmosphere was cheerful and cathartic. They
learned things and they did things. They organized fêtes, bazaars, youth
activities, sport, music, self-help and community projects. She got
involved in committees, meetings, debates, conferences. It was for her
a whole new venture into humancraft, and her personality blossomed.
Philemon gave her all the latitude she wanted.

Now, abiding by that silly ritual at home seemed a little thing . . . a
very little thing . . .

Then one day she decided to organize a little party for her friends and
their husbands. Philemon was very decent about it. He said it was all
right. He even gave her extra money for it. Of course, she knew nothing
of the strain he himself suffered from his mode of castigation.

There was a week of hectic preparation. Philemon stepped out of its cluttering way as best he could. So many things seemed to be taking place simultaneously. New dresses were made. Cakes were baked, three different orders of meat prepared; beef for the uninvited chancers; mutton for the normal guests; turkey and chicken for the inner pith of the club's core. To Philemon, it looked as if Matilda planned to feed the multitude on the Mount with no aid of miracles.

On the Sunday of the party Philemon saw Matilda's guests. He was surprised by the handsome grace with which she received them. There was a long table with enticing foods and flowers and serviettes. Matilda placed all her guests round the table, and the party was ready to begin in the mock-formal township fashion. Outside a steady rumble of conversation went on where the human odds and ends of every Sophia-town party had their 'share'.

Matilda caught the curious look on Philemon's face. He tried to disguise his edict when he said, 'Er . . . the guest of honour.'

But Matilda took a chance. She begged, 'Just this once, Phil.'

He became livid. 'Matilda!' he shouted. 'Get our visitor!' Then with incisive sarcasm, 'or are you ashamed of him?'

She went ash-grey; but there was nothing for it but to fetch her albatross. She came back and squeezed a chair into some corner, and placed the suit on it. Then she slowly placed a plate of food before it. For a while the guests were dumbfounded. Then curiosity flooded in. They talked at the same time. 'What's the idea, Philemon? . . . Why must she serve a suit? . . . What's happening?' Some just giggled in a silly way. Philemon carelessly swung his head towards Matilda. 'You better ask my wife. She knows the fellow best.'

All interest beamed upon poor Matilda. For a moment she could not speak, all-enveloped in misery. Then she said, unconvincingly, 'It's just a game that my husband and I play at mealtime.' They roared with laughter. Philemon let her get away with it.

The party went on, and every time Philemon's glare sent Matilda scurrying to serve the suit each course; the guests were no end amused by the persistent mock-seriousness with which this husband and wife played out their little game. Only, to Matilda, it was no joke; it was a hot poker down her throat. After the party, Philemon went off with one of the guests who had promised to show him a joint 'that sells genuine stuff, boy, genuine stuff'.

Reeling drunk, late that sabbath, he crashed through his kitchen door, onwards to his bedroom. Then he saw her.

They have a way of saying in the argot of Sophiatown, 'Cook out of the head!' signifying that someone was impacted with such violent shock that whatever whiffs of alcohol still wandered through his head were instantaneously evaporated and the man stood sober before stark reality.

There she lay, curled, as if just before she died she begged for a little love, implored some implacable lover to cuddle her a little . . . just this once . . . just this once more.

In intense anguish, Philemon cried, 'Tilly!'

Can Themba (Azania)

Return

(*Late afternoon to early evening. Outside* OKORO's *sitting room. He is grumpy, trying to shake dust from a bale of clothes that he has not been able to take to market, because he has had to stay to do the housekeeping.*)

OKORO: Several days gone and I've not been able to go to market, while other people are busy making money, all because of these foolish, misguided women. (KOKO *enters*) So you've come back?

KOKO: (*Going past him with something like a hobble*) Yes; we have and I'm kneeling.

OKORO: (*Following closely behind*) Rise, if you like. Now have you gone and bruised your toe on some stump on the road that you are walking like a hen that has just laid? Iyara is not such a long walk that you should have sore thighs.

KOKO: (*Looking around distractedly*) No; it's not such a walk, but where are the children? Are the children home?

OKORO: Why the sudden show of interest?

KOKO: (*Sitting herself down*) Oh, let's not go into that now.

OKORO: Why not? You didn't stop to think about the children before you took off on your foolish flight.

KOKO: (*Arranges her wrapper between her laps*) Are the children home, I asked.

OKORO: (*Stalks about the place*) I suppose you expected they would be standing here with me as a sort of reception committee to welcome their errant mother home?

KOKO: I expected no drums and cannons!

OKORO: So you didn't expect to be received into town like some white man or politician doing his campaign tour. Well, what then?

KOKO: Where are my children is all I asked.

OKORO: I've sent them off to Oguori's to play, if you care to know.

KOKO: (*Very frantic*) Good, good, for I have a confession to make, yes, immediately.

OKORO: (*Walks away*) What confession? That you ran away from home on some misguided feminine trail, leaving behind among others a child still feeding on your breast.

KOKO: Oh, will you listen! I have something serious to report. There is time enough on the floor to talk about these matters later.

OKORO: All right, all right! I'm listening now. After all, you've taken over the business of laying down the law in our land.

KOKO: (*Wringing her hands*) Okoro, I hardly know how to begin – I think I have got . . .

OKORO: Yes; got what?

KOKO: Oh, I can't say it!

OKORO: You can't say it out, did you say? Then let me find you pen and paper to write it down like our teacher does.

KOKO: Look, Koro, this is no laughing matter. You know I never went to school; so how can I write?

OKORO: Well, woman, I know you too well; you and the canary are mates. So when you suddenly run dry of words like a well at times of harmattan, there must be news across the country.

KOKO: Yes, there is. I think I've got the cross-piece.

OKORO: You've got what – the cross-piece – did you say – in your crotch? You don't know what you're saying.

KOKO: Oh, I believe I do.

OKORO: How do you know?

KOKO: See, I'm burning between my thighs.

OKORO: Oh, my mother who bore me! And do you say that to me sitting there without fear of the gods and the dead?

KOKO: (*Beginning to cry*) Oh, I don't know how this terrible thing came about.

OKORO: Oh, you don't know? Do say that again! When you were doing it, it was sweet; you didn't know it would turn out like this? That honey will become kola nut? Oh, women, deception is your bicycle, and you'll ride it all the way over a cliff, proclaiming you are on the straight path. You leave here, just a few nights away from home, from your husband and children, under a billowing banner bringing all women out of bondage, when in fact it was to go and meet your lover. That's what you should confess; Oh, confess it, woman, before I chop off your head with my cutlass!

KOKO: I'll confess, confess anything, if it will take away this fire burning up my skirts, up my middle. Oh, it's terrible, hotter than pepper taken by the Ijo with palm wine.

OKORO: Then may it burn you a hundred times as the seeds of the alligator pepper crushed and spat at your under-belly when distended with child.

KOKO: (*She goes to him on her knees*) Oh, curse me, kill me, 'Koro, if it'll take this pain from me. Oh, I can't bear it, I can't bear it! There, will you help blow it for me? (*She holds on to him.*)

OKORO: (*More dazed than angry*) Koko, who did this to you?

KOKO: The dead and the gods know I cannot tell who.

OKORO: What, shameless woman! Do you mean you had more than one man you cannot even tell who did it to you?

KOKO: Not one, not one did I do it with, I swear.

OKORO: Oh, this is too much.

(*He starts beating her with one piece of wrapper out of his unsold bale.*)

KOKO: (*Not caring to ward off the blows*) Oh, beat me, beat me dead! Your blows are not half as painful as this fire that has found a hob in my crotch.

OKORO: Woman without shame, gone to set up at Iyara, that hole of a place, all houses half-finished, earthworms at one end, and their floors running with gutters as houses in Isale Eko.

KOKO: It must be worse than the songs say, if it has done this to me.

OKORO: Harlot!

(*He keeps beating her.*)

KOKO: Oh, beat me; beat me dead! The dead and the gods know I don't know how it all happened.

OKORO: It was rape then!

KOKO: It wasn't. Oh, I don't know! I don't know!

OKORO: All done with full consent then, eh? And by a group of such number you don't remember who? Confess, confess!

(IDAMA *enters, and pulls* OKORO *away from* KOKO.)

IDAMA: Hey, confess what? Will you kill the woman?

OKORO: Keep away from this, will you? It's a private matter.

IDAMA: No! Now run, run, woman, run! Or do you enjoy beating by your husband so much you'll sit and take it all?

OKORO: I'll kill her today.

IDAMA: No, you won't. There, run, Koko, oh, I say run!

(*He pushes her gently but firmly towards her room.*)

OKORO: How can she run? Do you know what she says she's carrying, what she has brought back home with her from Iyara, the shameless woman?

IDAMA: (*Clasping his head in his hands*) Oh, no, don't say she too has it? So none escaped after all!

OKORO: Escaped what? Oh, stop laughing, will you! Now I know you've come indeed as my friend, when all you can do is laugh at this disaster that has crossed my doorstep.

IDAMA: Got it too, has she?

(IDAMA *goes on laughing, wiping the tears off his eyes first with one hand, then with the other.* OKORO *goes to hold him down while* KOKO *looks from one to the other not understanding.*)

OKORO: Now, are you going to speak sense and stop fizzing like a bicycle tyre that has lost its valve?

IDAMA: (*Sinking into a chair*) I'm no tyre that has picked up a nail. I came to tell you my wife came home with the thing.

OKORO: What – you mean she too has it?

IDAMA: Oh, yes, I'm afraid so.

OKORO: Titi also has it?

IDAMA: Yes, yes, right down to the itch.

(KOKO *goes in puzzled but somewhat relieved.*)

OKORO: Oh, 'Dama, what woman can we trust out of sight in this world? One man has had both our wives and now he has sent them back to us with a clear message. Let's go and demand damages, 'Dama. I shall die with him when I get to Iyara.

IDAMA: How then will you collect your damage fees from him?

OKORO: The adulterer! With my bare hands I'll wring his neck like a chicken.

IDAMA: If it were that simple there are many who will take the vow with you all across town.

OKORO: Stop that kind of talk, my friend. Has anyone suffered like me – of course, except you?

IDAMA: Oh, yes, every man with a wife in this town.

OKORO: The trouble with you, Idama, is that you exaggerate too much. Like your holy book, every story of yours must have to its one head limbs, fingers and toes by the dozen.

IDAMA: Well, you may not believe it, but it seems all our good women came back home carrying the same secret. Because each believed she was alone with her shame, none told the other.

OKORO: I do not understand. You mean they all went to Iyara to set up shop? I thought only my wife deceived me.

KOKO: (*From within*) Oh, you would, wouldn't you! You always believe the worst of me.

OKORO: Shut up there, will you? This is talk between men. But 'Dama, are you seriously saying all our women did the same act at Iyara – willingly and with one man who has sent them home with this thing? No, do not laugh. Idama, do not laugh. Can one man have such power, such stamina to take a townful of women in one night?

IDAMA: One man . . . ?

OKORO: Oh, give me his name, tell me his house, and if it is where the sun itself touches the earth, I shall be his special guest tonight, a suppliant for his unique gift and charm that lays a hallful of women in one night. I will pay any amount, do anything he wants to acquire his power.

IDAMA: One man? Who said one man?

OKORO: Well, am I to believe our women willingly and collectively surrendered themselves to public abuse by all and any comer from that crummy, scurvy, scabies-ridden crowd called Iyara?

KOKO: There, listen to him defaming us, listen to him!

OKORO: Shut up, woman, shut up, or have you no shame after what you've done? That you have company in your act of shame does not make you less guilty. Oh, yes, that a disease becomes an epidemic does not make it any less a disease. It makes it as many times terrible. Oh, so it's true women love the ugly and the bad!

KOKO: (*Clapping hands, with loud voices from within*) Shame, shame on you!

OKORO: Look, who's crying shame, you who went to shame a whole city.

IDAMA: It was not like that. Now, will you listen!

OKORO: All right, how was it then? Untangle the strands, since the thing has become a web in which we poor house flies flounder.

KOKO: Nobody called you a house-fly.

OKORO: Oko, shall I slap that woman across the mouth with my cutlass?

IDAMA: No, you keep your thing in its sheath, and listen to someone for a change.

J. P. Clark (Nigeria)
Excerpt from *The Wives' Revolt*

VIII — DEATH AND BEREAVEMENT

The Beautiful Playground*

The beautiful playground goes quickly to ruin,
The beautiful game field goes quickly to ruin,
Dense jungle soon becomes grass steppe, grass steppe,
Our beautiful town returns to open plain,
Our beautiful town returns to open plain.

Let the grave-diggers not bury me,
Let one bury my feet and leave my body free;
So that my kindred may come and see my face,
Come and look in my face.

The drum does not beat to joy,
The drum does not beat to joy,
'Misery, misery,' beats the drum,
Only to misery the drum beats.

If Death were game, a hunter would kill him, and I would be given a
   thigh,†
Would kill him, and I would be given a thigh,
A hunter would kill him, and I would be given an arm,
The slayer of my dear father,
A hunter would kill him, and I would be given an arm,
The slayer of my dear mother,
A hunter would kill him, and I would be given an arm,
The slayer of my dear brother.
Could not King Death be a game animal, so that a hunter would kill
   him and I be given a thigh?

Ewe (Togo)

†*Be given a thigh:* damage caused by an ox is compensated by the gift of a thigh when
the animal is slaughtered.

When Death Comes to Fetch You*

My husband rejects me
Because he says
That I am a mere pagan
And I believe in the devil.
He says
I do not know
The rules of health,
And I mix up
Matters of health and superstitions.

Ocol troubles my head,
He talks too much
And he heaps insults on me
As well as my relatives.

But most of his words are senseless,
They are like the songs
Of children's plays.
And he treats his clansmen
As if they are enemies.
Ocol behaves
As if he is a witch!

It is true
White man's medicines are strong,
But Acoli medicines
Are also strong.

The sick gets cured
Because his time has not yet come:
But when the day has dawned
For the journey to Pagak
No one can stop you,
White man's medicines
Acoli medicines,
Crucifixes, rosaries,
Toes of edible rats,

The horn of the rhinoceros
None of them can block the path
That goes to Pagak!

When Death comes
To fetch you
She comes unannounced,
She comes suddenly
Like the vomit of dogs,
And when She comes
The wind keeps blowing
The birds go on singing
And the flowers
Do not hang their heads.
The *agoga* bird is silent
The *agoga* comes afterwards,
He sings to tell
That Death has been that way!

When Mother Death comes
She whispers
Come,
And you stand up
And follow
You get up immediately,
And you start walking
Without brushing the dust
On your buttocks.

You may be behind
A new buffalo-hide shield,
And at the mock fight
Or in battle
You may be matchless;

You may be hiding
In the hole
Of the smallest black insect,
Or in the darkest place

Where rats breast-feed their puppies,
or behind the Agoro hills,

You may be the fastest runner,
A long-distance runner,
But when Death comes
To fetch you
You do not resist,
You must not resist.
You cannot resist!

Mother Death
She says to her little ones,
Come!

Her little ones are good children,
Obedient,
Loyal,
And when Mother Death calls
Her little ones jump,
They jump gladly
For she calls
And offers *simsim* paste
Mixed with honey!
She says
My only child
Come,
Come, let us go.
Let us go
And eat white ants' paste
Mixed with *shea*-butter!
And who can resist that?

White diviner priests,
Acoli herbalists,
All medicine men and medicine women
Are good, are brilliant
When the day has not yet dawned
For the great journey

The last safari
To Pagak.

Okot p'Bitek (Uganda)
Excerpt from *Song of Lawino*

Song of the Unburied

We, men, we are the oxen of the vultures,
We are cattle to be shared by the vultures,
To be devoured by carrion crows in the veld.

Basotho (Lesotho)

Dirge

He died; no song, no drumming, no sport, he is a poor man and his
    clan is poor.
One dies in fire, one dies in water. So do we all belong to death and
    go to our place.
I was at home alone, and I heard a bitter wailing; I went and found
    my brother dead and drummed in grief.

Ewe (Togo)

Girl's Song

O my cousin, my beloved,
Once I thought I did not love you.
When they came back saying they had left you dead,
I went up on the hill where my tomb will be.
I gathered stones, I buried my heart.
The odour of you that I smell between my breasts
Shoots fire into my bones.

Tuareg (Sahara and West Africa)

Hymn of the Afflicted

Older widows:
We are left outside!
We are left to grief!
We are left to despair,
Which only makes our woes more bitter!
Would that I had wings to fly up to the sky!
Why does not a strong cord come down from the sky?
I would tie it to me, I would mount,
I would go there to live.

The new widow:
O fool that I am!
When evening comes, I open my window a little,
I listen in the silence, I look:
I imagine that he is coming back!

The dead fighting man's sister:
If women, too, went to war,
I would have gone, I would have thrown darts beside him:
My brother would not be dead:
Rather, my mother's son would have turned back half-way,
He would have pretended he had hurt his foot against a stone.

All the women:
Alas! are they really gone?
Are we abandoned indeed?
But where have they gone
That they cannot come back?
That they cannot come back to see us?
Are they really gone?
Is the underworld insatiable?
Is it never filled?

Basotho (Lesotho)

Laws and Restrictions at the Feast of the Dead*

You have come to the festival,
Men and women.
Of quarrelsome people, let there be none among you.
The husband who has brought his wife
Must spend with her the night in the same place.
He who has no wife
Shall not take one belonging to someone else.
My whole village, I have pacified.
He who has the mastery over fetishes
Let him leave them in his own village.
If anyone wants to prowl at night like a witch,
Let him beware, our fetishes will make him jump.
It will be said: he has eaten bad food at the festival,
In truth, he will have devoured his own self.
He who is very hungry,
Let him not take food by force;
Let him ask for it, and he shall be satisfied.
He who wishes to dance,
Let him dance to the drum he prefers.
But let no one pick a quarrel.
I have convoked all of you,
I want you to return home in peace.

Bakongo (Zaïre and Angola)

Ceremonies for the Dead*

On the third day, the same comings and goings of friends, relatives, the poor, the unknown. The name of the deceased, who was popular, has mobilized a buzzing crowd, welcomed in my house that has been stripped of all that could be stolen, all that could be spoilt. Mats of all sorts are spread out everywhere there is space. Metal chairs hired for the occasion take on a blue hue in the sun.

Comforting words from the Koran fill the air; divine words, divine instructions, impressive promises of punishment or joy, exhortations to virtue, warnings against evil, exaltation of humility, of faith. Shivers run through me. My tears flow and my voice joins weakly in the fervent 'Amen' which inspires the crowd's ardour at the end of each verse.

The smell of the *lakh* cooling in the calabashes pervades the air, exciting.

Also passed around are large bowls of red or white rice, cooked here or in neighbouring houses. Iced fruit juices, water and curds are served in plastic cups. The men's group eats in silence. Perhaps they remember the stiff body, tied up and lowered by their hands into a gaping hole, quickly covered up again.

In the women's corner, nothing but noise, resonant laughter, loud talk, handslaps, strident exclamations. Friends who have not seen each other for a long time hug each other noisily. Some discuss the latest material on the market. Others indicate where they got their woven wrappers from. The latest bits of gossip are exchanged. They laugh heartily and roll their eyes and admire the next person's *boubou*, her original way of using henna to blacken hands and feet by drawing geometrical figures on them.

From time to time an exasperated manly voice rings out a warning, recalls the purpose of the gathering: a ceremony for the redemption of a soul. The voice is quickly forgotten and the brouhaha begins all over again, increasing in volume.

In the evening comes the most disconcerting part of this third day's ceremony. More people, more jostling in order to hear and see better. Groups are formed according to relationships, according to blood ties, areas, corporations. Each group displays its own contribution to the costs. In former times this contribution was made in kind: millet, livestock, rice, flour, oil, sugar, milk. Today it is made conspicuously in banknotes, and no one wants to give less than the other. A disturbing display of inner feeling that cannot be evaluated now measured in francs! And again I think how many of the dead would have survived if, before organizing these festive funeral ceremonies, the relatives or friend had bought the life-saving prescription or paid for hospitalization.

The takings are carefully recorded. It is a debt to be repaid in similar circumstances. Modou's relatives open an exercise book. Lady Mother-in-law (Modou's) and her daughter have a notebook. Fatimi, my younger sister, carefully records my takings in a note pad.

As I come from a large family in this town, with acquaintances at all levels of society, as I am a schoolteacher on friendly terms with the pupils' parents, and as I have been Modou's companion for thirty years, I receive the greater share of money and many envelopes. The regard shown me raises me in the eyes of the others and it is Lady Mother-in-Law's turn to be annoyed. Newly admitted into the city's bourgeoisie by her daughter's marriage, she too reaps banknotes. As for her silent, haggard child, she remains a stranger in these circles.

The sudden calls from our sisters-in-law bring her out of her stupor. They reappear after their deliberation. They have contributed the large sum of 200,000 francs to 'dress us'. Yesterday, they offered us some excellent *thiakry* to quench our thirst. The Fall family's griot is proud of her role as go-between, a role handed down from mother to daughter.

'One hundred thousand francs from the father's side.'

'One hundred thousand francs from the mother's side.'

She counts the notes, blue and pink, one by one, shows them round and concludes: 'I have much to say about you Falls, grandchildren of Damel Madiodio, who have inherited royal blood. But one of you is no more. Today is not a happy day. I weep with you for Modou, whom I used to call 'bag of rice', for he would frequently give me a sack of rice. Therefore accept this money, you worthy widows of a worthy man.'

The share of each widow must be doubled, as must the gifts of Modou's grandchildren, represented by the offspring of all his male and female cousins.

Thus our family-in-law take away with them a wad of notes, painstakingly topped, and leave us utterly destitute, we who will need material support.

Afterwards comes the procession of old relatives, old acquaintances, griots, goldsmiths, *laobés* with their honeyed language. The 'goodbyes' following one after the other at an infernal rate are irritating because they are neither simple nor free: they require, depending on the person leaving, sometimes a coin, sometimes a banknote.

Gradually the house empties. The smell of stale sweat and food blend as trails in the air, unpleasant and nauseating. Cola nuts spat out here and there have left red stains: my tiles, kept with such painstaking care,

are blackened. Oil stains on the walls, balls of crumpled paper. What a balance sheet for a day!

My horizon lightened, I see an old woman. Who is she? Where is she from? Bent over, the ends of her *boubou* tied behind her, she empties into a plastic bag the leftovers of red rice. Her smiling face tells of the pleasant day she has just had. She wants to take back proof of this to her family, living perhaps in Ouakam, Thiaroye or Pikine.

Standing upright, her eyes meeting my disapproving look, she mutters between teeth reddened by cola nuts: 'Lady, death is just as beautiful as life has been.'

Alas, it's the same story on the eighth and fortieth days, when those who have 'learned' belatedly make up for lost time. Light attire showing off slim waistlines, prominent backsides, the new brassière or the one bought at the second-hand market, chewing sticks wedged between teeth, white or flowered shawls, heavy smell of incense and of *gongo*, loud voices, strident laughter. And yet we are told in the Koran that on the third day the dead body swells and fills its tomb; we are told that on the eighth it bursts; and we are also told that on the fortieth day it is stripped. What then is the significance of these joyous, institutionalized festivities that accompany our prayers for God's mercy? Who has come out of self-interest? Who has come to quench his own thirst? Who has come for the sake of mercy? Who has come so that he may remember?

Tonight Binetou, my co-wife, will return to her SICAP villa. At last! Phew!

The visits of condolence continue: the sick, those who have journeyed or have merely arrived late, as well as the lazy, come to fulfil what they consider to be a sacred duty. Child-naming ceremonies may be missed but never a funeral. Coins and notes continue to pour on the beckoning fan.

Alone, I live in a monotony broken only by purifying baths, the changing of my mourning clothes every Monday and Friday.

I hope to carry out my duties fully. My heart concurs with the demands of religion. Reared since childhood on their strict precepts, I expect not to fail. The walls that limit my horizon for four months and ten days do not bother me. I have enough memories in me to ruminate upon. And these are what I am afraid of, for they smack of bitterness.

May their evocation not soil the state of purity in which I must live.
Till tomorrow.

Mariama Ba (Senegal)
So Long a Letter, Chapter Three
Translated from the French by Modupe Bode-Thomas

If Death were Not There*

If death were not there,
Where would the inheritor get things?
The cattle have been left for the inheritor;
Ee, how would the inheritor get things?
The iron-roofed house has been left for the inheritor;
Ee, if death were not there,
How would the inheritor get rich?
The bicycle has been left for the inheritor;
This inheritor is most lucky;
Ee, brother, tell me,
If death were not there,
Ugly one, whose daughter would have married you?
A wife has been left for the inheritor;
Ee, inheritor, how would you have lived?
The house has been left for the inheritor;
If death were not there,
How would the inheritor get things?

Acholi (Uganda)
Translated by Okot p'Bitek

Lament for Bala'nku*

1

Where shall I find one
      Like to Bala'nku,
         Mother!
      Like to Bala'nku,
         Mother!

Where shall I find one
            Like to Bala'nku,
                    Mother!
            Like to Bala'nku
                Mother!
      Mother, Mother, Mother,
        Ma–maï–ne',
            Like to Bala'nku.

2

He brought me unto goodly things,
All these I did possess;
He showed me joy,
                Mother!
          None like Bala'nku,
      Mother, Mother, Mother,
        Ma–maï–ne',
                Mother!
          None like Bala'nku.

3

All these sorrows have befallen me,
This misery is mine alone,
By myself I am left alone,
                Mother!
          None like Bala'nku,
      Mother, Mother, Mother,
        Ma–maï–ne',
                Mother!
          None like Bala'nku.

                      Vandau (Mozambique)

Lament for Ellsworth Janifer

The elephant has emptied the Imo River
The iroko has fallen to the bulldozer

Nothing is left in the village but old men, women and children
Power has deserted us for strange cities glittering with fancy
    lights

My brother and my friend
Why did you leave us so suddenly?

The ants will resume their lengthy processional, hauling and
    hoarding after the rains
The cock crows and the farmer rises from his mud bed
And ties his cloth about his waist
And sharpens his cutlass on the flintstone in the yard
His wife rises and his children rise, cold, reluctant and
    bleary-eyed

But no more shall you rise from your deep grave,
Nor make grand fiery speeches before the masters of the academy
Your fierce brain is at rest;
Its fierce see-saw jaws are at rest.
Slowly but surely the patient painter shall reconstitute the
    flood-soaked paintings of Venice
But who can blow the breath back into your crumpled lungs
Or restore the beat of your still heart-valves
Or the steam to your armpits?
Who can repair your complex machinery?
A punctured tyre, a crumpled fender,
        worn-out shocks
Spark plugs, generators and cooling systems –
These call for parts, skill and cosmetics.
But who can survive the shock of a head-on collision?

A broken arm may be mended

Torn cloth stitched back together
But an egg once broken is broken forever
All the wonder drugs and pride of technology are useless
You are now but an exposed film on which photographic image will
    not register

Projectors may retract, run film backwards
Speed it up or slow it down
Give us time to view at leisure
But words once spoken cannot be recalled
The ear cannot erase what it has heard
Lost virginity cannot be restored

Printer's errors may be corrected, a book revised
Whole editions destroyed and reset
But what is time that we cannot reverse it?

The clock stops, and is rewound or sent to the handyman
But your clock has stopped, your arms are still
Your vast maze of dials and rotaries, sensors and generators are
    forever motionless

The underground train will continue to clatter in its monotonous
    tunnel
The sun sets over Harlem
The street lamps come on, cars turn on their headlights
One by one as they crawl over the bridge into Bronx
All night long I sit at the window waiting
Waiting for you to return in the secret dark

Snow will return this year
Cold harmattan winds will blind dwellers of the open grassland with
    fine Saharan dust
And scatter wild fires through the villages and swamps
Sun will scorch the grass brown in March
And the yam will be reclaimed from the heavy rains of August
But you will not be there, O my brother

I shall look for you at the festival
My body painted red and white, the peacock feather dangling from
    my war cap
My grandfather's sword in the scabbard at my waist
george, ukpo akwete, a storm of loincloths
    criss-crossed at my waist

I shall listen for your voice in the successive reports of the
    dane guns and rifles
In the deep dictation of the tree-trunk drum
In the singing of young girls dancing round and round in a
    circle,
    their ripe young breasts naked and dancing
I shall listen for your voice in the sudden hysteria of birds
    startled from their city of nests atop the iroko in the square
Soon the birds return to their nests,
But will you return?

Like an empty stadium after an international soccer match,
Or the great auto raceway at Indianapolis,
All the noise and agitation of the air,
The gunning of the engines down the straightaway,
The feverish howling of the crowds,
The roar of the loudspeakers,
The collisions, explosions, fires and fights
Of player against player, fan against fan, crowd against
    referee,
All now lives but in echoes and echoes and echoes of the
    memory,
And on video-tape.

Death should be like an extended sojourn
In some foreign country
During which hope is kept alive
With occasional letters, photographs and gifts
To us loved ones waiting at home
Sent through some wayfarer

Who saw you in exile prosperous and happy
And with no more than your moderate portion of human sorrow

And as the birds return to their nests
As the goats return
As the dogs, cats, hens and sheep, cows and horses
Return to their barns at nightfall
So should you return to us from your foreign land of death
At the close of a less than eternal day.
The station-house, the house in which we were born.
And as children return from their play at nightfall
As they scatter from the moonlight when midnight draws near
And enter the cosy safety of the crowded sleeping mat
Spread on the floor beside the burning fireplace
So should you return.

And as the trader hawking his wares through the nine villages hurries
    home to his bride
As the young wife who ran away from her husband's house returns
    from her mother's house
So should you return to us
Whose love-longing is deeper than the roots of the silk-cotton tree,
Laser beams, X-rays, mechanical hearts
Firmer than the trunk of iroko.
But life is
Like the single railroad track at Uzuakoli
Whose end and beginning we cannot see
Only the brief stretch winding out of the brush at the left
Into the brush at the right,
And, in between.

                                   Onwuchekwa Jemie (Nigeria)

At The End

At the end,
One day I shall shut my eyes and close my mouth.
On that day shall a strip of cloth be tied over my eyes;
And my feet shall be made ready for a journey.
On that day shall I be an object of public display.
On that day there shall be a hubbub
Both in the sky and on earth.
On that day shall I refuse food
That there might be enough for the living.
On that day my kinfolk shall assemble.
Those who do not know me shall come to know me;
My enemies shall come to see
Whether it is really true that I am dead.
Then those who know me
And those who do not know me
Shall call out my praise names:
Artist!
The one whose calligraphy is a beauty on the page!
The one who writes what he sees!
Speaker of truth!
The one who weeps when the down-trodden weep!
Warrior who does not shrink from battle for fear of being shot
    dead!
Warrior who wears the customs of the land like a garment!
The one who sees what others do not see!
Warrior whose pen is sharp, like a double-edged sword!
The one whose pen is impartial to governor and governed alike!
It is now we recognize the beauty in his countenance.
Indeed, the value of a ragged basket is not realized
Until the day
When the remnants of a sacrifice are thrown away.

                              Nnamdi Olebara (Nigeria)
                    Translated from the Igbo by Chinweizu

PART THREE

Fields of Wonder

How the World was Created from a Drop of Milk

At the beginning there was a huge drop of milk.
Then Doondari came and he created the stone.
Then the stone created iron;
And iron created fire;
And fire created water;
And water created air.
Then Doondari descended the second time. And he took the five
    elements
And he shaped them into man.
But man was proud.
Then Doondari created blindness and blindness defeated man.
But when blindness became too proud,
Doondari created sleep, and sleep defeated blindness;
But when sleep became too proud,
Doondari created worry, and worry defeated sleep;
But when worry became too proud,
Doondari created death, and death defeated worry.
But when death became too proud,
Doondari descended for the third time,
And he came as Gueno, the eternal one,
And Gueno defeated death.

Fulani (Mali)

The Toad

When Death first entered the world, men sent a messenger to Chukwu,
asking him whether the dead could not be restored to life and sent back
to their old homes. They chose the dog as their messenger.

The dog, however, did not go straight to Chukwu, and dallied on the way. The toad had overheard the message, and, as he wished to punish mankind, he overtook the dog and reached Chukwu first. He said he had been sent by men to say that after death they had no desire at all to return to the world. Chukwu declared that he would respect their wishes, and when the dog arrived later with the true message he refused to alter his decision.

Thus, although a human being may be born again, he cannot return with the same body and the same personality.

Igbo (Nigeria)

Why the Sky is Far Away

In the beginning, the sky was very close to the earth. In those days men did not have to till the ground, because whenever they felt hungry they simply cut off a piece of the sky and ate it. But the sky grew angry, because often they cut off more than they could eat, and threw the left-overs on the rubbish heap. The sky did not want to be thrown on the rubbish heap, and so he warned men that if they were not more careful in future he would move far away.

For a while everyone paid attention to his warning. But one day a greedy woman cut off an enormous piece of the sky. She ate as much as she could, but was unable to finish it. Frightened, she called her husband, but he too could not finish it. They called the entire village to help, but they could not finish it. In the end they had to throw the remainder on the rubbish heap. Then the sky became very angry indeed, and rose up high above the earth, far beyond the reach of men. And from then on men have had to work for their living.

Bini (Nigeria)

The First Coming of Ulu*

A big *ogene* sounded three times from Ulu's shrine. The Ikolo took it up and sustained an endless flow of praises to the deity. At the same time Ezeulu's messengers began to clear the centre of the market-place. Although they were each armed with a whip of palm frond they had a difficult time. The crowd was excited and it was only after a struggle that the messengers succeeded in clearing a small space in the heart of the market-place, from which they worked furiously with their whips until they had forced all the people back to form a thick ring at the edges. The women with their pumpkin leaves caused the greatest difficulty because they all struggled to secure positions in front. The men had no need to be so near and so they formed the outside of the ring.

The *ogene* sounded again. The Ikolo began to salute the Chief Priest. The women waved their leaves from side to side across their faces, muttering prayers to Ulu, the god that kills and saves.

Ezeulu's appearance was greeted with a loud shout that must have been heard in all the neighbouring villages. He ran forward, halted abruptly and faced the Ikolo. 'Speak on,' he said to it, 'Ezeulu hears what you say.' Then he stooped and danced three or four steps and rose again.

He wore smoked raffia which descended from his waist to the knee. The left half of his body – from forehead to toes – was painted with white chalk. Around his head was a leather band from which an eagle's feather pointed backwards. On his right hand he carried *Nne Ofo*, the mother of all staffs of authority in Umuaro, and in his left he held a long iron staff which kept up a quivering rattle whenever he stuck its pointed end into the earth. He took a few long strides, pausing on each foot. Then he ran forward again as though he had seen a comrade in the vacant air; he stretched his arm and waved his staff to the right and to the left. And those who were near enough heard the knocking together of Ezeulu's staff and another which no one saw. At this many fled in terror before the priest and the unseen presences around him.

As he approached the centre of the market-place Ezeulu re-enacted the First Coming of Ulu and how each of the four Days put obstacles in his way.

'*At that time, when lizards were still in ones and twos, the whole people assembled and chose me to carry their new deity. I said to them:*
' "*Who am I to carry this fire on my bare head? A man who knows that his anus is small does not swallow an udala seed.*"
'*They said to me:*
' "*Fear not. The man who sends a child to catch a shrew will also give him water to wash his hand.*"
'*I said: "So be it.*"

'And we set to work. That day was Eke: we worked into Oye and then into Afo. As day broke on Nkwo and the sun carried its sacrifice I carried my Alusi and, with all the people behind me, set out on that journey. A man sang with the flute on my right and another replied on my left. From behind the heavy tread of all the people gave me strength. And then all of a sudden something spread itself across my face. On one side it was raining, on the other side it was dry. I looked again and saw that it was Eke.

'I said to him: "Is it you Eke?"

'He replied: "It is I, Eke, the One that makes a strong man bite the earth with his teeth."

'I took a hen's egg and gave him. He took it and ate and gave way to me. We went on, past streams and forests. Then a smoking thicket crossed my path, and two men were wrestling on their heads. My followers looked once and took to their heels. I looked again and saw that it was Oye.

'I said to him: "Is it you Oye across my path?"

'He said: "It is I, Oye, the One that began cooking before Another and so has more broken pots."

'I took a white cock and gave him. He took it and made way for me. I went on past farmlands and wilds and then I saw that my head was too heavy for me. I looked steadily and saw that it was Afo.

'I said: "Is it you Afo?"

'He said: "It is I, Afo, the great river that cannot be salted."

'I replied: "I am Ezeulu, the hunchback more terrible than a leper."

'Afo shrugged and said: "Pass, your own is worse than mine."

'I passed and the sun came down and beat me and the rain came down and drenched me. Then I met Nkwo. I looked on his left and saw an old woman, tired, dancing strange steps on the hill. I looked to the right and saw a horse and saw a ram. I slew the horse and with the ram I cleaned my matchet, and so removed that evil.'

By now Ezeulu was in the centre of the market-place. He struck the metal staff into the earth and left it quivering while he danced a few more steps to the Ikolo which had not paused for breath since the priest emerged. All the women waved their pumpkin leaves in front of them.

Ezeulu looked round again at all the men and women of Umuaro, but saw no one in particular. Then he pulled the staff out of the ground, and with it in his left hand and the *Mother of Ofo* in his right he jumped forward and began to run round the market-place.

All the women set up a long, excited ululation and there was renewed jostling for the front line. As the fleeing Chief Priest reached any section of the crowd the women there waved their leaves round their heads and flung them at him. It was as though thousands and thousands of giant, flying insects swarmed upon him.

Ugoye who had pushed and shoved until she got to the front murmured her prayer over and over again as the Chief Priest approached the part of the circle where she stood:

'Great Ulu who kills and saves, I implore you to cleanse my household of all defilement. If I have spoken it with my mouth or seen it with my eyes, or if I have heard it with my ears or stepped on it with my foot or if it has come through my children or my friends or kinsfolk let it follow these leaves.'

She waved the small bunch in a circle round her head and flung it with all her power at the Chief Priest as he ran past her position.

The six messengers followed closely behind the priest and, at intervals, one of them bent down quickly and picked up at random one bunch of leaves and continued running. The Ikolo drum worked itself into a frenzy during the Chief Priest's flight especially its final stages when he, having completed the full circle of the market-place, ran on with increasing speed into the sanctuary of his shrine, his messengers at his heels. As soon as they disappeared the Ikolo broke off its beating abruptly with one last KOME. The mounting tension which had gripped the entire market-place and seemed to send its breath going up, up and up exploded with this last beat of the drum and released a vast and deep breathing down. But the moment of relief was very short-lived. The crowd seemed to rouse itself quickly to the knowledge that their Chief Priest was safe in his shrine, triumphant over the sins of Umuaro which he was now burying deep into the earth with the six bunches of leaves.

Chinua Achebe (Nigeria)
Excerpt from *Arrow of God*

A Diviner's Invocation to His Ancestors

What will it be today?
Success or failure?
Death or life?
Ha! Flood does not run uphill.
What evil spirit throws his shade
To block the truth from me?
I raise my sacred staff against it!
Here is the east; there is the west.
Here the sun is bursting into life:
See how the truth comes riding on sun rays!
Sky and Earth are watching over me;
How can my tongue go zigzag?
Grey hair is enemy of lies.
Come, spirits of my forefathers, come!
Stand by your son!
Let us show this seeker of divination what we can do,
What we are famous for:
If the Ngwu tree is cut at noon,
It mocks its cutter with a new shoot
Before the sun goes down.
Answer! Answer your son!

Igbo (Nigeria)
Translated by Chinweizu

The God of War

He kills on the right and destroys on the left.
He kills on the left and destroys on the right.
He kills suddenly in the house and suddenly in the field.
He kills the child with the iron with which it plays.
He kills in silence.
He kills the thief and the owner of the stolen goods.
He kills the owner of the slave – and the slave runs away.

He kills the owner of the house – and paints the hearth with his
   blood.
He is the needle that pricks at both ends.
He has water but he washes with blood.

                                                    Yoruba (Nigeria)

Eshu*

When he is angry he hits a stone until it bleeds.
When he is angry he sits on the skin of an ant.
When he is angry he weeps tears of blood.

Eshu, confuser of men.
The owner of twenty slaves is sacrificing,
So that Eshu may not confuse him.
The owner of thirty 'iwofa' is sacrificing,
So that Eshu may not confuse him.
Eshu confused the newly married wife.
When she stole the cowries from the sacred shrine of Oya
She said she had not realized
That taking two hundred cowries was stealing.
Eshu confused the head of the queen –
And she started to go naked.
Then Eshu beat her to make her cry.
Eshu, do not confuse me!
Eshu, do not confuse the load on my head.

Eshu, lover of dogs.
If a goat gets lost in Ogbe – don't ask me.
Do you think I am a thief of goats?
If a huge sheep is missing from Ogbe – don't ask me.
Do you think I am a thief of sheep?
If any fowl get lost in Ogbe – don't ask me.
Do you think I am a thief of birds?

But if a black dog is missing from Ogbe – ask me!
You will find me eating Eshu's sacrifice in a wooden bowl.

Eshu slept in the house –
But the house was too small for him.
Eshu slept on the veranda –
But the veranda was too small for him.
Eshu slept in a nut –
At last he could stretch himself.

Eshu walked through the groundnut farm.
The tuft of his hair was just visible.
If it had not been for his huge size,
He would not have been visible at all.

Having thrown a stone yesterday – he kills a bird today.
Lying down, his head hits the roof.
Standing up he cannot look into the cooking pot.
Eshu turns right into wrong, wrong into right.

Yoruba (Nigeria)

At the Feast of the Ancestors*

Behold the things, ancestors,
Displayed for your feast.
You said: we have not had a decent burial,
But you have listened to what I have said.
Our raising of domestic animals has succeeded,
The women and the young people too are well.
For this reason I have come
To show you these animals.
Rise all, and dwell always in these animals!
May the leopard coming from the forest
Have his teeth on edge for these animals.

May the weasel coming from the forest

Be unable to take these fowls.
May the witch who twists his belongings
Fail to fascinate our goats.
May the thief on the look-out
Sprain his feet in his course.
Let all these animals prosper
And multiply,
Then the feast will be beautiful.
As for us, we shall return to the village,
To the village to dwell and prosper.
I have held out my hands to you in prayer,
And he who holds out his hands dies not.
I have shown you the animals of the feast,
And have brought you no other presents,
Except palm wine,
That you may favour the procreation of human wealth.
And here are the cola nuts I brought for you.

Bakongo (Zaïre and Angola)

Open the Windows of Heaven*

Open the windows of heaven,
Give us thy blessing!
Open the windows of heaven,
Give us thy blessing!
    Our Father, *Onyame!*
    Sweet Father of us, the Church membership.
Open the windows of heaven,
Give us thy blessing.

Fante (Ghana)

Looking for a Rain God

It is lonely at the lands where the people go to plough. These lands are vast clearings in the bush, and the wild bush is lonely too. Nearly all the lands are within walking distance from the village. In some parts of the bush where the underground water is very near the surface, people made little rest camps for themselves and dug shallow wells to quench their thirst while on their journey to their own lands. They experienced all kinds of things once they left the village. They could rest at shady watering-places full of lush, tangled trees with delicate pale-gold and purple wild flowers springing up between soft green moss and the children could hunt around for wild figs and any berries that might be in season. But from 1958, a seven-year drought fell upon the land and even the watering-places began to look as dismal as the dry open thorn-bush country; the leaves of the trees curled up and withered; the moss became dry and hard and, under the shade of the tangled trees, the ground turned a powdery black and white, because there was no rain. People said rather humorously that if you tried to catch the rain in a cup it would only fill a teaspoon. Towards the beginning of the seventh year of drought, the summer had become an anguish to live through. The air was so dry and moisture-free that it burned the skin. No one knew what to do to escape the heat and tragedy was in the air. At the beginning of that summer, a number of men just went out of their homes and hung themselves to death from trees. The majority of the people had lived off crops, but for two years past they had all returned from the lands with only their rolled-up skin blankets and cooking utensils. Only the charlatans, incanters, and witch-doctors made a pile of money during this time because people were always turning to them in desperation for little talismans and herbs to rub on the plough for the crops to grow and the rain to fall.

The rains were late that year. They came in early November, with a promise of good rain. It wasn't the full, steady downpour of the years of good rain, but thin, scanty, misty rain. It softened the earth and a rich growth of green things sprang up everywhere for the animals to eat. People were called to the village *kgotla* to hear the proclamation of the beginning of the ploughing season; they stirred themselves and whole familes began to move off to the lands to plough.

The family of the old man, Mokgobja, were among those who left early for the lands. They had a donkey cart and piled everything on to it, Mokgobja – who was over seventy years old; two little girls, Neo and Boseyong; their mother Tiro and an unmarried sister, Nesta; and the father and supporter of the family, Ramadi, who drove the donkey cart. In the rush of the first hope of rain, the man, Ramadi, and the two women, cleared the land of thorn-bush and then hedged their vast ploughing area with this same thorn-bush to protect the future crop from the goats they had brought along for milk. They cleared out and deepened the old well with its pool of muddy water and still in this light, misty rain, Ramadi inspanned two oxen and turned the earth over with a hand plough.

The land was ready and ploughed, waiting for the crops. At night, the earth was alive with insects singing and rustling about in search of food. But suddenly, by mid-November, the rain fled away; the rain-clouds fled away and left the sky bare. The sun danced dizzily in the sky, with a strange cruelty. Each day the land was covered in a haze of mist as the sun sucked up the last drop of moisture out of the earth. The family sat down in despair, waiting and waiting. Their hopes had run so high; the goats had started producing milk, which they had eagerly poured on their porridge, now they ate plain porridge with no milk. It was impossible to plant the corn, maize, pumpkin and water-melon seeds in the dry earth. They sat the whole day in the shadow of the huts and even stopped thinking, for the rain had fled away. Only the children, Neo and Boseyong, were quite happy in their little girl world. They carried on with their game of making house like their mother and chattered to each other in light, soft tones. They made children from sticks around which they tied rags, and scolded them severely in an exact imitation of their own mother. Their voices could be heard scolding the day long: 'You stupid thing, when I send you to draw water, why do you spill half of it out of the bucket!' 'You stupid thing! Can't you mind the porridge pot without letting the porridge burn!' And then they would beat the rag-dolls on their bottoms with severe expressions.

The adults paid no attention to this; they did not even hear the funny chatter; they sat waiting for rain; their nerves were stretched to breaking-point willing the rain to fall out of the sky. Nothing was important, beyond that. All their animals had been sold during the bad years to purchase food, and of all their herd only two goats were left. It was the women of the family who finally broke down under the strain of waiting for rain. It was really the two women who caused the death of the little girls. Each night they started a weird, high-pitched wailing that began on a low, mournful note and whipped up to a frenzy. Then they would stamp their feet and shout as though they had lost their heads. The men sat quiet and self-controlled; it was important for men to maintain their self-control at all times but their nerve was breaking too. They knew the women were haunted by the starvation of the coming year.

Finally, an ancient memory stirred in the old man, Mokgobja. When he was very young and the customs of the ancestors still ruled the land, he had been witness to a rain-making ceremony. And he came alive a little, struggling to recall the details which had been buried by years and years of prayer in a Christian church. As soon as the mists cleared a little, he began consulting in whispers with his youngest son, Ramadi. There was, he said, a certain rain god who accepted only the sacrifice of the bodies of children. Then the rain would fall; then the crops would grow, he said. He explained the ritual and as he talked, his memory became a conviction and he began to talk with unshakeable authority. Ramadi's nerves were smashed by the nightly wailing of the women and soon the two men began whispering with the two women. The children continued their game: 'You stupid thing! How could you have lost the money on the way to the shop! You must have been playing again!'

After it was all over and the bodies of the two little girls had been spread across the land, the rain did not fall. Instead, there was a deathly silence at night and the devouring heat of the sun by day. A terror, extreme and deep, overwhelmed the whole family. They packed, rolling up their skin blankets and pots, and fled back to the village.

People in the village soon noted the absence of the two little girls. They had died at the lands and were buried there, the family said. But people noted their ashen, terror-stricken faces and a murmur arose. What had killed the children, they wanted to know? And the family replied that they had just died. And people said amongst themselves that it was strange that the two deaths had occurred at the same time. And there was a feeling of great unease at the unnatural looks of the family. Soon the police came around. The family told them the same story of death and burial at the lands. They did not know what the children had died of. So the police asked to see the graves. At this, the mother of the children broke down and told everything.

Throughout that terrible summer the story of the children hung like a dark cloud of sorrow over the village, and the sorrow was not assuaged when the old man and Ramadi were sentenced to death for ritual murder. All they had on the statute books was that ritual murder was against the law and must be stamped out with the death penalty. The subtle story of strain and starvation and breakdown was inadmissible evidence at court; but all the people who lived off crops knew in their hearts that only a hair's breadth had saved them from sharing a fate similar to that of the Mokgobja family. They could have killed something to make the rain fall.

Bessie Head (Azania)

Talk

Once, not far from the city of Accra on the Gulf of Guinea, a country man went out to his garden to dig up some yams to take to market. While he was digging, one of the yams said to him:

'Well, at last you're here. You never weeded me, but now you come around with your digging stick. Go away and leave me alone!'

The farmer turned around and looked at his cow in amazement. The cow was chewing her cud and looking at him.

'Did you say something?' he asked.

The cow kept on chewing and said nothing, but the man's dog spoke up.

'It wasn't the cow who spoke to you,' the dog said. 'It was the yam. The yam says leave him alone.'

The man became angry because his dog had never talked before, and he didn't like his tone, besides. So he took his knife and cut a branch from a palm tree to whip his dog. Just then the palm tree said:

'Put that branch down!'

The man was getting very upset about the way things were going, and he started to throw the palm branch away, but the palm branch said:

'Man, put me down softly!'

He put the branch down gently on a stone, and the stone said:

'Hey, take that thing off me.'

This was enough, and the frightened farmer started to run for his village. On the way he met a fisherman going the other way with a fish trap on his head.

'What's the hurry?' the fisherman asked.

'My yam said, "Leave me alone!" Then the dog said, "Listen to what the yam says!" When I went to whip the dog with a palm branch the tree said, "Put that branch down!" Then the palm branch said, "Do it softly!" Then the stone said, "Take that thing off me!" '

'Is that all?' the man with the fish trap asked. 'Is that so frightening?'

'Well,' the man's fish trap said, 'did he take it off the stone?'

'Wah!' the fisherman shouted. He threw the fish trap on the ground and began to run with the farmer, and on the trail they met a weaver with a bundle of cloth on his head.

'Where are you going in such a rush?' he asked them.

'My yam said. "Leave me alone'!" ' the farmer said. 'The dog said "Listen to what the yam says!" The tree said, "Put that branch down!" The branch said, "Do it softly" And the stone said, "Take that thing off me!" '

'And then,' the fisherman continued, 'the fish trap said, "Did he take it off?" '

'That's nothing to get excited about,' the weaver said, 'no reason at all.'

'Oh yes it is,' his bundle of cloth said. 'If it happened to you you'd run too!'

'Wah!' the weaver shouted. He threw his bundle on the trail and started running with the other men.

They came panting to the ford in the river and found a man bathing.

'Are you chasing a gazelle?' he asked them.

The first man said breathlessly:

'My yam talked to me, and it said, "Leave me alone!" And my dog said, "Listen to your yam!" And when I cut myself a branch the tree said, "Put that branch down!" And the branch said, "Do it softly!" And the stone said, "Take that thing off me!" '

The fisherman panted:

'And my trap said, "Did he?" '

The weaver wheezed:

'And my bundle of cloth said, "You'd run too!" '

'Is that why you're running?' the man in the river asked.

'Well, wouldn't you run if you were in their position?' the river said.

The man jumped out of the water and began to run with the others. They ran down the main street of the village to the house of the chief. The chief's servants brought his stool out, and he came and sat on it to listen to their complaints. The men began to recite their troubles.

'I went out to my garden to dig yams,' the farmer said, waving his arms. 'Then everything began to talk! My yam said "Leave me alone!" My dog said, "Pay attention to your yam!" The tree said, "Put that branch down!" The branch said, "Do it softly!" And the stone said, "Take it off me!" '

'And my fish trap said, "Well, did he take if off?" ' the fisherman said.

'And my cloth said, "You'd run too!" ' the weaver said.

'And the river said the same,' the bather said hoarsely, his eyes bulging.

The chief listened to them patiently, but he couldn't refrain from scowling.

'Now this really is a wild story,' he said at last. 'You'd better all go back to your work before I punish you for disturbing the peace.'

So the men went away, and the chief shook his head and mumbled to himself, 'Nonsense like that upsets the community.'

'Fantastic, isn't it?' his stool said, 'Imagine a talking yam!'

Ashanti (Ghana)

Mussoco

In the morning, as soon as she was inside the house, Mussoco triumphantly announced:

'Hey, Auntie, I'm in luck! I've found lots of money!' – and she showed her a small parcel.

'Shh, don't shout, someone might hear you outside! Let's go into the room, advised her aunt who, sitting on a small stool, was calmly cleaning her teeth with a piece of coal and some salt.

Grandmother who was sweeping the yard, also with a coal and salt in her mouth, hurried up to them when she overheard what they were talking about.

'What? What's this?' she asked curiously.

'I've had bad luck ... I was caught ... in a snare ... for partridges! ...'

A dove could be heard cooing in the next hut.

Finally, the doors were closed; the three women sat down on the iron bedstead and, with beating hearts, nervously counted and recounted the money. Two hundred and ten escudos! That's something! The Lord is generous, he does not forget his sinners!

'Now keep your trap shut. You haven't seen anything, you hear? With this kind of money, daughter, you could buy a house and have a good life,' advised the grandmother.

'No, Grannie! What do I want a house for? We'll buy nice fabrics and expensive jewellery ... and a hand-turned sewing machine, if there's enough money ...'

'Of course, you can buy something for yourself ... But our hovel's a hovel, there's no other word for it ... Don't be a fool!' objected her aunt.

'A house! Nice clothes, yes! Can't I even handle my own money, then?'

Her head was spinning; she got up quickly and took a few quick paces round the room in order to shake off at least some of the feeling of joy that had overwhelmed her.

Two emotions were warring within her – self-respect and fear.

Smiling, the grandmother clapped her hands and then snapped her fingers:

'You see! Money makes people lose their heads!'

'Dance, daughter, dance; your patron saints have been kind to you ...' added her aunt jokingly.

A little time passed and one of the women neighbours began wailing all over the district:

'Who's found 210 escudos? Whoever's found them ought to give them back, because I've lost them. Come on! Who's found the money?

People, you work too, you know what a hard life it is for the poor, so don't hide my money from me! I've lost 210 escudos. Who's found them? For God's sake, let me have them back! If someone has a heart of stone, then his grave shall be of stone. Listen, folks, I appeal to you all!'

On hearing her neighbour's wails, Mussoco decided to return the money to its rightful owner. Two emotions were warring within her – self-respect and fear. It was one thing when you didn't know who the money belonged to, but now . . . knowing whose it was! No! And a neighbour too!

'Listen, Auntie. I'm going to give the money back to Donana. D'you hear what she's saying? If someone has a heart of stone, that person shall have a stone grave!' continued the girl agitatedly.

Auntie replied cunningly with an impassive face:

'What d'you mean return it? You didn't steal the money, did you? You found it on the street. That means it's yours. What are you scared of, then?'

'Don't turn down your own happiness! Finding isn't stealing. If somebody finds something, it's been found, there's nothing bad can come of that. Don't be a fool!' said the old woman in support of the aunt.

At the sight of the wretched Donana, her clothes in disarray, proclaiming her grief to the world at large, all the people felt sorry for her. So much money! Poor woman! But who had picked it up? No, they hadn't found anything. They weren't bloodsuckers. But how could anyone resist such a plea? Keep that money when the owner was in such distress over it? How cold-hearted could you get? No one could be guilty of such a crime; everybody knew how hard life was.

'Donana, where did you lose your money?' asked the passers-by as they gathered round her.

The unhappy woman repeated, as if by clockwork:

'I don't know, my dears. This morning, as usual, I left for Quanza to pay for the tobacco and find some work. I got as far as Alta station . . . And . . . Horrors! My God! I suddenly realized the money was gone! I went home as fast as I could and looked over every inch of the road. When I got home, I turned everything upside-down like crazy. I hunted through the trunks, the drawers, the clothes. Not a sign anywhere! I felt in all the nooks and crannies. Even in the mattress. But I still couldn't find it.' She groaned. 'All that work, all that hunger and fear in the forest, and all I went through in the market for those choosy customers – and what for ? To lose everything I worked so hard to earn! Oi!' and she wrung her hands in despair. 'I've already shouted it all over Ingombota. I've shouted it in Bungo, too. I've shouted it in Maianga. I've shouted it out at the fish and meat market as well. I'm done in! I've screamed my head off everywhere! Oi-oi-oi! I'm worn out! But nobody's turned up with the money – no one!'

'Ai-ai-ai! Who picked up the money, and why hasn't it been returned! Listen to the woman weeping, she's in agony, and they can't even give back what isn't theirs! Well, well! What mean folks there are in this world! Taking something that doesn't belong to them!'

'Yours, yours, yours, but it'll turn against you!' recited a little grey bird with a white breast, lightly hopping from branch to branch in a mulberry tree.

The days dragged on in wearisome tension. All the poor of Luanda, as if personally hit by the disaster, sympathized deeply with Donana in her grief. After all, how could the inhabitants, who were all in equally dire straits, react calmly to such unheard-of meanness? They all knew how hard it was to earn money, they tasted the bitter bread of work, they slept badly at night and so they were not indifferent to someone else's misfortune. No, a thousand times no! They would never do such a thing; the poor always help the poor! Washing or cooking in the houses of the masters, haggling in the streets or busy in their own hovels, they had never found life easy. At work they had to listen to the insults and abuse of their masters, obey their whims, deprive themselves of everything to satisfy them. And in their own homes, they had more than their share of worry and suffering. And God alone knew how many times they had to work themselves to the bone in order to earn some money and fill their bellies just once!

A warning that had travelled round the whole city was again heard in every spot. Not as an anguished complaint this time, but as an evil, fuming threat:

'I've prayed. I've screamed about the money I've lost, but nobody's answered. Listen, listen carefully and don't say afterwards that I'm a witch: I'm going to have spells cast. You hear me? I'm going to have spells cast! So don't complain about it afterwards . . . Whoever took that money is going to die. Whoever washes that corpse shall die. Whoever cuts its hair shall die. Whoever dresses it shall die. Whoever goes to bury it shall die. And whoever says "Woe is me!" shall also die!'

'Get away with you!' muttered the women in fright, although they understood deep down inside what was behind this hysterical outburst.

Others, in the grip of the same superstition, added with a bitter sneer: 'It's going to go badly for whoever took someone else's money.'

Mothers, some with small children slung behind them with a strip of cloth, promised themselves to check the children's hidey-holes carefully. Sometimes, as is known, children could find money (why not?) and spend it on all kinds of sweets and toys.

'A child is kindred to a lunatic,' babbled one old crone, thereby strengthening the mothers in their decision.

Chiming in the evening air that was lit by the glittering rays of the evening sun, the bells of Carmo church solemnly announced that an infant had been admitted to the holy faith. A little urchin, indifferent to the woman who was spreading such horror around, chanted something of his own to the music of the bells.

In the meantime, the premonition of death was already spreading round and sowing the horror of disaster everywhere. Lord, who had found that money? Begone, evil! Begone, evil! Where are you, heart of stone? Why don't you own up?

More terrified than anybody, Mussoco was no longer able to contain her growing sense of panic, in spite of her family's reassurances. Her neighbour's curses, which had disturbed their hut many times before, rang insistently in her ears: 'All you people who work, who know the sufferings of the poor, don't hide what I'm looking for!' A decline of spirits gradually took over from the initial exultation. The fine fabrics, the beautiful and expensive jewellery, the pleasures – all had fallen into a bottomless pit. She again spoke to her aunt and grandmother about returning the money. But both of them said: 'No, no; don't be a fool.' And again, as before, they talked her out of it. But now, under the stress of those curses, she ought to give up the money she had found, whether they liked the idea or not.

'Auntie!' she began meaningfully, 'have you heard what Donana's been saying?'

'Of course. Let her go and cast as many spells as she wants. Let her!'

'All that talk about spells . . . Well, she isn't joking! . . .' said Mussoco uneasily.

But the old woman, unwilling to lose their unexpected wealth and irritated by the girl's stubborn petty-mindedness, declared:

'You see! You too, now! Is the money burning your hands? Ignore that nonsense. It's all to put the wind up folks. I wasn't born yesterday, you know!'

'But Grandma . . .'

'Take no notice! And don't be such a nuisance! All that fear over nothing! If we'd stolen the money, then you could expect trouble. But you only picked it up in the street . . .'

'It's all just her talk! She's lying, she doesn't mean to do anything! So she'll go and have spells cast, only where? Don't give up the money, your luck's in! A fine one you are!' she added, smacking her lips. 'If she found that money, d'you think she'd hand it back?' added her aunt heatedly, lifting up her left eyelid with her index finger.

Morally crushed again, Mussoco weakly gave in to her former reasoning. Poor girl! Inwardly, this behaviour tormented her, consumed her with fire. Cursed be the moment when she had found that money! Just so that she could be tormented like this? Was the money burning her hands? her grandmother had asked. Yes, it was burning all right, only not her hands, but her heart; it was burning her whole life up all the time. 'I'm going to have spells cast! D'you hear? I'm going to have spells cast!' Oh, how that voice was torturing her! Oh, these cruel relatives, these cruel friends! The proverb was right: 'Honey outside, ice within!'

'I've wept, I've screamed about the money I lost, but nobody's answered. Listen, listen carefully and don't say afterwards that I'm a witch: I'm going to have spells cast! D'you hear! I'm going to have spells cast! So don't complain about it afterwards . . . Whoever washes that corpse shall die. Whoever trims its nails shall die. Whoever dresses it shall die. Whoever goes to bury it shall die! Whoever says "Woe is me!" shall also die.' So Donana went about, hurling curses everywhere.

That evening, perhaps because of what she had been through during the day, Mussoco felt a decision forming within her: she would return the money to its owner. Elated, she went out. Why tell her aunt and her grandmother first? No, they would only interfere.

Hiding the money in her clothes, she walked with uncertain steps through the dusk that was filled with the sound of people talking and the chirping of the cicadas. Her neighbour's hut was quite near, but as if in obedience to some unconscious impulse, her legs took her in the opposite direction. Calming down and panicking by turns, she argued with herself: Give her the money now? Yes, but how are you going to explain what happened? Won't you be ashamed to hand it over after so many days have gone by?

While lost in thought, she suddenly realized with astonishment that she was standing at the door of Donana's hut. Should she go in or not? And under what pretext? Yes, what pretext, indeed? Could she bring herself to do this? No, she certainly could not!

It was not her family but her timidity that got the better of her this time. She was ashamed, deeply ashamed! That damned money was destroying her peace of mind.

And so Donana appealed and threatened. But with no result. In spite of everything, the money had not been found. There was only one thing left now – vengeance to the death! Should she meekly tolerate her loss so that some cold-hearted stranger should enjoy what she had achieved at the cost of such labour and self-sacrifice? No, it must never happen! Whoever it might be, that person must have heard her prayers. Yes, must have heard; for her cries had attracted attention everywhere. Everybody had noticed. For eight days on end, her voice had rung out over all the districts in the city, even among the whining of the beggars and the shrieks of the insane. She had sworn to have spells cast, and now she was going to do just that. Pity? For whom? Had the person who found her money taken pity on her in her grief? To the heart of stone, a grave of stone!

To call up irremediable evil, Donana went to Ambriz. In those parts, as rumour had it, she would find the best witch-doctors. With the help of the *jimbambi* (evil spirits) they would quickly dispatch the culprit to the other world. Yes, and in no time at all.

'I have come to talk to the elders and their ancestors. I want you to bring down the evil spirits on whoever found the money I lost. Use your powers so that the elders and their ancestors will act quickly,' said Donana to one of the witch-doctors.

She went into the witch-doctor's cage that was stood about with idols and all the paraphernalia of witchcraft, knelt down , struck the ground with the flat of her hands and through her tears uttered oaths and appeals for revenge.

'To you, Honji and Vunji, Muene-Congo and the Lord, Lord Almighty, I appeal for justice. For eight days I have wept, cried out everywhere about the money I lost, but no one has answered at all. Those who could see merely looked at me, those who could hear merely listened. O, elders and your forefathers, if whoever found my money is far away and did not hear my appeals, let nothing bad happen to him; but if he heard and did not answer, I want you to rip him apart as with a knife, the way they cut up meat into pieces at the market. Let that person die who found the money and anyone who helps in spending it. And let that person die who washes the corpse, who trims its nails, who cuts its hair, who dresses it, or who says "Woe is me". May all die – all, all, all, because all heard me and no one opened his heart!'

Drawing sound out of a dusty goat's horn, the witch-doctor sent that curse out into space – first to the east, then to the west, and then repeated it before blowing on the horn.

'And now beware of the dead! Mind where you go, and don't say "Woe is me!" Remember your words – the *jimbambi* are no laughing matter,' the witch-doctor warned Donana.

At last! What joy! Soon, soon, when the rains come, the curse will begin to act. And the villain will never make fun of her; will the heart of stone fall into a stone grave? Is she a witch? No. How could they call her so? Didn't she warn everyone of her intentions? And who had confessed? No one. No, she had not acted like a witch: a witch doesn't warn you but brings death out of envy. But she was not consumed by envy. The gods could see that she had not brought death on anyone; it had been sought. It had been sought by the culprit who had ignored her pleas. Now let that person reap the fruits.

Mussoco had been feeling ill for several days. In spite of treatment at home, the sickness did not pass off: she had a constant temperature, fever and stomach cramps, and she kept spitting blood.

'Perhaps we ought to fetch the witch-doctor,' suggested her grandmother quietly during the night's vigil; she was already worried about Donana's curse.

The aunt yawned uneasily and nodded her head in agreement. She had been troubled by vague gnawings of conscience ever since the day when the confounded illness had begun. Although she was in sympathy with the grandmother, she did not want to admit her feelings: some sort of shame, cowardice, a morbid inadequacy spoke in her, making her wait for the tragic denouement. Yes, tragic, for she had already recognized the workings of the curse.

The local healer appeared next morning. But nothing, absolutely nothing could dispel the illness. According to *mumzamba*, the supernatural prophecy, if the accursed witchcraft entered a house, it would surely empty it in a very short space of time. And all because of money, money found in the street and hidden from the owner.

'Lord, I'm so young to die! And all because of the money I never even used,' sighed Mussoco as she faded slowly away.

That night, a thunderstorm raged. The aunt and the grandmother, faced with the ghastly truth, loudly gave voice to their repentance:

'Lord, Mussoco! What wrong have we done to you to make you leave us like this? Oi-oi-oi, our poor little girl! Who will we have left now?'

Their agitated neighbour hurried in on hearing the noise.

'Izabel, Sule! What's happened? What's the matter?' asked the bewildered Donana, not suspecting the truth.

'We don't know how it happened ourselves, dear neighbour! Our little girl's been sick for eight days ... and she's gone!' they said, pointing to the dead girl who was lying on the bed with a fixed expression of despair on her face.

Another eight days passed, and again the whole district was thrown into a turmoil.

'Have you heard? Donana is dead!'

'Dead?'

'It's the truth! And they say there was a red cock on her drain!'

'A red cock? That's a devil!'

'True, that's a devil. Of course, it's all because of witchcraft ... What else would make the rain fall when the evening mist was descending?'

'Yes, she went to Ambriz because of that money ...'

'She went to have spells cast . . . She wanted the *jimbambi* to find the culprit . . .'

'There you are! She wanted to bewitch someone and she came under the spell herself . . .'

'But what rain it was!'

'The *jimbambi* are like that . . . They only come with the rain or the wind: they're not like other spells . . .'

'Well, well. A devil on the drain. Yesterday it was banging away. I even trembled, brother!'

'When you hear a noise like that, it's beating its wings. In the forest, if he and she sit down and you don't make way for them, hey presto, you're done for, Mama mia! They look like a cock and a hen, but they run like partridges.'

'I know, I know. They sometimes even lose a few scales – that's their feathers . . .'

'Yesterday they saw the devil on the drain of the dead woman's hut. I don't know whether it was him or her . . .'

'That was a real disaster! But why cast spells like that? All she did in the end was bewitch herself . . .'

'That's what comes of witchcraft . . . If she had gone to church and prayed to St Antony, then whoever took the money would have been found . . . And the owner wouldn't have died . . .'

'It's fate, really . . .'

A few days later:

'Have you heard? Izabel's died!'

'There you are! The niece died the other day, and the aunt dies today. What a catastrophe!'

'Yes, it never rains but it pours!'

'The funny thing is that the people who were at the funerals of Mussoco and Donana were taken so ill that they passed away.'

'God forgive me, but I've already heard it was Mussoco who picked up the money.'

'Really?'

'I don't know, but they gossip such a lot round here. Anyway, other sinners like ourselves are saying she was the one who found the money. Poor thing, she wanted to give it back to the owner, but her aunt and grandmother talked her out of it.'

'O Lord! Those old women too! Why use other folks' money?'

'They were friends . . .'

'To hell with it! What sort of friends were they? Friendship outside and emptiness within?'

'Our old men were right: "We know the face but we don't know the heart." But I'm sorry for the poor girl, dying so young. She was such a nice person. And the aunt, now . . .'

'The lord forgive me, she's no longer with us. But why make her out to have been kind hearted? Our mothers are also saying a thing or two! They were so stubborn, the aunt and the grandmother, that the poor child died, and Donana too.'

'As for Donana, I've had enough of her. She didn't know how to cast spells. Why did she drag in other folks who had nothing to do with that money? Whoever washes the corpse shall die. Whoever goes to the funeral shall die. Whoever says "Woe is me!" To hell with it all!'

'More's already been done than she wanted. But anger means something too. A person weeps and shouts and nothing happens. It wasn't easy for her either. Let's drop all this. We'd have done the same!'

But death continued on its way.

'Have you heard the bad news? They're dying in the street now!'

'Impossible! Who's the unlucky one?'

'Didn't you know? Katarina!'

'Ai-ai-ai! Poor woman! Where?'

'In Cabino, near the railway. The poor thing was on the way to see the healer.'

'Fancy that! We're still walking about, but we're already dying.'

'That's the truth, my dear. The flesh is still alive, but the soul is already dead.'

So it went on, with fever, stomach cramps and the spitting of blood – the locals died one after another and the black terror crept deeper and deeper into their souls. As was said in the curse, when they went to the funeral, they paid with their lives for defying the taboo. Frightened friends, in spite of their natural solidarity, tried not to show up on such occasions. Even the parents, when struck by misfortune, did not carry out their sacred duty of tending the sick.

To climax it all, a new and terrible item of news started doing the rounds: to shake off the curse, Mussoco's family, already much thinned down, were scattering that accursed money about in the streets! How dangerous for the children! Even though they'd been warned, how would they be able to resist such a temptation? And if the whole sum . . . But no, they were scattering it about piecemeal, an escudo here, an escudo there. What a diabolical temptation! Damned money! Many innocent people had already died because of it; the Lord alone knew how many more were going to.

'Mind you don't pick up any money off the street! D'you hear? It's bewitched! Look how people are dying!' Mothers warned their children.

But death continued to lay people low. The vengeful curse took its inexorable course: 'Whoever washes the corpse shall die! Whoever trims its nails shall die! Whoever cuts its hair shall die! Whoever dresses it shall die! Whoever goes to bury it shall die. Whoever says: "Woe is me!" shall also die.' Salvation? Where was it to be sought? Before that abyss, the healer admitted that he was powerless to help – the curse was such a terrible one. Falling from the clouds, it entered the flesh of those who ignored the warnings and it secretly compelled them to obey the dread command: 'Die!'

'It's an epidemic,' declared the doctors.

But you can't fool the people, and along with the healers, the people protested:

'Rubbish. What epidemic? It's the bad *jimbambi*!'

'The whites! What do they know anyway?' say the blacks contemptuously.

'True! Witchcraft doesn't get at them! . . .'

'It's like that accident at Xamavo Market . . .'

'True! They say the roof fell in because of a high wind . . .'

'A high wind? It fell in because of the *jimbambi* . . .'

And those deaths, like the tragic year of 1921, for which various explanations were found, are still fresh in the memories of Luanda's inhabitants, not in terms of scientific conclusions, but in terms of the dogmas of their beliefs.

Oscar Ribas (Angola)
Translated from the Portuguese by Alex Miller

Chant

In the time when Dendid created all things,
He created the sun,
And the sun is born, and dies, and comes again;
He created the moon,
And the moon is born, and dies, and comes again;
He created the stars,
And the stars are born, and die, and come again;
He created man,
And man is born, and dies, and never comes again.

Dinka (Sudan)

X — EARTH AND SKY
AND THE MARVELS IN BETWEEN

A Libation Speech*

OLD MAN: Here in the state of Abura,
    Which must surely be one of the best pieces of land
    Odomankoma, our creator, has given to man,
    Everything happens in moderation:
    The sun comes out each day,
    But its heat seldom burns our crops;
    Rains are good when they fall
    And Asaase Efua the earth-goddess gives of herself
    To them that know the seasons;
    Streams abound, which like all gods
    Must have their angry moments and swell,
    But floods are hardly known to living memory.
    Behind us to the north, Aburabura
    Our beautiful lonely mountain sits with her neck to the skies,
    Reminding us that all of the earth is not flat.
    In the south, Nana Bosompo, the ocean, roars on. Lord of
        Tuesdays,
    His day must be sacred. We know him well and even
    The most unadventurous can reap his fish, just sitting on his pretty
        sands,
    While for the brave who read the constellations,
    His billows are easier to ride than the currents of a ditch.
    And you, Mighty God, and your hosts our forefathers,
    We do not say this in boastfulness
    (*He bends in the fingers of his right hand as though he were
    holding a cup, raises it up and acts out the motions of pouring
    a libation.*) but only in true thankfulness,

Praying to you all that things may continue to be good
And even get better.

Ama Ata Aidoo (Ghana)
Excerpt from the Prologue to *Anowa*

Daybreak

Have you seen the dawn go poaching
in night's orchard?
See, she is coming back
down eastern pathways
overgrown with lily-blooms.
From head to foot she is splashed with milk
like those children the heifers suckled long ago.
She holds a torch in hands
stained black and blue like the lips of a girl
munching mulberries.

Escaping one by one there fly before her
the birds she has taken in her traps.

Jean-Joseph Rabearivelo (Madagascar)
Translated from the French by John Reed and Clive Wake

The Boast of Niani*

The griots, fine talkers that they were, used to boast of Niani and Mali saying: 'If you want salt, go to Niani, for Niani is the camping-place of the Sahel caravans. If you want gold, go to Niani, for Bouré, Bambougou and Wagadou work for Niani. If you want fine cloth, go to Niani, for the Mecca road passes by Niani. If you want fish, go to Niani, for it is there that the fishermen of Maouti and Djenné come to sell their catches. If you want meat, go to Niani, the country of the great hunters, and the land of the ox and the sheep. If you want to see an army, go to Niani, for it is there that the united forces of Mali are to be found. If you want to see a great king, go to Niani, for it is there that the son of Sogolon lives, the man with two names.'

This is what the masters of the spoken word used to sing.

Mandingo (Guinea and Mali)

Excerpt from the epic *Sundiata* as recited by the griot Mamadou Kouyaté
Transcribed and translated into French by D. T. Niane. Translated from
the French by G. D. Pickett

Ibadan

The spirit of the rock protects the town.
Ibadan, don't fight!
We must ask for permission, before we enter the town.
Because this is the town in which the thief is innocent
and the owner of property is guilty.
Here peace is lying exhausted on the ground
and belligerence dances on his back.
Ibadan, the town where the owner of the land
does not prosper like the stranger.
Nobody is born, without some kind of disease in his body.
Riots in all the compounds are the diseases of Ibadan.
You think you have friends in Ibadan—
but they will sell your own child.
You may look at this town whichever way you like—
you will see nothing but war.

Yoruba (Nigeria)

Song of the Will-o'-the-Wisp

Fire that men see only at night, dark night,
Fire that burns without warming, that shines without burning,
Fire that flies without body and without support, that knows neither
    house nor hearth,
Transparent fire of palm trees, a man without fear calls you.

Fire of sorcerers, your mother is where? your father where? Who
    nursed you?

You are your father, you are your mother, you pass without a trace.
Dry wood does not beget you, you have not ashes for daughters, you
    die without death.
The wandering soul is changed into you and no man knows it.

Fire of sorcerers, spirit of the waters underground, spirit of the upper
    airs,
Flash that shines, firefly that lights the swamp,
Bird without wings, thing without body, spirit of the strength of fire,
Hear my words, a man without fear calls you.

Fang (Gabon and Cameroon)

Invocation to the Rainbow

Rainbow, O Rainbow,
You who shine away up there, so high,
Above the forest that is so vast,
Among the black clouds,
Dividing the dark sky,

You have overturned,
You have wrestled down
The thunder that roared,
Roared so loud, in rage!
Was it angry against us?

Among the black clouds,
Dividing the dark sky,
As a knife cuts through an over-ripe fruit,
Rainbow, Rainbow!

And it fled,
The thunder killer of men,
Like the antelope from the panther,
Rainbow, Rainbow!

Strong bow of the Hunter above,
The Hunter who hunts down the herd of the clouds
Like a herd of elephants in terror,

Rainbow, speak our thanks to him.
Say to him: 'Be not angry!'
Say to him: 'Be not wrathful!'
Say to him: 'Kill us not!'
For we are greatly afraid,
Rainbow, tell him so!

Pygmy (Cameroon and Gabon)

The Locust

What is a locust?
Its head, a grain of corn; its neck, the hinge of a knife;
Its horns, a bit of thread; its chest is smooth and burnished;
Its body is like a knife-handle;
Its hock, a saw; its spittle, ink;
Its underwings, clothing for the dead.†
On the ground – it is laying eggs;
In flight – it is like the clouds.
Approaching the ground, it is rain glittering in the sun;
Lighting on a plant, it becomes a pair of scissors;
Walking, it becomes a razor;
Desolation walks with it.

Malagasy (Madagascar)

Python

Swaggering prince
giant among snakes.
They say python has no house.
I heard it a long time ago
and I laughed and laughed and laughed.
For who owns the ground under the lemon grass?

---

†*Clothing for the dead*: particoloured like some mourning garments.

Who owns the ground under the elephant grass?
Who owns the swamp – father of rivers?
Who owns the stagnant pool – father of waters?

Because they never walk hand in hand
people say that snakes only walk singly.
But just imagine
suppose the viper walks in front
the green mamba follows
and the python creeps rumbling behind–
who will be brave enough
to wait for them?

Yoruba (Nigeria)

Sophiatowners*

The last bus to Sophiatown. About the eleven o'clock before midnight. Peter was waiting for the fish tin to rattle off. Then she came in.

'Hallo, Beautiful! Come sit with me,' someone called. Then a chorus of amateur wolves yelled, inviting her to come sit with them. And Peter noticed how she glanced round uneasily. She was looking for a safe seat near a gentleman. But he did not feel gallant. In Sophiatown you don't get gallant.

Then he saw a thug coming up from the back to take her in hand. Suddenly she saw Peter and made up her mind.

'Hallo, Jerry!' she exclaimed, and went to sit by his side. Peter did not know her from Adam and Eve, and he felt sick. The thug hesitated for a moment. Then he, too, decided. He was going to get tough.

But she addressed herself to Peter again.

'When did you get out of goal for murder, Jerry darling?' she cooed.

'Last week,' Peter muttered unhappily.

The thug shuffled past to the door discreetly.

Peter did not know whether his reputation had risen or fallen. But some girls do think fast, don't they?

Can Themba (Azania)

The Madman

He was drawn to markets and straight roads. Not any tiny neighbour-
hood market where a handful of garrulous women might gather at
sunset to gossip and buy ogili for the evening's soup, but a huge,
engulfing bazaar beckoning people familiar and strange from far and
near. And not any dusty, old footpath beginning in this village, and
ending in that stream, but broad, black, mysterious highways without
beginning or end. After much wandering he had discovered two such
markets linked together by such a highway; and so ended his wandering.
One market was Afo, the other Eke. The two days between them suited
him very well: before setting out for Eke he had ample time to wind up
his business properly at Afo. He passed the night there putting right
again his hut after a day of defilement by two fat-bottomed market
women who said it was their market-stall. At first he had put up a fight
but the women had gone and brought their menfolk – four hefty beasts
of the bush – to whip him out of the hut. After that he always avoided
them, moving out on the morning of the market and back in at dusk to
pass the night. Then in the morning he rounded off his affairs swiftly
and set out on that long, beautiful boa-constrictor of a road to Eke in
the distant town of Ogbu. He held his staff and cudgel at the ready in
his right hand, and with the left he steadied the basket of his belongings
on his head. He had got himself this cudgel lately to deal with little
beasts on the way who threw stones at him and made fun of their
mothers' nakedness, not his own.

He used to walk in the middle of the road, holding it in conversation.
But one day the driver of a mammy-wagon and his mate came down on
him shouting, pushing and slapping his face. They said their lorry very
nearly ran over their mother, not him. After that he avoided those noisy
lorries too, with the vagabonds inside them.

Having walked one day and one night he was now close to the Eke
market-place. From every little side-road crowds of market people
poured into the big highway to join the enormous flow to Eke. Then he
saw some young ladies with water-pots on their heads coming towards
him, unlike all the rest, away from the market. This surprised him. Then
he saw two more water-pots rise out of a sloping footpath leading off

his side of the highway. He felt thirsty then and stopped to think it over. Then he set down his basket on the roadside and turned into the sloping footpath. But first he begged his highway not to be offended or continue the journey without him. 'I'll get some for you too,' he said coaxingly with a tender backward glance. 'I know you are thirsty.'

Nwibe was a man of high standing in Ogbu and was rising higher; a man of wealth and integrity. He had just given notice to all the *ozo* men of the town that he proposed to seek admission into their honoured hierarchy in the coming initiation season.

'Your proposal is excellent,' said the men of title. 'When we see we shall believe.' Which was their dignified way of telling you to think it over once again and make sure you have the means to go through with it. For *ozo* is not a child's naming ceremony; and where is the man to hide his face who begins the *ozo* dance and then is foot-stuck to the arena? But in this instance the caution of the elders was no more than a formality for Nwibe was such a sensible man that no one could think of him beginning something he was not sure to finish.

On that Eke day Nwibe had risen early so as to visit his farm beyond the stream and do some light work before going to the market at midday to drink a horn or two of palm wine with his peers and perhaps buy that bundle of roofing thatch for the repair of his wives' huts. As for his own hut he had a couple of years back settled it finally by changing his thatch-roof to zinc. Sooner or later he would do the same for his wives. He could have done Mgboye's hut right away but decided to wait until he could do the two together, or else Udenkwo would set the entire compound on fire. Udenkwo was the junior wife, by three years, but she never let that worry her. Happily Mgboye was a woman of peace who rarely demanded the respect due to her from the other. She would suffer Udenkwo's provoking tongue sometimes for a whole day without offering a word in reply. And when she did reply at all her words were always few and her voice low.

That very morning Udenkwo had accused her of spite and all kinds of wickedness on account of a little dog.

'What has a little dog done to you?' she screamed loud enough for half the village to hear. 'I ask you Mgboye, what is the offence of a puppy this early in the day?'

'What your puppy did this early in the day,' replied Mgboye, 'is that he put his shit-mouth into my soup-pot.'

'And then?'

'And then I smacked him.'

'You smacked him! Why don't you cover your soup-pot? Is it easier to hit a dog than cover a pot? Is a small puppy to have more sense than a woman who leaves her soup-pot about . . . ?'

'Enough from you, Udenkwo.'

'It is not enough, Mgboye, it is not enough. If that dog owes you any debt I want to know. Everything I have, even a little dog I bought to eat my infant's excrement keeps you awake at nights. You are a bad woman, Mgboye, you are a very bad woman!'

Nwibe had listened to all of this in silence in his hut. He knew from the vigour of Udenkwo's voice that she could go on like this till market-time. So he intervened, in his characteristic manner by calling out to his senior wife.

'Mgboye! Let me have peace this early morning!'

'Don't you hear all the abuses, Udenkwo . . .'

'I hear nothing at all from Udenkwo and I want peace in my compound. If Udenkwo is crazy must everybody else go crazy with her? Is one crazy woman not enough in my compound so early in the day?'

'The great judge has spoken,' sang Udenkwo in a sneering sing-song. 'Thank you, great judge. Udenkwo is mad. Udenkwo is always mad, but those of you who are sane let . . .'

'Shut your mouth, shameless woman, or a wild beast will lick your eyes for you this morning. When will you learn to keep your badness within this compound instead of shouting it to all Ogbu to hear? I say shut your mouth!'

There was silence then except for Udenkwo's infant whose yelling had up till then been swallowed up by the larger noise of the adults.

'Don't cry, my father,' said Udenkwo to him. 'They want to kill your dog, but our people say the man who decides to chase after a chicken, for him is the fall . . .'

By the middle of the morning Nwibe had done all the work he had to do on his farm and was on his way again to prepare for market. At the little stream he decided as he always did to wash off the sweat of work. So he put his cloth on a huge boulder by the men's bathing section and waded in. There was nobody else around because of the time of day and because it was market day. But from instinctive modesty he turned to face the forest away from the approaches.

The madman watched him for quite a while. Each time he bent down to carry water in cupped hands from the shallow stream to his head and body the madman smiled at his parted behind. And then remembered. This was the same hefty man who brought three others like him and whipped me out of my hut in the Afo market. He nodded to himself. And he remembered again: this was the same vagabond who descended on me from the lorry in the middle of my highway. He nodded once more. And then he remembered yet again: this was the same fellow who set his children to throw stones at me and make remarks about their mothers' buttocks, not mine. Then he laughed.

Nwibe turned sharply round and saw the naked man laughing, the deep grove of the stream amplifying his laughter. Then he stopped as suddenly as he had begun; the merriment vanished from his face.

'I've caught you naked,' he said.

Nwibe ran a hand swiftly down his face to clear his eyes of water.

'I say I have caught you naked, with your thing dangling about.'

'I can see you are hungry for a whipping,' said Nwibe with quiet menace in his voice, for a madman is said to be easily scared away by the very mention of a whip. 'Wait till I get up there . . . What are you doing? Drop it at once . . . I say drop it!'

The madman had picked up Nwibe's cloth and wrapped it round his own waist. He looked down at himself and began to laugh again.

'I will kill you,' screamed Nwibe as he splashed towards the bank, maddened by anger. 'I will whip that madness out of you today!'

They ran all the way up the steep and rocky footpath hedged in by the shadowy green forest. A mist gathered and hung over Nwibe's vision as he ran, stumbled, fell, pulled himself up again and stumbled on, shouting and cursing. The other, despite his unaccustomed encumbrances, steadily increased his lead, for he was spare and wiry, a thing made for speed. Furthermore, he did not waste his breath shouting and cursing; he just ran. Two girls going down to the stream saw a man running up the slope towards them pursued by a stark-naked madman. They threw down their pots and fled, screaming.

When Nwibe emerged into the full glare of the highway he could not see his cloth clearly any more and his chest was on the point of exploding from the fire and torment within. But he kept running. He was only vaguely aware of crowds of people on all sides and he appealed to them tearfully without stopping: 'Hold the madman, he's got my cloth!' By this time the man with the cloth was practically lost among the much denser crowds far in front so that the link between him and the naked man was no longer clear.

Now Nwibe continually bumped against people's backs and then laid flat a frail old man struggling with a stubborn goat on a leash. 'Stop the madman,' he shouted hoarsely, his heart tearing to shreds, 'he's got my cloth!' Everyone looked at him first in surprise and then less surprise because strange sights are common in a great market. Some of them even laughed.

'They've got his cloth he says.'

'That's a new one I'm sure. He hardly looks mad yet. Doesn't he have people, I wonder?'

'People are so careless these days. Why can't they keep proper watch over their sick relations, especially on the day of the market?'

Farther up the road on the very brink of the market place two men from Nwibe's village recognized him and, throwing down the one his long basket of yams, the other his calabash of palm wine held on a loop, gave desperate chase, to stop him setting foot irrevocably within the occult territory of the powers of the market. But it was in vain. When finally they caught him it was well inside the crowded square. Udenkwo in tears tore off her top-cloth which they draped on him and led him home by the hand. He spoke just once about a madman who took his cloth in the stream.

'It is all right,' said one of the men in the tone of a father to a crying child. They led and he followed blindly, his heavy chest heaving up and down in silent weeping. Many more people from his village, a few of his in-laws and one or two others from his mother's place had joined the grief-stricken party. One man whispered to another that it was the worst kind of madness, deep and tongue-tied.

'May it end ill for him who did this,' prayed the other.

The first medicine-man his relatives consulted refused to take him on, out of some kind of integrity.

'I could say yes to you and take your money,' he said. 'But that is not my way. My powers of cure are known throughout Olu and Igbo but never have I professed to bring back to life a man who has sipped the spirit waters of *ani-mmo*. It is the same with a madman who of his own accord delivers himself to the divinities of the market-place. You should have kept better watch over him.'

'Don't blame us too much,' said Nwibe's relative. 'When he left home that morning his senses were as complete as yours and mine now. Don't blame us too much.'

'Yes, I know. It happens that way sometimes. And they are the ones that medicine will not reach. I know.'

'Can you do nothing at all then, not even to untie his tongue?'

'Nothing can be done. They have already embraced him. It is like a man who runs away from the oppression of his fellows to the grove of an *alusi* and says to him: Take me, O spirit, I am your *osu*. No man can touch him thereafter. He is free and yet no power can break his bondage. He is free of men but bonded to a god.'

The second doctor was not as famous as the first and not so strict. He said the case was bad, very bad indeed, but no one folds his arms because the condition of his child is beyond hope. He must still grope around and do his best. His hearers nodded in eager agreement. And then he muttered into his own inward ear: If doctors were to send away every patient whose cure they were uncertain of, how many of them would eat one meal in a whole week from their practice?

Nwibe was cured of his madness. That humble practitioner who did the miracle became overnight the most celebrated mad-doctor of his generation. They called him the Sojourner to the Land of the Spirits. Even so it remains true that madness may indeed sometimes depart but never with all his clamorous train. Some of these always remain – the trailers of madness you might call them – to haunt the doorway of the eyes. For how could a man be the same again of whom witnesses from all the lands of Olu and Igbo have once reported that they saw today a fine, hefty man in his prime, stark naked, tearing through the crowds to answer the call of the market-place? Such a man is marked for ever.

Nwibe became a quiet, withdrawn man avoiding whenever he could the
boisterous side of the life of his people. Two years later, before another
initiation season, he made a new inquiry about joining the community
of titled men in his town. Had they received him perhaps he might have
become at least partially restored, but those *ozo* men, dignified and
polite as ever, deftly steered the conversation away to other matters.

Chinua Achebe (Nigeria)

Amope*

Early morning.

*A few poles with nets and other litter denote a fishing village. Downstage
right is the corner of a hut, window on one side, door on the other.*

*A cycle bell is heard ringing. Seconds after, a cycle is ridden on stage
towards the hut. The rider is a shortish man; his feet barely touch the
pedals. On the crossbar is a woman; the crossbar itself is wound round
with a mat, and on the carrier is a large travelling sack, with a woman's
household stool hanging from a corner of it.*

AMOPE: Stop here. Stop here. That's his house.
   *The man applies the brakes too suddenly. The weight leans towards
   the woman's side, with the result that she props up the bicycle with
   her feet, rather jerkily. It is in fact no worse than any ordinary landing,
   but it is enough to bring out her sense of aggrievement.*
AMOPE: (*Her tone of martyrdom is easy, accustomed to use.*) I suppose
   we all do our best, but after all these years one would think you could
   set me down a little more gently.
CHUME: You didn't give me much notice. I had to brake suddenly.
AMOPE: The way you complain – anybody who didn't see what happened
   would think you were the one who broke an ankle.
   (*She had already begun to limp.*)
CHUME: Don't tell me that was enough to break your ankle.
AMOPE: Break? You didn't hear me complain. You did your best, but if

my toes are to be broken one by one just because I have to monkey on your bicycle, you must admit it's a tough life for a woman.

CHUME: I did my . . .

AMOPE: Yes, you did your best. I know. Didn't I admit it? Please . . . give me that stool . . . You know yourself that I'm not the one to make much of a little thing like that, but I haven't been too well. If anyone knows that, it's you. Thank you (*Taking the stool.*) . . . I haven't been well, that's all. Otherwise I wouldn't have said a thing. (*She sits down near the door of the hut, sighing heavily, and begins to nurse her feet.*)

CHUME: Do you want me to bandage it for you?

AMOPE: No, no. What for?

(CHUME *hesitates, then begins to unload the bundle.*)

CHUME: You're sure you don't want me to take you back? If it swells after I've gone . . .

AMOPE: I can look after myself. I've always done, and looked after you too. Just help me unload the things and place them against the wall . . . you know I wouldn't ask if it wasn't for the ankle.

(CHUME *had placed the bag next to her, thinking that was all. He returns now to unpack the bundle. Brings out a small brazier covered with paper which is tied down, two small saucepans . . .*)

AMOPE: You haven't let the soup pour out, have you?

CHUME: (*With some show of exasperation*) Do you see oil on the wrapper? (*Throws down the wrapper.*)

AMOPE: Abuse me. All right, go on, begin to abuse me. You know that all I asked was if the soup had poured away, and it isn't as if that was something no one ever asked before. I would do it all myself if it wasn't for my ankle – anyone would think it was my fault . . . careful . . . careful now . . . the cork nearly came off that bottle. You know how difficult it is to get any clean water in this place . . .

(CHUME *unloads two bottles filled with water, two little parcels wrapped in paper, another tied in a knot, a box of matches, a piece of yarn, two tins, one probably an Ovaltine tin but containing something else of course, a cheap breakable spoon, a knife, while* AMOPE *keeps up her patient monologue, spoken almost with indifference.*)

AMOPE: Do, I beg you, take better care of that jar . . . I know you didn't want to bring me, but it wasn't the fault of the jar, was it?

CHUME: Who said I didn't want to bring you?

AMOPE: You said it was too far away for you to bring me on your bicycle . . . I suppose you really wanted me to walk . . .

CHUME: I . . .

AMOPE: And after you'd broken my foot, the first thing you asked was if you should take me home. You were only too glad it happened . . . in fact if I wasn't the kind of person who would never think evil of anyone – even you – I would have said that you did it on purpose.

(*The unloading is over.* CHUME *shakes out the bag.*)

AMOPE: Just leave the bag here. I can use it for a pillow.

CHUME: Is there anything else before I go?

AMOPE: You've forgotten the mat. I know it's not much, but I would like something to sleep on. There are women who sleep in beds of course, but I'm not complaining . . . They are just lucky with their husbands, and we can't all be lucky I suppose.

CHUME: You've got a bed at home.

(*He unties the mat which is wound round the crossbar.*)

AMOPE: And so I'm to leave my work undone. My trade is to suffer because I have a bed at home? Thank God I am not the kind of woman who . . .

CHUME: I am nearly late for work.

AMOPE: I know you can't wait to get away. You only use your work as an excuse. A Chief Messenger in the Local Government Office – do you call that work? Your old school friends are now Ministers, riding in long cars . . .

(CHUME *gets on his bike and flees.* AMOPE *shouts after him, craning her neck in his direction.*)

AMOPE: Don't forget to bring some more water when you're returning from work. (*She relapses and sighs heavily.*) He doesn't realize it is all for his own good. He's no worse than other men, but he won't make the effort to become something in life. A Chief Messenger. Am I to go to my grave as the wife of a Chief Messenger?

(*She is seated so that the* PROPHET *does not immediately see her when he opens the window to breathe some fresh air. He stares straight out for a few moments, then shuts his eyes tightly, clasps his hands together above his chest, chin uplifted for a few moments' meditation. He relaxes and is about to go in when he sees* AMOPE's *back. He leans out to try and take in the rest of her, but this proves impossible. Puzzled, he leaves the window and goes round to the door which is then seen to open about a foot and shut rapidly.*

AMOPE *is calmly chewing kola. As the door shuts she takes out a notebook and a pencil and checks some figures.*

PROPHET JEROBOAM, *known to his congregation as* BROTHER JERO, *is seen again at the window, this time with his canvas pouch and divine stick. He lowers the bag to the ground, eases one leg over the window.*)

AMOPE: (*Without looking back*) Where do you think you're going?

(BROTHER JERO *practically flings himself back into the house.*)

AMOPE: One pound, eight shillings and ninepence for three months. And he calls himself a man of God.

(*She puts the notebook away, unwraps the brazier and proceeds to light it preparatory to getting breakfast. The door opens another foot.*)

JERO: (*Coughs.*) Sister . . . my dear sister in Christ . . .

AMOPE: I hope you slept well, Brother Jero . . .

JERO: Yes, thanks be to God. (*Hems and coughs.*) I – er – I hope you have not come to stand in the way of Christ and his work.

AMOPE: If Christ doesn't stand in the way of me and my work.

JERO: Beware of pride, sister. That was a sinful way to talk.

AMOPE: Listen, you bearded debtor. You owe me one pound, eight and nine. You promised you would pay me three months ago but of course you have been too busy doing the work of God. Well, let me tell you that you are not going anywhere until you do a bit of my own work.

JERO: But the money is not in the house. I must get it from the post office before I can pay you.

AMOPE: (*Fanning the brazier*) You'll have to think of something else before you call me a fool.

(BROTHER JEROBOAM *shuts the door.*

A woman TRADER *goes past with a deep calabash bowl on her head.*)

AMOPE: Ei, what are you selling?

(*The* TRADER *hesitates, decides to continue on her way.*)

AMOPE: Isn't it you I'm calling? What have you got there?

TRADER: (*Stops without turning round.*) Are you buying for trade or just for yourself?

AMOPE: It might help if you first told me what you have.

TRADER: Smoked fish.

AMOPE: Well, let's see it.

TRADER: (*Hesitates*) All right, help me to set it down. But I don't usually stop on the way.

AMOPE: Isn't it money you are going to the market for, and isn't it money I'm going to pay you?

TRADER: (*As* AMOPE *gets up and unloads her.*) Well, just remember it is early in the morning. Don't start me off wrong by haggling.

AMOPE: All right, all right. (*Looks at the fish.*) How much a dozen?

TRADER: One and three, and I'm not taking a penny less.

AMOPE: It is last week's, isn't it?

TRADER: I've told you, you're my first customer, so don't ruin my trade with the ill-luck of the morning.

AMOPE: (*Holding one up to her nose*) Well, it does smell a bit, doesn't it?

TRADER: (*Putting back the wrappings*) Maybe it is you who haven't had a bath for a week.

AMOPE: Yeh! All right, go on. Abuse me. Go on and abuse me when all I wanted was a few of your miserable fish. I deserve it for trying to be neighbourly with a cross-eyed wretch, pauper that you are . . .

TRADER: It is early in the morning. I am not going to let you infect my luck with your foul tongue by answering you back. And just you keep your cursed fingers from my goods because that is where you'll meet with the father of all devils if you don't.

(*She lifts the load to her head all by herself.*)

AMOPE: Yes, go on. Carry the burden of your crimes and take your beggar's rags out of my sight . . .

TRADER: I leave you in the hands of your flatulent belly, you barren sinner. May you never do good in all your life.

AMOPE: You're cursing me now, are you?

(*She leaps up just in time to see* BROTHER JERO *escape through the window.*)

Help! Thief! Thief! You bearded rogue. Call yourself a prophet? But you'll find it is easier to get out than to get in. You'll find that out or my name isn't Amope . . .

(*She turns on the* TRADER *who has already disappeared.*)

Do you see what you have done, you spindle-leg toad? Receiver of stolen goods, just wait until the police catch up with you . . .

(*Towards the end of this speech the sound of gangan drums is heard, coming from the side opposite the hut. A* BOY *enters carrying a drum on each shoulder. He walks towards her, drumming. She turns almost at once.*)

AMOPE: Take yourself off, you dirty beggar. Do you think my money is for the likes of you?

(*The* BOY *flees, turns suddenly and beats a parting abuse on the drums.*)

AMOPE: I don't know what the world is coming to. A thief of a prophet, a swindler of a fish-seller and now that thing with lice on his head comes begging for money. He and the prophet ought to get together with the fish-seller their mother.

(*Lights fade.*)

Wole Soyinka (Nigeria)
The Trials of Brother Jero, Scene Two

Ten-to-Ten
(Excerpt)

As the first bell rang, one Saturday night, a huge African policeman roused himself from the barracks. He was enormous. Nearer seven feet than six feet tall, he towered over his fellow men like a sheer mountain above the mites in the valley. Perfectly formed, his shoulders were like boulders, his arms like the trunks of elephants, the muscles hard and corded. His legs bore his magnificent torso like sturdy pillars under some granite superstructure. He had the largest foot in Pretoria, size fifteen, and people used to say, 'His boot is special made from the factory.' He was coal-black, with the shiny blackness of ebony, but had large, rolling, white eyes and thick, bluish lips.

He gave a last, critical scrutiny to his shining, black boots and black uniform with tinny buttons, before he stepped into the charge office to report for duty. His was the night beat. Every night at ten o'clock he went out with one or two other policemen to roam the dusty streets of Marabastad Location and clear them of vagrants. People looked at him with awe; nobody ever argued with him; when his immense shadow fell across you, you shrivelled, or, if you had any locomotion left in you, you gave way fast.

They called him Ten-to-Ten because of that night beat of his, and he was known by no other name. Ten-to-Ten's strength was prodigious and there were many legends in the location about him . . .

There was the one that he originally came from Tzaneen in the Northern Transvaal to seek work in Pretoria. One day he was sitting in a drinking-house when a young location hooligan came in and molested the daughter of the house. The girl's father tried to protest but the young hooligan slapped him across the face and told him to shut up. Ten-to-Ten was not accustomed to such behaviour, so he rose from the corner where he was sitting with his tin of beer and walked up to the young man.

'Look,' he said, 'you can't go on like this in another man's house. Please go away now.' He gently pushed the young man towards the door. 'Come on, now, go home.'

The young man swung round with a curse, hesitated a moment when he saw the great bulk of the man confronting him, then with a sneer drew a knife.

They say you can pester a Venda from the north, that you can insult him, humiliate him in public or cheat him in private, but there are two things you just cannot do with impunity: take his girl, or draw a knife on him.

That night, Ten-to-Ten went jungle-mad.

'Ha!' he snarled.

The knife flashed and caught him in the forearm, spurting blood. But before the young man could withdraw it, Ten-to-Ten had caught him by the neck and dragged him out of the house. In the yard there was the usual corrugated-iron fence. Swinging the boy like wet laundry, Ten-to-Ten lashed him against the fence repeatedly until the fence broke down. Then he started strangling him. Men came running from their houses. They tried to tear Ten-to-Ten off the boy, but he shook them off like flakes. Soon, somebody sounded a whistle, the call for the police.

By the time they came Ten-to-Ten was hurling all sorts of backyard missiles at the small crowd that sought to protect the boy.

The police stormed him and knocked him over, bludgeoning him with batons. They managed to manacle his wrists while he was down on his back, then they stepped back to wipe their sweat and wait for him to rise. Ten-to-Ten rose slowly on one knee. He looked at the police and smiled. The white sergeant was saying, 'Now, now, come quietly, no more trouble, eh?' when Ten-to-Ten spotted his enemy staggering from the crowd.

He grunted savagely and, looking at his bound hands, wrenched them apart and snapped the iron manacles like cotton. The police had to rush at him again while the crowd scattered.

They say the desk sergeant at the police station decided that very day to make Ten-to-Ten a policeman, and Marabastad became a peaceful location.

That is the kind of story you do not have to believe to enjoy.

Another time, legend has it, the coal-delivery man had some difficulty with his horse. He had a one-man horse-cart with which he delivered coal from door to door. On one occasion, the horse suddenly shied, perhaps having been pelted by mischievous boys with slings, and went dashing down the narrow avenue, scattering women with water tins on their heads. Just then Ten-to-Ten came round the corner. He caught the bridle of the horse and struggled to keep it still, being carried along a few yards himself. The horse reared and threatened to break away. Then Ten-to-Ten kicked it with his size fifteen boot under the heart. The horse sagged, rolled over and died.

But it was not only for his violent exploits that we thrilled to him. Ten-to-Ten played soccer for the Police First Eleven. He played right-back. For a giant his size he was remarkably swift, but it was his antics we loved. He would drop an oncoming ball dead before his own goalposts, and as the opponent's poor forward came rushing at him, he would quickly shift aside with the ball at the last moment, leaving the forward to go hurtling on his own momentum through the goalposts. Derisively, he would call, 'Goal!' and the excited spectators would shout, 'Ten-to-Ten! Ten-to-Ten!'

Sometimes he would approach the ball ferociously, with his rivals all about it, and he would make as if he was going to blast the ball and all.

They would scuttle for cover, only to find that he had stopped the ball and was standing with one foot on it, grinning happily.

When he *did* elect to kick it, he had such powerful shots that the ball went from one end of the field to the other. Once, they say, he took a penalty kick. The ball went with such force that when the goalie tried to stop it, his hands were flayed and the deflected ball still went on to tear a string in the net.

'Ten-to-Ten!'

Yes, he had a sense of humour; and he was also the understanding kind. He knew about his great strength and seldom exercised it recklessly.

In the Marabastad of those days there was a very quarrelsome little fellow called Shorty. He was about four feet six, but as they say, 'He buys a tickey's beer and makes a pound's worth of trouble.' No one but Shorty ever really took his tantrums seriously, but people enjoyed teasing him for fun.

'Shorty,' they once told him, 'Ten-to-Ten's in that house telling people that you're not a man, but just a sample.' Shorty boiled over. He strutted into the house with the comic little gait of the very short and found Ten-to-Ten sitting with a tin of beer in his hands.

He kicked the tin of beer out of Ten-to-Ten's hands, nearly toppling himself over in the process, and shouted, 'A sample of a man eh? I'll teach you to respect your betters. Come outside and fight.' The others quickly signalled Ten-to-Ten that it was all a joke and he caught on. But Shorty was so aggrieved that he pestered Ten-to-Ten all afternoon.

At last Ten-to-Ten, tired of the sport, rose, lifted Shorty bodily off the ground and carried him down the street with a procession of cheering people behind them. Shorty was raging; he threw futile punches at Ten-to-Ten's chest. His dangling legs were kicking about furiously, but Ten-to-Ten carried him all the way to the police station.

It was a startled desk sergeant who suddenly found a midget landed on his desk, shouting, 'I'll kill him! I'll kill him!'

'What's this?' the sergeant wanted to know.

Wearily, Ten-to-Ten explained, 'He says he wants to give me a fair fight.'

Shorty was fined ten bob, and when he came out of there, he turned to Ten-to-Ten disgustedly, and spat, 'Coward!'

Ten-to-Ten walked with two other policemen, Constables Masemola and Ramokgopa, up First Avenue into glittering Boom Street. It was like suddenly walking out of an African slum into a chunk of the Orient. They strolled slowly up the tarred Boom Street, past the Empire Cinema. Now and then they would stop to look at the exotic foods in the window of some Indian shop, and the pungent smells of Eastern cooking and Eastern toiletry would rise to their nostrils. A hundred yards ahead, you could see the Africans who had no special permits to be out at night, sorting themselves from the Indian and coloured night crowds and dodging down some dark streets. They had long noticed the stalwart shadow of Ten-to-Ten coming up. He knew it too, but did not bother.

He reasoned that as long as they were scampering home, it was a form of respect for the Law. Unlike some of the other policemen who ferreted out Africans and delighted in chasing them down the road, even when he caught one or two on the streets at night, it was enough for him to say, 'You there, home!' As they fled before him he felt duty to have been done.

Then they turned into the dark of Second Avenue of the location, away from where their eyes were guided by the blinking neons, into the murky streets where only their feet found the familiar way. It was silent, but Ten-to-Ten knew the residents were around, the silence was only because he was there. He was walking down the street, a presence that suddenly hushed these normally noisy people. In fact, he had heard their women, as he entered the street, calling down along it, 'Ten-to-Ten! Ten-to-Ten!'

Can Themba (Azania)

Soriatus

Passing through Mombasa
I remember Soriatus,
A child weaned before time.
Unfettered too, so goes the legend.
And all those burning licks his father gave him
Fell on dead skin.
Once he held him up high

Like a dead carcass on a hook
then let him go.
Soriatus never even groaned.
They all gave up.
No one could smooth his rough edges out.
It was common knowledge
he'd meet a terrible end.

A mere child then
He'd sneaked through the ship's portholes
docked at Bluff.
So goes the legend.
Sought refuge in the cool cargo;
was discovered half-dead at sea.
They should have tossed him on the waves, only,
The ship was about to enter Mombasa Bay.

All who passed there never found enough time to tell
the legend's exploits;
Endless knife brawls at seamen's bars
A nursery of fatherless kids
Or his regular brawls with prison inmates.
Only he had drowned himself
rather than hang.
His final destination was Chicago
he'd promised.
Because this was the toughest town in the roughest land.

Every mother warded off urchins with Soriatus:
If you don't want to die like him
you'd better do as you're told.
But in the tiny tin shacks and the mud
And those public toilet pipes
that burst according to some regular natural law,
There was plenty time, while elders broke their backs
in the nearby town
making a hard living,

For mock battles in an imaginary seamen's bar
And dress rehearsals for a human litter or brawls
With prison inmates,
Some showed more brawn than he
And ambitions far beyond Chicago.
Rather than visit the cemetery
I went to the seamen's bars
to meet the spirit of the man:
Roh, a sot,
boasting a battlefield of scars
Also Manzi
Who belonged in a nut-house.
All were bound for Harlem because
There the action was.

    Here lies Soriatus
    Surname: unknown
    Birthplace: unknown
    Age: unknown
    Parents:
    unknown
    An unknown who gave everyone for sure
    Hell.

                    Bhekokwakhe Langa (Azania)

Misra*

That night, cuddled up in each other's embrace, and in bed, she spoke
to you of a raid, so far undocumented in history books. Out of the raid,
out of the dust of triumph, emerged a warrior, she told you, a warrior
riding a horse, and as he hit his heels against the beast's ribs, the warrior
held tightly to a little girl, barely seven. The girl was his loot now that
the enemy had retreated in haste, defeated. Other men returned with
gold and similar booties – but not he. The little girl, now a young
woman, would remember for ever, her dog howling with fear and
anxiety and hunger, her cheeks shiny with mucus and with streaks of
tears running down them; and she cried and cried and cried, seated, as

though tied hand and foot to a bedpost, on the horse's back, a horse whose speed frightened her, as did the fact that he was taking her away from the world she had been familiar with so far. She was very pretty. Her hair had been shaven in the style your people shave children's skulls when suffering from whooping-cough, although the little girl's tuft on the skull was longer and slightly curlier. When the warrior arrived back in his hamlet, Misra went on telling you her story, his people intimated to him that they were afraid the girl might be traced to them – the soldiers of the Empire would follow the civilian invaders and the punitive expeditions would find many unburied dead. So he rode away, travelling as far south as he could, and the two of them, on a horse's back, ended up in the vicinity of Jigjiga.

In Jigjiga, the warrior, weary and fatigued from travel and worry, took ill. He stopped at the first house and knocked on the first door and spoke with the first man he met – luckily for him, the owner of the house, a very wealthy man. The warrior and the little girl were both given generous hospitality. A day later, the warrior died. And the little girl, who had been taken for his daughter, fell into the caring hands of the wealthy man. He raised her with his own children, making her embrace the Islamic faith, making her undergo the infibulatory rites, just like the other girls of the community. But he raised her with an eye to taking her as his wife when she grew up. And this he did, when she was seventeen. So, the man the little girl thought of and addressed as 'Father' for ten years of her life, overnight became a man to her, a man who insisted he make love to her and that she call him 'husband'. In the end, the conflicting loyalties alienated her, primarily from herself. And she murdered him during an excessive orgy of copulation.

To escape certain persecution, she joined a caravan going south to Kallafo, a caravan in search of grain to buy. She introduced herself as Misra Haji Abdullahi – taking anew the name of the man who became her father and whom she murdered as her 'man'.

And you asked, 'The girl's father and mother? Does anybody know whatever became of them? And whether or not they are still alive? Or if one of her parents has remarried or has had another child?'

You were surprised to learn that the girl was the offspring of a *damoz* union between an Oromo woman and an Amhara nobleman. She was the female child of the union, one in which her mother agreed, as is the custom, to live with an Amhara nobleman, none of whose other wives gave him a male child. The contract was for a period between a fortnight and six months. The girl was conceived by the 'salaried' concubine. Because the issue was a girl, the man lost interest in her, abandoning mother and child to their separate destinies and uncertain fortune. 'Yes, yes, but did the girl have a half-brother or a half-sister?'

'No one knew.' That was her answer.

'And then what happened?'

Again, she entered the household of yet another wealthy man. This time, she entered the household as a servant but was, in less than a year, 'promoted' to the rank of a mistress and eventually as a wife. By the time she found Askar, the woman had been divorced. She had two miscarriages and was discovered to be carrying, in secret, a dead child in her.

'A dead child in her, carrying a dead child in her living body?'

'That's right.'

'And then? Or rather, but why carry a dead child?'

'Then the living miracle in the form of Askar took the place of the dead child inside of her,' she said, holding you closer to herself, you, who were, at that very instant, dreaming of a horse dropping its rider. But you weren't alert enough to note a discrepancy in this and Misra's true story. For she had her own child who died at the age of eighteen months. Nor did you ever ask her why she told you this fictitious version. Or is your own memory untrustworthy?

Nuruddin Farah (Somalia)
Excerpt from *Maps*

To the Eminent Scholar and Meddler

You showed your dirty face first in Detroit
slandered me, in your ugly missionary voice.
If the season were right
I would have broken your bones across my knees.
I heard you have taken to playing an accordion
in the Washington night scaring foreign diplomats
with your horror show.

You joined the revolutionaries of Azania
only to betray them for multi-coloured blankets
and a battered copy of the *Pilgrim's Progress*.
You were caught eating hog in a synagogue in Rome,
uttering profanities during a rain dance in Navajo country,
screaming the sacred name of the Buddha across the Punjabi plain
taking a shit in a shinto shrine in Kyoto.
What manner of man are you?
a despoiler of natives, traducer of tribes and clans,
abuser of ancient homesteads?
Remember the night you were drunk in a tavern in Algiers
and I had to bail you out with my last dollar
and you turned around and insulted my mother,
You know your morality is a cheap alibi
for your lack of scholarship, and apology for your bad verse.
When we meet at the court of Prempeh, I will recount
all the historical oaths you broke,
and push the lie down your black throat.

Kofi Awoonor (Ghana)

Dissonant Voices

in the dark night
in the midst of a great darkness,
I heard the voice of the people,
dissonant voices,
saying:

'Someday, beside the barren hills,
you will stand as a signal
on a mound of dust,
and passing dogs will open their mouths
and howl at you, tails erect.
Do you not remember how
with a breath, you blew away the rain
for an age?

Or how with your fingers
   you stripped off the sky,
so that the sun's fire consumed us,
and our goats
   on the green, rock-studded hills,
and our cattle
   grazing beside the lisping brooks,
and our well-kept farms, from which
our grandfathers fed our fathers,
and from which our fathers
   gave us to eat?
And in that day we stood ashamed
before the faces of our weakening,
   goggle-eyed children:
because we could not give them
   food to eat.
Do you not remember, how every
    marriage
in this land

was an increase of your harem,
and every rich harvest
was only to swell your bursting barns?
You remember all these.
We, also, remember them:
   with clenched teeth
and burning fires in our hearts,
   we remember them.
Someday, beside the barren hills
you will stand as a signal
   on a mound of dust
and passing dogs will open
   their frothy mouths
and howl at you, tails erect.'

We shall sing anthems to thunder
when our throats are dry

when we are beheaded
and our heads have rolled
   on the bloody fields
we shall sing anthems to thunder
to pay first homage
   to the God-sent devil
our new king.

we still must question, secretly,
the face behind the mask

Who is he,
   that danced with us tonight
     at the requiem
  of those that died in mystery?

Who is he,
   we swear: we saw him kill them,
   we saw him drink their blood
     from calabashes
   and he most wept
     before their silent graves?

Who is he,
   shall we follow him to spiritland
   to see his face
     when he removes his mask
   to eat?

We still must question, secretly,
the face behind the mask
We see him on the streets
red-eyed with wind and blood
blowing like the wind

and the people dance with him
in the market-place
   without shame and naked
like mad men

in whispers we accuse him

and we decline to call him
by his name
we only murmur, pointing at him
with frozen fingers
   through our window blinds

Dream!

Why do we dream, in daylight,
with sunlight stark in our eyes,
burning out the fireballs of our
secret,
another Messiah shall come?

Dead men's bones still lie concealed
beneath our cobbled streets;
this year's rich harvest fed
on the flesh of our sons in mass graves

But we still shall sing our anthems
when our throats are dry
and when we are beheaded
in the fields;
and the bones shall also sing with us . . .

we still must question, secretly
the face behind the mask

we still must . . .

                    Ikechukwu Azuonye (Nigeria)

XI — AFFIRMATIONS, LAMENTATIONS, MEDITATIONS

I Thank You God

I thank you god for creating me black,
For making of me
Porter of all sorrows,
Setting on my head
The World.
I wear the Centaur's hide
And I have carried the World since the first morning.

White is a colour for special occasions
Black the colour for every day
And I have carried the World since the first evening.

I am glad
Of the shape of my head
Made to carry the World,
Content
With the shape of my nose
That must snuff every wind of the World
Pleased
With the shape of my legs
Ready to run all the heats of the World.

I thank you God for creating me black
For making of me
Porter of all sorrows.

Thirty-six swords have pierced my heart.
Thirty-six fires have burnt my body.
And my blood on all calvaries has reddened the snow,
And my blood at every dawn has reddened all nature.

Still I am
Glad to carry the World,
Glad of my short arms
   of my long arms
      of the thickness of my lips.

I thank you God for creating me black.
White is a colour for special occasions
Black the colour for every day
And I have carried the World since the dawn of time.
And my laugh over the World, through the night, creates the
   Day.

I thank you God for creating me black.

Bernard Dadié (Côte d'Ivoire)
Translated from the French by John Reed and Clive Wake

The Graceful Giraffe Cannot Become a Monkey

My husband tells me
I have no ideas
Of modern beauty.
He says
I have stuck
To old-fashioned hair-styles.

He says
I am stupid and very backward,
That my hair-style
Makes him sick
Because I am dirty.

It is true
I cannot do my hair
As white women do.

Listen,
My father comes from Payira,
My mother is a woman of Koc!
I am a true Acoli
I am not a half-caste
I am not a slave girl;
My father was not brought home
By the spear
My mother was not exchanged
For a basket of millet.

Ask me what beauty is
To the Acoli
And I will tell you;
I will show it to you
If you give me a chance!

You once saw me,
You saw my hair-style
And you admired it,
And the boys loved it.
At the arena
Boys surrounded me
And fought for me.

My mother taught me
Acoli hair fashions;
Which fits the kind
Of hair of the Acoli,
And the occasion.

Listen,
Ostrich plumes differ

From chicken feathers,
A monkey's tail
Is different from that of the giraffe,
The crocodile's skin
Is not like the guinea-fowl's,
And the hippo is naked, and hairless.

The hair of the Acoli
Is different from that of the Arabs;
The Indians' hair
Resembles the tail of the horse;
It is like sisal strings
And needs to be cut
With scissors.
It is black,
And is different from that of white women.

A white woman's hair
Is soft like silk;
It is light
And brownish like
That of the brown monkey,
And is very different from mine.
A black woman's hair
Is thick and curly;
It is true
Ringworm sometimes eats up
A little girl's hair
And this is terrible;
But when hot porridge
Is put on the head
And the dance is held
Under the sausage-fruit tree
And the youths have sung

> *You, Ringworm,*
> *Who is eating Duka's hair*
> *Here is your porridge,*

Then the girl's hair
Begins to grow again
And the girl is pleased.

*

No one, except wizards
And women who poison others
Leaves her hair untrimmed!
And the men
Do not leave their chins
To grow bushy
Like the lion's neck,
Like the chin
Of a billy-goat,
So that they look
Like wild beasts.

They put hot ash
On the hair
Below the belly-button
And pluck it up,
And they pluck the hair on their face
And the hair of the armpits.

When death has occurred
Women leave their hair uncombed!
They remove all beads
And necklaces,
Because they are mourning
Because of sorrows.
The woman who adorns herself
When others are wailing
Is the killer!
She comes to the funeral
To congratulate herself.

When you go to dance
You adorn yourself for the dance,
If your string-skirt
Is ochre-red
You do your hair
With ochre,
And you smear your body
With red oil
And you are beautifully red all over!
If you put on a black string-skirt
You do your hair with *akuku*
Your body shines with simsim oil
And the tattoos on your chest
And on your back
Glitter in the evening sun.
And the healthy sweat
On your bosom
Is like the glassy fruits of *ocuga*.

Young girls
Whose breasts are just emerging
Smear *shea* butter on their bodies,
The beautiful oil from Labwor-omor.

The aroma is wonderful
And their white teeth sparkle
As they sing
And dance fast
Among the dancers
Like small fish
In a shallow stream.

Butter from cows' milk
Or the fat from edible rats
Is cooked together with *lakura*
Or *atika*;
You smear it on your body today

And the aroma
Lasts until the next day.

And when you balance on your head
A beautiful water-pot
Or a new basket
Or a long-necked jar
Full of honey,
Your long neck
Resembles the *alwiri* spear.

And as you walk along the pathway
On both sides
The *obiya* grasses are flowering
And the *pollok* blossoms
And the wild white lilies
Are shouting silently
To the bees and butterflies!

And as the fragrance
Of the ripe wild berries
Hooks the insects and little birds,
As the fishermen hook the fish
And pull them up mercilessly,

The young men
From the surrounding villages,
And from across many streams,
They come from beyond the hills
And the wide plains,
They surround you
And bite off their ears
Like jackals.

And when you go
To the well
Or into the freshly burnt woodlands

To collect the red *oceyu*,
Or to cut *oduggu* shrubs,
You find them
Lurking in the shades
Like the leopardess with cubs.

*

Ocol tells me
That I like dirt.
He says
Shea butter causes
Skin diseases.

He says, Acoli adornments
Are old-fashioned and unhealthy.
He says I soil his white shirt
If I touch him,
My husband treats me
As if I am suffering from
The 'Don't touch me' disease!

He says that I make his bed-sheets dirty
And his bed smelly.
Ocol says
I look extremely ugly
When I am fully adorned
For the dance!

When I walk past my husband
He hisses like a wounded *ororo* snake
Choking with vengeance.
He has vowed
That he will never touch
My hands again.

My husband
Is in love with Tina

The woman with the large head;
Ocol dies for Clementine
Ocol never sleeps.
For the beautiful one
Who has read!

When the beautiful one
With whom I share my husband
Returns from cooking her hair
She resembles
A chicken
That has fallen into a pond;
Her hair looks
Like the python's discarded skin.

They cook their hair
With hot iron
And pull it hard
So that it may grow long.
Then they rope the hair
On wooden pens
Like a billy-goat
Brought for the sacrifice
Struggling to free itself.

They fry their hair
In boiling oil
As if it were locusts,
And the hair sizzles
It cries aloud in sharp pain
As it is pulled and stretched.
And the vigorous and healthy hair
Curly, springy and thick
That glistens in the sunshine
Is left listless and dead
Like the elephant grass
Scorched brown by the fierce

February sun.
It lies lifeless
Like the sad and dying banana leaves
On a hot and windless afternoon.

The beautiful woman
With whom I share my husband
Smears black shoe-polish
On her hair
To blacken it
And to make it shine,
She washes her hair
With black ink;

But the thick undergrowth
Rejects the shoe-polish
And the ink
And it remains untouched
Yellowish, greyish
Like the hair of the grey monkey.

There is much water
In my husband's house
Cold water and hot water.
You twist a cross-like handle
And water gushes out
Hot and steaming
Like the urine
Of the elephant.

You twist another cross-like handle;
It is cold water,
Clean like the cooling fresh waters
From the streams
Of Lututuru hills.

But the woman
With whom I share my husband
Does not wash her head;
The head of the beautiful one
Smells like rats
That have fallen into the fireplace.

And she uses
Powerful perfumes
To overcome the strange smells,
As they treat a pregnant coffin!
And the different smells
Wrestle with one another
And the smell of the shoe-polish
Mingles with them.
Clementine has many headkerchiefs,
Beautiful headkerchiefs of many colours.
She ties one on her head
And it covers up
The rot inside;

She ties the knot
On her forehead
And arranges the edges
With much care
So that it covers
Her ears
As well as the bold forehead
That jumps sparks
When lightning has splashed,
And hurls back sunlight
More powerfully than a mirror!

Sometimes she wears
The hair of some dead woman
Of some white woman
Who died long ago

And she goes with it
To the dance!
What witchcraft!

Shamelessly, she dances
Holding the shoulder of my husband,
The hair of a dead woman
On her head,
The body of the dead woman
Decaying in the tomb!

One night
The ghost of the dead woman
Pulled away her hair
From the head of the wizards
And the beautiful one
Fell down
And shook with shame
She shook
As if the angry ghost
Of the white woman
Had entered her head.

*

Ocol, my friend
Look at my skin
It is smooth and black.
And my boy friend
Who plays the *nanga*
Sings praises to it.

I am proud of the hair
With which I was born
And as no white woman
Wishes to do her hair
Like mine,
Because she is proud

Of the hair with which she was born,
I have no wish
To look like a white woman.

No leopard
Would change into a hyena,
And the crested crane
Would hate to be changed
Into the bold-headed,
Dung-eating vulture,
The long-necked and graceful giraffe
Cannot become a monkey.

Let no one
Uproot the Pumpkin.

Okot p'Bitek (Uganda)
Excerpt from *Song of Lawino*

If You Want to Know Me

If you want to know me
examine with careful eyes
this bit of black wood
which some unknown Makonde brother
cut and carved
with his inspired hands
in the distant lands of the north.

This is what I am
empty sockets despairing of possessing life
a mouth torn open in an anguished wound
huge hands outspread
and raised in imprecation and in threat
a body tattooed with wounds seen and unseen
from the harsh whipstrokes of slavery
tortured and magnificent

proud and mysterious
Africa from head to foot
This is what I am.

If you want to understand me
come, bend over this soul of Africa
in the black dock-worker's groans
the Chope's frenzied dances
the Changanas' rebellion
in the strange sadness which flows
from an African song, through the night.

And ask no more
to know me
for I'm nothing but a shell of flesh
where Africa's revolt congealed
its cry pregnant with hope.

Noémia de Sousa (Mozambique)
Translated from the Portuguese by Margaret Dickinson

Black Woman

Naked woman, black woman
Clothed with your colour which is life, with your form which is beauty!
In your shadow I have grown up; the gentleness of your hands was
    laid over my eyes.
And now, high up on the sun-baked pass, at the heart of summer, at
    the heart of noon, I come upon you, my Promised Land,
And your beauty strikes me to the heart like the flash of an eagle.

Naked woman, dark woman
Firm-fleshed ripe fruit, sombre raptures of black wine, mouth making
    lyrical my mouth
Savannah stretching to clear horizons, savannah shuddering beneath
    the East Wind's eager caresses

Carved tom-tom, taut tom-tom, muttering under the Conqueror's
   fingers
Your solemn contralto voice is the spiritual song of the Beloved.

Naked woman, dark woman
Oil that no breath ruffles, calm oil on the athlete's flanks, on the flanks
   of the Princes of Mali
Gazelle-limbed in Paradise, pearls are stars on the night of your skin
Delights of the mind, the glinting of red gold against your watered
   skin
Under the shadow of your hair, my care is lightened by the neighbouring
   suns of your eyes.

Naked woman, black woman
I sing your beauty that passes, the form that I fix in the Eternal,
Before jealous Fate turn you to ashes to feed the roots of life.

Léopold Sédar Senghor (Senegal)
Translated from the French by John Reed and Clive Wake

Western Civilization

Sheets of tin nailed to posts
driven in the ground
make up the house.

Some rags complete
the intimate landscape.

The sun slanting through cracks
welcomes the owner

After twelve hours of slave
labour.

breaking rock
shifting rock
breaking rock

shifting rock
fair weather
wet weather
breaking rock
shifting rock

Old age comes early

a mat on dark nights
is enough when he dies
gratefully
of hunger.

Agostinho Neto (Angola)
Translated from the Portuguese by Margaret Dickinson

Protest against Conscription for Forced Labour*

My penis wants to get erect,
When I find the sub-chief's mother,
I will fuck her all night long;
Ee, my penis wants to get erect,
When I find the chief's mother
I will fuck her in the middle of the road;
Ee, my penis wants to get erect,
I am mounting the bicycle,
I am hurrying to Gulu;
Ee, my penis wants to get erect,
When I find the District Commissioner's mother,
I will fuck her in the football arena at Pece;
Ee, my penis wants to get erect,
I will sit on the back of a kite,
We shall fly all night;
Ee, my penis wants to get erect,
When I find the king's mother,
Man, I will fuck her on top of a hill.

Omal Lakana, alias Adok Too (Uganda)
Translated from the Acholi by Okot p'Bitek

Telephone Conversation

The price seemed reasonable, location
Indifferent. The landlady swore she lived
Off premises. Nothing remained
But self-confession. 'Madam,' I warned,
'I hate a wasted journey – I am African.'
Silence. Silenced transmission of
Pressurized good-breeding. Voice, when it came,
Lipstick-coated, long gold-rolled
Cigarette-holder pipped. Caught I was, foully.

'HOW DARK?' . . . I had not misheard . . . 'ARE YOU LIGHT
'OR VERY DARK?' Button B. Button A. Stench
Of rancid breath of public hide-and-speak.
Red booth. Red pillar-box. Red double-tiered
Omnibus squelching tar. It *was* real! Shamed
By ill-mannered silence, surrender
Pushed dumbfoundment to beg simplification.
Considerate she was, varying the emphasis –

'ARE YOU DARK? OR VERY LIGHT?' Revelation came.
'You mean – like plain or milk chocolate?'
Her assent was clinical, crushing in its light
Impersonality. Rapidly, wavelength adjusted,
I chose, 'West African sepia' – and as an afterthought,
'Down in my passport.' Silence for spectroscopic
Flight of fancy, till truthfulness clanged her accent
Hard on the mouthpiece 'WHAT'S THAT?', conceding,
'DON'T KNOW WHAT THAT IS.' 'Like brunette.'

'THAT'S DARK, ISN'T IT?' 'Not altogether.'
'Facially, I am brunette, but madam, you should see
'The rest of me. Palm of my hand, soles of my feet
'Are a peroxide blonde. Friction, caused –
'Foolishly, madam – by sitting down, has turned
'My bottom raven black – One moment madam!' – sensing

Her receiver rearing on the thunder-clap
About my ears – 'Madam,' I pleaded, 'wouldn't you rather
'See for yourself?'

                                        Wole Soyinka (Nigeria)

Grandpa

They say they are healthier than me
Though they can't walk to the end of a mile;
At their age I walked forty at night
To wage a battle at dawn.

They think they are healthier than me:
If their socks get wet they catch a cold;
When my sockless feet got wet, I never sneezed –
But they still think they are healthier than me.

On a soft mattress over a spring bed,
They still have to take a sleeping-pill:
But I, with reeds cutting into my ribs,
My head resting on a piece of wood,
I sleep like a babe and snore.

They blow their noses and pocket the stuff –
That's hygienic so they tell me:
I blow my nose into the fire,
But they say that is barbaric.

If a dear one dies I weep without shame;
If someone jokes I laugh with all my heart.
They stifle a tear as if to cry was something wrong,
But they also stifle a laugh,
As if to laugh was something wrong, too.
No wonder they need psychiatrists!

They think they have more power of will than me.
Our women were scarcely covered in days of yore,
But adultery was a thing unknown:
Today they go wild on seeing a slip on a hanger!

When I have more than one wife
They tell me that hell is my destination,
But when they have one and countless mistresses,
They pride themselves on cheating the world!

No, let them learn to be honest with themselves first
Before they persuade me to change my ways,
Says my grandfather, the proud old man.

                    Paul Chidyausiku (Zimbabwe)

A Poem on Black and White

if i pour petrol on a white child's face
and give flames the taste of his flesh
it won't be a new thing
i wonder how i will feel when his eyes pop
and when my nostrils sip the smell of his flesh
and his scream touches my heart
i wonder if i will be able to sleep;
i understand alas i do understand
the rage of a whiteman pouring petrol on a black child's face
setting it alight and shooting him in a pretoria street,
pretoria has never been my home
i have crawled its streets with pain
i have ripped my scrotal sack at every door i intended entering
    in that city
and jo'burg city has never seen me, has never heard me
the pain of my heart has been the issue of my heart
sung by me
freezing in the air

but who has not been witness to my smile?
yet, alexandra's night shadow is soaked and drips with my tears.

Mongane Wally Serote (Azania)

The typical blackman

The typical blackman
forgiving and forgetful

If
a thief
rapes your mother, wife and daughter,
beats you up mercilessly
and escapes with all your property.

Then
years later
the law still having failed to catch up with him
you spot him at a party.
What do you do?
Forgive and forget?
Then you are a typical blackman,
and that is why we have progressed from
colonialism to neo-colonialism.

Naiwu Osahon (Nigeria)

Parables on the African Condition

1:The Missionary and the Elders (A Parable of Resistance)

When the missionary came to the forest city and was brought before
the elders he spoke earnestly to them about his god, how it was the one
true and all-powerful god, how it was only proper that all men should
worship him.

'You mean we should desert our ancestral gods and worship yours?' the amazed elders asked.

'Thus saith the Lord,' the missionary proclaimed: 'Abandon all false gods, worship me and be saved!'

'Tell us more about this strange, exclusive god you speak of.' And the missionary talked on and on till the elders interrupted him:

'Let us rest now and let us eat. We need new strength to hear all the magic of your god.'

But the missionary answered them:

'I will not sup with savages who make offerings to false gods,' and he brought out his canned food.

The elders turned to him and said:

'You have come over the broad seas to win our spirits to your god? Why won't you eat with us?'

But the missionary still would not eat, pleading the strangeness of the stew.

'Are we swine?' the elders asked. 'If you will not share with us that which sustains our life, which gives us strength, why should we take any interest in your god?'

Whereupon the missionary joined them, washed his hands and ate with them. And the elders ate, sitting on their mats of leopard-skin, drinking, talking, laughing, smacking their lips, licking their fingers, till their fingers gleamed, their lips shone with fat and the bottoms of their bowls held only bits of cracked bones. When the meal was over an old man turned to the missionary, smiled and said:

'What we have just eaten was your predecessor. He insulted our gods, our hunger and our ways.'

2: *Lambkin, Lion and Bear (A Cold War Parable)*

The head of the African lambkin was sticking out from the Western lion's mouth. The rest of him – hooves, tail, neck – was inside the lion's guts, soaking in the cosy warmth of the lion's digestive juices. Suddenly, the shadow of the Russian bear sauntered past at the far horizon; whereupon the lion's stomach churned and growled in anger. The lambkin grew afraid. With tear-filled eyes the lambkin cried: 'Lion, Lord Lion, protect me! That nasty bear, his hungry eyes are looking all over for me!' And the lion answered the lambkin and said: 'My poor, sweet thing! Duck your head into my mouth and you'll be completely safe.' And the lambkin, believe it or not, did what he was told.

3: The Wind and the Dog (A Parable of Underdevelopment)

There was once a dog who envied the wind his grace, his freedom and his speed. He tried to emulate the wind, but without luck. One day the wind came to the dog and said: 'Come, doggie! Race with me, and I'll teach you to run as fast and as gracefully as I.' And the foolish dog raced after the wind, panting, sweating, his red tongue hanging dry, till he dropped dead, his lungs burnt out. And the cunning wind laughed, and turned around, and whisked the corpse off to his dinner.

4: The Been-tos and the First-tos (A Parable of Disorientation)

At that gathering of African been-tos, when at last they had dropped the name of every place they had been to, each for the thirty-seventh time, they got bored with that, and plunged into their other favourite game.

One boasted that he was the first African to make a first in Classical Macedonian. Another boasted that he was the first person of African descent to earn a D.Sc. from Oxford in the special mini-field of Necropolitan Bird Warbles. Another boasted that he was the first African, of height exactly four feet seven and three-sevenths inches, and of weight 351 pounds, to be admitted to the Innermost Temple. Another boasted that he was the first African ever to read Sanskrit diagonally while standing on his own head. Another boasted that he was the first African ever to flunk out altogether from the great University of Leeds kindergarten at exactly age twenty-seven. Another boasted that he was the first African from his mother's almost royal womb to win the Pumpernickel Scholarship to the Antarctica College of Fishbait.

As the competition grew more desperate, their boasts became works of pure inspiration. One boasted that he was the first African from his two-hut hamlet in the dense equatorial forest to see snow. Another that he was the first African ever to kiss both ears of a pregnant Lapland reindeer. Another that he was the first African ever to chew gum and hum a Madison Avenue jingle and carry his pith helmet in his armpit and snore while sleep-walking in safari shorts across Lenin Square in a Moscow blizzard. Another swore that he was the first African ever to look out of the easternmost salient of the Fortress Tower of the Assassini. Yet another boasted that he was the first African ever to be buggered by a turbaned Arab in the market at Baghdad, right after the noonday prayer, on a perfumed rug embroidered in Samarkand gold. And another boasted that he was the first African to fornicate with a white sperm whale, not inside some aquarium, but out in the open seas, and he dared anyone to top that.

That was when he spoke up, the inordinately arrogant one whom everyone assumed was an albino. He said, with pride dripping from his voice and coating every syllable, that he was the first African ever to be reborn in the image of God. He had knelt down one night and prayed: 'O Lord, I have tried everything to remake myself in your image, but my black face won't scrub clean. Tell me, Lord, what should I do?' And the Lord, he said, had said: 'Have you tried scalding steam?' Whereupon, with great joy in his heart, he jumped into a boiling cauldron, and behold, came up white! It took a year, he said, to recover from his severe burns, five more of the most advanced plastic surgery to nurse his skin to its even texture. But God was with him, and saw him through it all, and it certainly was worth while, he said. He looked like an angel now, he said, white and clean! Whenever he put on his turban, he said, or conked his hair and wore a suit and tie, he could pass for an Arab or European, even in broad daylight.

Chinweizu (Nigeria)

The Transformation

Europeans with their civilization;
Africans confirmed in lechery,
lacking civilization.
Then came Freud and said
    'Fellow Europeans, copulation
    might not be that bad after all.'

And now they talk of their new morality
and of the positive assertion of drives

but give no credit to the savages.
Have we not invented lechery?

Europe indeed is changing
America following fast behind –

When all of us shall become confirmed lechers,
the black and white together,
one riffraff of passion.

Ifeanyi Menkiti (Nigeria)

The Impotent Observer

Don't just sit there
gaping at me
like an impotent observer
because life
is a
serious matter,
suffering is real,
and the man writhing
in pain
is
not
dancing for amusement.

Naiwu Osahon (Nigeria)

Song of Those Who Have Passed Their Prime

The body perishes, the heart stays young.
The platter wears away with serving food.
No log retains its bark when old,
No lover peaceful while the rival weeps.

Zulu (Azania)

King Tekla Haimanot Learns that His Daughter Mentuab Has Been Captured by the Enemy

Is he not there? Is he not there? Is Belau† not there?
Had Belau been there, he would never have let his sister go.
'My ox has died,' the peasant complains to me,
'My mule has died,' the soldier complains to me.
What afflicts me is Mentuab's fate.
Woe, woe, and woe! is no man spared?

Amhara (Ethiopia)

This World

> Sons of men
> frowning
> like their mouth is full of quinine
> daughters of women
> smiling
> like they won sweepstakes

Willy Nnorom (Nigeria)

Is the Chief Greater than the Hunter?*

Is the chief greater than the hunter?
   Arrogance! Hunter? Arrogance!
The pair of beautiful things on your feet,
The sandals that you wear,
How did it all happen?
It is the hunter that killed the duyker:
The sandals are made of the hide of the duyker.

Does the chief say he is greater than the hunter?
   Arrogance! Hunter? Arrogance!

†Princess Mentuab's brother and general of the army.

The noisy train that leads you away,
The drums that precede you,
The hunter killed the elephant,
The drum-head is the ear of the elephant.
Does the chief say he is greater than the hunter?
   Arrogance! Hunter? Arrogance!

Akan (Ghana)

New Yam

Cassava and maize are only the poor relations of yam.
Yam is a warrior who brings strife wherever he goes:
the children quarrel for the biggest portion
the landlord complains it was not pounded smooth like
   yesterday.
To plant yam is costly – but it amply repays its own debt.
You put the yam to bed in the ground
it will bring you money
that will plant you on top of a beautiful woman.

Yoruba (Nigeria)

Three Exist Where Three Are Not*

Three exist where three are not:

   Commoner exists where there is no king,
      but a kingdom cannot exist where there are no commoners;
   Grass exists where there is nothing that eats grass,
      but what eats grass cannot exist where no grass is;
   Water exists where there is nothing that drinks water,
      but what drinks water cannot exist where no water is.

Fulani (Nigeria)

Desperation

May the days kill me, that I perish!
May the years kill me, that I perish!
I call out 'Woe!'
I call the days!
Years – I do not believe that I shall live them.
Days – I do not believe that I shall live them.
Any measure of time – I do not believe that I shall live it.

Bergdama (Namibia)

Songs of Sorrow

Dzogbese Lisa has treated me thus
It has led me among the sharps of the forest
Returning is not possible
And going forward is a great difficulty
The affairs of this world are like the chameleon faeces
Into which I have stepped

I am on the world's extreme corner,
I am not sitting in the row with the eminent
But those who are lucky
Sit in the middle and forget.
I am on the world's extreme corner
I can only go beyond and forget.

My people, I have been somewhere
If I turn here, the rain beats me
If I turn there, the sun burns me
The firewood of this world
Is for only those who can take heart
That is why not all can gather it.
The world is not good for anybody
But you are so happy with your fate;
Alas! the travellers are back
All covered with debt.

Something has happened to me
The things so great that I cannot weep;
I have no sons to fire the gun when I die
And no daughters to wail when I close my mouth
I have wandered on the wilderness
The great wilderness men call life
The rain has beaten me,
And the sharp stumps cut as keen as knives
I shall go beyond and rest.
I have no kin and no brother,
Death has made war upon our house;

And Kpeti's great household is no more,
Only the broken fence stands;
And those who dared not look in his face
Have come out as men.
How well their pride is with them.
Let those gone before take note
They have treated their offspring badly.
What is the wailing for?
Somebody is dead. Agosu himself
Alas! a snake has bitten me
My right arm is broken,
And the tree on which I lean is fallen.

Agosi if you go tell them,
Tell Nyidevu, Kpeti, and Kove
That they have done us evil;
Tell them their house is falling
And the trees in the fence
Have been eaten by termites;
That the martels curse them.
Ask them why they idle there
While we suffer, and eat sand.
And the crow and the vulture
Hover always above our broken fences
And strangers walk over our portion.
                    Kofi Awoonor (Ghana)

Song of a Madman

However fast the yam runs the goat will eat him,
However fast the goat runs the tiger will eat him,
However fast the tiger runs the man will eat him,
However fast the man runs the earth will eat him,
However fast the earth runs something will eat him,
However fast something runs *something bigger* will eat him,
So, that's how it is, *something bigger* will eat him.

Emmanuel Obiechina (Nigeria)

We were Once Poor but Wealthy

If the rain catches you in Ikate
If the rain catches you in Aguda
I say
If the rain catches you in Lagos
Roll up your trousers
Get ready to swim.

We were once poor but wealthy
We are now rich but poor

If thirst catches you in Uwani
If thirst catches you in Ogui
I say
If thirst catches you in Enugu
There are many gutters for free
Police will not arrest you.

We were once poor but rich
We are now rich but poor

If hunger arrests you in G.R.A.
If hunger arrests you in Ugwu ndi Ocha
I say
If hunger grips you in Unibasity

Dustbins overflow like the Niger
And Sanitary will not arrest you.

We were once poor but wealthy
We are now rich but poor

They offered me crumbs
Thinking I would sing their praises
If they shut their doors on me
I say
If they shut their doors on me
Have they also shut my eyes?

Better to be mad and free
Than to be rich and blind

They stole the people's money
Lent it back to them
At 1000% interest
And they talk of philanthropy
      and chieftaincy
      and statues
    they speak of tradition
     of age and youth

If you shackle my feet
Have you manacled my ears?
If you pinion my arms
Have you manacled my tongue?

We were once poor but happy
We are now rich but hungry

Stealing gave them the eagle feather
Robbery gave them the ankle-string
Killing gave them the bronze staff
Tax-eating gave them their carved stools.

We were once naked but alive
We are now clothed but corpses

             Obiora Udechukwu (Nigeria)

Pray

Pray
if you believe in prayer
for those shipwrecked by love

else pity them:
the sunburst of your compassion
may heal their broken stems
may restore their crushed tendrils

they live in a drought-shattered continent
where the children are skeletal ghosts,
their music the hoarse death-low
of emaciated expiring beasts;
they cannot shutter their ears to the guttural rattles

those who should free them live in suave hotels
where chrome waiters glisten and glide
where magic is a signature on an authorized cheque
where rich food is discarded garbage
insulting the nostrils of famished children
where hope is a dead rat among the putrefying viands

in the cerecloth of devious stratagems
the healers are paralysed
in the formaldehyde of their wise inertia
our viscera grow noisome and decompose—
our tears are maggots battening on our corneas
acid rains hiss as they corrode our membranes

Forgive us our anorexia, our anomy, our accidie
forgive us our arid eyes, our unresonating ears
our vanished mouths:
forgive us and pity us
permit us our oblivion of grief
and the dry abrupt lusts
that spasm us

we have soared among cloudpeaks
and splintered our hearts on their marble whiteness
we were sodden in the drizzling harmattan of tears
now we sear, sere, in the sirocco of lost hopes

we have known the rocks and the shoals
the diapason breakers and talismanic spray
we have stood transfigured and effulgent
we have known the jagged edges and the taloned reefs

Pray,
if you believe in prayer,
for those shipwrecked by love;
or pity us:
for still it will not rain.

Dennis Brutus (Azania)

Caravaners' Song

In summer they even make the dust rise;
In winter they even trample the mud!
If they talk with the dark maiden,
And smile upon the red maidens,
Poverty will never leave them.
Poverty is a terrible disease;
It penetrates the sides,
It bends the vertebrae,
It dresses one in rags,
It makes people stupid;
It makes every desire remain in the breast;
Those who are long, it shortens;
Those who are short it destroys wholly.
Not even the mother that has borne the poor man loves him any
    longer!
Not even the father who has begotten him any longer esteems him!

Galla (Ethiopia)

What Makes You Proud?*

What makes you proud, cloth? you cover lepers.
What makes you proud, pearl? whores wear you.
What makes you proud, fortress? the lame climb on you.
What makes you proud, fountain? camels drink of you.

Berber (Morocco)

Blood

Blood
internal canals
ferrying food
underground red train
sometimes sabotaged
carrying viruses, disease.

Pitika Ntuli (Azania)

Differences*

'Women are for sleeping with, for giving birth to and bringing up children; they are not good for any other thing,' said Keynaan. 'They are not to be trusted with secrets. They can serve the purposes Allah created them for originally, and no more. It pains me to see you work hard and fail. Again and again.'
  'I don't agree.'
  'You never married. You don't know them.'
  'I still don't agree.'
  And the two walked side by side, they walked silently with their shoulders nearly touching. They were almost of the same height. But could they ever be of the same opinion? Could they share an idea, like two near-strangers might share a plate of anything, with hands coming into contact with one another every now and again, as their jaws munched, each with a morsel of something picked from the same source,

the same plate and hence the same idea, could they? Or did it depend on what use each made of the lungfuls of oxygen inhaled, as they walked side by side, hardly talking, hardly noticing what was going on outside their own heads. Could Keynaan and Loyaan see anything eye to eye? Would they forget their differences? Would they exchange their shoes, would each be ready to place his feet in the other's and walk in them? Would their feet feel comfortable? Would the shoes pinch, would a heel come off, some nails as well? When once addressing himself to these differences, Soyaan said: 'Not so much generational as they are qualitative – the differences between us twins and our father. My father grew up with the idea that the universe is flat; we, that it is round. We believe we have a perspective of an inclusive nature – more global; our views are "rounder". We believe that his are exclusive, that they are flat (and therefore uninteresting) as the universe his insularity ties him to.' That was Soyaan to Loyaan. *But now, Loyaan, now: talk to the same theme, pray. Say something.* 'My father sees himself as a miniature creature in a flat world dominated by a God-figure high and huge as any mountain anyone has seen. A miniature of a man before this huge mountain, and helpless too. When you confront him with a question of universal character, his answer is tailor-made, he will say: "Only Allah knows, only Allah." A miniature creature dependent upon his Creator to answer questions. Suddenly, however, he behaves as if he were the most powerful of men, the biggest. Suddenly, he is, as Soyaan called him, the Grand Patriarch. This happens when he is in front of his children and his wives.'

'What did you do to make the women so upset, Loyaan?'

'What do you think?'

'Did you refuse to eat the food your mother prepared?'

'You are being very mean, Father.'

'I could never upset them as much as you have. What did you do?'

'We disagreed. We saw that we viewed things differently.'

'You discuss your ideas with women? You disappoint me.'

Regardless of what went into their making, could the two share anything? Keynaan was nearly sixty, Loyaan not quite thirty . . .

'Women are like one's shadow, Somalis have a proverb,' quoted Keynaan. 'They follow at the heels of those who run away from them. They bully and boss and lead those who follow them.'

'We disagree, you and I.'

'You have no opinion on women.'

'Oh, yes. I do. That is why I disagree with you. If I had none, I would shut up and accept yours or your generation's as gospel wisdom.'

'You don't know them. You don't know your mother, for example.'

Of course, he did. A shower of abuse from Keynaan, and cheeks wet with tears, poor Qumman. Whenever some superior officer humiliated him, he came and was aggressive to the twins and his wife. He would flog them, he would beat them – big, and powerful that he was, the Grand Patriarch whose authority drenched his powerless victims with the blood of his lashes. She would wait until the twins grew up, she confided to a neighbour. She would wait. Patience, patience. A third pregnancy which resulted in Ladan. And a near-fatal fourth. There were no pills a woman could take those days. Society, on top of it, required women to be tolerant, to be receptive, to be receiving – and forgiving. 'Does one notice the small insects which die a suffering death under the eyeless heels of one's feet? Keynaan and his generation have never known women. Women are simply a generally generalized-about human species more mysterious than Martians,' Soyaan would argue.

Keynaan slowed down. Loyaan came level with him.

'Shall we rest awhile and have tea?'

Loyaan saw a terraced tea-shop with chairs arranged outside.

'Why not?'

Nuruddin Farah (Somalia)
Excerpt from *Sweet and Sour Milk*

For a Prostitute

A little pool without water!
Yet men drown in it.

Hausa (Niger)

O You Whose Eyes are Painted*

O you whose eyes are painted, O girls,
You and the rifle – what you command is done.

Berber (Morocco)

A Baby is a European

A baby is a European
he does not eat our food:
he drinks from his own water-pot.

A baby is a European
he does not speak our tongue:
he is cross when the mother understands him not.

A baby is a European
he cares very little for others:
he forces his will upon his parents.

A baby is a European
he is always very sensitive:
the slightest scratch on his skin results in an ulcer.

Ewe (Togo)

Hunger

Hunger makes a person lie down–
he has water in his knees.
Hunger makes a person lie down
and count the rafters in his roof.
When the Muslim is not hungry he says:
we are forbidden to eat monkey.
When he is hungry he eats a baboon.
Hunger will drive the Muslim woman from the harem

out into the street,
Hunger will persuade the priest
to steal from his own shrine.
'I have eaten yesterday'
does not concern hunger.
There is no god like one's stomach:
we must sacrifice to it every day.

Yoruba (Nigeria)

Streamside Exchange

Child: River bird, river bird,
Sitting all day long
On hook over grass,
River bird, river bird,
Sing to me a song
Of all that pass
And say,
Will mother come back today?

Bird: You cannot know
And should not bother;
Tide and market come and go
And so has your mother.

J.P. Clark (Nigeria)

On Truth

One thread of truth in a shuttle
Will weave a hundred threads of lies.
Vomiting one's liver cures the most severe biliousness;
The hatching of an egg is unpleasant for the shell:
Do not match yourself against Providence.
God is all-powerful:

He prevents the eye from seeing the eyelashes.
Eggs become lice:
The small man becomes the great man.
Stick to the truth:
Truth is like the light of dawn,
Untruthfulness is like darkness at sunset.

Kanuri (Nigeria)

Life's Variety

Why do we grumble because a tree is bent,
When, in our streets, there are even men who are bent?
Why must we complain that the new moon is slanting?
Can anyone reach the skies to straighten it?
Can't we see that some cocks have combs on their heads, but no plumes
    in their tails?
And some have plumes in their tails, but no claws on their toes?
And others have claws on their toes, but no power to crow?
He who has a head has no cap to wear, and he who has a cap has no
    head to wear it on.
The Owa has everything but a horse's stable.
Some great scholars of Ifa cannot tell the way to Ofa.
Others know the way to Ofa, but not one line of Ifa.
Great eaters have no food to eat, and great drinkers no wine to drink:
Wealth has a coat of many colours.

Yoruba (Nigeria)

INDEX OF CONTRIBUTORS

417

INDEX OF COUNTRIES

ACKNOWLEDGEMENTS

'The Rain-Man's Praise-song of Himself' and 'Song of a Bridegroom in praise of his Bride' from *The Unwritten Song* edited by Willard Trask: Macmillan Inc.; 'Arrawelo: The Castrator of Men' by Abdi Sheik-Abdi: Okike (no. 12); 'How the Leopard Got His Claws' (with 'The Lament of the Deer' by Christopher Okigbo) by Chinua Achebe and John Iroaganachi: the authors, Nwamife Publishers; 'An End to Sovereignty' and 'The First Coming of Ulu' from *Arrow of God* by Chinua Achebe: the author, David Bolt Associates and Harper & Row Inc.; 'The Madman' from *Girls at War* by Chinua Achebe: the author, David Bolt Associates and Doubleday; 'The Old Man and the Census' by Chinua Achebe from *Rhythms of Creation* edited by D I Nwoga: the author, Fourth Dimension Press; 'If Death Were Not There', 'Lightening Strike My Husband', and 'The Guns of Langalanga' from *Horn of My Love* by Okot p'Bitek: Heinemann Educational Books Ltd; 'Battle Hymn' from *People of the Small Arrow* by J H Driberg: Routledge & Kegan Paul; 'On Being Told that the Girl of his Desire is a Blood Relative' from *Africa's Cultural Revolution* by Okot p'Bitek: Macmillan Books, Nairobi; 'Anowa and Kofi' and 'A Libation Speech' from *Anowa* by Ama Ata Aidoo: the author, Longman; 'Is the Chief Greater than the Hunter?' from *Oral Literature in Africa* edited by Ruth Finnegan: the author, Oxford University Press; 'Mola My Husband' from *Myths and Legends of the Congo* edited by Jan Knappert: Heinemann Kenya Books Ltd; 'King Tekla Haimanot learns that his Daughter Mentuab Has Been Captured by the Enemy' from *The Unwritten Song* edited by Willard Trask: Macmillan Inc.; 'The Song of a Twin Brother' by Kofi Anyidoho from *Rhythms of Creation* edited by D I Nwoga: Fourth Dimension Press; 'Halfway to Nirvana' by Ayi Kwei Armah: the author, West Africa Book Publishers; 'Admonition to a Chief' from *A History of West Africa* by Basil Davidson: Longman; 'Talk' from *African Voices: An Anthology of Native African Writing* edited by Peggy Rutherford: Vanguard Press; 'To the Eminent Scholar and Meddler' by Kofi Awoonor from *Ride Me Memory* by Kofi Awoonor: Greenfield Review Press; 'Songs of Sorrow' by Kofi Awoonor: the author; 'Desire for a Woman' from *Witchcraft, Oracles and Magic among the Azande* by E E Evans-Pritchard: the author, Oxford University Press, 'Bird Riddle' from *Oral Literature in Africa* edited by Ruth Finnegan: the author, Oxford University Press; 'Dissonant Voices' by Ikechukwu Azuonye: African Arts, 1975; 'Ceremonies for the Dead' from *So Long a Letter* by Mariama Ba: the author, Les Nouvelles Editions Africaines; 'Song Composed under a Tyrannical King' from *African Music from the Source of the Nile* by Joseph Kyagambiddwa: the author, Praeger Publishers; 'Bride's Farewell Song' from *Oral Literature in Africa* edited by Ruth Finnegan: the author, Oxford University Press; 'At the Feast of Ancestors' and 'Laws and Restrictions at the Feast of the Dead' from 'Bakongo Incantations and Prayers' by J Van Wing: Journal of the Royal Anthropological Institute vol 60; 'The Apprentice' by Odun Balogun: Okike (no. 14); 'Love Strikes Queen Saran' from *Monson et le Roi de Kore* by Amadou Hampate: Review Présence Africaine, 1966; 'Song After Defeat' from *The Unwritten Song* edited by Willard Trask: Macmillan Inc.; 'Girl's Rejection of a Poor Suitor' from *Oral Literature in Africa* edited by Ruth Finnegan: the author, Oxford University Press; 'Hymn of the Afflicted', 'Song of a Woman Whose Husband Had Gone to the Coast to Earn Money', 'Memorial', 'What Makes you Proud?', 'O You Whose Eyes Are Painted', 'When I Make Love' and 'Desperation' from *The Unwritten Song* edited by Willard Trask: Macmillan Inc.; 'At the Hospital' from *Perpetua and the Habit of Unhappiness* by Mongo Beti: the author, Rosica Colin Ltd; 'Bride's Complaint' from *The Black Mind* by O R Dathorne: University of Minnesota Press; 'Why the Sky is Far Away' from *The Origin of Life and Death* edited by Ulli Beier: the author, Heinemann Educational Books Ltd; 'Pray' by Dennis Brutus from *Rhythms of Creation* edited by D I Nwoga: Fourth Dimension Press; 'Grandpa' by Paul Chidyausiku: the author; 'Originality' from *Energy Crisis* by Chinweizu: the author; 'Colonizer's Logic', 'Admonition to the Black World' and 'Parables on the African Condition' from *Invocations and Admonitions* by Chinweizu: the author, Pero Press; 'Protest Against Councillors' and 'A Diviner's Invocation to his Ancestors' translated by Chinweizu from *Poetic Heritage* edited by D I Nwoga and R Egudu: the translator, Nwamife Publishers; 'The Wives Revolt' by John Pepper Clark: the author; 'Streamside Exchange' from *Poems* by John Pepper Clark: Mbari Publications and Northwestern University Press; 'Peasants' from *The Graveyard Also Has Teeth* by Syl Cheney Coker: the author, Heinemann Educational Books Ltd; 'I Thank You God' by Bernard Dadié from *Poems of Black Africa* edited by Wole Soyinka: Martin Secker & Warburg Ltd; 'A Mother to her First-born' from *The Unwritten Song* edited by Willard Trask: Macmillan Inc.; 'Girls' Song for the Game of "Pots" ' from *People of the Small Arrow* by J H Driberg: the author, Routledge & Kegan Paul; 'Chant' from *The Unwritten Song* edited by Willard Trask: Macmillan Inc.; 'Justice' and 'How a Woman Tamed Her Husband' from *African Voices* edited by Peggy Rutherford: Vanguard Press; 'Konni and Uta' from *Lokotown* by Cyprian Ekwensi: the author, Heinemann Educational Books and David Bolt Associates; 'Dirge' and 'The Beautiful Playground' from *The Unwritten Song* edited by Willard Trask: Macmillan Inc.; 'A Baby is a European' from *African Poetry* edited by Ulli Beier: Cambridge University Press; 'A Shortage of Beggars' from *The Beggar's Strike* by Animato Sow Fall: the author, Les Nouvelles Editions Africaines; 'Song of the Will-o'-the-Wisp' and 'Fire Song at an Expiation Ceremony' from *The Unwritten Song* edited by Willard Trask: Macmillan Inc.; 'Open the Windows of Heaven' from *The Lyric of the Fante* by S G Williamson: African Institute volume XXVIII no. 2; 'Differences', 'Misra and Askar', 'Misra' and 'On the Brink of Manhood' from *Maps* by Nurrudin Farah: the author, Pan Books Ltd. and Pantheon Books; 'How the World was Created from a Drop of Milk' from *The Origin of Life and Death* edited by Ulli Beier: the author, Heinemann Educational Books Ltd; 'Three Exist Where Three are Not' from *Oral Literature in Africa* edited by Ruth Finnegan: the author, Oxford University Press; 'Love Song', 'Lament of a Woman Separated from Her Lover' and 'Caravaners' Song' from Enrico Cerulli 'The Folk-Literature of the Galla of Southern Abyssinia': *Harvard African Studies* vol. III edited by E A Hooton and Natica I Bates, Peabody

Museum, Harvard University: 'An Old Politician to a Novice' and 'Lull-a-Dirge' by Joe de Graft: Leone de Graft; 'Akosua 'Nowa' by Joe de Graft from *Poems of Black Africa* edited by Wole Soyinka: Martin Secker & Warburg Ltd; 'Getting off the Ride' by Mafika Gwala: the author, Ad. Donker (PTY) Ltd; 'The Death of Richard Corfield' by Muhammed Abdile Hasan from *Somali Poetry* edited B W Andrzejewski and I M Lewis: the editors: 'For a Prostitute' from *The Unwritten Song* edited by Willard Trask: Macmillan Inc.; 'Adamu and His Beautiful Wife' from *A Selection of African Prose* edited by W H Whiteley: Oxford University Press; 'Looking for a Rain God' from *The Collector of Treasures* by Bessie Head: the author, Heinemann Educational Books Ltd. and John Johnson Ltd; 'A Woman's Complaint to her Dance Group' translated by Onwuchekwa Jemie and Ihechukwu Madubuike from *Poetic Heritage* edited by R Egudu and D I Nwoga: the translators; 'The Toad' from *Law and Authority in a Nigerian Tribe* by C K Meek: Oxford University Press; 'War Sweeps Umuchukwu', 'Obu's Classroom' and 'The Ogbanje Healer' from *The Potter's Wheel* by Chukwuemeka Ike: the author, Collins Sons & Co Ltd; 'Colonel Chumah's War' from *Forty-Eight Guns for the General* by Eddie Iroh: the author, Heinemann Educational Books Ltd; 'Letter From a Contract Worker' by Antonio Jacinto from *When Bullets Begin to Flower* edited by Margaret Dickinson: East Africa Publishing House; 'Lament for Ellsworth Janifer' by Onwuchekwa Jemie from *Rhythms of Creation* edited by D I Nwoga: Fourth Dimension Press; 'Why, O Why, Lord?' by Zephania Kameeta: World Council of Churches, Geneva; 'On Truth' from *The Heritage of African Poetry* edited by Isidore Okpewho: Longman; 'My Cousin Mohammed' from *The Myth of Freedom* by S Anai Kelueljang: the author, New Beacon Books; 'A Mother Praises her Baby' from *The Unwritten Song* edited by Willard Trask: Macmillan Inc.; 'The Day of Treachery' from *Zulu Poems* by Mazisi Kunene: Africana; 'Protest Against Conscription for Forced Labour' by Omal Lakana from *Horn of My Love* edited by Okot p'Bitek: Heinemann Educational Books; 'I Heard Small Children Ask' by Ben J Langa from *South Africa: A Different Kind of War* by Julie Frederikse: James Currey; 'Soriatus' by Bhekokwakhe Lange from *Rhythms of Creation* edited by D I Nwoga: Fourth Dimension Press; 'The Goldsmith' from *The Dark Child* by Camara Laye, translated by James Kirkup: Farrar Straus & Giroux, Collins Sons & Co. Ltd; 'Yoruba Love' by Molara Ogundipe-Leslie: Okike (no. 19); 'Ritual Song by Parents of Twins' from *Outcasts* by Bonnie Lubega: the author; 'Children's Planting Song' from *Popular Culture of East Africa* edited by Taban Lo Liyong: Longman, Kenya; 'As Beer Has Made Me Drunk' from *Popular Culture of East Africa* edited by Taban Lo Liyong: Longman, Kenya; 'The Battle of the Elephants' by Ihechukwu Madubuike from *Rhythms of Creation* edited by D I Nwoga: Fourth Dimension Press; 'The Song of the Bottle' and 'The Locust' from *The Unwritten Song* edited by Willard Trask: Macmillan Inc.; 'On the Eve of Krina', 'The Destruction of Sosso the Magnificent', 'The Boast of Niani' from *Sundiata* by D T Niane, translated by G D Pickett: the author, Longman; 'Mate' by Bicca Maseko: the author, Ad. Donker (PTY) Ltd; 'The Call' from *Thunder from the Mountains* edited by Maina wa Kinyatti: Zed Books; 'Veterans Day' and 'The Transformation' by Ifeanyi Menkiti from *Rhythms of Creation* edited by D I Nwoga: Fourth Dimension Press; 'Dialogue' and 'I Am A Child Without Friends' from

The Unwritten Song edited by Willard Trask: Macmillan Inc.; 'Boy on a Swing' by Oswald Mtshali: the author, Ad. Donker (PTY) Ltd; 'The Killing of the Cowards' from *Chaka* by Thomas Mofolo translated by Daniel P Kunene: Heinemann Educational Books Ltd; 'Tirenje or Monde?' from *Chirundu* by Eskia Mphahlele: Ravan Press; 'Nehanda Nyakasikana' from *Zimbabwe Prose and Poetry* by Solomon Mutswairo: the author, Three Continents Press Inc.; 'The Rout of the Arabi' from *Africa is my Witness* by Vusamazulu Mutwa: Blue Crane Books; 'Lament for Bala'nku' from *Songs and Tales from the Dark Continent* by Natalie Curtis: G Schirmer; 'Simangele and Vusi' from *Fools and Other Stories* by Njabulo Ndebele: the author, Ravan Press; 'Refugee' by Stephen Ndichu from *Rhythms of Creation* edited by D I Nwoga: Fourth Dimension Press; 'Western Civilisation' by Agostinho Neto from *When the Bullets Begin to Flower* edited by Margaret Dickinson: East Africa Publishing House; 'The Song of a Child Who Survived Nyadzonia' by Emmanuel Ngara from *None But Ourselves* by Julie Frederikse: the author, Heinemann Educational Books Ltd; 'This World' by Willy Nnorom from *Rhythms of Creation* edited by D I Nwoga: Fourth Dimension Press; 'A Story of Our Times, 'In My Country', 'Two Worlds' and 'Blood' by Pitika P Ntuli: the author; 'Song of a Madman' by Emmanuel Obiechina from *Rhythms of Creation* edited by D I Nwoga: Fourth Dimension Press; 'Elegy for Slit-drum' from *Labyrinths* by Christopher Okigbo: the author, Africana Press; 'A Warrior's Lament' and 'At the End' by Nnamdi Olebara, translated by Chinweizu: the translator; 'The Typical Blackman Forgiving and Forgetful' and 'The Impotent Observer' from *Fires of Africa* by Naiwu Osahon: the author, Di Nigro Press; 'Madam Universe Sent Man' by Naiwu Osahon: the author; 'The Trial' from *Gods Bits of Wood* by Sembene Ousmane: Heinemann Educational Books Ltd; 'The President's Wife' from *The Last of the Empire* by Sembene Ousmane: the author, Heinemann Educational Books Ltd; 'Meka's Medal' from *The Old Man and the Medal* by Ferdinand Oyono: Heinemann Educational Books Ltd and Georges Borchardt Inc.; 'The Graceful Giraffe Cannot Become a Monkey' and 'When Death Comes to Fetch You' from *Song of Lawino and Song of Ocol* by Okot p'Bitek: East Africa Publishing House; 'Jubilant Throng' from *Two Songs* by Okot p-Bitek: the author, East Africa Publishing House; 'Invocation to the Rainbow' from *The Unwritten Song* edited by Willard Trask: Macmillan Inc.; 'Daybreak' from *Translations from the Night* by Jean-Joseph Rabearivelo, translated by John Reed and Clive Wake: the translators and Solofo Rabearivelo; 'Mussoco' by Oscar Ribas: *Lotus* no 40–41 1979; 'Laugh with Happiness' by Shabaan Roberts from *Anthology of Swahili Poetry* edited by Ali A Jahadmy: Heinemann Kenya; 'Song of the Bridesmaids' from *African Poems and Love Songs* by Charlotte and Wolf Leslau: the authors, Peter Pauper Press; 'Bride Price' by Mabel Segun: the author; 'My Name' by Magoleng wa Selepe: the author, Ad. Donker (PTY) Ltd; 'Black Woman' from *Selected Poems* by Leopold Sédar Senghor: Atheneum; 'A Poem on Black and White' by Mongane Wally Serote: the author, Ad. Donker (PTY) Ltd; 'Song of the Unburied' from *The Basuto* by Hugh Ashton: the author, Oxford University Press for the International African Institute; 'If You Want to Know Me' by Noémia de Sousa from *Poems of Black Africa* edited by Wole Soyinka: Martin Secker & Warburg Ltd; 'Azania is Tired' from *South Africa: A Different Kind of War* by Julie

Frederikse: James Currey; 'Telephone Conversation' by Wole Soyinka from *Reflections* edited by Frances Ademola: African Universities Press; 'Amope' from *The Trials of Brother Jero* by Wole Soyinka: Spectrum Books; 'The Guest in Your House' from *African Poems and Love Songs* by Charlotte and Wolf Leslau: the authors, Peter Pauper Press; 'Ten-to-Ten' and 'The Suit' by Can Themba from *The World of Can Themba* edited by Essop Patel: Ravan Press; 'Sophiatowners' by Can Themba from *Drum* edited by Anthony Sampson: the editor; 'A False Hero of Independence' from *A Grain of Wheat* by Ngugi wa Thiong'o: the author, Heinemann Educational Books Ltd; 'Girl's Song' from *The Unwritten Song* edited by Willard Trask: Macmillan Inc.; 'The 'Wraith-Island' from *The Palm-Wine Drinkard* by Amos Tutuola: the author, Faber and Faber Ltd and Grove Press; 'The God of the State' from *The Witch Herbalist of the Remote Town* by Amos Tutuola: the author, Faber and Faber Ltd; 'We Were Once Poor but Wealthy' by Obiora Udechukwu from *Rhythms of Creation* edited by D I Nwoga: Fourth Dimension Press; 'I Spoil Everything' from *The Black Mind* edited by O R Dathorne: University of Minnesota Press; 'Truth and Falsehood' from *Tales of Amadou Koumba* by Birago Diop: Longman; 'Eshu' from *Oral Literature in Africa* edited by Ruth Finnegan: the author, Oxford University Press; 'Hunger', 'New Yam', 'Python', 'Ibadan' from *Yoruba Poetry* edited by Ulli Beier: Cambridge University Press; 'The God of War' from *African Poetry* edited by Ulli Beier: Cambridge University Press; 'Song of a Hungry Child' from *Yoruba Poetry* edited by Ulli Beier and Bakare Gbadamosi: Cambridge University Press; 'Olorum Nimbe' from *Oral Literature in Africa* edited by Ruth Finnegan: the author, Oxford University Press; 'Life's Variety' from *The Heritage of African Poetry* edited by Isidore Okpewho: Présence Africaine; 'Not Even God is Ripe Enough to Catch a Woman in Love' from Not Even God is Ripe Enough by Bakare Gbadamosi and Ulli Beier: the authors, Heinemann Educational Books Ltd; 'Keep it Dark' from *African Voices* edited by Peggy Rutherford: Vanguard Press; 'Song of Those Who Have Passed Their Prime' from *African Voices* edited by Peggy Rutherford: Vanguard Press.

Faber and Faber Ltd apologizes for any errors or omissions in the above list and would be grateful to be notified of any corrections that should be incorporated in the next edition of this volume.

72470